Journey To Aviad

Allison D. Reid

ISBN: 1-4563-2965-0
ISBN-13: 9781456329655

Dedication

In memory of my beloved grandmother, Agatha Irene Gibson (1929-2010), who always encouraged both my imagination and my own personal journey to Aviad (although I came to know Him by another name in this world).

To Donna,
may you find peace
and healing in the
love of christ.
Allison Reid

Table of Contents

Prologue

The veil of night has not yet lifted. Even so, I find myself climbing the familiar stone steps that spiral up to my office. I have trod them so many times before that I do not need the light of my lantern to navigate their steep incline. This ancient staircase, cut by masons long dead, has been worn smooth by the feet of generations of my ancestors. No place in the world do I feel the pressing weight of time more strongly than here, where there is no other distraction for my mind, and no other task for my body but to climb, with the voices of all those who came before me echoing in the sound of my footfalls. Reaching the top of the staircase, I push open the heavy wooden door and light a lantern. While I may not need it to navigate the stair, my aging eyes will need light for the task I begin on this day—a task that I have left for far too long. With the world sleeping in the quiet before dawn, I smooth out a fresh piece of parchment and lift my pen in thought...

I have always been amazed by the way time unfolds itself; slow and subtle as the petals of the morning glory open to the first rays of sun. At first, you will see naught but a tightly closed bud, but allow yourself to be distracted by a passing breeze for only a moment, and you miss the flower's brilliant heralding of the new dawn. I implore you, whoever you may be, to look around you. Open your eyes to every detail of the present as it lives, as it breathes. Do not be distracted by a fleeting wind and miss the coming of the dawn, for the events of today very soon become tomorrow's folklore.

No doubt someday many will wonder if these lands that sustain us, the cities we inhabit, the shrines at which we worship, our language, our literature...our very lives...ever truly existed, just as we continually struggle to unearth the traces of our own history from the rubble of our past. Our collective memory diminishes with each passing generation, leaving us with only tomes and trinkets to remind us of who we once were, and to show us who we are yet destined to become. Our descendants will look through our libraries, the remnants of our dead, and our rubbish alike, trying to discover if the tales they've heard of us are truth, or merely the imaginative ravings of some drunken bard of days long gone. And most likely they will find part truth, part fiction, mesh it together and call it "history." Our existence will be neatly summed up into a list of significant dates, and squabbles over land, and rulers whose power was as over-inflated as their egos. That is not history. It fills the minds of the intellectuals, no doubt, and allows them to feel rather smug in their knowledge, but such things do not feed the soul, they do not represent the truth as it was breathed and bled by those who lived its everyday reality. The beauty of the flower cannot exist without its roots, its stem, the rain, the soil, the sun, and any number of other things we do not see, though they are rarely given the same adoration as the colorful bloom.

Of course, I suppose the more frightening thought is that no one will wonder at all—that we will be here and gone in an instant, with none left to remember our families, sing songs of our exploits, or learn from our triumphs and failures. Perhaps that is why I find myself here in the silence before the sunrise, driven to commit all that I know to parchment, so that the truth is not buried with me, forever lost to the coming ages. No doubt the men of this age would shift uncomfortably in their seats and try to deny my writings as false, if they knew that a young girl of our own time grew up to hold the fate of the world in her hands. They have no idea how close they came to suffering the utter destruction of everything they hold dear.

But there is no point to telling a story's end before its beginning, and even the greatest heroes known to legend have made their entrance into the world as children. While it is true that we make our own choices as we grow, before we have even drawn our first breath Aviad the Creator has called to us each by name, and continues to call to us on our journey through this life. So often it falls to those who truly listen for His voice to rise and fight for us all. So it is with young Elowyn, who came into the world of base birth and unknown lineage, like a single seed planted in the garden whose tender shoots sprouted unnoticed in a world unwary of its fate. This is where my tale truly begins.

May the Ancients look kindly upon one man's humble retelling of her life, as it has been made known to me over the course of many years. For though Elowyn's physical form must inevitably someday perish, I write this tome in the hope that the essence of her life, and the knowledge of her mark upon this world, will not.

Chapter I

The Coin

A lone man slipped cautiously through the quiet of the forest just before dawn. The sky was draped with a thick gray mantle of clouds, covering any waning moonlight that might have guided him along the treacherous path before him. The man lowered his face as he raised his hood against a sudden, heavy burst of rain. Only the most urgent of tasks could have brought him to the very edge of the Deep Woods at this early hour. But he was a man of honor, and he had made a solemn vow that would not be broken. His nerves and muscles were stretched taut as he made his way slowly forward. He prayed for an end to the rain, so that the sight of the sun's first gentle rays might break through the clouds and ease his troubled mind. The rain diminished, but the darkness persisted.

A twig snapped somewhere in the underbrush behind him. The man lowered his hood and instinctively turned to peer back down the path. Cursing the darkness under his breath, he listened intently for a moment. Unable to see, and hearing nothing more, he continued on, walking at a faster pace than before. Another twig snapped, from somewhere to the right this time. He withdrew an arrow from his quiver and held it ready in his hand. His senses were all on edge now as he broke into a run, only to hear more sounds of movement from somewhere ahead of him. He was being surrounded, by what he could only guess. He veered to the left, off the footpath, running erratically in the direction of a small stream he had crossed earlier. Any hope to shake his pursuers was futile; the noose they had drawn around him had already tightened. The man was quickly surrounded by a pack of wild beasts, larger than wolves, with red glowing eyes and fiery breath. Leading them was an enormously tall figure with an antlered helm who carried a staff taller than himself.

The man raised his bow and released as many arrows as he could into their midst, unsure if such beasts could even be harmed by them. He screamed as they set upon him, their teeth and claws tearing through his leather armor and into his flesh. But there was more at stake than his life. That was the difficult message he had received in prayer the night before. Perhaps his demise was fated, yet there still might be hope if he could only get to the stream. In spite of the agonizing pain, he rammed his way through the beasts, pulling a small cloth-wrapped object from beneath his shirt. The rain stopped and the clouds thinned. His prayer had been answered after all. The sun had not yet risen, but the moon still shone bright enough to reflect off the surface of the stream. He could see it now, bubbling and flashing not much farther ahead of him.

The man dashed toward the stream with the last of his strength. He dropped his bow, and frantically unwrapped the object. He flung it into the rushing water just as the beasts brought him to the ground with such force that his helm flew off. For a brief instant the moonlight caught the object's silvery surface, flashing so brightly that he was blinded by it. His last moment of awareness was filled with hope as the creatures around him shrieked in painful fear of its brilliance.

Elowyn awoke to the warm sensation of the sun gently caressing her face. She smiled in recognition of its touch, slowly allowing each of her senses to greet the morning. There had been a brief, but heavy rain shower just before dawn. The smell of damp earth was nearly overpowering...a rich, musty smell that made her nose tingle, her lungs draw in deeply, and her spirit come completely alive. Her wool cloak clung heavily around her small frame, but beneath it her dress was still warm and dry.

Slowly she opened her eyes to see long fingers of light sifting through the brilliant green of newly opened spring leaves. To her utter delight, she found that the entire forest was covered with droplets of water, shimmering and sparkling as though someone had strewn it with thousands of the most rare and beautiful gems. Then she realized that of course someone had—they belonged to Aviad, the Ancient One as so many called him, the Creator of all things. She beamed joyfully at the glistening drops, and whispered to herself, "Aviad's diamonds".

Pleased by this revelation, Elowyn stretched her stiff muscles, and slid effortlessly down the trunk of the tree she had been sleeping in. It had taken her a long while to learn how to sleep sitting up, with her back against the trunk and her legs straddled over a large limb. She'd had to start with very small trees with limbs that were close to the ground so that when she fell in the night she wouldn't get hurt. She rarely fell anymore and it was so much safer to sleep off the ground, away from the damp and the beasts of the night. Certainly it was much more pleasant than sleeping at home, squeezed with her mother and two sisters into a stuffy cottage that smelled too much of tallow.

Elowyn crossed a small clearing and made her way through a copse of young trees. She loved the way they stood so thin, and straight, all clustered together as if they were whispering secrets to each other. As a slight breeze rustled their leaves, she could almost believe they were giggling. There was an older tree with a thick, knotted trunk right above them, sheltering the young ones under a canopy of branches.

"If that tree were a person, she would be round and jolly, with long braided hair. I'll bet she's their mother," she said wistfully, wishing she had such a mother herself. The young trees seemed to giggle again as she brushed past them with a smile.

Elowyn climbed up a small ridge and slid down the rocky bank on the other side to reach the large stream that wound its way through the woods. It bubbled up from a spring in the ground some distance away, its bed wide, shallow, and filled with many colorful stones. At this time of year the water ran cold and clean—perfect for drinking, and sometimes bathing if the air was warm enough. She splashed her face, enjoying the shivering chill that ran through her body, then paused to take a long, satisfying drink. Elowyn settled herself on a sun-drenched boulder and nibbled on a bit of bread from her pouch. Captivated by the simple beauty of her surroundings, she gave a contented sigh as she watched the light dance off the water, casting its quivering reflection on the leaves above her. Nothing could possibly make this morning any more glorious.

A quick flash of light suddenly caught Elowyn's eye—something silvery in the stream was glinting out at her. Almost indistinguishable from the sun's rays dancing merrily on the water's surface, the object had nearly escaped her attention. But Elowyn was an observant child by nature, and always seemed to find things out in the woods that other people had lost or discarded. She waded into the stream and lifted the object out of the water. It was a silver disc of some sort, with well-worn markings she did not recognize. Perhaps it was a Pilgrim's medallion or an unusually large coin, though it wasn't like any coin she had ever seen before, even during Faire time when the rare and exotic became commonplace. She shrugged. Tyroc was a large port city, a center of trade. It was not unusual to meet foreign visitors who wore strange clothes, uttered seemingly indecipherable languages and carried mysterious looking coins with them. She could only imagine who might have dropped this.

Placing the disc safely within the pouch at her waist, Elowyn looked about with a more scrutinizing eye. One lesson she had learned rather well—when there was one lost item, there might be others, especially if a group of travelers had recently camped nearby. It did not take long for her to discover a warrior's helm peeking out from the dense undergrowth along the stream's edge. Knowing how valuable such an object was, her eyes lit up with excitement. But the stab of joy that coursed through her was brief. Such an item was not likely to have been left behind either willingly or by accident. Elowyn looked about and listened intently. The only sounds she could hear were the birds calling out overhead and the gentle gurgle of the stream. No one was nearby. She was sure of that.

The helm couldn't have been lying there for long, for it was in perfect condition, still buffed and shined with only a few scuffmarks. It had a family crest imprinted in a subtle location along the side, which meant there was no chance she would be able to sell it. She grimaced at the thought of being hailed a thief by the local merchants. They already thought her to be odd and seemed uneasy when she was around. She could sometimes hear them whispering about her as she passed their stalls. She had caught words like "wild," and "strange," and "unkempt," and "How will her mother ever find someone to marry her?" Elowyn did not care about any of those things, and so she stuck out her chin defiantly, pretending not to hear them.

Inching forward on her hands and knees, Elowyn cautiously probed the long grasses with her fingers to see if anything else had been left behind. The undergrowth slowly revealed several well-made, expensive-looking arrows; one sunk deep into the base of a tree, two more angled into the earth, and one lying broken where someone had stepped on it. She then came to a place where the ground was stained with something dark that she could not at first identify. She rubbed some of the damp soil between two fingers, catching her breath and backing away as her fingers turned dark red with blood. Whether it had come from human or beast she could not tell. Trembling and feeling queasy, Elowyn wondered if it was wise to continue looking—she had no wish to come across anything dead. But in the end, her desire to know what happened overruled her fears. She stopped searching for objects in the brush and stood up to survey the entire area.

As she looked around, it was soon obvious that a great struggle had taken place, and she had happened upon the scene of some unknown warrior's defeat. The whole area was covered with footprints, the foliage trampled, and the limbs of young trees broken. As she followed the footprints, tracing her way back in time to the very point where all the trouble began, she could see where the man with the helm had been walking, alone, at a normal pace. Then his steps began to grow farther apart, as if he were still walking, but much more rapidly. Then she found the point at which he broke into a full running stride, careening wildly through the brush, until his footprints suddenly became muddled with many others. But these were not the distinct prints left by men's boots. They were those of beasts—strange beasts different than any she had ever encountered before.

Allison D. Reid

Whatever these creatures were, they left tracks almost like those of wolves, or wild pack dogs, and yet they indicated an animal far larger than any ordinary wolf. Besides, it was not the custom of wolves to run in such large groups and attack well-armed men.

There were also strange black scars on several of the trees, as though they had been singed by fire. More blood had seeped into the soft earth along the edge of the path, which was still damp from the morning's rain shower. In the midst of the beasts' tracks, there was another set of footprints. She could tell by the depth of the prints and the length of the stride that whoever had left them was tall, and carried some sort of staff or walking cane, but she could tell nothing beyond that.

At some point, the pursued man must have broken away, limping terribly and taking erratic shots with his bow. He made a painful dash in the direction of the stream, only to be brought down close to the water's edge. His bow still lay there where he'd dropped it, nearly buried in the tall grass. No archer, no matter how skilled, would have been able to fight off such a direct ambush. The strangest part of all, the part that made the hair on the back of her neck stand straight up, was that there was no body. If a wild pack of animals had truly attacked the bowman, they would have devoured him on the spot, leaving behind what remains of his corpse could not be eaten...his bones, scraps of torn clothing, armor. Instead, she found a trail where his body had been dragged along, seemingly whole, in the direction of the Shadow Wood—the true wilderness wasteland, where few dared to travel unless heavily armed and in large groups. Many such groups came to this place, because just to the east was the narrowest ford in the river which marked the border between Tyroc and the Shadow Wood. Strange tales were told about that wood—the kinds of tales that even the most careless parents strive to protect their children from.

It was no surprise that Elowyn had heard whisperings of people entering the Shadow Wood and never returning; it was rather the expected outcome for anyone so foolish. She herself had watched countless bands of armored warriors head in the direction of the Shadow Wood, and she could not recall having seen any of them come back. But she had never heard of anything emerging from its depths to drag people into it either. That was the sort of thing that would keep one lying awake at night, jumping at every rattle of the wind.

Elowyn's breath caught in her throat and she began to shiver as she looked down at the tracks again. Something about them greatly disturbed her—something beyond the pain of knowing that a life had ended so violently. She examined the area again to see what it was that she might have missed. She retraced the bowman's final steps, stopping as she approached the second set of footprints. Not only was there no indication that the second man had helped the first, been chased off, or fled in terror, the contrary seemed to be the case. It appeared to her as if the tall man with the staff had led the animals to the bowman, stood by as they attacked him, and followed the pack of beasts into the Shadow Wood as the corpse was dragged away.

Suddenly the sun no longer seemed warm or comforting, and all of Aviad's diamonds had dried up. A little bud of fear was balling up in the pit of Elowyn's stomach, and no matter how hard she swallowed, it refused to stay down in its place. She knew she was nearing the same panicked state that must have made the bowman break into a doomed run. She snatched up the helm, the arrows, and the bow, and as she ran for dear life, she came to another startling realization. The previous night, she had stayed up much later than she should have, star gazing. When she'd finally dropped off to sleep, the ground had not been wet enough to leave such clear footprints. Indeed it had not rained in more than a week, save for that small shower just before dawn. This attack had happened while she was blissfully sleeping, completely unaware that a life and death struggle was taking place but a few moments' walk away. If she'd been seen, she might very well have been caught and dragged off with the unfortunate bowman.

Ordinarily the walk home from her favorite place by the stream was a lengthy one. That day it took her half the time. She could not keep herself from breaking into a run whenever she thought about the narrow escape she'd had. She slowed her pace as the trees thinned and she began to see signs of other people about. For the first time in her life she breathed a sigh of relief at the sight of civilization.

Moments later, she saw her own thatched-roof cottage coming into view. Before going inside she went to stash her latest treasures into her own private chest. She had found it some time ago, broken and abandoned in a rubbish heap, and decided it was worth saving. She had hidden the chest in the hollow of a huge tree not far from the cottage, well away from her mother's prying eyes. The ancient tree was covered with vines, and the opening was not obvious to the casual passer-by, so her things were safer there than any place else she could think of.

Space in the chest was precious. She only kept her most special items there...some bright, smooth stones from the river, a writing tablet her tutor from the Temple had once given her, bits of twine and rope (one never knew when such things might be useful), a knife with a broken handle someone had cast away, a few beads, and pressed leaves that were bright red, orange and purple, carefully caught and saved last autumn. Most precious of all was a pair of old trousers that she thought must have been her father's. They were well worn and smelled of the sea. She had found them in an old trunk in the cottage years ago, and carried them off without anyone knowing. The newly found helm just barely fit into her little chest of treasures, but the bow and arrows were simply too large. She left them resting on top, their length extending upwards into the tree. She would decide what to do with them later.

Walking toward the cottage, Elowyn was filled with an entirely different kind of anxiety. Her heart, her step, her breathing...all suddenly seemed extraordinarily heavy. There was always an uncomfortable stillness that descended when she returned home. She hesitated outside the door, kicking up dust with her toes, gathering the strength to enter. Her mother rarely looked at her or spoke to her, as if ignoring Elowyn would negate her actual existence. Morganne, her older sister was cautiously kind, with an apologetic look in her eye that was almost a condescending form of pity. Perhaps it was only Elowyn's imagination, but she always felt that if Morganne could have put her facial expression into words, they would have been "I'm sorry you can't be more like me—then maybe mother wouldn't dislike you so."

Two springs had passed since Elowyn noticed that her mother was going to bear a child—Adelin she came to be called after she was born. Their mother avoided Adelin as much as possible, passing on the responsibility of her care to Morganne. That was about the only thing that Elowyn had in common with Adelin, whose arrival had been a strange surprise. But her existence was not something their mother would voluntarily speak of, and Elowyn did not dare ask. Adelin regarded Elowyn with an equal amount of suspicion. If Elowyn tried to pick her up, she would cry loudly for Morganne.

As much as Elowyn dreaded returning home, she knew she couldn't stay away forever. She had already been gone for two straight days, and had no desire to sleep out in the dark alone that night, not after what she'd seen. With a heavy sigh, she pressed against the wooden door until it swung open. Adelin was sitting alone in a corner, attempting to untangle herself from a great deal of yarn. Her expression became very intense and focused as she tried to comprehend the puzzle placed before her. Apparently the yarn had been a clever attempt to keep Adelin quiet and out of the way for a while. Morganne was sitting at the work table, casually sewing a plain linen chemise. The relaxed curve of Morganne's shoulders told Elowyn that their mother had gone into the city for the day. A wave of relief swept over her as she plopped herself down on the rough stone floor.

The shutters were open, allowing a single sunbeam to illuminate Morganne's figure, her fair hair catching the light like spun gold. A delicious-smelling spring breeze filled the room, flushing out the unpleasant odor of the tallow candles their mother burned so readily through the winter months. It was such a rare moment of peace that Elowyn dared not so much as breathe, lest whatever benevolent spell hung over the cottage be broken. *This is how it should be*, she thought to herself. *This is what's real.*

Morganne paused from her sewing and gave Elowyn a probing look. "Are you well?" Elowyn nodded. She was more than just well—she was content. Such moments were more precious than all the wealth of Tyroc. Morganne continued her sewing. "I was starting to worry about you, being gone so long. Those renegades attacked again along the north road—left ten of the city guards dead, but not one of the renegades was even wounded. They laid out another ambush," she said in a disapproving tone.

Elowyn's ears perked and her heart stirred with a curious indignation. She couldn't help but think of the man with the helmet. An ambush certainly wasn't fair. It was the kind of attack made by cowards, and by strange wolf-like beasts, not by honorable men. Yet there was another part of her that had to admire their cunning. These renegades, from all reports, were only a small band, but they were exceptionally wood-wise. They had successfully challenged the ruling family of Tyroc without ever being caught, or losing a single member. That was the way the stories went anyhow. It was almost as though they were invincible.

"One of these days, you're going to get into trouble out there, and what then?"

"I don't go near the north road, or any other road for that matter."

"You know that's not the point."

Elowyn sighed; she had no desire to argue. She noticed that a dingy gray cloud had swallowed up the sunbeam. She stared hard at the open window, wishing that the sunbeam would come back. Normally she would have shrugged off Morganne's comment without a thought, but she couldn't forget what had made her come running home in the first place. She had felt threatened, and it wasn't by any renegade group. Somehow running into them seemed much less frightening than running into whatever had dragged off the bowman. As a general rule, men could be moved to pity, they could be reasoned with, but what of these other roving creatures? Stifling a small shiver, she quickly changed the subject.

"I wonder what the renegades are after anyway. Why do they keep attacking?"

"I don't think anyone knows for sure. I heard some women talking about it in front of the tailor's stall last time I went into town. One had heard that the renegades are a group of the City Guards that went bad after the Sovereign died. They had been among his most loyal men, who by some accounts went mad with grief. Another said they were traitors who made a botched attempt to overthrow the Sovereign's sons and then fled the city to keep from being executed. Yet another claimed they were under an evil curse, though I don't believe that. The most reasonable explanation I have heard so far is that they are poachers trying to cover up their hunting of forbidden quarry in the Sovereign's forest. One thing for certain—they don't seem to care who they kill. All the stories agree that they are ruthless, bloodthirsty murderers," Morganne said with a tone of certainty. "Please stay home for a while?" she softly pleaded.

Elowyn looked at Morganne thoughtfully. There were days when she acted as though she cared, and yet there were others when she seemed to enjoy rubbing Elowyn's face in the fact that her own mother didn't want her. "Besides," Morganne returned to her usual practical tone, "Mother has been weaving incessantly all winter, and none of the wool cloth has been fulled yet. I am going to need your help soon."

Elowyn made a face and groaned. Fulling was a nasty, smelly, tedious job—even worse than making tallow for candles in the fall. Normally Elowyn was kept well away from the cloth with her always slightly grubby hands. Their mother was meticulous when it came to keeping the house free of dust and dirt. Most cottages like theirs had floors of beaten earth covered with rushes or hay. But their mother would have none of that, and paid to have a stone floor laid. She complained that the earthen floors soiled her wool and cloth, and that rushes only gave the mice and other pests a place to hide. Every morning before her work began, the cottage was swept out, and whenever possible, strewn with absinthe and wild thyme to keep the moths and mice away. The trestle table was set up and wiped clean. Then their mother would either spin, or sit at her loom, and make it known that she was not to be disturbed. It always seemed to Elowyn that she loved her loom more than she loved all three of her daughters put together. Mother did all of the weaving, leaving Morganne most of the sewing—that was how they made their living throughout the year. The quality of their work was known well enough in Tyroc shops that her mother's many eccentricities were graciously overlooked. By all rights, she should have had her own shop in town. But she wanted none of the hassles of running one, especially the part of dealing with a constant stream of noise from the street and interruptions from customers. She much preferred to work in solitude, selling her finished product to cloth merchants, or to other tailors.

It was a mystery to Elowyn that she had not yet been apprenticed to one of them. Many of the other girls her age and class already had been apprenticed to someone, or at the very least, they were learning the family trade well enough to one day continue it. But no mention of an apprenticeship had ever crossed her mother's lips, nor did she teach Elowyn the craft that she and Morganne knew so well. Elowyn had no real interest, truth be told. Still, she could not help but feel slighted that she was purposely left out. This is not to say that Elowyn did not contribute in her own way. Survival was always a precarious thing, and each had to do their share. Even little Adelin was made to help with the most simple of tasks. It was Elowyn's job to fetch water, keep the garden, bring in the firewood, run errands, and collect wild foods and herbs when she went out roaming in the woods. Sometimes she was given the washing to do, though her small size made doing a good job difficult, and their mother was as particular about the laundry as she was the cleanliness of the cottage.

Fulling was the most dreaded chore Elowyn was required to help with, and she never managed to get out of it. Her mother would lay a length of newly woven wool cloth in the big wooden trough behind the cottage, then pour over it warm water and stale urine that had been saved up from the chamber pots. She and Morganne would have to hike up their dresses and walk across it for hours, until the weave was tightened, and the cloth slightly shrunk. After that it would have to be stretched out on a wooden tenter, and its surface brushed with teasles from the garden. Once dry, Morganne would use long flat shears to smooth off

12

the nap—once for common cloth, and several times for fine cloth. If it was to be sold to a merchant, the cloth was then brushed, pressed, folded, and stored away until their mother was ready to cart it into the city. Cloth that was to be used for Morganne's sewing was set aside for washing with soapwort, or sometimes for dyeing. Typically their mother wove linen over the winter months, preparing for summer demands for cooler cloth, and because linen did not need to be fulled. But whatever wool cloth she did make was saved up until the first warm weather, and then the dreaded trough would make its appearance. Elowyn's legs and feet ached just thinking about it.

Living among weavers and seamstresses wasn't all bad though. For one thing, Elowyn never ran out of clothes, and they never went unmended, no matter how many times she ripped her dresses on trees and thorns. There was something satisfying too, about laying out dull looking linen on the grass, then watching the dew and sun work together to bleach it white. But what she really looked forward to were the times when their mother bought raw wool that had not yet been dyed. Some colors were too difficult, too expensive, or too dangerous to make at home, and for those she was willing to pay the dyer in town. All the rest were made with Elowyn's help.

Elowyn loved getting up in the dark hours before dawn, and starting a blaze beneath the enormous dye cauldron. It was big enough that Adelin could curl up comfortably in its bottom, and none would know she was there unless they looked inside. Their mother paid two men from a neighboring farm to hoist it onto the trivet for her, to empty it when needed during dyeing season, and take it down for storage at the end. It took Elowyn and Morganne many trips back and forth from the stream to fill the cauldron with water, and it took hours for the fire to heat.

With some small amount of pride, Elowyn would watch as the dyes were made using plants she had grown in the garden or collected out of the woods. Not that her mother ever acknowledged it, but that was the only time when Elowyn really felt deep down that she was part of something bigger. Those plants were her contribution to Mother's sought after cloth, and Morganne's famed needlework. Elowyn tended and nursed the garden with the same care she would give a wounded animal, and her plants always grew straight, healthy and strong, even when other gardens yielded a stunted crop.

Once Mother had the mixture she wanted, Elowyn would watch the fire and stir the pot so that all the wool dyed evenly. There was something about that big bubbling cauldron that always captivated her imagination. She would pretend that she was brewing potions like the great alchemists she had heard about in the old stories. They were forever attempting to find the elixir of life, or a formula that would change lead into gold. Even though they had failed, their attempts had brought forth a variety of useful concoctions over the centuries that were used to aid Aviad's armies in their fight against the Shadow Spirits. The old tales were full of desperate battles, and heroic feats, in a world filled with miracles brought forth by the very hands of Aviad. Elowyn's soul felt a great sense of loss, and a longing for such times now long passed into history. Nothing remarkable ever happened in the present day, certainly nothing worth preserving in tales of glory for generations to come.

After dark, when everyone else had gone in to bed, Elowyn would lie on her back near the fire, and watch the sparks spiral upward to meet the stars. She would dream of far-off lands ruled by benevolent monarchs—places of peace, and wealth, and pristine beauty. Sometimes she dreamed of going off to find her father. In her dreams he was always strong, kind, intelligent, and loving. If only he knew where she was, he would come for her...wouldn't he? But somehow, once all the dyeing was done, and the cauldron had been dried out and stored away, the magic and the dreams went away with it. The reality was, she knew nothing about her father, not even his name. Her mother refused to speak of him, though neither she nor Morganne knew why. To bring the subject up at all risked a beating, and they no longer dared to ask.

After a long day spent haggling over cloth prices, their mother would typically come home tired and irritable. But when she returned late that particular afternoon, her eyes were bright with excitement.

It was unusual to see her in such high spirits. For a fleeting moment, Elowyn saw a beauty in her mother that stood in such sharp contrast to her volatile nature. Her hair was a lovely light golden brown, her eyes the blue of the deepest ocean. She had a strict profile, with every feature outlined to perfection. Rarely was a hair on her head, or a fold of her clothing out of place. But it was difficult for Elowyn to perceive her as beautiful. Elowyn realized that it was because she never smiled—to the contrary, she was usually scowling about one thing or another. While Mother's creations were often praised by others, she rarely expressed any satisfaction with her work. She just continued on; spinning, weaving, and selling, without ever pausing to admire the exceptional beauty brought forth by her own hands.

Barely glancing at Elowyn and Adelin, their mother swept straight past them to the table where Morganne was still sewing. On it she dropped a large pouch filled with silver coins.

"There was a wealthy man from foreign parts in town today. He bought up every bit of weave I had, and paid well for it too. Better than those cheap scoundrels at the shop, who are always trying to cheat me." Her eyes flashed with anger for a moment, before they cooled with vengeful satisfaction. "He liked your needlework too, and wants to commission us to fill an order. He's willing to pay for velvet and even silk. The silk is being sent by ship and will be here by month's end, but the velvet will need to be purchased. I will spin and weave the linen and wool myself—it will have to be the finest cloth I have ever made. None of what I have left in store will do. I've signed the contract already. The order must be ready by late summer when he returns, as he will be bringing back with him the Lady the garments are meant for. She will be wintering at the Castle. Apparently she is a family friend to the Sovereign and his house!"

Their mother's eyes glinted proudly, as though by being the one selected to make this woman's clothes, she too had some connection to the ruling family of Tyroc. "You can do final fittings when she arrives, but once I get the weave ready you'll have to work by these measurements alone." She handed Morganne a piece of parchment with detailed figures on it. Elowyn couldn't tell by Morganne's expression if she was happy or terrified. She looked very much like a stunned animal as she stared at their mother in complete disbelief.

"How many garments does she want by summer's end?" Morganne asked. Their mother produced a roll of parchment, with all the details of the order on it.

As Morganne perused it, Elowyn could see her body tense with anxiety. "I...I don't know if I can make that many so quickly...if I already had the material, it would be easier, but..."

The look in their mother's eye grew dangerous. Elowyn knew that look. It was usually accompanied by a swift blow. Morganne wisely kept silent.

"The contract is signed. You *will* make them," their mother said icily. She dug into the bag, pulling out a single coin and dropping it on the table. Morganne cautiously reached for it, her face flushed. Though her expression was masked, Elowyn could tell that on the inside Morganne was seething with emotion. Exactly what emotion Elowyn could not tell—she always had such a difficult time reading Morganne's thoughts. Morganne picked up the coin without even looking at it, tucked it in her belt pouch, and quickly turned away, avoiding their mother's gaze. She continued her sewing, head bent low, her fingers working furiously and trembling ever so slightly. Elowyn wondered if she would ever get anything so valuable from her mother. Elowyn's contributions to their trade, though important, were never acknowledged. Suddenly Elowyn remembered the strange coin she had found and pulled it out of her pouch.

"Look," she announced brightly, "I have a coin too—I found it in the stream." She held it up with pride, secretly hoping that it was valuable enough to get her mother's attention, even if only for a brief moment. Their mother gave it a skeptical glance.

"Worthless," she pronounced callously, barely giving it a glance. "I have warned you about bringing other people's refuse into the house. Get rid of it."

Elowyn's heart sank. She began to feel a tightness in her throat, and hot indignant tears welled up, ready to spill over. Whether to spite her mother, or in spite of her, Elowyn refused to let them fall. The effort stirred an angry defiance within her, and her expression grew sulky. She had so hoped that this time she had found something important, but she was used to such disappointments, especially where her mother was concerned. Even if the coin was of value, she realized that her mother was not likely to admit it openly. The object would simply vanish, no doubt finding its way into the pouch at her mother's waist. Elowyn tucked the coin out of sight, fully intending to keep it regardless of its worth. Its strange markings interested her, even though she had no idea what they meant, and Elowyn liked the way the cool raised metal felt under her fingers.

By late afternoon, the dingy gray cloud that had come between her and a beautiful sunbeam earlier that day, had turned into a billowing mass of large, black, threatening clouds that swallowed up the entire sky. The wind had picked up too, and through the half-open shutters, Elowyn could smell the rain coming. She had managed to keep the morning's events out of her thoughts, but as her fingers caressed the coin in the pouch at her side, and the musk of damp earth filled her lungs, Elowyn couldn't help but remember. How it gotten so far out into the stream she didn't know, but she felt sure that the coin belonged to the slain bowman.

Dusk came early, and swiftly. As complete darkness descended on the cottage, the shutters were secured, the fire banked, and everyone dressed for bed.

Elowyn had a tenuous relationship with storms. Their power was beautiful and exciting; she could feel their living energy flowing through the air. If only she could forget their dangerous nature, she might enjoy storms more. Somehow tonight was different. She felt none of the usual awe-filled excitement. Her stomach tightened into sickening knots and her heart pumped fast and hard. For once she was relieved not to be sleeping outdoors. Elowyn usually enjoyed nighttime, because she could look up and see the whole sky blazing with stars. How could one ever feel alone or afraid in the company of stars? But in the midst of a storm there are no stars, and no moon either. Tonight the only light to comfort her came from the dim glow of the fire, burning low in the hearth. Looking up from her mat on the floor, there was nothing above her to gaze upon except for the rafters and straw of the ceiling, and the dwindling store of dried herbs and fish hanging from them.

The whole cottage shuddered under the force of the growing wind, and one corner of the roof began to leak almost as soon as the rain began. Elowyn wondered if it would withstand the beating, or come collapsing in on top of them as they slept. The blackness outside was oppressive, and she felt very small in the midst of it. She had always thought that if one was afraid of something fearsome emerging from the darkness, it would be most sensible to face the darkness and at least see it coming. She now understood why groups of men traveling through unfamiliar lands huddle close to the fire through the night, staring blankly at the light with their backs to the darkness. Sensible or not, facing the fire was a way of creating a world within a world. Staring stonily into the heart of the hypnotic flames, she could almost let herself believe that this cottage was the only thing that existed. There was no storm, no slain bowman, and there were no strange beasts emerging from the Shadow Wood to drag in unsuspecting passers-by. She could even lull herself into believing that the Sovereign was still alive, and there was no rebel group ambushing the city guards, who served as the City's only protection against whatever else was out there lying in wait. Elowyn shivered, pressing as close to the fire as she could. Morganne lay next to her in silence, staring at the ceiling. Her face still held no expression, but the tightness of her lips betrayed her anxiety.

"Morg?" Elowyn asked cautiously.

"Hmm?" Morganne absently responded, still absorbed by her own thoughts.

"What kinds of things live in the Shadow Wood?"

Morganne was shaken out of her thoughts for a moment. "The Shadow Wood? Why do you ask such a question?" Her tone became stern. "You haven't been going there have you?"

Elowyn shook her head furiously, and with some indignation. "Of course not!" But she couldn't tell Morganne the true reason as to why she wanted to know, lest she be forbidden to go back into the woods at all.

"Never mind then," Elowyn said hastily. "I was only curious. There are so many strange tales about that place."

Morganne nodded. "Especially since the Sovereign died, and everyone is so uneasy. The tension among the merchants is almost unbearable. But I have to wonder if most of those stories about the Shadow Wood aren't made up. Some people will say just about anything to call attention to themselves, or their shops," she said dryly. "I have often heard the head seamstress tell her apprentices that 'good gossip makes for good business.'" Morganne yawned deeply and turned away from Elowyn with her back to the fire. "Don't think about it any further, and go to sleep. Dawn will come early enough."

But sleep that night was difficult for Elowyn. She tossed and turned on her mat, restless as the wind that raged against the cottage in erratic gusts. The rain pounded on the shutters with seemingly sinister intent, as if trying to get in and drag her out into the darkness. "But that's silly," she thought. "It is only rain after all...isn't it?"

Sudden storms weren't unusual—sea squalls frequently came and went without warning. There was something more to this storm though, something dark...disturbing...unnatural. All of Elowyn's instincts were on edge, and she didn't know why. She felt like a small, frightened animal desperate to burrow into the ground, but finding no place to dig, and no place to hide.

Telling herself that it was simply the day's events that had her so spooked, she eventually lapsed into a half-sleep state. She wasn't certain if it was moments or hours later when she was startled by a loud and demanding rapping on the door. At first she tried to ignore it, her heart pounding wildly, hoping whoever it was would go away. Instead, the knocking grew louder and more persistent. Elowyn shook Morganne awake, but even though the sound was deafening to Elowyn, Morganne seemed not to hear it at all. Morganne told her that she was imagining things, rolled over, and went back to sleep. Elowyn didn't dare wake her mother, not unless she wanted to risk a hard beating. There was nothing for her to do but get up, open the door, and face whoever might be standing there. With trembling fingers, she lifted the latch on the heavy wooden door and slowly opened it just far enough for her face to peer out.

At first Elowyn saw nothing but the swirling blackness of the storm's fury. Then the lone figure of a man stepped forward. The firelight behind her softly illuminated his figure, as her eyes slowly adjusted. His face was hidden in shadow, but she could see that he was dressed in heavy leather armor. There was something odd about it though, as if it didn't fit him quite right. She squinted and concentrated her efforts, trying to make sense of what she was seeing as the flickering fire light and shadows of the night danced together before her eyes. Her face twisted into an expression of nauseated horror when she realized what was wrong with the man's armor. It had been completely shredded, stained red with his blood. He reached out to her in a pleading gesture for help, but his hands and arms were mauled to the bone.

Too terrified to scream, too numb to move, Elowyn looked up at the man's face. For a brief moment the firelight caught his features before the shadows reclaimed them. She saw that he wore no helm, and blood ran down the side of his head and across his cheek. But it was the look in his eyes that would haunt her dreams for the rest of her life. They were staring straight into hers, filled with shock, unbearable pain, and panicked desperation. She could feel his suffering as though it were her own. Her legs swam under her, and she tried to back away. The doomed man did not make a sound as he followed her movement. He tried to speak, yet all she heard was a low hissing noise that might very well have been the wind. He brushed past her to where her pouch hung on the wall and gestured toward it emphatically. When he tried to touch it, his hands passed right through both the pouch and the wall behind it. Suddenly he looked over his shoulder in terror, as though all the minions of the underworld were pursuing him. Letting out what would have been a loud scream of anguish if she could have heard him, he dissolved into a cold mist and was gone.

Elowyn shrieked in fear, quickly slamming the door and latching it. She dropped to her knees and whispered a fierce prayer to Aviad. Grabbing her little satchel of protective herbs, she hung it around her neck, hoping it was strong enough to ward off any presence of evil. Her nightclothes were damp with sweat, and she was shivering uncontrollably. She pressed herself against the heat of the fire until she was so close that it burned her skin. Still, the chill refused to leave her.

Elowyn huddled with her knees pulled tightly against her chest, jumping at every sound. She dared not go to sleep, and so the hours passed as the darkness pressed against her mind, trying to bend her spirit to its will. But she clutched the satchel tightly in her fist, breathing another prayer, refusing to let the panic of absolute terror control her thoughts. She took the coin out of her pouch, examining the raised markings on its face. As her fingers traced the intricate pattern of curves and lines, she sensed that there was a deep mystery about this coin. She wondered if it carried an evil curse. She was more certain by the moment that the vision she had seen was of the slain bowman, and that he was indeed the one who had lost the coin in the stream. Certainly he had not come to a very good end.

The storm eventually subsided. The black fury of the night gave way to a still, damp, deep gray dawn. As tired as Elowyn was, she knew that she could not sleep, not yet. Her heart was resolved to set things right so that the bowman's tormented soul might find rest. Quietly, she dressed and dropped the coin once again into the pouch at her waist. Before the rest of the house had begun to stir, she slipped out, her small form disappearing into the woods.

Chapter 2
A Chance Encounter

Elowyn did not pause to enjoy the bold fragrances awakened by the previous night's storm. She did not gaze upon the leaves, or drink at the stream, or search for animal tracks. Her only thought was to get to the place where the bowman had fallen, before dawn broke across the sky. She ran with the swiftness of a young deer, allowing her heart, her limbs, her breathing, her mind, all to fall in with the rhythm of her steps. She could force her body to run long distances when she had to, but it took all of her concentration. Every part of her being had to be in perfect alignment.

Elowyn was convinced that by removing the coin so soon after the man's brutal death, she had somehow interfered with his ascension into the afterlife, causing his spirit to appear before her in the night. How else could she explain it? He had sought her out from beyond the dead, and pointed directly at the pouch that held the coin. It was quite obviously an object not meant for her to keep, and it had to be returned at the proper time of day. Elowyn knew very little about the workings of magic, but it was common knowledge that the rites of good magic were most effective at sunrise. That was usually when cures were tried, when newly planted crops were blessed, and when pilgrims to the Shrines petitioned their most desperate prayers. Nearly any ritual of importance, even the harvesting of garden herbs, was best performed at sunrise. If she did not make it before then, she would have to wait another day, and perhaps risk another terrifying vision in the night.

The sky was a pale, watery gray when Elowyn finally slowed her pace and approached the stream. She paused at her favorite sun rock to allow her breathing to slow and her aching limbs to rest. There was still enough time before sunrise to complete her mission. As much time as she had spent in this place, getting to know every detail of its character, today it seemed completely foreign to her. Whatever had once made Elowyn feel at home here was now gone. The very way the leaves shifted above her gave her an uneasy feeling. Was it really only yesterday that she was sleeping happily in a nearby tree, blissfully unaware of the bowman and his accursed coin? It did not take her long to realize what was so disturbing about the rustling leaves above her; there was not so much as a breath of wind. All the other trees around it held perfectly still. She backed away, peering warily into its branches. There was not enough light yet to see well, but she didn't sense any signs of a creature there. The tree itself seemed to be attempting to speak with her, just as the strange apparition had. She huddled some distance away, in the shelter of a huge boulder. Coming had been a mistake. She no longer felt welcome in this place—it had changed.

A twig snapped somewhere close by. Elowyn quickly stood up, her body tense and alert. The sound did not seem to have been made by an animal, because the silence that followed was too profound. Whoever was out there had made a mistake in his movements, and was now trying to mask his presence. She could feel eyes upon her, and the flesh on her head and neck began to tingle.

"Who is it? I know you're there!" She had nothing to gain by stealth at this point, since obviously she had been seen. Her only hope was to provoke her stalker into showing himself. Before she quite knew what was happening she found herself knocked to the ground, winded and gasping for air, her face shoved into the muddy earth. A huge weight pressed upon her back so that she could not get up or look over her shoulder to see her attacker. She could only smell some horrible odor—like sulphur or brimstone—that made her gag. The weight was crushing her. She could not move, or breathe, or cry out for help. The hot stench of her attacker's breath was wet against her neck, the tips of gigantic teeth pressing down, ready for the kill. Then she heard the twang of arrows being released, and a heavy thud as the weight dropped suddenly off her. Elowyn picked herself up and wiped the mud away from her eyes, as she

24

half scurried, half crawled, attempting to put as much distance as she could between herself and her attacker.

What Elowyn saw lying on the ground before her in the dim light was an extraordinarily large, muscular wolf-shaped beast. The thing was hideously ugly, with glowing red eyes, and horns protruding from the top of its head. One arrow had penetrated the beast neatly between its shoulder blades; another had passed through its skull. As she pieced together what had nearly happened to her, she started to let out a shriek, her muscles tensed to flee. Strong arms instantly wrapped around her, and a hand was firmly cupped over her mouth.

"It's all right, you're safe now, but don't yell," a soft voice whispered. "You'll only attract others. Now, you promise you won't scream if I let go?" Elowyn nodded. She was released from her defender's grip, and turned to see a young man with sandy colored hair, deep hazel eyes, and skin darkened by the sun. His nose was long and finely sculpted, his cheeks ruddy as though he had spent a lifetime outdoors. The clothes he wore, once of a fine quality, were now dusty and travel worn, and in desperate need of both washing and mending.

"We're not safe here, even now," he continued to whisper. "Follow me...softly." There was nothing to do but follow. It didn't occur to Elowyn that it might be unwise to follow a strange man to an unknown destination. There was something about him that she instinctively trusted. She was amazed by the way he deftly moved like water across the ground, blending in perfectly with the woods around him, making not so much as a single leaf stir as he passed. Elowyn had taken great pains to learn how to move swiftly and silently, when others went tromping through the brush so clumsily that half the wood must hear them. Many times she had sat frozen in place, observing with great interest travelers who had camped by the stream. Not once had she been caught, nor even roused suspicion of her presence. But this man's skill was far beyond hers. She felt a thrill of pleasure at being able to mimic his movements, correcting the flaws in her own.

Elowyn felt her connection to her surroundings deepen so intensely it was almost unbearable. Her heart surged with longing, enticing her to stop, close her eyes, breathe deeply, and just melt into everything around her. The sun was finally rising, licking the sky with bright orange and gold, setting the whole wood ablaze with color. But she did not have the luxury of stopping. If she took her eye off the man for even a moment, she would no doubt lose sight of him. It was difficult enough to keep up with his long stride and still maintain the stealth of her movements.

He suddenly ducked around the edge of a low-ridged hill, and vanished. That was her first moment of awareness that she really didn't know much about this man, or where he was leading her. This was a part of the wood she did not know. She pressed against the exposed rock of the hill, and looked around anxiously.

"Come, this way," came his whisper from somewhere behind her. His face peered out of a small opening, masked by the rock face and an overhang of tree roots. She crawled in after him, finding herself in a dark corridor made of rock and packed earth. It was barely tall enough for her to stand in, and narrow enough that she could touch both sides.

"Feel your way forward carefully. At the end of this tunnel there is a larger room. There we can talk." Nervously, Elowyn did as he instructed, shuffling her feet along the floor, her hands extended along the walls as they twisted and curved, the whole time sloping downwards until she knew she was well underground.

Elowyn greatly disliked dark underground places because they cut her off from the outside world. Morganne's warning suddenly ran through her mind, "One of these days, you're going to get in trouble out there, and what then?" Yes, what then? She had already nearly met her death once that morning. If this man's intent was to hold her prisoner in this hole, who would ever find her? The passage suddenly grew wider and the air became less oppressive. The soft sounds made by her movements changed, and even without the ability to see where she was, she knew she was now standing in a rather large space.

"Step forward a bit," the man said in a low whisper. As she did so, she heard the sound of a heavy door closing behind her. It took every ounce of courage she had not to scream and try to claw her way out if she had to. In the midst of that unforgiving blackness, her eyes were suddenly drawn to the comforting glow of a hot coal, and then to the brighter flame of a small candle. Moments later, the room was lit from end to end by many lanterns. "Better?" the man asked. Elowyn nodded, holding her tongue so that he would not hear the quiver in her voice.

"I do apologize, little Maiden. Forgive this inadequate dwelling," he bowed with casual politeness. It was the first time Elowyn had heard his true voice, which was strong and melodic, with a slightly bitter edge. "I would much rather be out in the open myself, enjoying the sunrise and a low fire, with a breakfast of fresh fish cooking in the embers. But, alas, the times do not allow it. By the way, you need not worry that I have shut you in. I have in fact shut everything else out. There is no point in attracting unwelcome visitors. Here, we are safe from everything, save famine." Elowyn relaxed and looked about the cavern, which was completely empty. The walls were rough. She could see where they had been carved by hand. This was not a natural place; someone had built it, though for what purpose she could only make wild guesses.

He took off his cloak and spread it on the floor. "I am afraid there is no water for washing up, and this is the only seat I have to offer you. Truly a young maid of your beauty and grace deserves better. Perhaps in more peaceful times I shall be able to show you better hospitality." Elowyn blushed. She was not at all accustomed to being spoken to in this manner. She knew she must look frightful, with mud smeared all over her face and thoroughly soaked into the front of her dress. But it couldn't be helped.

"Now to business," the man said, once Elowyn had settled comfortably onto his cloak. He sat on the bare floor a respectable distance away from her. "You came very near to perishing this morning. Though it was an incredibly foolish thing to do, had you not called out, that beast would have had little girl for breakfast."

Allison D. Reid

Elowyn finally found her voice. "Thank you," she said, shuddering. "I don't know what I would have done…"

"You would have been dead," he replied matter-of-factly, "or worse. That entire area has been swarming with Alazoth's Hounds the last two nights. You might say they have taken it over completely. The one you encountered was merely a scout. He must have sensed you. A large pack of them was lying in wait across the stream. That is why I brought you here, though in doing so I break faith with those who wish this location to remain secret. To rescue you from one Hound, only to send you off to be torn to pieces by the rest, would have made me a murderer. At least here you are safe, for the time being. I mean not to pry, but what was a maid so young as yourself doing that close to the Shadow Wood alone?"

"I am often there, both day and night. But I have never before seen such a beast as that, nor heard their name spoken."

"Well, if you continue to frequent that place, especially by night, you are likely to see many more of them. And no one may be there next time to save you. You have never seen one before, because up until recently, they have been neatly contained within the Shadow Wood itself by the river. Somehow they have found a way to cross it in significant numbers. They are attacking anyone they find."

"Please, I owe you my life, and I do not even know your name."

The man smiled. "Aye, very true little maiden." He stood up and bowed. "I am Einar, son of Thaine, at your service. But to most of my friends, I am simply known as Einar. Have I yet earned the pleasure of knowing yours?" His lips curled with amusement.

Elowyn nodded solemnly. "Elowyn," she said, shifting uneasily in her seat as she felt him waiting for the rest. "Just Elowyn…" her face flushed, though he most likely couldn't see it beneath all the mud.

Einar dusted himself off, extending his hand to help her to her feet. "Well then, 'just Elowyn,' it is time we get you safely away from here so that I may return to my duties. Though I would love nothing more than to spend the day indulging myself in the pleasure of your company, I have serious matters to attend to this day."

Elowyn didn't quite know how to take this man. His compliments lavished so freely upon her were flattering in their own way. Certainly no one had ever called her a beautiful young maid before. Yet everything he said was diffused through the bitterness in his voice and the gleam in his eye. She could not tell if his words were sincere, if he merely spoke them out of courtesy, or if he was mocking her.

"I will take you close enough to Tyroc that you can find your way safely home. I strongly suggest that henceforth you remain within the protection of the city walls."

The look on Elowyn's face was one of intense pain. "Oh, but I can't!"

"Can't?" Einar seemed perplexed at first, then a flash of understanding passed over his features, and he smirked in what she was discovering to be his usual way. "How is it that one of your youth has already found the disfavor of the Sovereign's sons?"

It was apparent that he had misunderstood her completely. This was nothing unusual; Elowyn was used to being misunderstood in just about every way. He thought her aversion to the city was because she was a criminal of some kind. Turning red, she tried to explain. "No, it's nothing like that. But the city...if you told me that I must spend my life locked up behind a wall...I would prefer death," she said emphatically.

He laughed in a condescending way that irritated her. "Strong words for such a young girl. What do you know of death? Though I am certain that it could be arranged—no doubt the Hounds would oblige your wish."

Elowyn grew sulky. "You don't understand; I *belong* out here, among the trees and the wild beasts."

"Have you no home then? Are you an orphan?"

"No," she said, grimacing. "I am no orphan. I live with my mother and two sisters in a small cottage on the road outside the East Gate, but I rarely sleep there. I much prefer a tree branch under the stars for a bed. That place...where you found me...that is my favorite place, or rather, it was. I shall miss it." Elowyn's mournful expression caught Einar by surprise and some of the bitterness faded from his heart. Lost in thought, he seemed to be remembering a former time, a former self perhaps. For just that moment, he glowed with a luminous, child-like wonder, and Elowyn found him to be fascinatingly beautiful.

But then something disturbed his thoughts, like a pebble thrown into a still pond, dragging him back to the present. The dark thought spread until it had crossed the whole length of his mind. His jaw hardened and the bitterness returned. The smirk she was beginning to dislike was back, smothering that lovely glow until it was thoroughly extinguished.

"But things have changed, haven't they," he said to himself. It was more a statement than a question. He sighed, and shook his head regretfully as if his spirit carried a heavy weight. "Like it or not, the city is the only secure place for you. Even if I should show you areas of the wood that are safe right now, I cannot guarantee that they will remain so for long. I want no part in hastening your death. If against my advice you do go beyond the gates of Tyroc, and I can see by the look in your eyes that you intend to, at least remain close and stick to the north as much as possible. Carry a weapon."

"But I have none."

"Not even a dagger?" He seemed shocked by the thought that she habitually roamed the wilds alone with no weapon. It was not something he would imagine doing himself.

Elowyn shook her head in response. Where was she supposed to get such an expensive object? "But I did find a bow," her eyes brightened as she remembered.

"Oh? You *found* a bow?" He asked inquisitively.

Feeling insulted, Elowyn stiffened. "Yes, I *found* it, lying in some tall grass. The same beasts that attacked me killed a man and hauled his body away. They left his bow and helmet behind. I didn't steal anything." She folded her arms indignantly.

"Nay, little maiden," Einar's tone softened, "I meant not to accuse you of it. What can you tell me of the man who was killed?"

"Nothing, I'm afraid. I never actually saw him."

Einar appeared to struggle with his thoughts for a brief moment. His curiosity intensified, and a look of great desire crossed his features before he regained his composure. "If you wish, I will teach you how to use it. It is a pity that a young maid should have to think about such matters, but in this dark age..." his voice trailed off.

"Why do you speak so?" Elowyn's tone became somewhat irritated. "You talk as if the whole world were coming to an end. It can't be all that bad."

"But it is." Einar grew solemn and edged closer to her, looking about nervously. "Don't you feel it? You are no ordinary child—that is plain to me. Have you not sensed the darkness encroaching? Have you not felt the fingers of evil reaching out from the depths?" Elowyn's scalp tingled, and the hair rose on her neck. He drew so close to her that she could feel his breath upon her ear as he whispered, "The emergence of the Hounds is only the beginning."

The wild look in Einar's eyes made her wonder if he was a bit mad. His sudden change in demeanor thoroughly startled her, yet even as she backed away from him, she knew exactly what he meant. She *had* felt it. She had felt it at the stream when she discovered the bow. It was what had made her race at break-neck speed to seek the protection of the very place she most loathed. She had felt it in the growing darkness; she had felt it in the wind; she had felt it in the height of the storm. And most of all, she had felt it deep within her soul, at the first knocking on the door.

Elowyn's expression turned to one of immeasurable fear, as she recalled the night's events that had impelled her to come to the stream that morning. Only instead of leaving the coin behind as she had planned, she had been attacked by yet another evil presence, one that was entirely new to her. Her fear intensified as she realized that there was no way to return the coin to the stream. What if the vision she had seen haunted her again, and again, every night without respite? Her breathing quickened and she began to panic. Frantically she made a dash for the door. She could not bear feeling trapped in this cave any longer. She needed to feel the sunshine and know that it was more real than the darkness, that it was indeed real at all.

Before she could lift the latch, Einar gently blocked her and said in a soothing voice, "My apologies, little maiden; I did not mean to frighten you so. Shame be upon me and my children forever for my carelessness."

In a trembling voice, Elowyn asked, "Is there no way at all to get near that stream where you found me?"

"Nay, I am afraid not. I was only there looking for someone, but it is obvious he is not there. Even I would not dare return, lest I had a whole army at my side. The other bank of the stream is blackened with Alazoth's Hounds. Though by day they sleep and stay in the shadows, for it is my understanding that they cannot bear the sunlight, to go anywhere near them is a risky business. Once the sun has set, they will follow your scent. That is partly why I brought you here rather than escorting you straight home. If a Hound does track us to this place after sundown, it will not find anything. Your home would be another matter."

Elowyn's heart fell.

"Come child, it is time that we leave this place. I must resume my search, alone. It is highly important that I find my friend, now more so than ever."

"Will I see you again?"

Einar paused and considered her question thoughtfully. "Aye, I believe you shall. I cannot promise you when, but it will be soon. Now, follow me again, silently."

The return journey was as glorious as the first. Again, Elowyn mimicked his fluid movements with sheer delight, and even made up a few of her own in order to keep up with the pace of his adult stride. It seemed to her that he was very much aware of her attempts, and that he purposely threw in difficult moves just to watch her reaction. Not to be undone, as they neared their destination, he disappeared into the brush, leaving her standing in the middle of a clearing, searching for any sign of his form. She found it increasingly disturbing that another human could be so close, yet remain beyond her senses. She heard nothing, saw nothing, smelled nothing. Had she not known better, she would have thought herself quite alone.

After a few moments he emerged with a glimmer of amusement in his eye. "Well, at least you cannot mimic that one yet." She took his comment as the compliment he intended it to be. He did not realize how many months she had spent, figuring out how to move stealthily through the forest simply by trial and error. His motions were highly perfected, yet he made them seem so simple. His skill completely awed her. She had never met anyone so adept.

"Just through those trees, you will see the city wall. It is here I must take my leave. Farewell, most worthy Maiden of the Wood, we shall meet again. Remember all the things I told you, and stay to the North of Tyroc if you must leave the city. There you will be watched after." Then he bowed to her, slipped silently into the trees without stirring so much as a leaf, and was gone.

Chapter 3
Vision of Darkness

News reached the cottage three days later that a member of the renegade group had been caught. Such a thing had never happened before. Everyone had begun to believe that this mysterious group was completely impenetrable, beyond capture, injury, or even death. The latest rumor going about was that they weren't people at all, but an elusive band of evil spirits. Whether they were made of spirit or flesh-and-blood would be revealed soon enough. By proclamation of the Sovereign's sons, all were required to attend the renegade's execution. This was a momentous victory for the two sons, and they wanted everyone to know it.

Elowyn worried that their mother was going to throw the crier out on his ear when he came knocking at the door. She had just settled at the loom with some newly spun, fine linen thread and was beginning the rhythm of the weave. Interrupting her weaving hours was dangerous, usually resulting in a backhand across the face. But the crier was not at her mercies, and even their mother realized it was ill-advised to oppose his demands. Irritated though she was, there was nothing she could do so long as she lived under the rule of Tyroc. So when the time came, she grudgingly dropped her threads and dragged Morganne, Elowyn, and Adelin out the door, grumbling the entire way.

To their mother, this execution meant nothing more than time away from her loom she could not afford to waste. She cared nothing for the politics of Tyroc, but she was keenly aware of the games the nobles often played with the simple tradesmen and artisans. Even the slightest delay or variation in what they asked for could give them cause to claim that they did not have to pay. She in turn would have little recourse against them. Considering that she had borrowed heavily to purchase the velvet and other materials she needed, if they refused to pay her, she would be ruined. But if all was precisely to their specifications, and the money was paid in full, this order would bring more wealth than she had seen in her lifetime. The risk made her anxious, which had the effect of making her more cross than usual.

They traveled the road together in an uncomfortable silence, each focused their own thoughts. Adelin was too young to know what was happening. She bounced contentedly on Morganne's hip, pointing and babbling to any bright object that caught her attention. Morganne's expression was solemn and somewhat tense. Elowyn could not guess what her thoughts were, but that was nothing unusual. Morganne usually kept to herself. Elowyn felt a kind of fluttering in the pit of her stomach and was dragging her feet, hoping somehow they would arrive too late. However, the end result was that their mother kept barking at her to hurry up, and each time she said it, she became more irritable.

There were others traveling with them, flooding in from the outskirts of Tyroc. Even laborers from the southern farming villages were given a reprieve by their lords so that they might attend. People flocking in on the smaller roads continued to join together like streams flowing into a river, until they became a massive flood of humanity surging forward. The main road took a sharp curve and sloped upward, running along the colossal eastern wall of the city. Rows of strategically placed guards stared down at them from the battlements, bows in hand. Elowyn could sense the tension in their muscles as they stood ready to shoot at the least sign of trouble. As the procession drew closer to the city gates, the crowds increased to an unbearable level. They were jostled along, pressed closer and closer together until one could only move forward, swept along in an unrelenting current.

Elowyn felt as though she were riding amidst a sickening sea, a swirl of men, women, carts, and livestock. There were other children too. The youngest ones clung to their mother's skirts as shipwreck victims might cling to floating bits of wood. The whole mass swelled and moved along the wall in a gigantic wave, pushing, pulling, and roaring with an incomprehensible cacophony of shouts, laughter, jumbled conversations, and the groans of overburdened carts. The closer they came to the gates, the hotter and more foul smelling the air became. Elowyn felt as though she were being smothered. Every sound seemed louder than it really was, adding layers to the nervous ball that was beginning to form deep down in her stomach. One of the carts near her had a squeaky wheel. Though it was such a small sound in the midst of all that chaos, it completely unnerved her. She held her ears trying to block it out, but it only seemed louder with the dampening of the other sounds. It was like a tiny, desperate scream for help that went ignored.

Every once in a while a faint whiff of fresh air brushed Elowyn's face, and she drank it in greedily as though it might very well be her last. She closed her eyes and tried to calm herself, hoping that once they were all squeezed through the gate into the city, there would be more room on the other side. But in that she was greatly disappointed. When they finally approached the gate, and were shoved through by the pressing mob behind, the inner city was just as crowded. She continued to push forward, through narrow streets lined with corbelled buildings that leaned out precariously over them. The doorway of every shop was jammed with buyers haggling over goods. The rest of the crowd attempted to converge in the central square where the execution was to be held. Not only was the square packed with eager spectators, but merchants had set up their carts any place they could, not willing to miss the opportunity to sell their wares to such a multitude. It was almost like faire time.

Elowyn was tired of being jostled and elbowed and nearly run over by carts. She felt trapped in a prison of legs and long dresses, and was not tall enough to see what was going on ahead of her. A heavy-set woman with an edgy basket on her shoulders was pushing her way through the crowd. She shoved full force into Elowyn, nearly toppling the basket.

"Now then," the woman said gruffly, "watch where you're going."

Never mind that Elowyn had been standing perfectly still, and it was the woman who should have been watching. But Elowyn knew better than to say anything. As the woman and her basket moved forward, a throng of people tried to follow in her wake. The result was that Elowyn found herself being separated from Morganne and her mother. There was no way she could help it. Soon she would be swallowed up by the mass of people around her.

To Elowyn, who never came into the city unless she absolutely had to, and who avoided even the smallest of crowds as a general rule, this whole venture was a complete nightmare. She looked around desperately for a way to break free. The only things she could see were the tops of nearby buildings, and one lone tree standing above the crowd to the east. Gritting her teeth, she made her way toward the tree, not caring whose leg got pushed out of the way, or whose toes got stepped on. After what seemed like an age, she finally reached it and scrambled up the trunk with experienced ease. A few people looked at her strangely, and a group of rough-looking boys pointed at her and laughed, but she didn't care. She was relieved to be above the fray and felt safe in this small bit of nature amidst the ugliness of the city.

"Poor tree," Elowyn said as she examined it. She was accustomed to the beautiful, healthy trees growing freely in the wilds. This one was bursting forth like an unwanted weed, stunted and sickly. Its roots strained at the cobbles, forcing them to bubble upward in rolling swells. Its trunk was full of nails, and holes, and deep scars from carts being rammed into it. She fingered a pale, listless leaf. The city was choking it, and yet it defiantly lived, even in this place where it surely didn't belong. Or perhaps, she thought, the tree was the only thing that really belonged, and it was the city that was encroaching.

Down below, something was starting to happen. First came a crier, announcing the royal procession. Guards with long spears began to shove through the crowds, holding them back to make a wide pathway up to the platform in the town center. Then came members of the Circle—the late Sovereign's most trusted personal guards. A mysterious bunch they were, with their faces always covered. They were supposed to be the best fighters anywhere in the Sovereign's realm, and they guarded the Sovereign with their lives. Elowyn supposed now that the Sovereign was gone they belonged to his sons.

Sure enough, the two brothers appeared next, along with a figure she did not recognize who was wearing a rich black cape. The Sovereign's sons wore gold circlets on their heads, and held royal scepters in their hands. Long brilliant red robes trailed behind them, the ends held up by servants. The extravagance of their clothing and jewelry was like nothing Elowyn had ever seen, even on the wealthiest of her mother's clients. But Elowyn found that instead of making them look majestic and powerful, the excess of their attire only appeared gaudy and overbearing. After the brothers came the remainder of the Circle, and then the prisoner; a hooded figure bound around his chest, arms and wrists. Following the prisoner were more guards like the kind she had seen on the walls of the city. They carried short spears that were pointed at the prisoner's back.

It was rumored among the people of Tyroc that there was something strange about the brothers. Everyone whispered that the eldest in particular "wasn't quite right," but because he had been favored by the Sovereign, none dared to speak against him openly. No one really knew anything about the younger son, who had remained aloof and mysterious. Indeed, this was one of the first times he had appeared before them as a public figure. Everyone was hoping that today the question on everyone's mind over the last months might finally be settled—who would succeed as the next Sovereign? Though the elder had clearly been the beloved son, the people were uneasy about the idea of being ruled by a man who was quite possibly insane. However little they knew about the younger son, at the least he seemed of sound mind and body.

Once the procession was settled on the platform and the crowds had been stilled, the younger of the two brothers came forward to speak. Elowyn found that she was close enough to see his face, and she studied it thoughtfully. His expression was surprisingly vacant, cold, and arrogant. Before he had even opened his mouth, Elowyn knew that she disliked him. His elder brother sat behind him in silence with a dazed look, as if he was not really sure where he was, or what was going on around him. There was no question as to why people whispered that he wasn't quite right.

Allison D. Reid

"Good people of Tyroc," the younger brother addressed the crowd. His voice was forceful and clear, but its tone betrayed his youthful age. "It has been nearly four months since the passing of my beloved father from this world into the one beyond. To find him taken so suddenly in the prime of his age was a great shock to us all. Regrettably, he left no clear will or documentation to establish the succession of rule. Were these normal circumstances, it would be clearly my brother Avery's birthright. However these are not normal circumstances. My brother's health is far too delicate to bear the strain of leadership, and I, according to the laws of our realm, am not yet come of age to claim the title of Sovereign. Therefore, the decision has fallen to the Council of Elders. They have spent these last months in grave deliberation as to what would be in the best interests of the people. I am pleased to announce that our good Lord Braeden, my father's trusted Chief Steward, and my long-time, most learned tutor, has graciously agreed at the Council's request, to serve as Protector of Tyroc, and to mentor me into my rightful place as Sovereign."

The man in the black cape neither spoke nor smiled, but faced the crowd and made a low, dignified bow. Elowyn gazed at him intently, probing his features to figure out what sort of man he might be. His eyes were dark, nearly as black as the cape draped around him, and deeply set, leaving pronounced shadows above his cheekbones. Perhaps they seemed even darker due to the fact that his face was unusually pale—nearly as white as newly bleached linen. It was stretched thin in an unnatural way, almost as though he was wearing someone else's skin. His nose was twisted, and his lips were hard and cruel. She had never before felt such a deep sense of distress just from looking into someone's face. For a moment, his glance fell in her direction. She felt their eyes lock as he peered at her form through the branches of the tree. Elowyn suddenly felt uncovered and instinctively tried to shield herself, nearly losing her balance in the process. The strength of his gaze seemed to penetrate her clothing and her body, reaching through to the very depths of her soul as if to see if he could snatch away a piece of it.

40

An intense sensation of dread overcame Elowyn and a cold chill violently shook her small body. She felt the same sickness in her stomach that she had suffered several days earlier when she had found the ground by the stream soaked with blood. As she stared at the man in the black cape, unable to look away, it seemed to her that a thick, dark cloud suddenly descended upon him. From where she could not tell, as the sun was blazing brightly in the midst of a flawless sapphire sky. She gasped and shut her eyes tightly, praying that whatever hold this man seemed to have over her would be broken. Gathering her courage, she cautiously opened her eyes. The dark mist had dissolved away, and despite his pallor, the Sovereign's steward appeared once again to be an ordinary man in a black cape. Elowyn could not explain the experience, though it left her trembling and uneasy.

Elowyn glanced over the crowd below her. No one else seemed to have seen what she had, or felt that deep sense of foreboding in their blood. The crier had urged them to cheer at the moment when the man stepped forward to take recognition, and they had mindlessly complied. As far as they were concerned, the anxiety of not knowing who the Sovereign's successor would be had ended, and now they could continue living their lives just as they had before. Tyroc was the largest city anywhere within close reach, and it had enjoyed peace for so many years that perhaps the populace had forgotten how easily and swiftly the winds of fortune could change.

"And now!" the younger brother said, holding up his hand for quiet once more. Elowyn saw the look of arrogance intensify as the cheering crowds made him bolder. "Now we come to the less pleasant task of dealing with the traitor in our midst. It is truly sad," he paused for effect, "that one of our own would take advantage of our weakness in this time of mourning. This rebel group, whose members were once loved and trusted by my father, and who for so many years gladly partook of his bounty and endless generosity, have turned his grave into a stepping-stone. In a most dishonorable fashion, they have used our turmoil against us, striking out at the innocent while they themselves hide in the shadows like cowards.

"They have haunted our forests and roads, killing our guards on sight, unprovoked. Our many attempts to stop them failed until several days ago, when we caught this man skulking along the city walls. Even in these difficult circumstances we have tried to be fair. We asked what grievance this group has against us, and tried to understand their demands, but all we got for our efforts was silent defiance. These are not men who can be reasoned with. They are thirsty for nothing more than blood and power. They slaughter without cause, and without conscience. They are murderers and thieves, and our laws will punish them according to their deeds, for even in our hour of darkness, we are a just people." He paused long enough to look upon the rapt faces of the crowd as they drank in every word of his carefully rehearsed speech.

"This man," he said, pointing to the bound and hooded figure, "will serve as an example to the rest. Others will now know what happens to groups such as these, who strike out against the people of Tyroc. Justice shall be served here today as we avenge the innocent blood these men have spilled. Executioner, bring the condemned man forward so that the people may get a good look at one of the many who have caused them so much anguish."

The hood was finally removed, revealing a fair-haired young man who was blinking painfully in the brightness of the light. The crowds were jeering at him and yelling insults. They might have thrown stones and rotten food as well, had there not been a chance of mistakenly hitting one of the Sovereign's sons.

Elowyn's stomach ached. The younger brother's speech sounded noble, and it rang true with all of the rumors she had heard. Yet there was an uneasiness stirring deep within her being. The look on the captured man's face did not speak of blood lust or greed. His eyes did not lack conscience. He stood there amidst the jeers with his chin high and a look of peace on his face. With shock, Elowyn realized that as horrified as she was at having to witness this man's execution, he was not afraid to die.

Perhaps that was what unnerved her so. He was supposed to argue, and struggle, and try to break free—what had he to lose if they were to kill him anyway? What animal in the wood sees the hunter and just stands there without any attempt to outrun the arrow or outwit the blade?

The younger brother continued, "Our law allows you final words before your execution. Do you have anything to say for yourself?"

"Only that such blatant lies do not become one of your stature, Milord. But, praise be to Aviad that He is beyond such deception. In my death, shall the truth someday be revealed." He said it not with anger or bitterness, but as a quiet statement of fact. There was no question that he believed what he said.

The younger brother's face flushed with emotion for the first time that day. He glanced at the man with the black cape as though asking for direction. He had not yet learned how to make a seamless recovery when something unexpected rattled his performance, and his inexperience was showing. The man in the black cape appeared to be completely unruffled, even slightly amused, as he whispered something in the brother's ear.

The younger brother turned once again to the crowd. "Yes, fine sentiments from a thief and murderer," he said in a smug, condescending tone. "Fortunately our laws are swayed by evidence rather than impassioned words."

He pulled out a small scroll and waved it before the crowd, "This scroll certifies that this man has been convicted of treason before a court of Tyroc. He is found to be in league with those who have slain our people without cause or mercy. The customary punishment for treason is death by public impalement—a slow, torturous death. But we are prepared to show this man more mercy than he has shown, in the hope that his comrades will be brought to repentance, and return to the lives they once had. The prisoner, alas, must still answer for his crime, but we have granted him a swift death by the executioner's axe."

A drum began to beat, slowly, steadily. The prisoner was grabbed roughly by the ropes that bound him and forced onto his knees. Two guards shoved him facedown by his shoulders against the block and bared his neck. Elowyn felt severely ill. Nothing could compel her to watch such brutality. Her tear-filled eyes roved the boisterous crowd. At that moment, they were nothing more than a vengeful mob. They craved this. They enjoyed the spectacle, and afterwards they would go on just as before, selling their wares, planting, reaping, plying their trades…and this man's death would be utterly forgotten. Did not one of them have the same sense she did that something was very wrong? Or was she simply being swayed by her own emotions and the man's powerful calm as he spoke his final words, "In my death shall the truth someday be revealed." What was the truth, and who would reveal it? Who in this crowd would care enough to look for it?

Among the many jeering and scornful faces, Elowyn found one lone man who seemed to care. His head was bared in respect, and his eyes were filled with unspeakable grief and sorrow. He wore a simple gray travel cloak, the type that so easily slips by unnoticed because it is so common. She wondered if he were perhaps one of the condemned man's family. The drum suddenly stopped, and the sound of the axe fell several times before its grisly work was finished. Callous cheers and catcalls rang out from the crowd while Elowyn and the gray-cloaked man wept their silent tears. As Elowyn expected, it was not long before the masses began to go about their business as though nothing had happened. When the crowds had thinned, Elowyn slid down from her place in the tree, made her way through the maze of narrow streets to the northern gate, and vanished into the woodlands on the other side. The man's body was taken and buried by his family, but his head was placed on a stake and displayed on the outer wall of Tyroc until there was nothing left of it but the skull, hanging as a reminder and a warning to the rest of the rebel group. No one realized at the time what a prophetic omen this visage of death would be for the dark days yet to come.

Chapter 4
The Storm Breaks

Elowyn passed through the northern gate, which opened out onto dense woodlands that stretched for several days' journey. Even without Einar's warning, she would have avoided the Eastern gate, which was sure to be flooded with people returning to the nearby towns and farms to the south. She felt the need to be by herself, to try to understand what she had just experienced, and why it had sickened her so. She had witnessed the cruelty of the Sovereign's punishments before. Over the years she had been forced to watch hangings, and beatings with the lash, and had walked by any number of people locked in the stocks on the edge of the square. Such sights had always greatly disturbed her, but never before had she felt such cause to question whether or not the sentence was just. This particular execution had felt very wrong to her, and her heart could not endure the casual way in which the crowds had accepted it. As Elowyn struggled with her emotions, she came to realize that she was upset by more than just the day's events. She felt an impending sense that the world was changing around her, far more quickly than she liked. Something within herself was changing too. The events of the past week had put an enormous strain on her spirit, and she knew not where to turn for relief. She, who so passionately enjoyed her solitude, did not like feeling alone.

Even though Elowyn had closed her eyes during the execution, the sound of the axe striking the block repeatedly still rang in her ears, tormenting her. Against her will, her imagination conjured up its own images to go along with the sounds. They kept repeating until she was ready to fall upon her knees and beg Aviad to have mercy and quiet her mind. She wanted so much to be able to cry, to mourn for this man she did not know. Somehow she thought that might make her feel better. But the tears simply would not fall. It was as though part of her had been executed too, a piece of her humanity severed. She could only stumble forward blindly, in a kind of dazed numbness.

Elowyn eventually realized that she was gaining no joy or comfort from her walk; she was merely getting herself lost. Never having traversed the woodlands beyond the north gate, she didn't know the trees here. The direction of the beaten paths, the locations of the streams, and the patterns of the animals were all a mystery to her. She was beginning to feel hungry, too. Finding a tree that seemed inviting, she sank against its trunk. A gentle wind pressed a few young, low branches so close around her that the tips of their leaves tickled her face. She felt almost as if the tree sensed her despair and was giving her a loving hug. Perhaps she was silly to imagine such things—Morganne would no doubt think so—but she felt it all the same. Whether real or imagined, the thought made her feel a little better.

Elowyn closed her eyes and tried to let the warmth of the sun melt away the shadows in her heart. The sounds of the forest grew deeper and more vibrant; the chatter of birds all around, the rustle of small animals disturbing the winter's remaining blanket of dead leaves, running water in the far distance, and the hypnotic sound of the west wind caressing the tops of the trees. She could hear the soft but growing rumble moving toward her, like an impending wave that would soon wash over her and continue on throughout the whole of the wood. Her breathing deepened and she began to relax for the first time since that last blissfully innocent night she'd spent stargazing from her favorite tree by the stream. She was startled out of her thoughts by a voice that was familiar.

"I wondered how long it would take you to show in the northern wood. I had begun to fear that the Hounds had devoured you after all."

Elowyn looked up to see Einar leaning against a nearby tree. He seemed different today than when he had saved her from the wolf-beast. His voice was like a still pond, low and heavy-laden with some unspoken burden. His face showed no sign of joy; even that familiar bitter smirk had been wiped away.

"No, I didn't get eaten. I've had to stay home and tend the garden. It was time to pull the weeds away from the spring herbs..." Elowyn stopped abruptly. She realized that it didn't matter what she had been doing for the past three days, nor did he want to know. It was the way he said things that made her feel as though she must straighten her shoulders and give an accounting of herself.

"How did you find me here? I haven't been walking anywhere in particular. To be truthful," she flushed, "I have no idea where I am. I was just going to rest a few minutes and then get my bearings."

"Did I not tell you that you would be watched for in the northern wood?"

Elowyn felt a slight chill. Had he been silently watching her all this time? She stood up and peered nervously through the brush. Until Einar had spoken aloud she had not felt any presence but her own, and it unnerved her that she had not sensed his approach. Were others watching as well without her knowledge?

Einar motioned for her to sit again. "Not like that, little maiden. The wood is not full of spies set to follow you. I only meant that very little happens in this part of the wood without my knowledge. I live out here, you know. This is my home." He gestured grandly with his arms in a way that included everything within sight and beyond. "Every curve of these hills is burned within my heart and soul."

That was one sentiment Elowyn could relate to. She relaxed again, though part of her still did not know whether it was fully safe to trust this man.

"So, what did you think of Tyrocian Justice, eh? Quite a spectacle today." Einar's tone gave Elowyn the impression that he was trying very hard to hold back an immense flood of anger, though she could not tell exactly what he was angry about. She scanned his features carefully, wondering how she was expected to respond. But his expression was closed and tight. She fidgeted nervously. Saying the wrong thing could be dangerous, yet she had to say something.

"I only went because I had to. Mother dragged me." As soon as the words came out of her mouth she felt terrible. They were true of course, but the event had much more of an impact on her than that. In truth she was horrified by what she had seen, and was rent with compassion for the executed man. Considering the crowd's response and the serious charges brought against him, she was afraid to speak out on his behalf, even to Einar. After all, what if he really had been guilty of all they accused him of? Would she want someone like that roaming free? Mixed in with the horror of brutality was a wellspring of confusion that nagged at her. Usually she had such a clear sense of what was right, and what was fair. Today that sense was clouded.

But Elowyn was an honest child at heart, and she felt compelled to speak as much truth as was safe. "Everyone seemed happy to watch him die. I don't know what he did, or if he did anything at all. But killing him did not make me feel glad, or safe." She looked up to gauge his reaction and was surprised to find his head was bent low over his knees. He was not even looking at her. She finally understood that the burden Einar bore so heavily that day was grief, and it occurred to Elowyn that perhaps he had known the executed man.

After a long silence, she asked timidly, "Did you know him?"

"You could say that. He was like a brother to me."

"Did he really do all that they say?"

Einar paused for a long time, wrestling with his own thoughts before letting out a weary sigh. "Things are not always the way they seem. Someday, when you are older, you will understand that. But, no, he did not murder innocents. He did nothing more than was necessary to preserve the life of his family and the families of others." Einar's muscles tightened and the anger returned to his face, wiping out all traces of grief save the shadows under his eyes.

His statement left her with more questions than answers. Einar quite obviously knew far more than he was telling her, but she dared not pry.

"I didn't like the man in the black cape." Elowyn shivered slightly, remembering vividly the way she'd felt when his eyes had lifted to meet hers.

Einar's eyebrows rose with interest. "Eh, what man is that?"

"The man standing next to the brothers. He's supposed to take the Sovereign's place until the younger son is old enough. I don't remember his name."

"I was not there young maid, I only heard about what went on. But I understand now of which man you speak. What do you know of him?"

Elowyn shrugged. "Nothing at all. I just didn't like him. He...he didn't seem right somehow."

Einar nodded, studying her thoughtfully. "So, you didn't like him," he said as he began to chuckle to himself. The sound was completely unexpected, and Elowyn wasn't sure how to take it. "A little child indeed..." He stared absently, consumed for a moment by some unspoken thought.

"I don't know what you mean."

"It is from an old rhyme.

'In the night the shadow will come
It will pay no heed to the morning sun
O'er every hill and valley it will creep
Washing o'er us while we reap
But while the world stands blinded in the dark of day
A little child will show the way.'

"Actually," Einar said, standing up and dusting himself off, "it is an old prophecy if you hold with that sort of thing."

"But what does that have to do with the black-caped man?"

"Everything."

Elowyn liked Einar. She couldn't help it. He had showed her kindness. He spoke to her as though she was worthy of being spoken to (which was far better treatment than she was usually accustomed to), and of course, most of all, he had saved her life. Because of that, she felt a certain devotion to him, and an inner need to repay her debt. Certainly she admired his wood skills and hoped that someday he might teach her. But she had difficulty understanding him at times. He made strange remarks, and more than once he had referred to an impending darkness which Elowyn found to be extremely troubling.

Einar scanned the blue sky overhead. The sun was beginning its afternoon descent as wispy white clouds passed over. "You had best not sleep out among the trees tonight, little maiden, the storm will be upon us soon."

"What storm?" There was no sign of bad weather anywhere in the sky, or on the wind.

"You must trust me on this, it will be here. Before night falls you will see it on the horizon."

"How do you know this?" Elowyn asked with awe. She thought perhaps he was gleaning some clue from their surroundings that she was unaware of.

"That is the one thing I beg you not to ask. I can only see into the night ahead because my eyes, unlike yours, are no longer shielded by innocence. May they remain so for a while longer. But before you go, I have both a gift for you, and a boon to ask. Whether or not you grant my boon, little maiden, it is my greatest desire that you accept the gift. My heart might rest more easily knowing that you have it."

He handed her an object bundled in heavy cloth. She eagerly pulled away the wrapping to reveal a new belt and a long, nimble dagger in a plain, but well made, leather sheath. Gasping in surprise, she closed her fingers about the cold, heavy hilt and drew it out. The blade was so finely polished that she could see the leaves above her reflected in its surface.

She looked up at Einar in wonder and disbelief. No one had ever given her such a gift before, and she didn't know quite what to do, or what to say. He smiled warmly at her, probably the first genuine smile she had seen cross his features since they had met.

"I bought it especially for you, so wear it well. A dagger is not a toy, nor is it a tool to be used for crude, mundane purposes that will dull and weaken the blade. This is a weapon of defense, something to protect you while you are wandering about in the wilds."

He showed her the proper way to hold and wield it, and taught her the best strategies he knew of to use her small size to her advantage; how to twist herself free from a predator's grasp, and how to keep an opponent from using her own blade against her. In the end, he gave her a strong warning that she would need to practice a great deal in order to truly master the weapon's use.

"With this blade," he said, "I mean not to give you cause to run headlong into danger. Rather, I hope that it just might give you enough of an advantage to get out of it in dire circumstances. Your best hope of survival, little maiden, is still to remain within the protection of Tyroc's walls." He made the statement not as a chastisement, but with just a hint of bemusement in his eye. He knew very well that she would not follow his advice, nor did he expect her to.

"And now," Einar's tone grew serious, "the boon I must ask." His expression saddened again, as though he did not much like what he was about to ask of her. "When we first met, you told me that you had found a bow, left by someone the Hounds had slain and carried off. Do you still have it?" Elowyn nodded. "I would very much like to see it—not take it, mind you, but simply examine it. It may aid my search for my lost friend."

Elowyn felt relieved. From the look on his face, she had expected he had a difficult and unpleasant task for her.

"Of course you may look at it. I will bring it to you," Elowyn said without hesitation. She hoped that he would not insist on following her home. It would not do at all for her mother to see her walking about with a strange man, nor did Elowyn want her to see the bow, or any of the other little treasures she had hidden away from prying eyes. But Einar did not offer to walk her home, and indeed seemed somewhat relieved that she did not ask him to. Elowyn sensed more than ever that a great mystery hung about him. He was clearly more than a mere woodsman, but he didn't seem willing to offer much information about himself.

Allison D. Reid

"Where should I meet you? All the places I knew are overrun now," Elowyn said mournfully.

"Look that way. See the hill and the large boulder? On the other side of that lies a small cluster of ruins. It was once a glorious temple and shrine to Aviad, but was felled during the Great War and never rebuilt. The new temple was erected inside the city walls to protect it from being destroyed a second time. When you are able, I want you to meet me there. I will keep watch for you as long as I can. But for now, young maid," he said, scanning the skies again, "you had best begin your journey home. The sun will soon set, and the storm will be upon us."

Elowyn searched again for signs of bad weather and found nothing. He spoke with such confidence it was difficult not to believe him. As much as she wanted to sleep under the comfort of the night sky to soothe her fears, she instead picked her way carefully back to Tyroc, making certain that she could remember how to get back. She left little markings for herself every so often, imprinting the landscape on her mind—taking special note of an unusually shaped tree here, an interesting rock face there, until the great wall of the city finally loomed before her. There, behind the cover of some thick brush, she strapped her new belt and blade to her chemise so that they would remain hidden beneath her clothes. The dagger would only draw questions from Morganne and her mother that she was not yet prepared to answer.

Elowyn discovered that she had emerged about half way between the north and east gates. She followed the city wall until she came to the road that would lead her back home. By the time she reached the cottage, the sun was hanging low on the horizon. Ahead of her, the sky was clear and perfect, with a vibrant wash of colors smeared across it. She paused to drink in their beauty and wondered if perhaps Einar could be wrong. But when she turned to give a fleeting glance back in the direction of Tyroc, her heart sank.

Great swells of dark clouds were beginning to form. They were the most foreboding clouds she had ever seen, and some primitive instinct urged her to run and hide before they were close enough to overtake her.

52

She could tell that they were moving very fast, billowing up and out like thick smoke, rising higher and higher into the sky as they formed. Everything beneath them had an eerie, unnatural greenish-yellow cast. The first hint of thunder rumbled in the distance, and Elowyn could see bright, jagged streaks of lightning spreading out from cloud to cloud. She flung open the door and raced inside. Her mother was immersed in her weaving and paid no attention, no doubt trying to make up for time lost earlier that day. Morganne was stirring some pottage over the fire for supper, the beginnings of a new garment spread out across the trestle table.

"There you are!" Morganne exclaimed. "And whatever is the matter?"

"There is a bad storm coming this way." Elowyn grabbed Morganne's hand, dragged her outside, and pointed in the direction of the quickly massing darkness. Morganne was usually stout of heart at such times, but even her face paled as she stared dumbfounded for a few seconds at the huge mass moving toward them. But she quickly gathered her wits, running behind the cottage to bring in several lines of cloth that had been hanging out in the sun. Elowyn closed the shutters as securely as possible and barred them from the outside. She hoped they would hold in spite of the oncoming wind. She also dragged in as much wood as she could in order to keep their fire going through the night. For a brief time the storm seemed to stall, hanging a good distance away, but growing darker, higher, and more threatening. The wind blew in erratic bursts, nearly knocking Elowyn down one moment, holding perfectly still the next. Just as the girls raced inside and Elowyn prepared to fasten the front door behind her, the storm was upon them. It struck as suddenly and sharply as a blow across the face. The wind tried to rip the handle out of Elowyn's grasp, but Morganne helped her pull it shut and secure it. The little cottage shook and groaned, the shutters rattled and the rain began. The sound of it was like an army on the march...steady, terrifying, and relentless. Adelin was frightened and began to cry. Morganne instinctively picked her up to soothe her.

To Morganne this was simply a very bad storm. She was apprehensive, of course, hoping that the roof would hold, and praying fervently that entire crops would not be laid to waste. Such outpourings of nature's fury could easily destroy them, not so much in the short term, but over many years. Storms such as this one often marked the beginning of bad times, bringing about widespread famine and plague. The balance was so delicate, so easily disturbed. Too much rain would drown crops, just as surely as too much sun would dry them up. Bad harvest led to low stores and starvation through the winter months; starvation led to weakness of the body. Weakness of the body led to sickness, and sicknesses spread like wildfire in the close quarters of Tyroc. Morganne tried not to think about these possibilities. She continued preparing their evening meal as she balanced Adelin on her hip, suddenly grateful for the abundance they had enjoyed for so long.

Elowyn's young mind was far less practical. She was not thinking about crops, or floods, or famine, or plague. Deep down, some part of her knew that she could survive on what the wilds provided her. Elowyn was, however, thinking very hard about the last storm, and how it had seemed unnatural in the same way this one did, only this storm was far more powerful. And no matter how she tried to push away the memory, she could not help but recall the apparition who had appeared at the door. The strange coin was still in her pouch. She fingered it with trepidation, wishing with all her might that she had been able to rid herself of it in the stream.

She wondered how Einar had known that the storm was coming. There had been no visible signs, she was sure of it. He was holding something back; he had even admitted as much. What did she really know about him anyway? Who was he? Where did he live? He said the woods were his home, but even hermits in the wilds have a place of shelter from poor weather, a place to store food, clothing, and other personal items. Where was he now? Certainly not out in the storm, and the hewn place below ground he had taken her to was not exactly suited to live in. There were no provisions there, no water and no blankets for warmth. It was a shelter for hard times, not a residence. Einar had not given her any reason to fear him, but the cloak of mystery that surrounded him only peaked her curiosity more each time she encountered him.

A large crack of thunder followed by a deafening crash startled her from her thoughts. A nearby tree had probably been hit by lightning. The rain and wind pounded the cottage harder than ever, making eerie, mournful whistling sounds through the cracks in the shutters. She surveyed Adelin with envy. Elowyn was frightened too, and longed for some form of comfort. But she felt too young to be strong, like Morganne and her mother (who didn't seem to care that a storm was raging outside), and yet too old to be held and comforted like Adelin. All Elowyn could do was sit trembling by the fire, consumed an endless stream of fears and questions that had no answers.

Her mother suddenly jumped up, cursing and flinging her work aside in a fit of temper. The roof had begun to leak above her, just barely missing the loom where she had been completely engrossed in weaving a very fine, beautiful linen cloth. Morganne and Elowyn both froze, barely daring to breathe, lest they call attention to themselves. However frightful the storm was, it was not half as dangerous as their mother would be if her weaving was ruined with water.

Elowyn found it difficult to understand her mother, even in the best of times. In all visible ways, she assumed the grace, attitude, and proud posture of the nobility. At any rate, she had no trouble looking them in the eye, and did not fear them. She often demanded rights and privileges not given to women of her class, and she typically got them. For instance, she had insisted from the beginning that all of her daughters be given an education, and she wanted a scholar from the Temple in Tyroc to give it to them. The wisdom of their mother's request was questioned by many, to no avail. In the end, she pounded the High Priest's desk with her fist, a large sum of silver in hand, and asked whether her money was less valuable than anyone else's. She explained that she never worked on large orders without a signed and sealed contract, and she needed her daughters to be able to read and work from them just as she did. The High Priest, eager to be rid of her, finally agreed that Elowyn and Morganne could be taught reading and writing privately, but explained that the laws of the Temple forbade them from learning with the young boys taking classes there. Accepting this solution as a victory, she grumbled defiantly under her breath on her way out that no child of hers would grow up to be an ignorant street urchin.

Elowyn could not tell if their mother had done so out of pride, or necessity, or as a rare act of good will towards them, but the effect on Elowyn and Morganne was a positive one. Not only did they learn to read and write; they also got their first gleaning of knowledge about the Ancients. Morganne in particular had absorbed everything she could in utter fascination. She pored over book after book, until their tutor finally had to admit that there was nothing more he could teach her in regards to language. He was, however, greatly impressed with Morganne and asked that she be allowed to continue her studies on a more spiritual basis at the Temple. The idea was resolutely rejected by their mother, who growled that she was not paying him to teach her fairy tales. That was the end of their tutoring sessions. Morganne's reading skills were immediately relegated to reviewing contracts their mother had signed, though occasionally on trips to town, Morganne would sneak visits with her old tutor and he would loan her books to read on the sly—usually by candlelight when their mother had gone to sleep.

As offended as some were by their mother's ways, she instilled a certain confidence in her work that went unquestioned. Indeed few would dare to. Morganne was convinced that half of those who came to her for material, did so not only because of the outstanding quality, but because they were afraid to go anywhere else. Despite the regal air she donned when doing business or dealing with the upper class, she had a coarse side too. She could string curses together as if they formed a kind of high poetry, and she was extraordinarily tough. At times she could be downright brutal and seemingly devoid of all compassion when her temper flared, and it tended to flare quite often. Morganne had learned to tiptoe her way around trouble most of the time, and Elowyn could not really fault her for that. It was Morganne who was forced to work so closely with her day after day, trying to keep orders filled on time.

There were times when Elowyn was painfully jealous of their closeness...the way they worked together so flawlessly without needing to speak. Far too often Elowyn mistook it for affection, which she felt was so purposefully and acutely withheld from her. Morganne had even been named after their mother, Morgan, implying a special bond between them. But then there were also times when Elowyn came home to find Morganne bruised and bleeding and swollen, with "all the willfulness beat out of her," as their mother said. In those moments Elowyn understood the truth—that is to say, she understood it in the fleeting and somewhat vague way that children do. That truth was just as quickly forgotten again the next time her mother overtly rejected her, or ignored her existence while depending on Morganne's.

Elowyn watched her mother's movements as she scrambled to protect her loom with a large piece of waxed cloth. The water kept coming, but at least it could be directed away from her work. A tub was placed to catch the drips rolling off of the cloth, and a delicate peace was once again restored. Their mother continued weaving, Morganne went back to the pot over the fire, and Elowyn was left again with nothing to focus on but the worrisome storm swirling outside.

It was unbearable...sitting helpless, listening to the wind tear at the world just beyond their door, knowing the only barrier between them and it was a very small cottage with a leaky roof. Their mother weaved, and the storm went on. They ate in tense silence, and it still continued. Adelin got tired of being afraid of it and fell asleep. Morganne, unable to sleep, picked up her sewing and got nearly an entire garment done before she finally laid out her mat by the fire and closed her eyes. The storm even outlasted their mother, who at some point stood, stretched out her back, yawned, and withdrew to the small room that served as both her sleeping area and storage space for cloth and other materials. It was separated from the main room by a heavy curtain and was the only place of semi-privacy in the whole cottage.

Elowyn poked the fire, watching the flames jerk violently back and forth in the draft. She felt terribly alone. The door rattled and she jumped, her heart leaping to her throat. What if the apparition from the last storm was back to torment her? She grabbed her satchel of protective herbs and stared hard at the door, though she wasn't all that certain of their powers against this particular spirit. At the least, holding it brought her comfort. Morganne had made the satchel for her when she was young. Elowyn's name was stitched on one side of it, and the symbol of Aviad on the other. It reminded Elowyn of the days when she was innocent enough to believe that it could magically protect her from absolutely anything.

Thankfully there was no knocking this time, just a rattling, scratching, snuffling sound, as if something were sniffing at the crack under the door. A great wave of relief and compassion swelled through her. "Poor thing," she whispered to herself. "Some wild creature is seeking shelter." She didn't dare let it in though, whatever it was.

The sound soon stopped, and Elowyn's body began to succumb to exhaustion. It was not long before she fell asleep, a troubled sleep though it was. All night, she had shadowy dreams about the brothers, the black-cloaked man, the coin, and the bowman. None of it made logical sense as a story might. When she woke she just had vague memories of people and places, and of feeling a great burden crushing down on her heart.

The morning was a dismal one, gray and wet. They all ventured out to survey the damage and found that the outside of the cottage had taken a considerable beating. There was no question that the roof would need immediate repair, for all of them could see where patches of it had blown away and the whole thing sagged heavily in the middle. If not tended to, it would eventually fall in. Sometimes they could patch up weak spots themselves, simply by weaving in more straw and reeds, but this was beyond their capabilities. Their mother cursed and grumbled about the cost and inconvenience of having to get it fixed.

Behind the cottage, lightning had indeed split a great tree in two, felling it dangerously close to the cottage. There were many more branches and tree limbs strewn about as well that would make easy firewood. Their mother's trivet had been uprooted and knocked over by the wind, but did not seem to be damaged. It would need to be reset into the ground over the fire pit once the ground had dried. At that moment, the earth beneath their feet was still swelled with water—small ponds had formed all around, and the rain barrel had overflowed. If the rain did not stop soon, they might be flooded out. Elowyn prayed that everything in her treasure-hiding tree was all right, especially the bow. There was no way she could check it now, not without revealing its location to Morganne and their mother.

It wasn't until she rounded the back of the cottage that she noticed tracks and remembered the animal scratching at the door. She was curious as to what sort of visitor the storm had brought to her door, but the prints on the side of the house were far too muddied to be distinguishable. She could only tell that they had been made by a large, heavy creature. As she neared the front of the cottage the tracks became clearer, until finally, just beside the front step, there was one perfect print—the print of a Hound. It hardly seemed possible that these horrid creatures, once held safely at bay in the Shadow Wood, should suddenly appear not only in the Tyrocian woodlands, but right at her very doorstep. She wondered if, despite Einar's precautions, it had followed her scent and she was responsible for leading it home. How long she stood staring at its footprint she wasn't sure, but the pallor of her face must have betrayed her anxiety.

"What is wrong?" Morganne asked, coming round the corner after her. A dozen different misleading answers raced through Elowyn's mind. Telling Morganne the truth was out of the question, at least for now. Morganne knew very little about animal tracks, but she was quick to tell when Elowyn was holding something back, so Elowyn gave her the most believable answer possible.

"Last night during the storm there was something scratching at our door, probably a rather large wolf. I'm glad it wasn't more determined to get in." Elowyn quickly ducked inside the cottage and hung her dripping

59

cloak on a hook by the door. She hoped Morganne had been satisfied by her answer and would not ask about the tracks any further.

Elowyn wanted to grab the bow and find Einar. She needed to speak with him, more now than ever. But to her frustration, she was instantly sent her into town to fetch someone to fix the roof. Their mother could not spare Morganne who was once again sewing in earnest. So Elowyn went, and with each step, her entire being felt as though it would burst—this would take up her entire day and Einar was waiting for her. The urgency of his request pressed upon her like a huge immovable weight, crushing the very breath out of her body.

Finding a thatcher wasn't easy. Buildings were damaged all over Tyroc, and several of the older and less sturdy ones had caved in completely. Every able-bodied person was out helping to clean up the wreckage, carting away debris, shoring up leaning homes, fixing broken shutters, tending to those few who had been hurt, and assessing roof damage. Those who could repair their own homes would do so with help from their neighbors. The rest would be given to the thatcher and his apprentices in priority order…that is to say, the most important people got theirs done first, and the rest would have to wait. After seeing the state of Tyroc, Elowyn knew she would not be very high on that list, even with the extra money her mother had given her to "bargain with." She gave the most imploring and desperate looks she could muster, hoping that someone would take pity. In the end, she settled for the lowest of the thatcher's apprentices, who was not yet trusted with the important jobs. And she mainly got his attention by promising to slip him the extra coins without telling his master about it.

Elowyn was relieved that she had secured a small assurance of temporary peace at home. Nothing was ever certain, of course, but she could not imagine anything that would wear worse on her mother's temper than the roof falling in on her loom.

The apprentice was not much older than she, and rather awkward. He walked with his shoulders stooped and head lowered in the same way as one who has just entered a room with a low ceiling. Elowyn wondered what he thought he would bump his head on out in the open air. Silently he shuffled along behind her, looking warily about as though he were embarrassed to be seen with her. Elowyn walked faster. She wasn't especially thrilled about having him drag behind her like a corpse either. The sooner this unpleasant business was over with and she could escape into the woods, the better. In her soul she felt that she had been spending entirely too much time locked away behind walls and shutters.

Upon reaching the cottage, the apprentice intently surveyed the roof with his eyes without making the apparently gargantuan effort of lifting his head. He shrugged.

"The whole thing has to come down," he said matter-of-factly in the most monotone voice Elowyn had ever heard. "I'll come back tomorrow morning with the tools and materials. It should hold the night if we don't get more rain." Then he took the money she had promised and shuffled his way back to town.

If her mother was pleased by her victory, she didn't show it. She grumbled something unintelligible in Elowyn's direction, which most likely meant that she wanted to be left alone. Elowyn was more than happy to fulfill her wishes, and after quietly grabbing an empty sack and a few provisions, she skipped off to her treasure tree. She was horrified to see that the rain had drenched everything inside. Her chest and the bow were both sitting in a deep puddle. Elowyn quickly grabbed the bow and dried it off with her cape the best she could, though she could do nothing about the string. She hoped it was not so damaged that Einar no longer wanted it. She slung the bow over her shoulder, stuffing the arrows and the helm in the sack. Perhaps if he was upset about the bow he could be won over with the helm. Looking over her shoulder to make sure no one was looking, Elowyn slipped quietly into the cover of the forest.

Chapter 5
Vivid Dreams and Tree Sailing

Contrary to her usual manner, Elowyn tried to stay close to the city wall for as long as she could. The presence of the Hound tracks had shaken her, and the best part of the day for traveling was already gone. She urgently wanted to get to the place Einar had shown her before nightfall, hoping that he would already be there, awaiting her arrival beside a blazing hot campfire. For the first time she was forced to admit her own fears about the wilderness—fears she had not known before, that she never thought she, of all people, would succumb to. How could her world have changed so completely, and so quickly?

Elowyn's progress was slowed considerably by her desire to make as little noise as possible. She was starting to incorporate the movements she had watched Einar make into her own, but they were difficult, forcing her to concentrate intensely on every footfall. In one sense, she was grateful to have something methodical to concentrate on, something she could lose herself in and forget everything else. In another, she was left more vulnerable. She could not focus on perfecting every movement of her body, while watching and listening for signs of danger at the same time.

Truth be told, the journey was a miserable one. She was not used to traveling with so much baggage. She found that the constantly shifting weight was tiring and made her muscles ache. Everything was off balance. It did not help that portions of the forest floor were either very slippery, very muddy, or completely under water. She was soaked through to the skin and covered in mud. And all the while that little voice inside was urging her to go faster, to get there before dark, or else.

Dusk came early upon the wood. Though the rain had ceased, the skies had not yet cleared. The thick gray clouds stubbornly blocked out what little daylight yet remained. The wind grew increasingly cooler, leaving Elowyn shivering under her thin summer cloak. She longed for dry clothes and something hot to eat, knowing she was not likely to get either. In the last moments of twilight, just as she had resigned herself to stopping, she stumbled unexpectedly upon her destination. It had crept up on her as stealthily as a shadow in the night. Rising above her were the remnants of a crumbling stone archway, so entangled in vines that she almost missed seeing them. Elowyn pushed aside some of the leaves so she could trace her fingers across the surface of one of the pillars. The stone had once been polished smooth, like marble, and engraved with intricate designs. Time had obliterated many of them, but a few had survived to tell their stories.

At the peak of the arch was the carved symbol of Aviad; an outstretched hand holding three flaming spheres. She remembered the story of the creation of the world...of how Aviad gathered the stars together, and from them molded the earth, the sun, and the moon. There was no question that this was the temple she sought, only now that she was here, did she dare enter? Instinctively Elowyn felt that, abandoned or not, on the other side of that archway lay holy ground. Once the threshold was crossed, she would be wholly in the realm of Aviad the Creator, who still guided humanity from the world beyond. She wasn't sure why that thought made her tremble so, for she loved Aviad. She had learned much about his ways from the scholar in the temple who had taught her to read and write, and she knew that those ways were kind and just. Yet, in her heart, she was afraid to step forward.

Perhaps she did not feel worthy, she who held no status in the world of men, she who was of little importance even to her own kin. Why should Aviad accept her into a place that once held the greatest of his priests and scholars and Tomes of Knowledge? Surely if this temple still stood erect, she would not be permitted to enter and approach the altar, any more than she had been allowed to study alongside the sons of the wealthy. She felt like a thief, sneaking in by broken window to a place where she did not belong, and would not be welcomed. How long she stood and stared at the archway she wasn't certain. Time seemed to stand still. Nothing else in the world existed but her, the gateway before her, and the symbol of Aviad staring down upon her from above.

Elowyn realized that she must make a decision. There was barely any light left for making camp and she needed to find a suitable place, quickly. Far in the distance she heard something baying and howling at the rising moon. The night creatures would soon be out, perhaps the Hounds were among them. She stared up at the carved image of Aviad's hand, and remembering the way she had been taught to properly address Him in prayer, whispered, "May I enter, Lord? Is it right for me to enter?" Her heart instantly felt comforted, and all her fears and uncertainty fled. She even thought she received a response—though no one spoke aloud—in the kindest, softest, most loving voice she had ever known.

"Come in, Child."

Elowyn closed her eyes and stepped through the archway. Squinting one eye open, she looked around. Nothing bad befell her...no lightning had come down to strike her for entering the temple, neither had she been torn to pieces by fierce guardians of the holy ground. Aviad had indeed welcomed her.

Elowyn cleared away more vines to get a better view of where she was. Though the roof was long gone, enough of the walls remained that she was never quite sure what awaited her around each corner. Normally she would not have entered such a place in the dark. She did not know these ruins, and she could not see more than a few feet ahead. There could be anything—anything at all—hiding in wait, and she would never know until it was on top of her. She was taking a walk of faith as she cautiously moved forward, trusting in Aviad to protect her.

In what was once the center of the temple, Elowyn found that one corner of the inner room still stood with the vaulted stone ceiling above it intact. It was a place of shelter for which she was thankful. Apparently someone else had recently been there, for there was a blackened ring on the floor and some dry leftover wood that had once been part of a fire. In the last moments of light, she scrambled together any dead wood she could find close by, wet though it was. From her bag of provisions she pulled out some dry tinder and a smoldering coal, taken from the cottage hearth. It wasn't long before she had expertly started a small fire. She placed some of the wet wood near the flames to dry it out.

Now there was nothing for her to do but sit back and wait for Einar to come. Elowyn removed her overdress and laid it alongside her boots as close to the fire as she dared. She knew it would be foolish to sit all night in wet clothes. Huddled in the corner, she nibbled on some bread and dried fish while she watched the fire dance and allowed her tired body and spirit to rest. It was unlikely that Einar would arrive by night, but at least she felt fairly protected from wind, rainfall, and anything that might try to sneak up on her from behind. Though she didn't know it at the time, her instincts had been right about the ruin. Abandoned by the folly of men, it was indeed holy ground, and remained one of the greatest places of power in the world. There was no need for her to be concerned about Hounds approaching it. Had they dared to tread there, the very soil would have burned their flesh.

By the time Elowyn's overdress had dried, her thin summer chemise had dried as well, the heat of the fire radiating through it to her skin. She made a futile attempt to brush off the mud before pulling the dress over her head. Her clothes were in such sorry shape, she could already hear Morganne chastising her for not being more careful. But that voice of disapproval was growing more distant as she felt herself being lulled to sleep by the warmth of dry clothes and the comforts of the fire. She murmured a simple prayer for protection while she slept, and then she knew no more until the morning sun fell across her.

In those first few moments of half consciousness, Elowyn forgot where she was. She felt the sun's warmth on her skin, and her mind took her back to that favorite place by the stream where she had awakened peacefully so many times before. She was convinced that once she opened her eyes, there would be a canopy of green leaves overhead, with the light shining behind them so that they looked like the stained glass in the windows of the Temple.

What she did open her eyes to was far more glorious. Spread before her were countless stone pillars and archways where once great halls and chambers had stood. Rising up around them were trees and flowers and grasses that had pushed their way up through the stone. On one end stood a large portion of wall completely covered in vines, its secrets yet to be revealed. But the best part so far was the ground beneath her. Patches of brightly colored mosaics shone through the dirt and fallen leaves, still speaking their silent tales should anyone care to listen. They remained as a lingering tribute to the days when the Prophets lived and walked among them. She wished that she could have seen these mosaics as they once were, and not in their present state of decay, which served as a painful reminder of better days now passed into history.

Elowyn felt a sudden urge to care for this place that had lain unloved for so long, and having something to do would help pass the time as she waited for Einar. First, she set to work clearing away all the vines that had grown up and around everything. This was more difficult than she had expected, since many of them were old, thick, knotted vines which had not been cut back in any number of years. Those that were hard and rooted in the ground like trees she could do nothing about. But the young, thin, green ones pulled away nicely when she put her weight into it. Guessing what might be revealed beneath the leaves became an amusing game—sometimes there was plain stone, at other times she found carvings or even bits of paint where once there had been pictures on the walls.

When the walls revealed images of the Ancients, or Prophets, or once great heroes, Elowyn clapped delightedly, smiled and bowed to them in greeting. She felt as though she were releasing them from the bonds of time, awakening them from a long, lonely sleep. She made a good effort to figure out who each one was, though most remained a mystery. There was often not enough of the image left for her to tell much about it, or her knowledge of the Ancients and the spiritual texts was too limited for the given clues to make any sense to her. But there was no question that each one was important. The only one she felt sure of, which was repeated over and over throughout the ruins, was the image of Aviad, most often portrayed holding the heavens in his hands.

The last ivy-covered wall in the innermost part of the ruin turned out to be the best preserved. Nearly all of the carvings remained intact and in fair condition. Each set of carvings was separated, which made it seem as though she were looking at different pages of a book. The pictures progressively told a story when strung together. Elowyn tried very hard to understand the message of the story, but the images were filled with people, places, and objects that she did not know. She hoped Einar would be able to tell her what it all meant once he arrived.

Breaking a branch off a nearby tree, Elowyn set to work sweeping away dust and fallen leaves. She then decided that she would do a bit more exploring to see what other mysteries this place might hold. There was, unfortunately, little left to be found. The further out she got from the central room, the less preserved the ruins were. In many places, only the stones of the foundation remained, with rubble scattered all around. She did, however, find an old well, for which she was grateful. Like the fire ring, the well had also been used recently. There was a new rope and wooden bucket for drawing the water, which was fresh and pure.

Close to the well, Elowyn found a stone basin, half sunk in the mud and covered by a blanket of fallen leaves. She had seen similar basins at the Temple, sitting atop pedestals and filled with holy water. This one seemed to have once rested atop a pedestal too, the pedestal itself now broken and indistinguishable from the rest of the rubble. Carefully, she scraped the mud away with a flat stone, hoping that the basin would still be intact underneath. Miraculously, it was still whole, though too heavy for her to lift and carry. She had to drag it to the well to be washed off. With no small amount of guilt, she then removed her overdress and used it to drag the basin the rest of the way back to her camp. As she saw it, her dress was already so mud-stained it was beyond hope. It was more important to her that she not risk damaging the beautiful mosaics or breaking the basin.

Elowyn nestled the basin carefully in the center of the great room, filling it with water from the well. The trees and sky overhead danced on the surface of the water with mirrored perfection. She had intended to wash up her hands and face, yet somehow this did not seem appropriate now that the basin was sitting in the midst of Aviad's greatness. No longer simply a convenient vessel filled with well water, it had become once again a sacred object that belonged to the glory of the temple. Many times Elowyn had watched the learned monks and priests of Tyroc dip their hands in the holy water, and ceremonially bathe themselves before approaching the altar room. But the hands they dipped were clean, their hair and clothes well kept. Looking down upon herself with disappointment, she saw all too clearly her mud covered skin and clothes…the uneven fingernails so black underneath from scratching in the dirt that she doubted they would ever come clean again. Her hands were rough and calloused, even at her tender age, from both hard work and too much time spent climbing rocks and trees. She was glad that she could not see the state of her hair or face. Though she would have liked to wash herself in the basin, she felt that she would only contaminate its purity, and that it was not enough to cleanse her. Instead, she sat and gazed upon its simple beauty while feasting on some bread and wild apples from her bag. By now the sun was high overhead and she was quite hungry from all her work.

Elowyn was torn as to what to do next. There was still no sign of Einar, and she did not have an endless amount of provisions. She would need to stock up on wood for her fire before nightfall, perhaps even find something to eat. Somewhere nearby there was a stream where she could wash herself and find some small fish to catch, if she was lucky. But what if she left and Einar came? Would he wait? And then the most uncomfortable thought of all…what if he didn't come? How long was she expected to stay with the Hounds inching closer each night? In the end, she decided that she did not have much choice but to leave the camp in search of the stream. Before she did, she scratched a short note in a patch of exposed earth near her campfire, saying, "I am here. E." She hoped that he would understand and wait. She slung her bag over her shoulder and went exploring on the other side of the ruined temple where she had not yet been.

The terrain there was more rough and broken, with large boulders strewn about. She found several dead trees knocked over by the latest storm, many of the branches already shattered into manageable pieces that she could break without the need of an axe. That would take care of her wood supply—now to find the stream and food. Following the sound of the water was more difficult than she had anticipated. It seemed to be leading her into more and more difficult terrain, with gigantic tangles of thorns, jagged rocks, and fallen trees whose roots had pulled up massive amounts of earth when they fell. They formed unstable walls that could not be safely climbed, and which housed all sorts of crawling things and spiders' webs that Elowyn had no desire to become intimately familiar with. Eventually she came to the edge of a ravine, with the stream rushing at the bottom. Elowyn sat down on a rock, frustrated by this sudden obstacle in her way. Even if she could scramble down the cliff edge, there was no surety of being able to climb back up without falling. She would need to find another way down, but which way?

Elowyn decided to walk downstream. She was certain that the cliffs must eventually give way to gently rolling woodlands as she got nearer to the city walls. Tyroc on the whole lay rather flat along the coastline. More importantly, she would rather be heading in the direction of Tyroc than away from it should she run into any trouble. Though the painstaking journey along the ravine's edge seemed endless, she did eventually come to a place where she could safely climb down.

The stream was full of small rushing waterfalls, swirling pools, and brightly colored pebbles winking at her like gems from their sandy bed. It really was a lovely place to spend an afternoon—almost as lovely as the place she had lost to the Hounds. Elowyn cleaned herself up the best she could without having to completely immerse herself in the frigid water. For Morganne's sake, she attempted to wash her overdress as well. She flung it hard against the rocks, while the frothy stream tried to grab the heavy folds out of her hands. When she felt that she had gotten the dress as clean as she could, she laid it across a warm boulder and began to look for trapped fish in the shallow pools further upstream.

By the time Elowyn had finished her afternoon expedition, she had caught several small fish, found a patch of promising looking berries, some wild onions and mushrooms, various types of pottage plants, and a stash of herbs to dry and take home with her. Overall, she'd had a successful day. But as the sun got lower in the sky, she felt a sudden sense of urgency to return to the ruins. What if Einar had come and was waiting for her? She grabbed her things and hastily made her way back, guided only by her sense of direction. She hoped that by starting out at the lower end of the stream, closer to Tyroc, she would find a more gentle pathway and bypass the difficult terrain of the ravine above. In that, she was correct and the return journey turned out to be far less difficult. Rushing to the place where she had made camp, Elowyn looked around desperately for any sign that Einar had been there. To her disappointment, the ruin was completely undisturbed, including her simple note scratched in the earth.

Elowyn still had plenty of time to gather more dead wood and get her fire going before nightfall. She revived the fire and laid her overdress before it to finish drying while she gratefully prepared a dinner of freshly caught fish, meager though it was. She washed her smelly hands at the well and filled her water skin to its fullest before settling in for the evening. As dusk began to close in on the wood, Elowyn realized with great apprehension that Einar was not coming. She was about to spend another night alone in the ruins.

Once the sun had fully set, and the rim of the world was but a quickly fading streak of blue, the howling began. The eerie sounds seemed even closer, and stronger than before, filling Elowyn's heart with dread. She pressed herself against the wall, allowing the fire to stand as a vigilant barrier between her and the oppressive darkness beyond. Though the danger was nearer, Elowyn found that she was less afraid than she had been the previous night. Now that she knew some of its secrets, the ruin itself was far less foreboding. The red-gold light from her fire flickered against the bare walls she had cleared away. Each time the flames were revived with the poke of a stick, or the addition of new wood, she could see the face of Aviad smiling down upon her. Far above, the sky's nightly journey had begun. The stars had always been such a comfort to her—now they were more so as she thought of Aviad's place among them. To her mind, the stars were messengers of the living Aviad, winking at her through the dark uncertain hours of night, reminding her that she was ever watched over.

Elowyn's dreams were exceptionally vivid that night. First she dreamed that she heard a voice, the same voice that bade her to enter the Temple two days earlier. This time it told her that she must clean herself. She looked down to find that her dress had been renewed, and there was not so much as a smudge of dust anywhere on her. Even her hair had been washed.

So she asked, "How must I clean myself, since I am already bathed?" The voice insisted that she must be clean for the journey.

"What journey?"

But to that question came no answer. Somehow she understood that the voice meant for her to wash in the basin, as she had seen the men doing at the Temple. Elowyn approached the basin, looking up at the great carving of Aviad above her on the wall. She knew it was the image that had spoken, though how she could not say. She just knew. She cupped her hands and filled them with water, pouring it over her head. Beyond that she did not know what to do. She did not know the prayers and songs that the monks sang in the holy places.

"I am only a child," she stammered, "I do not understand what these things mean. Is that enough? What else must I do?"

"Believe, and remember. The Journey begins," the voice said.

Then the voice left the carving—at least that was how it had seemed to her in her dream. Elowyn woke to find that she had already been asleep for many hours, and her fire was almost completely out. The howling had stopped, and the wood was blanketed in the complete silence that only comes about in the deepest part of the night. She restarted her fire and tried to fall back asleep, only to find herself staring at the carving of Aviad, wondering if what she had experienced was real. She half expected the wall to come to life before her eyes. But it remained cold and silent, and Elowyn eventually fell to sleep again, this time dreaming of the wood and the stream and the sunshine dancing through the swaying branches overhead. She even dreamed about the young, thin, giggling trees that watched over her old stomping grounds, and of their jolly mother with the thick, knotted trunk. They were the most pleasant dreams she'd had in quite some time.

When Elowyn finally roused herself, late in the warmth of the morning, she let out a great sigh of contentment. She ate a small breakfast then approached the basin with great curiosity as she remembered her dream. She immersed the tips of her fingers in the cool water, looking up at Aviad's image. There was no sound, no movement. She reminded herself that it had only been a dream after all, and yet she wondered if the elements of her dream were instructions meant to be followed. This was a peculiar place, no doubt still touched by the presence of the Ancients from when it was a sacred site. Perhaps it would be best to do as she had been told, just in case what she had experienced had been more than a mere dream. She cupped some of the water in her hands and poured it over her head. The drops ran along the length of her hair and down her face, dripping off her eyelashes, nose and chin. She looked up again at the carving, smiled brightly and skipped off into the trees humming to herself. She felt as though all of her burdens were lifted that morning. Her body felt light, her spirit refreshed.

Elowyn decided to do something she had not done in a long while. She called it tree sailing. Morganne called it utter madness. And just past her camp, standing in a patch of soft, springy green moss, was the perfect tree for it...tall, but not too tall, strong, flexible, and with a great number of canopy-like branches fanning out from the trunk. Elowyn scrambled up the tree, inching forward on her belly across the strongest of the overhanging branches, grabbing the smaller ones to her chest. She pushed herself forward as far as she dared, hanging on with her whole body. As the wind caught the branches, she was swayed up and down. It was the closest she had ever come to experiencing what it must be like to sail on the ocean—something she had always felt a great longing to do. Once caught in the rhythm of the tree and the breeze, she could close her eyes and relax without any fear of falling. She felt so free suspended weightless in the air. It was almost as though she were part of the tree itself, growing tall and graceful, joining the wind and sky in their daily song, year upon year, age upon age. Time seemed motionless, meaningless.

Elowyn had been in the tree for a long while when her senses slowly became aware of movement below her. Peering through the leaves, she saw someone moving about where her camp was. His form seemed familiar, but she had to be sure...yes, it was Einar. Finally he had come! She called out to him, laughing as he looked about unable to find her.

"Up here," she called, "in the tree!"

Einar seemed both startled and amused at the same time. "By the Sovereign's name, what are you doing up there, child?"

"Can't you see?" Elowyn smiled joyfully. "I am riding the wind!"

Surely if anyone could understand this unique habit of hers, it would be Einar. He shook his head at her but did not scold. That beautiful, wondrous, youthfulness that she had recognized in him only once before, shone through his features.

"You are indeed a most unusual child..." Einar looked around the ruins as Elowyn eagerly climbed down the tree to retrieve the helmet and bow. "I see that you have not sat idle while you waited for me. Making a new home for yourself?" Elowyn could see that Einar did not regard this place with the same reverence she did. As his eye roved from crumbling wall to fallen pillar, he saw little more than a jumble of old masonry.

"It is a special place...it seemed to need me. Everyone has forgotten it." Though Elowyn said this with the utmost humility, she could feel her face growing warm.

Einar began to laugh in that jaded tone of his, until he saw the crestfallen look on her face. "Aye, such a tender soul. I suppose if I had

74

been forgotten for hundreds of years, I would want one such as you to find me again."

"I was hoping you could tell me what the carvings mean. They are all about people and places I don't know, except, of course, for Aviad. He is everywhere."

Einar seemed a bit uncomfortable as he scanned the numerous images spanning the walls. "I'm afraid I will be of little help to you in that regard. I have not put much thought into the old tales of Aviad and the like." He shrugged.

To Einar it all seemed no more than a fairy tale, and a dangerous one at that. How long had the Temple leadership interfered in the affairs of the Sovereign for the sake of its own gain? How often had they swayed the people, based not on the issue at hand, but simply on their word and desire? He thought the Temple leadership to be imminently corrupt, and the people who blindly followed them to be no better than drunks, addicted to a never ending supply of ale, packaged neatly and sold as religion. However, he could not say this to Elowyn, her innocent face raptly gazing into his, desperately craving his wisdom and approval.

"Perhaps one day I shall be able to introduce you to a friend of mine who knows of such things." Quickly changing the subject, he put on the brightest expression he could manage and said, "Come now, sit with me and show me this bow that you've found."

As Einar sat down, the breeze lifted his cloak, revealing a heavy bandage wrapped around his left arm from elbow to shoulder.

"You're hurt!" she exclaimed. "What happened?"

Einar quickly covered his arm with his cloak. "Let's just say we ran into some...trouble, two nights ago. We had to move camp, which is why I am so long in getting to you. My sincerest apologies for the wait. It could not be helped."

Elowyn's ears attended to every word. This was the first time he had ever mentioned "we" or "camp." Again, she wondered about him. Where did he go? Where did he live? Did he have a family? Why was he always so secretive? What was he hiding? Perhaps in showing him what he had come for, she would get some answers.

Pulling the bow out of her sack, Elowyn handed it to him. All of the joy instantly left his face, and he held it close to his body with his head bowed heavily.

"Please, tell me again exactly what you found, and where you found it." His voice was low and somber.

Elowyn recounted the tale of that last night by the stream, of finding a stray coin, which led her to find the helm and the bow and the arrows. She told him about the tracks she had found, and what she thought they meant, which seemed to be confirmed by the attack on her the next day. She showed him the helm as well, and he wept over it when he saw the crest.

"It is finished then. My friend is lost, and so is the accursed quest that sent him to his death. There is no hope to recover either, the Hounds and their Master have seen to that."

Elowyn shuddered at the mention of the Hounds and their elusive Master. "The night of the storm, one of those Hounds was scratching at our cottage door. It left a footprint. The last two nights that I have been here, their sounds have drawn closer. Einar, what are we to do if they come to the cottage? It is only my mother, two sisters and I. We are not warriors, and we have no weapons to fight off such horrific beasts. I told my sister the print was from a wolf, so as not to scare her. But I am scared."

"If you were not, after what you have seen, child, then you would be a fool." His words troubled her. She had expected him to say something comforting, or at the very least give her some practical advice.

Einar rose and said abruptly, "I must take my leave, and report back what you have told me. I am sorry." Elowyn felt her heart being squeezed by a mixture of emotions. Sorrow first, for she felt the loss of Einar's friend, who apparently meant much to him. Second, hurt, for she had anticipated that once she brought Einar what he asked for, he would be more open with his own business. Instead she found him even more closed off, and curt with her in a way he had never been before. She knew it was not because of anything she had done, but it left her sore just the same. Third, fear. Einar was the closest thing to a brother, or even a father, that she had ever known. She wanted him to make things right, to protect her, to assure her that she was not in danger, or tell her what to do, just as he had given her instructions on how to use the dagger. Though Elowyn knew she was miserably clumsy with it, at least she was not completely vulnerable so long as she carried it. There was always a chance. But now she was left feeling helpless, paralyzed. She handed him the bow and arrows with the helm.

"Keep them, or give them back to your friend's family. I do not want them any longer."

"Thank you," Einar nodded. His eyes had grown cold, and all the muscles in his face hardened. She felt as though she were standing with a total stranger.

"When will we meet again?" Elowyn asked, hoping that he would look at her, and that she would be able to see some remnant of the kind gentility she had come to know in him.

"Soon," was all he would say. Then he departed, vanishing into the trees, as was his custom. Elowyn felt hurt, and betrayed, and very uncertain about Einar. She had done his bidding, waited at the ruins patiently for two days, knowing that if it had taken a week or more for him to come, she would have waited. This was not exactly the way she had expected his visit to turn out. She sat in front of the little basin and cried until the hurt gave way to a quiet resentfulness. She decided that if she was going to continue meeting Einar, she wanted to know more about him. She needed to know that she could trust him. "Next time I see him," she vowed to herself, "I will demand some answers."

But then as she stared at the ground, she noticed something. A footprint, deep and clear. It was Einar's. Glancing in the direction he had gone, she saw more. The ground was still extremely soft from all the rain the storm had brought, especially in the thick wooded places where the sun did not reach. It would be impossible for him to leave no tracks on a day such as this, no matter how great his skill. She sat and debated for a moment. Was it right to follow uninvited? What if she were caught? Surely he would be furious. It would be his fault though, wouldn't it? If he had been more honest from the start, she wouldn't need to sneak after him looking for answers. And then the most dreaded thought of all; what if she followed him, and did not like what she found? Was it better to know than not know? She told herself that she would just follow a short bit, to see in what direction he had gone. But curiosity grabbed hold of her; she could not stop herself. She needed to know, once and for all, what his secret was, and she might not get the chance again, for she realized that she did not have the ability to follow him any other way undetected.

Einar was heading well away from Tyroc, up along the ravine but more to the west. Where the soil became thin and sandy, his footprints were shallow and difficult to follow. Several times she thought she had lost the trail, only to pick up traces of it again further ahead. Eventually she came to the bottom of a long, sloping valley. On the other side, a steep hill crested and she could not see what lay beyond it. Many separate plumes of smoke rose above the hill, and Elowyn guessed that they came from the camp he had spoken of. She eased her way slowly along the edge of the trees, not wanting to draw attention to herself if anyone was on the lookout. As she got closer, she began to hear the bustling sounds of an active camp—axes at work, people calling out instructions to one another, bits and pieces of casual conversation, and warm greetings passed between friends. Elowyn strained to see, but was not yet close enough. The camp was masked by thick, tangled underbrush, much of it sporting nasty looking thorns. Carefully she inched herself up a nearby tree so that she might get a better look.

The camp was full of makeshift tents, many of which were wind-blown with patches sewn on to cover the rips. It was a bedraggled group she saw—most dressed in what were once fine sturdy clothes, now worn thin with use. A group of men were digging a large pit on the far side of the camp against a rock face. The rest were busy setting up tents, preparing food, and taking care of other menial chores. Several seemed to be wounded. There were no women, and no children.

One man was tied up against a tree near the edge of the encampment. Elowyn wondered who he was, and why he was being held prisoner in such a way. Then she saw Einar emerge from a tent. He strode over to the prisoner and had some sort of argument with him. She could not hear what they were saying, but both seemed very upset. The prisoner spit on Einar, and instantly several large men rushed over to pull Einar away before he had the chance to strike him. An older man approached who had an aura of authority about him. As he and Einar spoke, the man's expression grew increasingly concerned. He dismissed the other men and motioned in Elowyn's direction. At first she panicked thinking she had been seen, but then realized that he was motioning to a tent near to where she was hiding. Perhaps if she could get close enough to it, she could finally hear what was going on. Elowyn slithered down the tree as quietly as she could and crawled over toward the back of the tent where she could hear but not be seen.

"I realize it is tempting Einar, but you know that is not our way, and it is not yours either. I have known you since you were but a lad bouncing on your father's knee. Worry not, Justice will be served tonight at the appointed time, and I have decided to give you first rights."

"I fear even that will not be enough to quell my grief, my lord. It festers deep within my soul. It haunts me, consumes me...I cannot rid myself of it."

"Aye, and so it shall be...for a time. You know that we all share the same grief, for all of us have lost these past months, in one way or another."

"Yes, my lord. I do not mean disrespect to you or any other in this camp." Einar's tone softened, "I beg your patience, for this latest news is a fresh wound that I must learn to bear."

"Indeed. And now that we are in private, I wish to hear of it. What news do you bring?"

"Nevon is dead. The Hounds have devoured him."

The two men fell silent for a few moments before the elder finally asked, "How do you know that he is perished?" Einar relayed to him the whole tale of tracking his friend as far as the clearing where he had saved Elowyn from the Hound. He told him of their rapid advancement and of his inability to travel any further east because of their numbers and the encroaching storms. He told him also of what Elowyn had seen, and of what she had found and returned to him.

"This girl you speak of, can her word be fully trusted?" Elowyn bristled slightly at the question, listening intently for Einar's answer.

"Yes, my lord. I have worked to slowly gain her trust, and she has proved herself to be honest and forthcoming with what she knows. I have found no reason to doubt her sincerity."

"And she knows not who you are or where you are from? One careless word to the wrong person..." Elowyn saw the shadow of the elder rise and begin to pace with what she perceived to be anxiety.

"No, I have been careful not to reveal myself, though I am not sure how much longer I can continue to question her while leaving all of her questions unanswered. Eventually she is sure to become suspicious." Elowyn's ears perked with great interest at this remark, wondering if his secret would now be revealed. Einar's answer made her wonder about the sincerity of his friendship. True, he had saved her when she was still but a stranger to him, and he had showed her kindness. But what if he was only using her to glean information for whatever purpose he was tasked with? The other man continued with his questioning.

"There was no body? Not even a trace of one? Even for Hounds, that is strange. And no sign of the package he was carrying either? Of course, he would have held it close to his body and well hidden. If the Hounds' Master has Nevon's remains, so also he must have the package. If that object is now in his possession...I fear to think of what may become of us."

Einar spoke once again, his voice carrying an edge that meant he was trying desperately to stay his anger. "Despite our disagreements in the past, I know that you and Nevon both truly believed in the quest, and

I am sorry that it failed. But with all due respect, I cannot believe that my fate, or that of the world, rests with any single object.

"Ever since we found the dying Monk in the forest, the men have been rattled and uneasy. His presence, his tales, his relic, and most of all, this quest, have been a distraction from our true purpose here. What do we go out and tell the men? How many of them have hung so much upon this that they will now give up all hope that they can save themselves? Nerves are frayed enough. We are weary and wounded, and our families, our very lives, have been taken from us. Is that not enough pain to endure?

"There is plenty of evil to be fought right here, with Braeden's wicked deeds, his evil magics, his outright manipulation of the courts, and of the people, too, for that matter. Have you forgotten that he was recommended to the Sovereign by the Temple? If he is what the Temple represents, then I want no part of it—its relics, its monks, or of its so-called deities."

"You know not what you say," the elder man interrupted with a slight growl to his voice. "Think what you will in private, but speak not against the Ancients in my presence. How convenient that you believe so readily in the powers of evil, but not in the ones that might save you."

"How am I to do otherwise?" Einar challenged. "The fingers of evil reach far, and deep. I can see their workings all too readily. The dark minions call out, and they are answered and aided. Every day they grow in number and strength. Those of us who can see through the darkness, those of us who are willing to stand against it—who answers when we call out in desperation? The most righteous people I have known in my lifetime, those most devoted to the Ancients, and the Temple...where are they now? What help has come to them? They are all either dead or suffering in exile while their families are trapped on the other side of that damned city wall. I for one will not stand idle, waiting for some unknown power to save me. Whatever has become of the relic Nevon carried is of no real consequence to me. As long as I have breath, I will

Allison D. Reid

continue to fight, on my own terms. I believe in the power of my bow more than in the wisdom and power of the Temple or its god.

"Let us assume for the moment that all who serve in Temple are truly innocent of corruption. How wise can they be if they are duped by such a blatant scoundrel as Braeden, even that they recommend him to the Sovereign with their highest praise, so that he was the one chosen to shape the heirs and the future of all Tyroc? How powerful can their deity be to allow one such as Braeden to defile the Temple for so many years? Once again, my lord, you are like a father to me, and I respect that we differ on this greatly. But now that Nevon is dead, and I am no longer bound by my oaths to him, I must speak my mind, at the least just this once, even should you cut out my tongue and hang me by it for doing so."

Elowyn listened to the long silence that followed with great anxiety. Would the other man really do such a thing? Then she heard him speak in a low voice.

"I will not deny that to hear you speak thus fills my heart with the greatest sorrow I have ever known. Such bitterness is poison only to the soul that bears it. You are still filled with youthful rage, and given our circumstance I have no cause to blame you for that. So long as you do not destroy yourself with it, you may yet live long enough to know the folly of what you have just said. You have spoken your mind to me openly, and I know that nothing I say will change it. But I now want your oath, that you will not speak with the other men in a way that will cause dissent among them."

"That is an oath I gladly give. I have no desire to inflict the doubts I suffer upon my brothers. They may cling to their fantasies for as long as they wish. If things continue to go as they have, those fantasies may soon be the only comfort they have left. And now I must also ask a boon of you, my lord, if you will hear it."

"What sort of boon?"

"That should you decide to send out another to recover the relic, and finish the quest Nevon began, you would consider sending me."

82

"What?" the elder said with utter astonishment. "You? After all you have just said? Why would you of all people desire to be sent on such a mission?"

"Because I know these woods better than anyone here, and I am familiar with the patterns of the Hounds. I have no desire to see yet another brother given up to them as a sacrifice. But mostly because I can think of no better way to honor Nevon's memory than to take up the quest he believed in enough to die for. Besides," he added, "I know the girl Elowyn and how to find her. She may need to be questioned again in the future about what she has seen."

"You really are arrogant," the other voice chuckled gruffly. "All the same, it is a noble gesture, and I know that Nevon would be deeply honored. But I am not sure that we can spare you here. It is partly your knowledge of this region that has allowed us to survive for so long against such odds."

"If this relic is all that you believe it to be, what difference will it make if our little band lasts another week, or another month? The Hounds draw closer each night, and we have not the strength to fight them off for long. It is more likely that we will perish at their Master's hand than at the hand of Tyroc. The only other option we have is to abandon this place altogether, with no hope of serving justice and re-claiming what is ours. I doubt that most of these men are prepared to leave just yet. *That* certainly is not our way."

"No, it is not. I must consult with the other commanders about all of this. Your request will be seriously considered. In the meanwhile, gath-er the camp and make all necessary preparations to take care of Mavek. I want that sordid business finished before night falls. Are you still com-pletely certain that you desire first rights?"

"Aye. I have thought carefully on it and I will accept the burden. My soul will not be able to mend until the deed is finished and I may lay the visions that haunt me to rest."

"So shall it be then."

Einar and the other man parted company, leaving Elowyn to sort through everything she had just heard. Could it be that this was the renegade group everyone was talking about? Clearly they were not welcome in Tyroc. Yet they spoke of some great wrong that had been done to them—they spoke of justice, and honor, and of fighting evil. Those were not the words of common criminals, nor bloodthirsty murderers. What was the purpose Einar had spoken of? What was the quest on which his friend had perished, and what sort of mysterious package had he been carrying?

Elowyn's feelings about Einar in particular were rather mixed. She was shocked to hear him speak against the Temple, and most especially against Aviad. She expected such words from her mother, whose only care in life was her loom, but she did not expect it of Einar. How could anyone who knew and loved the wood as he did, not know the hand that had so lovingly made it? Most of all, she wondered what "sordid business" Einar had agreed to carry out. There was nothing for her to do but sit and wait while the camp made their preparations, and hope that she was not caught. There was no turning back now.

Near to where the prisoner was tied, a great bonfire was being lit and torches were being staked in a circle around it. Elowyn crept slowly around the outskirts of the camp to get as close as she dared to the prisoner, so that she would be able to see, and possibly even hear what was going on, without being seen herself.

As evening closed in, the torches were lit, and a bell began to ring. Not a cheery high-toned bell, but rather a low, mournful one. It was the kind of bell that was rung in honor of the dead. The men approached the prisoner one by one, each dropping an unseen object into a container near his feet before gathering around the fire and waiting in silence.

Soon after came a group of men in dark robes. Among them was the man she had seen earlier with Einar, and she guessed that these were the other commanders he had spoken of. Each of them also dropped something into the container. One of the commanders then took the container and poured out its contents at the prisoner's feet so that all could see. They were little stones, about the size that could be squeezed comfortably into your fist. All of them were dark in color except for two, which were white.

The elder looked directly at the prisoner and said, "Your peers have judged you."

"These men are not my peers," the man snarled. "My peers are now in the castle of Tyroc, making ready to either rescue me or avenge me if I am dead."

"You willingly joined us. You accepted our rules, lived among us as a brother, and took your oaths with us. When you found those oaths to no longer be convenient, you went behind our backs and betrayed us to our enemies. Innocent blood was spilled because of your actions, and that we cannot accept. You well know the penalty."

"I did my duty."

"And now, as much as it pains us, we must do ours."

The elder then turned to address the men, but Elowyn could not make out the words, as he was looking away from her. After a few moments someone emerged from the crowd dressed entirely in black, and with a hood and mask covering his face. He carried a black bow and black-feathered arrows. He received some sort of blessing from the man who had spoken, and words of acceptance from the rest.

"Which one of you cowards has been appointed to the task?" the man provoked angrily. "Which one of you am I to curse with my last dying breath?"

The man in black approached the prisoner, close enough that Elowyn could clearly hear the response, even though it was no more than a low seething hiss. "It is I, my old friend." The voice was unmistakably Einar's, but never had his tone seemed so frightening to her.

"Three friends have I lost, friends that were like kin to me. One perished of his own will delivering dusty trinkets for holy men. He was slain by a horde of nameless beasts, and I have no way to truly avenge his death. But the other two...they were betrayed by you, whom they once trusted and called 'friend' and 'comrade.' I have tried to forgive, but I cannot. What you have done breaks every code of honor and decency we strive to follow. It is the worst form of treachery one man can inflict upon another. Fear not that I have been unhappily appointed to this task; I have asked for it. I desire it." Einar's voice trembled with emotion.

The prisoner snarled at him. "I am not sorry for what I have done. Do what you will to me, my death will not bring them back."

"No, it will not. But it may allow their spirits to rest. I know it will greatly ease mine."

Einar kissed the first arrow, nocked it, and drew the string back tight with practiced perfection.

"This one is for Orrin." The arrow was released. Elowyn with thumping heart could hear it pass through the man's chest and into the tree he was bound to. He gasped and shuddered in agony, still alive, while Einar slowly brought his next arrow to the string.

"And this one," he said, looking directly into the prisoner's eyes with a cold fiery stare, "this one is for Elias." The second arrow released and met its mark. The gasping stopped, and Elowyn hid her face into the ground, biting her lip to keep from crying out.

"May they rest in peace," Einar whispered, forcing the ends of his remaining arrows into the ground, and disappearing into a nearby tent.

More than anything Elowyn wanted to run from there. But now she realized the danger she had put herself in. If she were caught spying, what would they do to her? This was nothing like the execution she had witnessed in Tyroc, where the crowds cheered mindlessly and went on with their business. The camp was so quiet that any movement at all would betray her presence. She looked at the faces of the men. They were somber, reflective. They did not hunger for this man's demise like the crowds who merely saw death as some form of grisly entertainment. They had all voted to put this man to death, this man who was once one of their own. They took it seriously—they meant it. They were fully aware of what they were doing.

Elowyn wished that she had never followed Einar; indeed, that she had never known him at all. He had looked that man in the eye as he drew his arrows back. It was with satisfaction that he let them fly. There had been no hesitation in his movements, no sense of remorse or sorrow in his voice. Perhaps this group was indeed no more than a bunch of murderous outlaws after all. She lay there not moving while the body was taken down and buried, while the men sat and spoke with each other in hushed tones. She lay there until the torches were snuffed out, the fire banked, and the camp made ready for sleeping, with only a few sentries on duty to keep watch. Her muscles were stiff and sore, but she held perfectly still until eventually her nerve broke.

When she thought no one was near enough to notice, she dashed as quickly and quietly as she could into the wood. There she ran blindly through the dark as though the whole of the camp pursued her, not caring that thorns and branches clawed mercilessly at her skin all the way. When she tripped on roots or stones, she picked herself up and went on. At last when she felt that she could run no more, not even to save her own life, she sought shelter in the nearest suitable tree. She knew not where she was, and she could hear the Hounds baying to each other in the distance. Terrified and shaking, there was nothing more for her to do but sit and wait and hope for the dawn.

Chapter 6
A Robe for Gareth, and Alazoth's Hounds

At some point in the night Elowyn fell asleep in spite of herself, exhausted by the emotion of the day's events. When she awoke, she felt completely different than she had that first morning in the ruined Temple. There was a heavy, sick feeling in the pit of her stomach, and her limbs and head ached. Instinctively she felt the need to go home, and after listening carefully to make sure there was no one else close by, she slid out of the tree. Though Elowyn did not know precisely where she was, she knew the general direction of Tyroc and began to slowly make her way toward it. The sun had risen high by the time she reached Tyroc's familiar outskirts and shifted her course to the road beyond the eastern gate.

The young apprentice had apparently made good on his promise to return, for the cottage had a new roof. Fragrant wisps of white smoke were rising from it, quickly becoming indistinguishable from the drifting clouds above. Elowyn felt as one coming home after a very long journey, knowing that things would never be quite the same as they were before.

To Elowyn's great relief, when she opened the cottage door she saw that their mother was not at home. Morganne was working furiously on another chemise, and not the rough woolen type that Elowyn was so accustomed to wearing all through the winter. This one was made of very finely spun linen thread that only spinners of their mother's expertise could achieve. It flowed and rippled like silk when Morganne shifted it in her lap.

Elowyn knew that this type of undergarment was not meant to be completely hidden the way common ones were. It was meant to be trimmed with ribbons, or lace, or embroidery, and then let to peek out just enough to show everyone how well to do was the lady who wore it. Very few could afford to wear such things, especially since the rest of the dress was likely to be extremely elaborate and expensive.

Elowyn had tried her hand at spinning before and was a miserable failure at it. Her fingers always sifted either too much wool onto the spindle or not enough, and somehow she could never keep it turning at an even speed. Her thread came out thick and lumpy in some places, and thin and weak in others, so that the fibers pulled apart and she would have to begin again. Her mother had been doing it so well for so long, she gave it little thought, and didn't have the patience to teach Elowyn. She could balance the distaff on her shoulder, carry her spindle, and keep it going while doing her other household tasks at the same time. Even Morganne, who could spin thread well enough to be used for more basic cloths, held a grudging respect for their mother's spinning ability.

When Morganne finally paused her sewing and turned to look at her, Elowyn saw that her face sported a fresh bruise. Her cheek and the side of her mouth were badly swollen and turning a sickly purple color. Elowyn winced. There was no point in asking what had happened. Apparently their mother was in one of her violent moods. Elowyn quietly asked if she wanted a poultice. Morganne declined, not wanting to stay her sewing even to tend her injury. She did not ask where Elowyn had been for so many days. Her thoughts were completely turned inward, her eyes and hands focused on the work in front of her.

A wave of guilt swept over Elowyn. Though she knew she could not have stopped her mother, she also knew she should not have been away for so long. The cottage had not been swept; the woodpile and store of herbs were dwindling. She was almost afraid to see the state of the garden. Her chores were left unfinished and Morganne was too frantic to take care of them. And though Morganne had no doubt been working her needle by day and night until her fingers were stiff and aching, she did not scold Elowyn.

Despite the fact that she was exhausted from lack of sleep and the emotional duress of the night before, Elowyn went to work. She brought in wood from the large pile stacked behind the cottage, and then replenished the pile with some of the dead wood that had fallen during the storm. She swept the floor, laid out fresh strewing herbs, and opened the shutters to allow fresh air and sunlight to flood out all the stale, smoky air. She bundled together the herbs she had found near the temple ruin and hung them from the ceiling. Then she went to survey her garden.

There was a lot to be done. Spring was working its magic on the soil and the plants, as well as on the weeds. Everything was bursting forth in a huge rush, spurred on by the heavy rain and bright sunshine that had followed it.

Elowyn carefully pulled the weeds away from her tender young plants, giving them room to breathe and grow. She cupped the soil back around the places where the hard rain had washed it away, in some cases exposing the roots. To many, this would have seemed like hard, disagreeable work. But for Elowyn it was soothing. Her garden was full of close friends that she had not seen since the onset of winter, when they all settled silently below ground for a long sleep. The trouble of the previous day began to melt away like a bad dream in the midst of all the delicious smells of new life growing.

For many days, Elowyn did not stray far from home. She watched from what felt like a little island of safety as the Hound tracks increased in number, moving closer to civilization, then going past toward the north woods where Einar's camp lay. Several prints appeared just on the edge of the wood near her garden, but did not come closer. At night she could hear the Hounds calling out mournfully to each other with their bone-chilling howls. Morganne noticed the sounds and wondered at them, but she did not realize what they were. She thought they were made by migrating wolves that had roamed curiously close to town. They frightened Adelin at first, but when Morganne did not seem worried, Adelin ignored them.

Their mother was characteristically oblivious, or at the very least, indifferent. Elowyn wondered, if her mother came face to face with one of the Hounds, would she be afraid of it, or would it be afraid of her? She could not imagine her mother being afraid of anything. Even though remaining at home was unpleasant at best, she gleaned some comfort from her mother's total disbelief in the supernatural, and her lack of attention to anything beyond her work. Elowyn could almost believe that things were not really so bad as they seemed, and that once the Hounds had passed by there would be nothing more to threaten their tenuous existence in the little cottage beyond the eastern gate. Deep down Elowyn knew it was not so. But as long as she could lull herself into half-conscious sleep, she could go on with her daily chores and forget about the razor teeth she had once felt grazing the back of her tender neck.

Other things were much harder to forget. When she let her mind wander, she found herself re-living the horror of the execution she had witnessed. She could hear the sound of the arrow as it pierced its victim, binding him to the tree. She could hear his labored breathing, the rattle of excruciating pain in his lungs. She could see the cold, seething anger in Einar's eyes. It was a look she had never suspected him to be capable of, and never wanted to see again. She did not really know him as well as she thought—he frightened her now. Einar had saved her life, yet callously taken another. He had purposely avoided telling her who he was, while at the same time he was using her to gather information. How could she ever trust him again?

Two nights after Elowyn had returned home she dreamt that she was the man tied to the tree. Shadowy figures of men in robes cast dark colored stones at her feet. She cried out, asking what she had done, but no one would answer. Einar stood before her, his venomous stare eating through to her very soul, yet his voice was the one she knew. "I apologize, little maiden...perhaps if the times were different I would offer you better hospitality. But as things are, I am afraid I have little choice..." He bowed to her graciously then raised his bow, so that the black tip of his arrow was pointed directly at her heart. She awoke screaming and drenched in perspiration, with Morganne and her mother both leaning over her, shaking her awake. Morganne looked concerned. Her mother scowled at her, unhappy that she had been disturbed in the night.

Elowyn felt a cool hand pressed against her forehead, and heard Morganne's voice swimming around her. "She is burning up with fever." An afternoon soaked through with rain and cold, followed soon after by a harrowing night on the run were enough to test the strength of Elowyn's young body. The emotional duress of watching Einar execute a man, and the way in which the event had haunted her every thought, only weakened her further.

Elowyn felt Morganne's arms around her chest, pulling her away from the hearth to the coolest corner of the room. Violent chills shook her. She felt so unbelievably cold, she could not understand why Morganne was laying wet rags across her, drenching her with cool water directly from the rain barrel. Elowyn gasped with the shock of it and struggled against her, but did not have the strength to do much beyond flailing her limbs about and whimpering. A hot drink that smelled of chamomile and willow bark was pressed to her lips. She drank what she could of it, enjoying the warmth, though not the taste.

Through the night, Elowyn passed in and out of wakefulness, vaguely aware of Morganne's form always just within reach. Each time she fell asleep again, her dreams were restless and disturbing. Something dark was chasing her. No matter how fast she ran, it was always just behind, so that if she stumbled, even for a second, it would be on top of her. At times the fever was high enough to make her delirious, and she saw visions of people standing in the cottage staring at her. Morganne caught snippets of incoherent conversations Elowyn seemed to be having with the empty air and worried that her sister was near death. Morganne tended to her carefully, attempting to lower the fever with more cool rags and herbal remedies. She was much relieved when two nights later the fever finally broke and Elowyn fell into a restful sleep.

For several more days, Elowyn was alert but very weak. Morganne went back to her sewing with renewed ferocity to make up for time lost.

There was nothing for Elowyn to do but lay back and watch the rhythm of her daily routine. It was so well rehearsed that Morganne and their mother had no need for words. At first, Elowyn welcomed the silence and found it to be peaceful. But as time went on, she began to feel the unmistakable tension seething beneath. Theirs was a silence that was building up, layer upon layer, ready to ignite at the slightest spark. It ate away at Elowyn until she could hardly bear it. The moment she was well enough to dress and go outside, she sought refuge in her garden. She longed for the woodlands, and surprisingly for the Temple ruins where she had come to feel at home in the short time she had known them. But she could not go there again, not with the chance that Einar would be there waiting for her.

The people of Tyroc, especially those on the outskirts, soon took notice of the presence of the Hounds, though few knew what they truly were. Most had only heard them after dark and were too alarmed by the sounds and the size and number of the tracks to investigate. A very few had reported seeing them from a distance—mainly guards held high and secure by the outer walls of the city. Their descriptions were hazy at best. Only one man had reportedly stood toe to toe with the Hounds and lived to tell about it. He was an old farmer whose wife had passed on some years ago, and whose children had all grown and gone. He lived alone, save the company of his faithful servant and the hired hands who came during the daytime to help him in the fields. He was a great believer in the Ancients and the old ways, much to the amusement of his neighbors. He had often borne ridicule for his stubborn belief in all the old tales and superstitions.

As the story went, he heard a disturbance among his animals one night, put on his hat, tucked a knife in his belt, and went out to see what was bothering them. He saw a great host coming at him from across the field. A tall man, shrouded in darkness and wearing a horned helm, was in the midst of the Hounds. In his hand he carried a staff or hunting pole of some sort. The farmer described the Hounds themselves as being as large as lions, with great red glowing eyes, and horns growing out of their

94

heads. They breathed fire, and from them came a horrible smell like the depths of the eternal abyss. The farmer's animals had gone crazy with fear, trapped as they were in their pens.

The farmer, thinking that this was to be his end, stood between the Hounds and his animals, and did the only thing he knew how. He threw down his knife, knelt on the ground, and prayed to the Ancients, waiting to be devoured. After a few moments when nothing had happened, he opened his eyes and found that the entire host had vanished. They had either passed him by, or disappeared. He and his animals were all unharmed. He rushed in and told his servant what had happened, and his servant said with trembling voice that he must go straight away to the Temple in the morning to tell the High Priest his story, and to give thanks to the Ancients with an offering.

The farmer took this advice, but found the High Priest to be somewhat skeptical. So he began to tell anyone who would listen, causing such a stir among the crowds that he was eventually hustled back to his farm by two burly soldiers who thought he had lost his mind. The last thing they wanted was some strange old man stirring up fear and causing a riot.

Those inside the city gates still felt relatively secure, but their concern was growing by the day as more and more tales reached them from the outside. Though the Sovereign's youngest son tried to make light of the matter in public, he ordered the number of men on night watch to be doubled, and everyone in his court was advised to travel only by day, and with great caution. Those whose homes and farms lay beyond the walls, along the roads, or in the southern farmlands, felt the most vulnerable. Doors and windows were barred by dusk, weapons clenched more tightly in the fist. The authorities assured the population that the unusual migration of what they called "wolves" would pass, and things would be back to normal soon. What actually happened was that the precautions against the Hounds became normal, until the freedom people had enjoyed before the Hounds' appearance became a distant and pleasant memory, then ceased to be thought of all together.

Allison D. Reid

The changing events in Tyroc brought a visitor knocking at the cottage door one quiet afternoon. Morganne opened it to find her old tutor, Gareth, standing on the step in his traveling robe with a book in his hand. Their mother looked up from her loom with an irritated curiosity.

The young scholar addressed her respectfully, "Mistress Morgan, it is good to see you so well and prosperous."

"And what might you want of me?" She looked at Gareth's time worn clothes and said gruffly, "If it is a new robe that you desire, you shall have to speak with Morganne. I've not the time for it."

"Aye, you have guessed it," he said in a relieved tone. "But on this, the eve of our Summer Rogation days, I am not permitted to enter any house that has not been cleansed by the High Priest. Would your daughter be permitted to take my order and measurements outside?"

Morgan shrugged and went back to her weaving. She had no use for holy men and took even less interest in their rules and rituals. Morganne, with some suspicion, stepped outside and half closed the door behind her. She began to take his measurements, and then said loudly enough for her mother to hear, "Step this way, please, where the ground will be more even under your feet." She then whispered, "You didn't really come here for a robe, did you."

He shook his head and grinned. "Nay. And may the Ancients forgive me for the falsehood I just spoke to your mother, but I feared that she would not allow me to see you otherwise, and my time is short. I am leaving Tyroc."

"Leaving? But why?"

"The reasons are complicated, and your mother will be suspicious if we tarry long out here. The short of it is, my mentor and I, and several others, have been asked to leave because we have had a...disagreement... with the leaders of the Temple. More than that I cannot tell you here and now. But I have written what I can in a letter, which you must destroy in the fire as soon as you have read it. Do you swear it?"

Morganne nodded.

96

Gareth thrust the book he was carrying into her hands. "The letter is inside. The book is one I want you to have, and keep well, as I will not be able to carry it. My load will be heavy enough with the things I need to survive the journey, which will take us quite far from here. No one left at the Temple is more worthy of this gift than you, and I want you to have something more wholesome than contracts by which to practice your reading."

He looked at her with a tormented expression. "You have the gift inside of you, and you have the spirit to use it. If only you had been permitted to study at the Temple a while longer..." He shook his head wistfully. "Somehow, some way, you are destined to follow the ways of the Prophets. With faith, I know you will find your path." He then took from his pouch a handful of copper coins. "Give these to your mother for the robe I told her I was ordering. It is all that I can spare. Do not worry about actually making it. I know the time is too short."

"I can manage it," Morganne said. "You'll need something to keep you warm and dry. The robe you are wearing is more fit for the rag pile than a long journey. It is the least I can do to repay your years of kindness to me. You shall have the robe before you leave."

Gareth backed away from her and bowed sadly, ready to turn back toward Tyroc. "Stay safe. Open the door to no one after dark, and go not into the wood. May the Ancients bless you and watch over you."

Morganne was left feeling distressed by what he had said, especially the last part. She wondered what the letter might contain, and what sort of disagreement had caused her tutor's expulsion from the Temple. She walked back into the cottage and was given an inquisitive look by her mother. Morganne laid down the coins in front of her.

"He had to barter for the robe. All he had to spare were these coins and one of his books." Morganne knew she had to play this moment very carefully.

"I've no interest in books. You should have consulted with me before accepting it."

"He is not a man of means, Mother, the Temple requires poverty. I did not want to offend him by taking the coins and refusing the book." She took the silver coin her mother had given her and placed it with the copper ones. "Take this to cover the rest of the cost, and I will keep the book...to practice my reading with."

Morgan grumbled that she was a fool, but took the money and went back to her loom. Morganne was greatly relieved, and quickly went to work making the finest quality robe she could manage with the time she had. Elowyn had seen her sister work fast before, and she had seen the care and perfection that went into every task Morganne undertook. But there was something personal about this robe, and about that book. She did not completely believe the nonchalant demeanor that Morganne had displayed in front of their mother. Of course Elowyn also knew of the books that continuously changed hands between Morganne and their old tutor. She had tried to read some of them herself, but often found them too laborious and flowery, and heavily laden with allegory. They did not read like children's tales and were not meant to. Elowyn was curious, more because she was trying to figure out why Morganne was so fascinated by them than because she had an interest herself.

Morganne worked on the robe until Morgan had gone to bed. When she was certain that their mother was asleep, she dropped her work and grabbed the book with an anxious fervor. Morganne held the book before the firelight and withdrew from it a letter, sealed with the mark of the Temple, and written in the hand of their long-beloved tutor. Elowyn looked at her with questioning eyes.

"Gareth is leaving Tyroc," Morganne blurted out in a whisper. "I don't know why, he couldn't tell me. He just said it would all be explained in the letter."

Morganne opened it with care, smoothed out the parchment on her lap, and read aloud softly.

> To Morganne and Elowyn, my two dearest students of whom I have such fond memory. I write to you with a heavy, yet hopeful heart. By now you know that I must leave Tyroc. I realize that you

have little cause to follow the politics of the Temple, and there is much that I do not have the time to explain. But to be plain, it is my belief, and that of several others, that the leadership has lost its way and fallen prey to the lures of wealth and prestige.

No doubt you have heard the howlings and bayings by nightfall, and have been assured that the beasts that utter them pose no true threat. We have searched and prayed, read through prophecy, and endured frightening visions that tell us otherwise. We believe these creatures to be the Hounds of Alazoth (whose name we rarely speak, and then only with great caution, for our enemies are ever listening). Their appearance is a most ominous sign, for their Master, Alazoth, was banished into a great Rift and left prisoner there more than a thousand years ago when the Prophets still lived among us. It was thought that he would never again emerge, but it is apparent that something, or someone, has set him free to torment humanity once again.

Alazoth is the Master of Destruction. His Hounds have always come before him, ushering in the first wave of his endless, unstoppable calamities. They bring with them all sorts of evils, pestilence, plague, and strife. As you were taught when you were under my study, there are the three Good Ancients, Aviad the Lord of Life and the Creator, Immar the Lord of Divine Love and Mercy, and Emeth the Lord of Truth. These are the Three whom we serve as the Prophets did before us, and to whom our spirits will someday return. I have also told you, that while we recognize them separately in name, Immar and Emeth are born of Aviad and yet have been with him from the beginning. Thus the Creator, Divine Love and Mercy, and Truth are truly One.

But there are also the three Shadow spirits whose overwhelming desire is to take that which belongs to the Ancients and make it their own. They are ever trying to deceive us, to lead us away from the Divine and into eternal darkness. They are Death, whose true name is unknown to us, Tieced, the Dark Lord of Deceit, and lastly, Alazoth, the Dark Lord of Destruction. They would have us believe that they are also One, but they have done nothing more than create a false mockery of the Divine. They desire to twist the Truth, to destroy Aviad's creation and enslave His children into the misery that is their vision for this world. They have great power, but unlike Aviad, they are not all-powerful. Therein lies our hope, that their victory is not inevitable so long as we continue to recognize their influence and stand against them.

Their circle of power has been weakened ever since Destruction was sealed in the Rift. We have never before had to battle their full force without the aid of the Prophets and the heroes of old. And now the times are changed. Many people have fallen away from the Temple. They no longer make pilgrimages to the shrines of power, or call upon the Ancients in daily prayer. Those who still believe do so more with their mouths than with their lives.

We spoke our concerns to the Temple leadership and they have turned us away, calling us blasphemers and trouble makers. They are more interested in pleasing the Sovereign's sons than in remembering their duties to the Ancients and to the people of Tyroc. I, along with my mentor, and the others who have followed him in this matter, have been asked to leave. We are going far from here, to the region that was once the home of the Prophets of Emeth, the Ancient of Truth. There is a monastery which, as we have heard it told, remains devoted to the old ways, and has preserved many of the sacred texts. As dark as the days are, and as dark as they are likely to become, I shall probably never return to Tyroc. This is a bitter farewell. Yet I make it with the hope that we can look into these happenings with the monastery's assistance, and learn whether Destruction has truly been released upon the world once again. If it is true, then I fear greatly for all of us, and pray that the hearts of men are strong enough to resist what is sure to come.

I say these things not to frighten you. Still, it would be far more cruel to withhold what I know, for knowledge is our greatest weapon against the Shadow Spirits, far greater than the sword could ever be. Always remember that. It is probably the greatest piece of wisdom I can offer you. I am sorry to say that there will be no one left willing to loan you books from our library. Treasure this book, for it was given to me by my mentor when I entered the Temple as a youth. May you find comfort in it, and remember all that I have taught you, for we both know that your most important lessons were not how to form letters with a pen, or how to read the words on a page. Believe and remember. The journey begins!

Until we meet again, whether in this life or the one beyond, I remain faithfully yours,

Gareth

Elowyn stared at the letter in complete disbelief. She had heard those words before...believe and remember. The journey begins...she had heard them from the Aviad in her dream at the temple. She wondered now, had it been a dream at all? What did it mean? She felt her skin and scalp tingle, just as it does when one first senses that he is being stalked by an unknown something lurking in the dark. Elowyn's muscles involuntarily tensed, gathering their strength to break into a wild run. She needed to find someplace safe to hide, but where? Elowyn was unable, at her age, to fully grasp the spiritual implications of what their tutor had said. She only knew that she was in the path of a danger that she could not see and did not know how to fight.

In all honesty, Elowyn was even more unsettled by the possibility that Aviad had really spoken to her in the ruins. It was not that she didn't believe in Aviad truly in her heart. But to hear him directly, to have him speak to her in a vision...that was something meant for holy men and Prophets, not little girls. She felt as though she had accidentally taken some priceless heirloom and was now afraid to be caught holding it. If the vision was not a mistake, that meant she was supposed to understand it and do something with it. That kind of responsibility was overwhelming and terrifying to her.

Elowyn looked to Morganne for guidance, but her expression was blank, dumbfounded. Whereas Elowyn had already experienced the Hounds intimately and been warned numerous times by Einar that some great evil was already upon them, all of this was new to Morganne. She had overheard vague rumors while going about the shops in Tyroc, but for the most part she brushed them off as gossip. And she had gone into the city less and less over the last weeks, absorbed as she had been with her sewing tasks. Her world, up until now, had been very neatly divided. Isolation in the cottage, with nothing else to focus on but her work, made it very easy to forget the outside world, and even the realm of the spirit. The prick of her needle felt far more real than anything else.

There was no question that the Ancient writings fascinated Morganne, and she wholly believed in them. But she had always thought direct involvement with both the Ancients and the Shadow Spirits to be a thing of history. She had certainly never witnessed or felt anything beyond the ordinary, nor had anyone else she knew. It was shocking to think that the howling and baying which had haunted her sleep for so many nights came not from ordinary wolves, but mythical beasts found thus far only in what she had thought to be long-forgotten legend. What else might be happening to her, and around her, that she had not recognized because she had not remembered and believed? And now that she knew, what was she to do with that knowledge? Though Morganne's life had been hard, and forced a maturity upon her that was beyond her years, she was still only a girl. Her life was not yet her own; it belonged to her mother, who had no belief in the Ancients at all. Was she meant to sit and sew, and simply wait for doom to come upon them all?

Morganne turned to Elowyn and said sharply, "You already knew about them, didn't you?" Elowyn nodded slowly, not wanting to speak of her direct encounter with the Hounds.

"But how? How did you know of them?" Elowyn remained stubbornly silent in a way that typically infuriated Morganne.

Morganne suddenly felt trapped and restless. She felt the need to do something, but what? For the first time she thought of leaving, perhaps even traveling with her mentor to whatever far off place he was destined for, so that she might learn more. Gareth had said that she possessed a gift, that she was destined to follow the Prophets. Over the years she had learned to trust his wisdom, but doubts still consumed her. Why must he leave now when she was in such desperate need of guidance? She was quite sure that a girl would not be permitted to go and study with the monks. Even if by chance they did allow it, Morganne was not prepared to suffer a journey through the wilds to a place where she knew no one. She had not so much as a silver coin to her name, having given that up to her mother in exchange for Gareth's book. She would only be an added burden on the group's limited resources. Besides, what would happen to Elowyn and Adelin if she left? Surely their mother's wrath would be taken out on them tenfold. The contract her mother had signed would not be filled, and she could possibly lose everything. Morganne could not bear to live with that on her conscience for the rest of her life.

Morganne read the letter carefully many more times, determined to burn every detail of its contents into her mind. Once satisfied that she would be able to recall Gareth's words adequately, she threw his letter into the fire as she had promised. Morganne then went back to work on his robe, making it light and strong and well waxed against the rain. She also made him a new pouch to hang at his side. It was very late in the night when she finished and finally lay down by the hearth to sleep. Early the next morning, before her mother had a chance to protest, she took the robe and pouch and made her way into the city.

When Morganne walked up to the Temple and asked for Brother Gareth, she was at first told that he was not available for visitors. Protesting vehemently, she explained that she had stayed up all night making a new robe he had commissioned for his journey, and now needed to make sure that it fit him properly. The man at the entrance took the things she had made and disappeared inside without saying a word.

As she patiently waited to see if he would return, Morganne watched a group of young boys, all sons of wealthy merchants, pass by her unchecked into the Temple. They were in their school clothes, with cropped hair, writing tablets and books tucked under their arms. They would be learning the old tongue (in which most of the tomes were written), reading by repetition from sacred texts as well as books of verse, history, and legend. They would be learning about astronomy, and arithmetic, and all sorts of things that she, as a weaver's daughter, could only dream of learning. And she knew that she could learn them too, if only given a chance.

The brief glimpse into the tomes that she had gotten under Gareth's tutelage was to her like a sip of water to one dying of thirst. Her desire to know more, to learn, to grow…it entirely consumed her being so that she could hardly bear it. Day by day, stitch by stitch, the cottage, and the gift of her needle, began to feel like a cage in which she was to be held prisoner until the end of her days. She longed to go with her tutor on his journey, but dared not ask. She looked up to see Gareth walking toward her, wearing the new robe and a large beaming smile.

"It is wonderful!" he exclaimed. "I have never owned, nor hoped to own, such a marvelous garment. The Temple will think that I have broken my poverty vow!" he said as he winked.

Morganne managed a smile, but was still disturbed by her new-found knowledge. "I wish that I could go with you," she said timidly, wondering how he would respond.

Gareth shook his head. "Nay child, it would be far too dangerous. There is no guarantee that we shall ever reach our destination."

"But from what you have told me, I have no guarantee of safety here, either. Now that I know, what am I to do? I feel so…helpless."

Gareth nodded in understanding. "As do I. But sometimes it is when we feel the most helpless, and the most alone, that we are actually the closest to knowing our true nature. There are none that we can rely on, not even ourselves. We must trust the Ancients alone to guide us and protect us. Even if it is our fate to perish, we die knowing that, because of Aviad, our spirits never shall. That is the greatest hope we have, and the purest joy we will ever know. Worry not about what you must do—for now this fight is in the hands of others. Just keep your faith, and take care of your family the best you can. If Aviad calls upon you to serve in his army, you shall hear it, and he will tell you what to do. But now I must go and finish my preparations. As the Prophets commonly said upon part-ing, 'Go in Wisdom until we dance once again among the stars.' Farewell, dear Morganne. Farewell." Then Gareth disappeared into the Temple, and that was the last she saw of him.

Chapter 7
The Scattering of the Circle

Elowyn noticed that Morganne's mood changed greatly after Gareth's departure. She was silent, pensive, and less attentive to her needle than she had been. She made mistakes in her stitching, which was very much unlike her. Their mother noticed the change too, and the tension between them rose to an unbearable level. They snapped at each other, and their mother's temper flared perilously. Elowyn spent as much time as she could in her garden, which turned out to be a good thing, since the weather had become far more nasty and unpredictable than usual. She was able to devote enough time to its care that her garden continued to flourish in spite of the weather.

One day Elowyn went out to tend her plants and felt a presence other than her own. She didn't hear or see anything that indicated someone else was around, but she couldn't shake the feeling that she was being watched. She kept glancing into the brush, trying to catch a glimpse of color or movement, or anything that might betray the watcher. Nothing. Yet there *was* something there, she was sure of it. Elowyn inched closer to the edge of the brush and listened. Her muscles were tense and alert. She was unsure whether it would be wiser to investigate further, or just go back inside the cottage until the feeling passed. But being the curious child she was, she could not seem to resist the temptation of stepping past the tangled wall of brush that edged her garden to take a look.

There, leaning against a tree, patiently waiting for her, was Einar. Elowyn froze, her eyes wide with uncertainty, her body ready to bolt at any sudden move. Should she run or call for help? Einar slowly laid down his bow and raised his open palms toward her in a friendly gesture.

"I have no cause to harm you, child. It pains my heart to see such fear in your eyes."

Elowyn remained silent and kept her distance.

He continued softly, "I know what you saw must have been difficult to understand. I would like the chance to explain."

"How did you know I was there?" she asked in a suspicious tone.

Einar smiled. "No doubt the same way you knew how to find my camp. The rain betrayed us both, I'm afraid."

There was a long and uncomfortable silence between them before Einar finally said, "I am truly sorry, little wind rider." His voice was so tender, and so sincere, that for the moment it wiped away the last memories of him that had haunted her so persistently.

"Such events were not meant for your tender eyes to witness. I owe you a great debt for not betraying the location of our camp to the guards, and I know that you have no obligation to help me further. But I do ask that you come and sit with me, and allow me to tell you my tale now that there is no longer need to hide it. Then you may judge me as you will, and should you choose to never speak with me again, I will honor your wish. Will you at least grant me that?"

Elowyn hesitated for a moment before nodding in agreement. She was willing to trust him just once more. She followed him into a small clearing where he had already set up a makeshift camp. He uncovered hot embers from the previous night's fire and nursed it back to life. He offered her food and drink—wild rabbit he had caught himself earlier that morning, greens, and medlars. It was a simple fare, but to Elowyn it seemed like a feast. She rarely enjoyed the luxury of any meat other than dried fish or salted pork.

"I suppose I should start at the beginning, back before all the trouble began. As a young lad, I grew up in the castle at Tyroc. Aye, I thought that might surprise you. Yes, I knew the Sovereign and his sons quite well enough, and better than I would have liked, for I was a solitary child, much as you are. I was always escaping off into the north woods when I was supposed to be working on my studies, or practicing my fencing, or making appearances at extravagant court feasts." Einar sat back against a young tree and slowly stoked the fire as he gathered his thoughts.

"I had a sure love for the bow, but my father said that it was the weapon of wall sentries and poachers, hardly befitting for one of my social standing. Thankfully a man in the Sovereign's court, who had far more prestige than my father, saw things differently. He had me taught by the finest archer he could find, and then entered me in the Nobles' competitions, where no doubt he placed and won a good number of sizeable bets. I did not care that he was exploiting my talent, so long as I was able to shoot. My swords skill suffered terribly, and I know it was a great embarrassment to my father.

"As far as the average fighter went, I was good enough to hold my ground. But you see, my father was one of the Circle, the Sovereign's chosen elite guard, and swordsmen all. I was not supposed to be good. I was expected to be among the best of the best. It put a great deal of strain on our relationship until the man who had seen to my archery studies felt that he was in danger of losing his side income. He brought the matter to the Sovereign, who made a point to come watch me in competition one afternoon. He was impressed enough that he personally assured my father that there would be a place for me when my time came to serve.

"As it turned out, this was a good thing, because my father died unexpectedly shortly thereafter, leaving me an orphan. I was too young to join the Circle, but had no family to watch out for me. So the Sovereign took me in, so to speak. What this meant was that he had his servants see to my physical health and my studies, and when it was his desire that I amuse him with my skill, I was brought before him and expected to perform. Sometimes I was included in his hunting party and rode alongside his sons.

"I actually enjoyed the company of the eldest, Avery. Back then he was strong, and noble, and kind of spirit. The younger son's company, however, I enjoyed not at all. Darik was sullen, spoiled, and madly jealous of his elder brother. He mistreated the servants because they were afraid of him. He mistreated me because I was living on his father's charity, and was therefore no better than the servants. One day he infuriated me to the point where I completely lost my temper and knocked him down.

He ran back to the castle with a bloodied nose and his eye beginning to swell, screaming threats the entire way. Avery, who without my knowing had seen the entire incident, walked up to me with a big grin on his face and said, 'I wondered how much more you could possibly take off him.'

"'I don't find it so amusing,' I said, truly frightened by what I had done. Men of the Circle were supposed to protect the Sovereign's family, not attack them. Had I been an adult, I could have easily been charged with treason and executed. 'I shall have to leave now before the Sovereign has me flogged or beheaded, or worse.' I was honestly ready to flee for my life, but Avery stopped me.

"'You will stay. I shall take care of this.' His manner was so firm, and his voice so commanding, I felt as though I had to obey. It was, after all, the way I had been taught and trained my whole life. What he did I shall never know, but the matter was not brought up again by anyone, including Darik, who from then on kept a safe distance from me. Somehow though, I always felt that the incident was not forgotten, and that someday I would be paid back for both the insult and the injury.

"Then came the day when Avery and Darik were expected to take on more advanced studies, and one of the priests was brought in from the Temple. His name was Braeden. I took an instant dislike to him, and he viewed me with as much disdain as Darik had. The two took up a strange companionship for a tutor and pupil to share, whispering secrets, and keeping unusual hours together when no one else was about. I noticed too, that after Braeden arrived, the trouble between Avery and Darik increased tenfold. Royalty or not, they were brothers, and they felt a deep need to be in constant competition with each other. Braeden encouraged this to a brutal level, and as Avery usually won in the end, the effect on Darik was unquestionably bad. Braeden would soothe his feelings with false praise and words spoken in secret for a time, yet he continued to pit them against each other.

"While Avery excelled, much to the Sovereign's pride, Darik became more ill-tempered and violent, ever clinging to Braeden's robes. It wasn't right. It should have been stopped. But no one could see what was coming, because no one was paying attention. And then it was simply too late. Even afterward, most lamented what happened as nothing more than a tragic accident. A few had their suspicions, mainly based on their dislike of Darik rather than on any true knowledge of the events that transpired. But I saw more than I was meant to.

"The brothers were running about on one of the outer walls. I saw them from the edge of the wood where I had been sitting quietly for some time, carving arrows. It was the part of the wall that rose up into an open, flat-topped tower, with a steep and narrow winding staircase from its top, down into the outermost courtyard of the castle. I heard them laughing and calling out to each other in a harmless manner and thought nothing of it. Then the tone of their exchange shifted, and they were no longer calling out, but yelling. I could not understand what the argument was about as their precise words were carried off and lost on the wind. From my vantage point, I could only see them from about the waist upward. They started to shove and wrestle with one another, then Avery took a swing and Darik was down. Avery said something to Darik that I couldn't make out, turned his back, and began to walk away toward the staircase. Darik got up, seething with rage. He ran toward Avery and shoved him down. For a few moments, I could see neither of them. But then Darik came running back into view, looked around anxiously, and sped off along the wall out of sight.

"When Avery did not reappear, I began to get nervous. I raced to the closest gate to tell the guards there what I had seen, and warn them that Avery might be hurt. They ordered me to remain where I was while two of them went off to investigate. An age seemed to pass before one of them finally came back. His step was slow, his expression disturbed, and his armor and clothes were smeared with blood.

"'You, boy. Come with me.'

"I was marched away in the most frightening silence I had ever experienced, through dark, roughly carved corridors with no windows and no fresh air. We finally came to a dank, torch-lit room wherein sat a large, imposing-looking man who was introduced to me only as the

Allison D. Reid

Captain. Beyond him was the doorway that led to the castle prison. I swallowed hard, but stood my ground and wondered what they wanted of me. I knew that I had done nothing wrong.

"'This is the boy,' the guard said.

"The Captain stared at me for a moment, smiled and said, 'I know who you are. You're Thaine's son, peace be to his soul. Your father was a good man and a credit to the Circle. Now then,' his face became serious again, 'I'm told that you are our only witness.'

"'Yes, Sir' was all I could manage to say. I was still very much alarmed by the blood I had seen on the guard, and by the very fact that I'd been brought down to the prison for interrogation.

"'Please, Sir, Avery is the closest thing I have to a friend. What has happened to him?'

"'First you must tell me exactly what you saw.'

"With great anxiety I relayed everything I could remember, which didn't seem like very much to me at the time. Afterward I was told that Avery had fallen head first down the staircase and was so badly injured no one knew if he was going to live or die. I was asked if I knew where Darik had gone, but of course, I didn't. It was Braeden who reportedly found him hours later, huddled and frightened in one of the tower cellars.

"Whatever state he had been in when Braeden first found him, when they finally emerged together, Darik seemed cold and hardened. He claimed that his brother's fall had been an accident, that Avery had lost his balance near the staircase, and that what I had perceived from below as a shove, was really an attempt to grab Avery and keep him from falling. Upon seeing his brother's body after the fall, he took him for dead, was frightened, and hid. Darik stuck to this story, and was sure to repeat it over and over again to anyone who would listen with a sympathetic ear. It was my word against his, and who was I?

"The Sovereign was heartbroken. He wandered through the halls with a pale face and darkened eyes. He clung to his son's bed sheets and wept as only a King can without his honor being called into question.

110

To everyone's amazement, Avery lived. His body eventually healed, but he was never the same after that. When I was finally allowed to see him, it was like being with a stranger. His mind was muddled. There were a good many things he couldn't remember, and he was easily confused and prone to strange mood swings that were unlike him.

"He looked different, too. All the intelligent wit and good humor that had once shone in his eyes were gone. He would very often stare blankly into space for long periods of time, then start laughing, or shouting angrily, or sometimes even crying until the tears fairly poured down his cheeks. Then he would stop as suddenly as he'd started and stare into space again as though nothing had happened. If you asked him what he had been laughing or yelling or crying about, he would only shrug as if he wasn't really sure himself. This state improved slightly over time, but not enough that he was ever a whole person again. There were times when I secretly thought it would have been better had he died at the bottom of that staircase, and I'm sure there were others who felt the same.

"Darik went smugly on, with no one now to fight him on anything. He grew more spoiled and contemptible by the year, and he and Braeden were totally inseparable. Braeden, it seemed, had completely bewitched him, and the Sovereign as well. The Sovereign trusted him without question, even appointing him to serve as his chief steward, in charge of his lands and finances. No one challenged the wisdom of this. They were all too relieved to be absolved of responsibility toward Darik, who was greatly despised by the court as a whole. The Sovereign, consumed by grief over his favorite son, had no use for Darik either. The Sovereign did speak with me about the tragic event once, and only once. I was brought to his chamber, and all of his servants were told to wait outside.

"'Darik claims that he was trying to save Avery when he lost his balance and fell. Yet I have known Darik to be less than truthful in the past. Even so, he is now my only capable heir. It has been hard for me to reconcile myself to him as long as the question of what really happened has not been resolved in my mind, and my elder son cannot remember how he came to fall. The Captain of the Circle has told me what you saw, but I want to hear it from your own lips. Was Avery deliberately pushed?'"

"I was so fearful that I just stood there for a time, wide-eyed. What did he want to hear? Did he want to hear that his less-than-favorite son had told the truth, so that he could mend his relationship with him, or did he want to hear his suspicions confirmed in order to serve out some sort of punishment on his wayward son? I answered with the truth in the safest way I could at that moment.

"'My Lord and gracious Sovereign, I only know that I saw them fighting, and when Avery turned away, Darik grew angry and pushed him. I could not see well enough to tell you if he was deliberately pushed down the stairs, or if he was simply pushed near enough to them to lose his balance and accidentally fall.'

"This answer was apparently not to his satisfaction. He walked over to the window and stared out blankly for a while before sending everything on the tabletop next to him crashing to the floor in one violent, angry motion. One of the Circle came bursting through the door when he heard the clamor, then stood silently waiting for orders.

"'A curse was brought upon me the day that child was born,' he hissed under his breath, 'A curse that took my wife, and left a devil in her place.' To the guard, he said gruffly, 'Einar is free to go.'

"I was escorted back to my room and left to wonder if I had angered the Sovereign. But the incident was never again spoken of, and nothing bad befell me because of it. Soon after that my formal training to enter the Circle began in earnest, and I had no time to dwell on past events. My time was no longer my own, save for the precious few hours I spent each week alone in the northern wilds. My place in the Circle was a unique one—a lone archer among an army of swords. Those who initially laughed stopped laughing when they saw that I could shoot with consistent and deadly accuracy, whether on foot or horseback. The most difficult part of my training was not learning how to use my weapon, but learning my place within a large group of men, where each of our lives might one day be dependent on the skill and cunning of any of the others.

"This was probably made harder by the fact that while the others went home at night to their families, I was very much alone. For a long while, I felt disconnected from everyone and everything. But this feeling did not last. For the first time I made true friends who eventually became like brothers to me. Nevon, Orrin and I became nearly inseparable, choosing to spend even our free time together. They spurred my interest in the sword and helped me to increase my skill. In turn, I taught them both to shoot with a bow. Nevon actually became quite good at it and preferred its use when he was out alone on his own business. I also became rather close to one of the older men who saw to our training, and who would later become my commander. Though by that time I was practically grown, he appointed himself as my surrogate father and kept a close watch on me.

"The years passed, and I was eventually accepted into the full fellowship of the Circle. We were, in fact, the seventh generation of men to follow this prestigious line of work, which is traditionally passed down from father to son. It was a life different from any other that one can imagine, for part of the price of our prestige was total public anonymity. We kept company only with our own. If we were to marry at all, we must choose wives from among those already living within the castle or among its grounds, with the exception of direct descendants of the Sovereign himself should he have any daughters. All of our needs were provided for, so that there was no cause to venture into Tyroc. When as a group we did appear in public, we were always masked and in uniform, and we were never to tell anyone who we were or what we did. Our first allegiance was not to ourselves, or our families, or the Temple, or the court, or the Council of Elders, but to the Sovereign and his family. It was our sole duty to protect them with our lives, and it was always said that no Sovereign would fall to the sword lest the entire Circle be extinguished first.

"No better system of self-protection was ever devised. We had total security, and luxury beyond anything we could have earned on our own.

Allison D. Reid

As men without names in the greater world, we were beyond approach, beyond threat or bribery. We were bred and brought up to serve this one purpose, and it never entered our heads that we could, or would want to, do otherwise. When I took my vows, it was with a sense of honor and pride. My only hesitation was that I might someday be called to give my life for Darik, whom I thoroughly hated. But when I thought of the Sovereign, who had shown me great leniency and charity all my life, and when I thought of Avery, whom I felt extremely protective of, I knew that there was no other way I would choose to live, or die, except in their service. In my heart I swore my allegiance to them personally, and not to Darik.

"I'm afraid that time did nothing to heal the relationship between the Sovereign and his younger son. With each passing year they grew more estranged, until the rumors began to circulate that the Sovereign was trying to find some legal way to disinherit him completely. Whether it was true or not, I never found out. But Darik believed that it was true, and that was enough to set him very ill at ease. He had always suffered an insatiable craving for power, and ever since his brother's fall he had gotten quite used to the idea of being the next Sovereign of Tyroc. I started to notice strange goings on at night between Braeden and Darik…strange even for them.

"Now, Braeden had made it quite clear from his first days at the castle that when his duties were finished, and he was in his chambers for the night, he wanted to be left alone. He would answer the door for no one, save the Sovereign himself. When it was my turn for night patrol, and I would go past his window, strange lights and sounds sometimes emerged. Once as I passed through the corridor, I heard dark laughter coming from his chamber, of the sort that made my blood run cold. I even once thought that I heard thunder, and felt a damp wind blowing from the space under his door. I wondered why he was so adamant about not wanting to be disturbed.

"I became even more curious when from afar, I saw Darik approach his door, look about as though he did not want to be seen, and then

114

knock in a particular rhythm. Braeden opened it just a sliver to see if it was truly Darik. He also looked about, then quickly pulled Darik in, shut the door, and bolted it. When several nights later the Sovereign was found dead in his sleeping chamber, and no obvious cause of death could be found, I had my suspicions. I dared not say anything openly, not before I had some sort of proof.

"With the Sovereign gone, and my suspicions about the cause of his death aroused, the intense dislike and mistrust Darik and I held for each other only increased. My position was now even more precarious. I knew not from one day to the next if I would be singled out and dismissed, or dragged down to the prisons at Darik's whim, or even if one night I would go to sleep like the Sovereign had and simply not wake up again. And so I did something that I knew was forbidden, for I felt that I had little to lose should I get caught. I slipped into Braeden's chambers while he was away and took a good look around. What I found were a great number of books related to dark magics, all neatly disguised as Tomes of Wisdom from the Temple, and vials of strange concoctions, and a variety of other evil-looking objects that I could not identify. I knew then that Braeden was not quite the man he claimed to be, but of course I still had no proof of actual wrongdoing. And before I had the time to find it, the whole of my world came crumbling apart.

"A great tension suddenly arose between the Circle, the Council of Elders, and Darik. By law, Darik was yet too young to become Sovereign, and it was well known that he was not at all favored by his father. The Council desired very much to have Avery, who was old enough and the clear successor, to become Sovereign in name only, and keep the actual ruling power for themselves as his 'guardians.' The leaders of the Circle were very much against this. Their personal feelings about Darik aside, they had no interest in seeing the sacred position of Sovereign, which they had had served faithfully for seven generations, to be completely stripped of its power. They felt there was no guarantee that even should Avery produce heirs, a highly unlikely prospect in itself, that power would ever be willingly returned to future Sovereigns.

"On a more personal level, the leaders of the Circle felt very strongly that it was an insult to use Avery, whom they had loved and protected from infancy, as a means to power in such a shameless way. Better to allow Darik to succeed in his father's place, and to survive through one despotic ruler's lifetime, than to be forever captive under the control of an entire group of despots. Then the Council began to accuse the Circle of plotting to take power for themselves and produced all sorts of forged letters and documents implicating us in a conspiracy. It was all rubbish, of course, but how to prove it? No one could pinpoint where the letters had come from, or who had written them.

"Unknown to the rest of Tyroc, behind the walls of the castle, the order of rule was slowly disintegrating, with groups forming into different factions. None could come to agreement, and the Sovereign had not made his wishes clear. Had Avery been deceased or Darik well liked, such a power struggle might never have played out. But as it was, each group had a lot to gain, or a lot to lose, and each was defended with a violent ferocity that brought Tyroc near to the brink of anarchy.

"And then, in the dark of the night, the Circle's fate was sealed, and Tyroc's along with it. Armed men awoke us from our beds where we lay defenseless. We were told to leave our weapons where they lay, to dress in ordinary clothes, and to grab whatever of our personal belongings we could carry on our backs. At spear and sword point we were marched out of the castle and into the northern wilds where none from Tyroc could see what was happening. We were told only that we were now exiled from Tyroc, and given stern warning that if ever we showed our faces there, we would be killed on sight. Then we were abandoned without food, without shelter, or any means of protection. At the time, we guessed that we were either expected to die of hunger and exposure, or drift off to neighboring towns and never be seen or heard from again. We were greatly underestimated.

"I found my commander among the confused and bewildered men, and pulled him aside in quiet. I told him that I knew these woods well, and that there was a place a good distance away where we could hide ourselves, if we were cunning and covered the evidence of our numbers as we went. He understood, and after speaking with the other commanders bade everyone to follow me single file, and to step where I told them to if they valued their lives. I wound them by ways that were not easily tracked, through water, and over stone, and finally to the only suitable shelter I knew of—the room carved into the rock that I took you to the first day we met. I know not who built it, so many ages ago, but I had discovered it as a child and knew that it had been forgotten. There we spent a dark and desperate night, trying to understand what had happened to us and why.

"We noticed right off that there were some among us who were not from the Circle, but from the regular guard. They too had been approached in the night, and told that they were to be given a difficult mission. If they completed their appointed task, they were to be richly rewarded, and if they failed they would be severely punished. When it was apparent that their task was to force the Circle into exile, these men had laid down their arms and refused to comply.

"In spite of the fact that we were told to dress and leave our weapons behind, some of us had managed to slip them by undetected in our clothes, or among our things. I had folded up my bow and a few arrows neatly inside a blanket while the man watching over me became distracted by a rebellious guard. There were a few of the guard who complied with their orders merely out of fear for their families, but who were sympathetic to our plight. They silently urged us to hide daggers and knives among our things, even if swords were too large to go unnoticed by their overseers. In the end we were not completely defenseless, though we would need to find some means of fully arming ourselves later. Some of the men had stuffed their bags with money, others with food, blankets, and other provisions. By pooling everything we had together, we had enough to get by in the short term. When everyone's stories had been told, and all the facts had been gathered (however few they might be), the only thing we really knew for certain was that the trail of our misfortune seemed to lead back to Braeden.

Allison D. Reid

"At sunrise I got up and went out alone to have a look around. At the place where we had been left, I found fresh tracks, and a good number of them, too. They spread out around the area in a search formation. Someone had been looking for us. When apparently no trace of us could be found, the group had headed back toward Tyroc…all except for one. One set of tracks headed off in the opposite direction, so I decided to cautiously follow them. Not far off I came upon a fair-haired young man sitting at the base of a great tree. His uniform was that of the regular guard of Tyroc. He had not heard my approach, and I took full advantage of my position.

"I strung an arrow and aimed it directly at his heart, calling out, 'You there! Stay where you are! Speak honestly to me, and you will live. But any false moves or false words, and I will let loose my arrow. You can trust me when I say it does not easily miss.'

"He did not look alarmed, but said carefully, 'Indeed I trust to that, for I know of you, Einar, son of Thaine. It is for your sake and the sake of the others that I find myself here alone.'

"'How is it that you know my name, for I swear we have never met.'

"'For as long as I have lived in the Sovereign's service, there has been only one true archer among the Circle. Your name, and your reputation, are well spoken of.'

"I lowered my weapon but remained alert to his every move. Though he did not seem threatening, I was still apprehensive and wanted to know more before I let down my guard. The man went on to introduce himself as Elias. He was a member of the regular guard who had been roused in the night and given the choice between reward or punishment. He had been in such shock over the whole affair that at first he complied, thinking perhaps the Circle had committed some crime worthy of exile, for he had long trusted the Sovereign and those who spoke on his behalf. But as the night wore on, and he began to ask questions, his trepidation grew. He felt that something was seriously amiss.

"When at last he and a group of others were told to go back into the wood in secret and murder us in cold blood while we slept, he knew

118

that he had unwittingly played part in a great treachery. He went along, fully intending to turn on his companions and fight with the Circle to the death. It was much to his surprise, and that of his overseers, that we were nowhere to be found. There weren't even tracks to follow, which seemed truly inconceivable to them, considering our numbers. The tracks leading to the drop off point were obvious, but after that, there was nothing...it was as though we had simply vanished.

"From Elias' account, this had greatly disturbed those among the guard who were superstitious or lacked even the most basic wood skills. The others tried desperately to figure out how they had been outwitted, even discussing how it might have been possible to leap from tree to tree as an ape might, if you can imagine anything so ridiculous. No doubt, any tale they could come up with was better than returning empty-handed and with no trace of a trail to report to their superiors. Elias warned me that they were not likely to give up so easily, and might return to the wood seeking clues to our whereabouts. He advised us to stay hidden, and to leave as little trace of ourselves as possible.

"Elias was a wise and righteous man, and he offered himself in the way he thought would do us the greatest service. Since we had nothing, he felt that joining us in exile would only burden our meager resources. Instead, he returned to the castle and resumed his life, reporting that he had accidentally gotten himself lost in the dark while following what he thought to be a lead. Instead of getting more lost, he had decided to wait until dawn to get his bearings. As it turned out, the lead he had thought so promising in the dark was nothing more than a deer trail in the harsh scrutiny of daylight.

"But when he was off duty, he came to us in secret, bringing us bit by bit the supplies we needed; armor, weapons, food, clothing, and sometimes gold, though it was rare that we dared to enter Tyroc to buy anything with it. When it was necessary, we donned the simplest clothes we had, and wore a rough gray peasant cloak and hood to hide our faces. We never knew if we might be recognized by those on gate watch, for surely they were told to keep an eye out for us.

"Elias also brought us news, which in some ways was worth more than all the rest put together. Many of the men had wives, children, parents, and siblings still living in the castle. They would be left unharmed so long as they kept silent, and did not ask questions about where their loved ones had been taken. Elias, at great risk to himself and his own family, broke that silence, assuring each and every one of them that we were alive and well beyond the city walls.

"No doubt such news was bittersweet, with separated families in a never-ending state of worry and grief, mixed with the hope that one day they might be together again. The castle that had once been their home and shelter was now a prison in which they were kept against their will. They were not permitted to leave under any circumstance. In the meanwhile, the people of Tyroc were completely oblivious to the events taking place. A new Circle was formed, created from the guards who were willing to swear loyalty to Braeden. They donned our uniforms, took up our swords, our masks, and our lives. Who on the outside would ever know the difference?

"The guards continued to search for us while we remained in hiding, gathering our full strength together. We were all sworn to secrecy regarding the underground chamber since our lives depended on it. We were wary of lingering there too long, for as a place of hiding it worked well, but it was not defensible. If ever it were discovered by the guard while we were inside, it would become our tomb, but it served its purpose. Before we could make a more defensible camp in the open we needed materials to make shelter. I had to teach my comrades wood skills, and how to fight from the shadows. Though it went against all that we had been taught about honor in our years of training, this was the only way we would be able to survive, and possibly claim our lives back. At any rate, we felt no obligation to fight honorably against those who had no honor themselves, especially when traditional ways of fighting put us at a fatal disadvantage. Those who had learned archery for sport or for hunting would now need to use it in a more serious fashion. Elias brought us bows, and we crafted our own arrows by lamplight when there was naught else we could do.

"There were a few close calls, when the guards came near to our hiding spot, but passed by. We felt a great sense of urgency to move out into the open as soon as possible. We did this gradually, a few men at a time, to a place of high ground with thorny vegetation and hard, stony earth. It was easier to mask our presence that way. When we felt we were ready, we went on the offensive.

"We left obvious traces for them to follow, allowing them to think they had found us, when really we had led them to a place of our own choosing. In this way we ambushed them time and time again, killing as many of our enemy as we could while purposely hiding any evidence of casualties on our side. When the guards began to take numerous losses, Braeden and Darik made our struggle public, claiming that we were a rebel faction taking advantage of the Sovereign's death. In this way, they further covered their treachery with the people, so that we who were once beloved and well respected were thought of as murderous villains.

"Our circumstance became exceedingly difficult. Elias was in the most dangerous position of all. Braeden was obviously aware that someone had been supplying us, and his spies were on the watch. Elias was not able to come as frequently or bring as much. It was time for us to rely on what we had and finally sustain ourselves alone. Some of the men were growing weary of this life on the run and became discontent, a few even desiring to go back and face whatever punishment might await them, if only they could see their families again one last time. But deep down, they knew the folly of this and fought on in spite of their restlessness.

"However, our situation only grew from bad to worse. Elias reported strange happenings taking place in the castle. Dark menacing clouds would form just above it, rumble threateningly, then dissipate. Each time it happened the clouds grew a little bit stronger. He said that he didn't wish to sound like a madman, but whenever the gathering of clouds began, they seemed to form directly above Braeden's chamber. Though he had no proof, he was certain that somehow the storms were Braeden's doing. I shared with him what I had observed before we were ousted, and my personal belief that Braeden was somehow involved in dark magics. There was no doubt in our minds that he was evil and intent on taking control of Tyroc, using Darik as a front. Only what were we to do about it? Surely we were exiled for this very reason. We were a threat to his real and true purpose so long as we remained in Tyroc. Braeden was now comfortably surrounded by those who would not question him.

"Then, just as we thought that our situation couldn't get any worse, it did. Late one evening, as we were heading back toward camp, we heard someone calling out in desperation. Following the sound cautiously, we came upon a monk lying in the ruined temple, dripping wet from head to toe, and half crazed with pain and fear. He had been badly injured, though by what we could not have yet imagined. Even when he told us his tale we could hardly believe it, for he spoke of creatures known only from legend. He described to us a horde of fierce four-legged beasts, with glowing red eyes and short, curved horns growing from the tops of their heads. They had hunted down the monk and his companions as they were making their way to the ford in the river that led from the Shadow Wood into Tyroc. He even had a name for them...the Hounds of Alazoth. A few of the men who had been educated at the Temple and knew the name shook their heads in pity and whispered that the poor old fool was delusional in his suffering. But the monk heard them and grew extremely angry and excited.

"He shook his finger at them. 'Do not laugh at that which you do not understand! Your doom is coming, do you hear me? It lies just across the river. It has not found a way to cross yet. Not yet, but it will, and you had best be ready. Did I imagine these wounds on my body? Did I imagine the sacrifice my companions made so that I might cross with the relic and save us all?'

"I tried to soothe the monk and clean up his wounds with water from the well, which we had often used ourselves to drink from. A few of the men made herbal poultices to dress his injuries, while another gave him mandrake to ease the pain.

"'Do not waste your energies trying to cure me. I can already hear Emeth's call. He beckons me to join my companions in Aviad's realm once my appointed task has been completed.' He searched our faces and soon latched upon Nevon's. 'You,' he said, grabbing at Nevon's sleeve. 'You are the one. I can see that your faith is strong. Come closer.'

"He lowered his voice and grasped Nevon's hand tightly, thrusting into it a small object wrapped in linen. 'This is what we have lost our lives to find and preserve. It must not get into the hands of Alazoth and his followers, or the whole of the world will be lost. You will see... as his Hounds cross over, they will bring with them all manner of death and misery. I do not know how their Dark Master has escaped from the Rift that should have been his prison for all time, but somehow he has. There is something or someone here that he seeks, which is drawing him close, desiring to fully restore his destructive power. When that happens, if it is not stopped, I weep for the people. My suffering now is pleasure compared to the trials they will face. You must get the relic away from here, take it to my people, the Guardians of the Ancients—they know what must be done with it. This relic is old, and it is powerful—more powerful than you can imagine. I dare not say more in this open place, nor would it be wise or safe for you to know its secrets.'

"The monk's life began to fail him. His breathing became shallow, and his pupils grew so large they seemed to swallow up the rest of his eyes. 'Swear to me!' He gasped and clutched Nevon's sleeve in earnest. 'Swear to me that you will do as I have asked!'

"Nevon stared at him, blank with shock, searching our faces for any sign of what he should do. He found nothing beyond perplexed and uncomfortable expressions. 'I...I do not know how to do this...' Nevon stammered. 'I have never heard of your people and do not know the way to find them.'

"'Aviad must guide you,' the monk breathed weakly. 'There is no other way. Please, I beg you, end my pain! Swear that you will do this so that I may join my companions in Aviad's realm. I cannot depart this world until I know the quest will be continued.'

Allison D. Reid

"Nevon nodded with helpless resolve, grasping the man's hand. 'I swear it.' Then the monk died, and we were left feeling greatly troubled by what we had just heard and witnessed. Those who had at first laughed at the old man's tale were no longer laughing. We bore his body back to our camp in silence. There we buried him, and curiously enough, no one would speak of the experience.

"By daylight a small group of us made our way to the ford the monk spoke of, to see if we could find any trace of his companions. Crossing the river, we found evidence of the beasts he had described. There were bits of rough fur caught in the brambles, scorch marks on many of the trees, and hundreds upon hundreds of their strange looking tracks covering the earth. Searching further, but daring not to go too deeply into that accursed forest, we eventually found the remains of two men and buried them there. With heavy hearts we returned once more to camp, and people gradually began to talk, but in small numbers and with hushed voices, as though they were afraid of who, or what, might be listening. The righteous outrage that had so successfully sustained us thus far was disintegrating into exhaustion and fear. This was a new enemy—one that we had no idea how to fight. Those who had been brought up in the Temple's teachings, but had never taken them very seriously, were the most alarmed.

"Still somewhat skeptical, I kept close watch on the river and the goings on across it, hoping to find that it was wild beasts of the ordinary kind that had killed the monks. By day, I saw nothing unusual. But twice I went in the dark of night and saw the beasts first hand, pacing and howling at the water's edge, unable for some unknown reason to cross it. I even saw what I took to be their Master; a great figure draped in shadow, far taller and more massive than a man. He wore black horned leather armor that creaked ominously when he moved, and a great antlered helm atop his head. In his hand, he carried a hunting pole or staff of some sort that was as tall as he. Seeming to sense my presence, he kept roving the underbrush intently, calling out to his Hounds in an eerie, guttural, primitive language that sounded as old as time. They growled and paced,

124

seeming to stare straight at me with their glowing red eyes, breathing smoke and flame. Though I knew I was well hidden, I felt completely exposed. There was no question that they saw through my cover and into the darkness beyond with perfect clarity. These were beasts of the night.

"I carefully traced my way back to a nearby stream and waded through it all the way to the outskirts of Tyroc. If indeed they crossed the water, I did not want to lead them back to our camp. I dared not go back to that place again by nightfall, but by day watched the ground on the riverbank for any sign of Hound tracks. I reported everything I had seen to my superiors, who, against my advice, shared my findings with the rest of the men. A great chill hung over everything we did, until Nevon finally approached our commander and told him that he must take his leave and do the Monk's bidding, lest a curse come upon him for breaking his oath. I begged him not to go—I thought it incredibly foolish and a waste of a good fighter. If a new danger was encroaching upon us, it seemed to me that pressing our cause and returning to our castle duties was far more urgent than going on some wild chase with a useless relic. I certainly held no belief that it would be of any use to us, unless it could magically oust Braeden or restore Avery to the man he should have grown to become.

"On this point Elias, Nevon, my commander, and I greatly disagreed. Elias and Nevon were both convinced that Braeden was indeed the "someone" who was drawing the Hounds to Tyroc. The closer they came, the greater were the weather disturbances about the castle, and the stranger the happenings in general. Braeden now rarely emerged from his chambers—only Darik was permitted to come and go, and the whole household walked about with unease. They tried to hide it by bustling about their normal business and making more merriment than usual. But it was a false merriment that belied the tensions brewing underneath. Nevon and Elias wholly believed in what the monk had told us, and they believed in the relic. Our commander was also a spiritual man, but even more so, a man of strict honor. He said that whether or not the relic turned out to be of any value, an oath had been made and Nevon was now bound to fulfill his promise.

"Before taking up his journey, Nevon went to the temple ruins where we had found the monk and spent the night there in prayer. He emerged convinced that he had heard Aviad calling to him, and that he must undertake the journey, regardless of what would become of him. He relayed to me the Prophetic rhyme that I told to you the day of Elias' execution. He had learned it in lessons as a child, but had forgotten it until that night, and felt that it was significant to his quest. I asked him what that significance might be. He thought that it must relate to Braeden in some way, though he could not be certain of its full meaning. What he felt most strongly at the time was that, whatever it meant, it must be told to me. I told him that I had no use for such things, and tried once more to get him to reconsider this quest, which was surely folly, regardless of his oath. He would not heed my warnings, and there was nothing more I could say to persuade him.

"What concerned him most was not his safety, but that he still did not know who the Guardians of the Ancients might be, or how to find them. We only knew that the monk and his party had crossed the river from the east. Nevon decided that he would go north, circumventing the Shadow Wood, and then east to the nearest village. There he would seek guidance from the religious community. With luck, the monks had sought a room or supplies there before continuing toward Tyroc. It was the best chance he had. I cautioned him strongly not to travel along the river, nor go anywhere near it, and to seek shelter at night. He left us in the dark hours before dawn, and as you well know, it was the last any of us saw him.

"After Nevon left we began to hear the howlings, even as far off as our camp, and the wilds took on a sinister feel. That night it stormed like never before. It came upon us so suddenly that we did not have time to seek the shelter below ground. We huddled together in our dripping tents. When the wind blew them down, we simply clutched them tightly over us with our fists and waited. Never had I spent a more miserable night in all my life. Not knowing that Nevon was already dead, I was

126

sick with worry about how he was faring this weather alone in the wilds with no shelter at all.

"When the storm finally stilled, and before dawn broke, I started out for the river to watch for signs of the Hounds just as I had been doing all along. Only I didn't get that far. As I approached the stream that I had so often used to cover my trail, I saw the Hounds and their tracks all about. They had crossed, and no barrier I knew of would halt their approach now. My concern for Nevon increased a hundred fold, for I could see what I thought to be traces of his presence near the stream, but had no way to follow them safely. I could not tell if he had passed by this place before the Hounds had found it, or if he had been caught unaware. I was just ready to return to camp with this news when I heard you calling out, and saw that you were being stalked by one of the Hounds. Mind you, I had no idea if such beasts could even be killed with arrows, but I could not stand by and watch one devour a young girl.

"When you told me that you had found a bow, you must now know that I was burning with curiosity. Part of me wanted to settle the question of Nevon's fate, while the other clung to hope that he had passed safely. But I did not feel at liberty to ask too many questions, out of fear that I might accidentally reveal more than I ought. It was not only my secret and my safety at risk, but that of all those other men in hiding as well. I needed to seek the permission of my commander, and also to learn if I could trust you completely. I sent you on your way, fully intending to find you again when the time was right.

"When I returned to camp and told of the Hounds' crossing, the spirits of the weakest men finally broke under the strain. Two of those who had been regular guard had relatives in the small farming villages to the south of Tyroc. With the blessing of our commanders, they and a few of the others took leave of us, vowing that they would do what they could to send us provisions to further the cause. They were not yet giving up, but all could see that their health was quickly deteriorating. We did not fault them for parting company with us.

"There was only one who lost complete faith in our fight, who instead of leaving us in an honorable fashion, preferred to try to destroy us. That was Mavek. He secretly sent a message to Braeden through one of the guards at the gate. He wrote that he had been wrong to side with the Circle and that he desired to return to his former post. He said that he knew the name of the traitor who had been smuggling supplies to the Circle. He promised to aid in the traitor's capture, as well as share all the knowledge he had regarding the Circle's activities, so long as he was promised a safe return to his old life. He vowed to come back the next day to get an answer to his offer. Braeden was more than happy to give Mavek what he desired in exchange for our lives.

"Two days later, when Elias met with Orrin and myself at the appointed place, he slipped a note on rolled parchment into my hand as we greeted one another. In that brief moment, I sensed that something was wrong. I whispered to them that we were being watched just as a group of men burst out from hiding and attacked us. Elias was captured alive, and Orrin and I were both wounded. We fought as long as we could, but when it was apparent that we were beaten and could do nothing to rescue Elias, we escaped into the woods and hid. There I watched and wept helplessly as Orrin's life slipped away, knowing that Elias' would be equally short in Braeden's keeping.

"The parchment Elias had slipped to me was a hastily scribbled note of warning. It said, 'I have found out too much, and my doom is imminent. Braeden's eyes see everywhere, his hands reach far. With every victory evil gains, his power to conjure and sustain the storms increases. He is making way for the Hounds. It is he who calls them and their Master to his side. There is no way back to the lives you once knew—everything has changed. The monk knew the truth, he tried to warn us. Fly while you can. Destruction is coming.'

"I took the note to my commander, but did not share it with the others. He sent me out to find any trace of Nevon and the relic, while he and the rest of the men made ready to move camp. There was no doubt that Mavek had betrayed its location, and Braeden's forces would be coming for us soon. I knew that I had to find you again, that I had to see the bow you found, to settle once and for all what had happened to Nevon.

"Braeden wasted no time making an example out of Elias. The very next day he was executed. There was no legitimate trial before the court—what use would that have been, when all those in position to judge were safely tucked in Braeden's pocket? There was no attempt, nor was there the need to attempt, to discover our grievances or understand our demands. Everything that Darik proclaimed so loudly from the public platform was false, all designed to stir hate against us while covering his own murderous deceit. One of our own risked his life to be there for the execution and to report back to us everything that was said. That was the day I found you in the north woods and asked that you bring me the bow. That was also the day we bore the brunt of a fierce attack as we tried to relocate our group. Not surprisingly, Mavek was in the lead, showing them straight to us. We fought hard, killing many and capturing Mavek alive. We took several losses ourselves, and a good number were wounded. As evening drew closer and the storm approached, the guard retreated. For once Braeden's foul sorcery worked in our favor, as his men did not want to be caught out in its fury. Perhaps, too, they thought it would weaken us, or even kill some of us.

"Several of the men wanted to seek shelter in the underground place we had once used, but I reminded them that Braeden would now know about it, and expect us to go there. I took them instead to higher ground, where there were cliffs and caves I had known about since childhood. We sought shelter there the best we could, splitting up into three's and four's, squeezing into narrow cracks in the rock, and caverns so small that they had to be crawled into. It was not a very pleasant place to spend the night, but at least we were dry, and out of the wind, and the immense flood of rain the storm produced washed out all traces of our footsteps. When, after two days, there was no sign that we had been followed, we re-established our camp nearby. That was when I finally came to find you at the temple ruins.

"When you confirmed my worst fears about Nevon, I'm afraid I did not take the news very well. I had lost too much too recently. My grief burned to anger as I strode back to camp. I wanted Mavek to pay for all the pain he had caused, and for the innocent lives that had been lost because of him. It is true—when our commanders met and decided that Mavek's life would be put to a vote, I asked for first rights. I wanted to be his executioner, because I thought it would ease the pain of loss. Given the choice to go back, I would most likely ask for that right again. Even so, my soul is no less weary of this living death we face each day, and my suffering is no less acute. I lament the bitterness I feel rising up in my soul, and yet know not how to purge myself of it. I must learn to live with the fact that I will never gain my life back. I am destined to wander without home or heritage for the remainder of my days.

"Those who had hung all their hope on the relic took Nevon's death especially hard. Everyone assumed that when he was killed, the relic was taken from him, and that everything the monk told us was now coming to pass. We were at a breaking point. The Hounds moved closer each night. The guard was no longer sent out to look for us. Either Braeden was weary of losing men in our pursuit, or he knew that the Hounds would rid him of our presence soon enough. By watching their pattern of movement carefully I surmised that they would overtake our camp in another day or two. As much as we despised the thought of giving up, our days in the north wood were finished.

"Most headed south toward the farming villages where they expected to find the welcoming faces of those comrades who had already left us. But I, and a very small group of others, have decided to follow the path Nevon took, to find his body if we can, and to seek out the Guardians of the Ancients. Even if we cannot fulfill the quest as planned, we can let the Guardians know what became of their own, and what became of the relic. Perhaps they know some way of fighting the overwhelming evil enveloping all of Tyroc. It is a fool's chase more likely than not, but what else have we? To settle down to laborer's work and a pittance of a wage that will barely keep bread on our tables? Shall we die of old age, alone, and in despair that we never regained that which was taken from us? I would rather take my own life here and now than to succumb to such an empty, meaningless end. We were born to serve Tyroc, to serve the Sovereign and Avery. We will gladly die trying to save them.

"Judge me, and all of us as you will, Elowyn Wind-Rider, now that you know our story. If you think of us as nothing more than brutal renegades, we shall part ways and I shall leave you in peace. If you judge us kindly, we would ask for your help one last time. What say you?"

Elowyn was overwhelmed by a confused jumble of emotions. Instinctively she knew that Einar was telling the truth, and yet how could it be? How could such terrible things be happening all around her? She shuddered to think that not long before she had spent those lovely, peaceful days at Aviad's temple, the monk had died an agonizing death there. It was horrible to imagine their beloved Sovereign being murdered by his own son. She remembered vividly the dark aura that had surrounded Braeden the first time she saw him, and the way his gaze had made her shiver. Even if she should doubt everything else Einar told her, there was no question that Braeden was evil. The mysterious fair-haired prisoner now had a name and a past, and she finally understood what truth Elias had spoken of before he was executed. How sad that the only man there who had wept over his death was one of Einar's companions, one of the true Circle.

The unbearable, maddening pain of injustice welled up inside of Elowyn. She wanted to cry and yell and pound her fists. Most of all, she wanted to right the wrong that had been done. But what was there for her to do? This was too big for her. If the entire Circle together could not change things, what chance had she?

"What is it you want of me?"

"You have told me where Nevon fell and what you saw. Now I need for you to show me. Show me exactly where you found the tracks and his things, and recount to me every detail you can possibly remember, no matter how insignificant. The smallest thing may very well help us. The stream bank has been clear of Hound prints for days. The beasts have hopefully moved on, but I must tell you honestly that I cannot guarantee your safety. I realize that I am probably the last person you would choose to trust. Even so, I swear to you, by whatever name you hold most dear, and by Nevon's spirit, wherever it may rest, that I will protect your life with my own. My companions will swear the same. You shall not perish, lest all of us together have perished first in your defense."

Elowyn searched the depth of his eyes and realized that this might be her only chance to help him. Einar's request was such a simple one, and yet for the first time she saw in him fear and desperation. He had one last hope to cling to, and it hinged on her trust alone. He sat across the fire from her, breathless in anticipation of her response, wondering if he had completely destroyed her faith in him.

Elowyn's gaze did not falter as she gave him her answer. "I do not fear the woods. I will go."

"Thank you," Einar whispered gratefully, unable to hide the emotion in his voice. He lifted a small hunting horn off his belt and blew steadily into it three times. Gradually his companions emerged from the wood where they had been waiting patiently in hiding.

A weary, travel-worn group stood before her in absolute silence. Their clothes hung loosely on their bodies, and their rough, gaunt faces wore the haunted expressions of men who have learned to live as prey. Elowyn was startled to think that these were the same men she had seen the night she had spied on their camp. The once proud and imposing men of the Circle looked so different to her now. She did not fear them, or find them contemptible. She felt, instead, as though she wanted to weep for them, to embrace them, comfort them. But she knew that a child's pity would not be accepted by such men, who had once stood by the Sovereign's side. She looked down shyly, unsure of what to say, or how to act without betraying her true feelings.

Einar took her unease to be nervousness and tried to reassure her. "Do not fear them, they are quite safe." She nodded and began to walk. It was better to let them think she feared them. They instantly spread out to surround her in a protective fashion, and even though, at first, it felt strange and uncomfortable to be the object of such attentiveness, she did feel much safer. She had underestimated how much this walk would affect her. The closer she got to her once favorite place by the stream, the more nervous she became. She had not been back since the day Einar had saved her from the Hounds.

Elowyn almost didn't recognize the place once they reached it, for its character had completely changed. Everything around her seemed cold, lifeless, and uninviting. She could clearly see evidence that the Hounds had camped there in great numbers not so very long in the past. They had even managed to foul the water so that it carried their unmistakable stench. The smell brought back the memory of their attack. Every nerve was on edge, every muscle ready to move. When a small animal scrambled through the brush nearby, she jumped and spun around toward the sound before her mind had time to reassure her body that it was not a threat.

Einar moved toward her, put his hand on her shoulder and said in a low, soothing voice, "Steady now. They aren't anywhere nearby, I promise."

Elowyn felt her face grow hot with shame. When she had stated so boldly that she did not fear the wood, she had meant it. But now that she was here, she was terribly afraid. She just could not bear to admit it openly.

Elowyn took a deep breath and began to retell her story to all of them, moving about to show them all the places where there had been tracks and burn marks. She pointed out where each object of Nevon's had been found. The one thing she could not bring herself to recount to them was the visage of Nevon appearing at her door in the night. She was unsure herself if the encounter had been real or just a horrible nightmare, but she was certain that the telling would be both painful for Einar to hear and frightening for her to relive. She still feared that she would be haunted by the spirit again each time the storms came. She wished she had the coin with her so that she could give it to Einar, or at least be rid of it in the stream where she found it. But she had been gardening when she decided to investigate the sounds of Einar's movement in the wood and was not wearing her pouch.

Elowyn said as much to Einar, but he told her not to think of it further, that it was hers to keep. Because the coin had been found so far out in the stream, Einar was skeptical that it had even belonged to Nevon, despite Elowyn's insistence. He knew that Nevon had not been carrying any foreign coins with him at the time of his disappearance. The relic itself had been well wrapped in heavy cloth and tucked away close to Nevon's body, so that it would be well protected from thieves and accidental loss.

Finally, Elowyn showed them where the drag marks had been, and in what direction they had gone. She shuddered as she peered ahead into the tangled darkness of the Deep Wood, wondering for what twisted purpose the enemy might want poor Nevon's remains. They all stood for a moment in silence, heads bowed, hats and helms removed out of respect. One of the men lifted a large stone from beside the stream and placed it on the spot. They had nothing to mark it with that the first rainfall wouldn't wash away, but they felt the need to express their grief in some tangible fashion. Standing in the place where Nevon had fallen made the loss even more real, and deepened both their anguish and their resolve to succeed.

"Well, my friends," Einar pointed toward the Deep Woods, "this is where we begin." He turned and looked at Elowyn. She understood what he wanted to say, but couldn't. It was not very likely that she would ever see him again. And the hard truth was that her situation was just as precarious. The darkness surrounding Tyroc was growing stronger, building up to some unknown cataclysm. There was no longer safety within or without its walls. Einar's presence, knowledge, and strength had been a comfort to her, though until now she had not fully realized how much. She did not want him to go, yet she knew that there was no way for him to stay. She especially did not want him to depart wondering if he had been forgiven. He needed to know that she had accepted him, that she believed him, and that she finally understood why he had done the things he had. But words completely escaped her.

Einar watched as she struggled with her thoughts, and waited patiently for her to speak. Though the words never came, he was startled to find himself gripped tightly around the waist in a tearful embrace.

"Poor little wind rider," he said gently. "Be cautious and wise, and if you must flee, seek my companions in the southern cities. They will care for you. I still have hope that one day we might return."

Elowyn looked up at him with a child's eyes, so large and innocent, fully betraying every trace of the pain she was not yet skillful enough to hide. They were the same gray-blue as the ocean on a winter's day, and for the rest of Einar's life, the image of that rapt, anguished face looking up at him remained burned into his memory. When he closed his eyes at night, he saw her face…when he was at rest, if he let his mind wander even for a moment, her face was there, peering up at him.

Einar felt something small and soft being thrust into his hand as Elowyn released him from her embrace and quickly fled into the cover of the trees. He opened his fist to find a small, worn cloth bag with a drawstring top, stuffed with dried herbs and flowers. On the outside the name Elowyn had been neatly stitched. Only then did he know for certain that he had been forgiven. He tied the little bag securely to his belt and moved forward, motioning to the rest of his weary group to follow. He knew that whatever trials they had already faced, the most difficult part of their journey was yet ahead.

Chapter 8
In the Arms of the Enemy

The day Einar left marked the start of a great change in Elowyn's life. Gone completely were the carefree days and nights of frolicking among the trees, and gazing up at the stars. She could still hear the hounds moving about in the dark and knew they were lurking, even though she rarely saw any visible trace of them. There was no one in the wood to protect her now.

The storms became less intense, but persisted longer. Everything seemed to be wet all the time. The insects were thriving, and every kind of vermin was determined to force its way indoors through the cracks in the walls, or the thatch of the roof. Fireweed (and sometimes Yew wood when Elowyn could get it) was kept burning in the hearth to drive them away. Extra garden rue was hung from the ceiling, and tansy strewn on the floor against the insects. As unpleasant as things were indoors, Elowyn reminded herself that they were preferable to the alternative. These were not ideal conditions for sleeping outside, and Elowyn knew she was greatly needed at home. It was now mid-summer. There were a good number of chores awaiting her at this time of year, including many that were not customarily hers. With Morganne so busy, there was simply no one else to do them.

Elowyn carefully gathered as many herbs, lichen and other useful plants as she could from the surrounding meadows and woodlands. Much to her relief, she found that she did not have to forage in as deep as usual to find what she needed. Elowyn was apparently not the only person who was wary of straying too far from Tyroc's borders. Some of the wild plants were faring quite well with the unusually wet weather, while others were sickening and rotting where they grew. Her garden plants were no different, and Elowyn found that she was forced to harvest some of them far earlier than she liked, and give up on others all together.

This was always the hungriest time of the year. The previous winter's stores were nearly gone, but the new harvest had not yet come in. There was growing concern that the grain harvest might either fail or be badly tainted with ergot, which could be deadly if not carefully removed before milling. Those who still had large amounts of good grain or flour tucked away suddenly became less free with it. Prices rose at the market for bread and baked goods of any kind that required flour or meal. Morgan either could not, or would not, pay the high prices, and so they went without bread, relying on ground cinquefoil root for flour and porridge.

Elowyn found, however, that the biggest hardship she had to endure was not the lack of bread or food, but her newly given responsibility of trying to keep Adelin out of trouble. Adelin was used to having Morganne's full attention. She could not understand why she had suddenly been passed to Elowyn, who was trying her best to keep Adelin entertained and still get her own work done. For the first time, she began to fully understand and appreciate the daily toil Morganne endured without complaint. If Elowyn looked away for even a moment, she would find Adelin pulling on Morganne's dress or trying to climb into her lap. There were times when Elowyn had to resort to penning up Adelin with her in the garden, behind the makeshift fence that was used to keep the animals out. Adelin would stand and cry in the direction of the cottage until Elowyn was so unnerved that she teetered on the brink of tears herself. But eventually even Adelin would grow weary of crying and drop to the ground with a surly expression, crossing her little arms angrily in front of her. When it rained, however, the garden was not an option, and they were all stuck inside together.

Rainy days were by far the worst. The cottage was overflowing with cloth, finished garments, and garments that were in various stages of completion. At times Elowyn was used as a dress form, or was made to carefully press, hang, or fold different pieces as they were handed to her. She was always very apprehensive about touching the finished garments, and it certainly did not help that Morganne's watchful eye scrutinized everything she did. Elowyn wanted nothing to do with these garments in particular. Never had she seen their like before…precious velvet gowns in deep, rich colors, luxurious fur lined mantles, full and flowing linen dresses covered in delicate beadwork and trim, weightless silk that was as smooth as water between her fingers. She thought that to wear such a garment must feel like wearing air. Some of the dresses had elaborate embroidery, or were couched with gold thread that glittered brilliantly in the firelight. If she damaged even one of these, she feared what her mother would do to her. She would almost rather face the Hounds again.

There came a fateful week when it did nothing but rain…the long steady kind that soaks through everything. Trapped inside together for so long, with pressure mounting to get the order completed on time, everyone's nerves were frayed. Adelin was impossible to occupy, and her constant crying for Morganne only made the tension worse. Their mother kept looking up from her loom to glare at them. She growled at Morganne to keep Adelin quiet, while Morganne and Elowyn exchanged helpless glances, unsure of what else to try. Morganne would then sit Adelin on her lap for a while, but the work she was doing was far too delicate to have Adelin moving about or pulling at the fabric, and she did not want her curious little fingers to get caught on the needle. Elowyn made more attempts to keep her occupied and quiet, to no avail. Their mother demanded silence again in threatening tones that chilled Elowyn's blood. But what could she do? Stand with Adelin out in the rain until they both caught their deaths? Bitterly she thought that it was not likely her mother would mourn their passing.

Elowyn did her best to keep up with Adelin, until at last she had chased after her so many times that Adelin was starting to see it as a game. She began to run from Elowyn on purpose just for the sake of being chased, laughing the whole time. Elowyn did not find it amusing at all. Finally, Adelin tried to make a wide pass around Elowyn by running toward her mother. Her young, unsteady feet stumbled and got tangled up in the threads being fed into the loom. She fell, pulling the threads with her, and damaging some of their mother's weave in the process. Elowyn stood frozen and wide-eyed as she watched her mother's face grow white with intense anger. Morgan rose from her stool to her full height and breadth, her lips curling into a thin, snarling line. She raised her hand to strike the oblivious Adelin with blows that were likely to kill her at that young, fragile age. Before Elowyn quite knew what was happening, Morganne had thrown down her sewing, snatched Adelin into her arms, and backed away. Their mother's first blow whistled through the empty air. The shock of being defied in such a way by her eldest daughter was the last for Morgan. Her anger grew to an uncontrollable rage the likes of which they had never seen, nor ever wanted to see again in their lifetimes.

Morganne pushed Adelin behind her, gazing up coolly. She stood there, facing their mother, taking one strike after another without apology. Elowyn was paralyzed with terror, not knowing what to do. Adelin began to shriek as she watched Morganne fall to the floor, half-conscious and bleeding. Elowyn held tightly to her squirming, wailing sister, wondering if their mother would now turn on them, too, only Elowyn was prepared to run with Adelin and hide, or even fight back, rather than just stand there and willingly take an undeserved beating. Instead, their mother leaned over Morganne and jeered at her in a tone of complete disgust.

"This was a lesson, not only for you, but for your sisters. First, let your pain serve as a reminder of what happens when I am crossed. You belong to me, and I may deal with you in whatever manner pleases me. But the second lesson is the greater, and the earlier you learn it the better. Kindness is weakness, Morganne, and there is no place for the weak in this world. You should have let Adelin take her own punishment. You see now what happens when you risk yourself to save others? Look at yourself, if indeed you can. I despise you, and what you are becoming." Then she strode out of the cottage and left them alone for a good many hours. She could have been mistaken, but Elowyn thought she heard Morganne softly laughing to herself before she completely lost consciousness. Adelin, still terrified, crawled into a corner and cried herself to sleep. Elowyn treated Morganne's wounds the best she could with wet rags and herbal poultices, and lay next to her in silence all through the night.

It was many days before Morganne could go back to her full routine, and even then she did so with great pain. But if their mother was sorry for her actions, or regretted the loss of time worked on the order, she made no sign of it. Indeed, for about a week she said absolutely nothing at all to any of them. She threw herself into her weaving as though nothing else in the world existed.

The effect all of this seemed to have on Morganne was a mystery to Elowyn. Morganne was different, but not in the way Elowyn expected. Her back stood straighter, and she did not lower her eyes when their mother addressed her. Instead she stared straight back at her with the same defiant look she had displayed before. She seemed to now enjoy provoking their mother in subtle ways that were sure to get her attention, but could not be pointed to as outright disrespect. Morganne appeared to regain the focus she had lost when Gareth left, and it showed in her work. Elowyn did not understand the transformation at all. Yet somehow it made her feel more secure, especially now that Einar was gone. Their mother's reaction was a mystery too. When Morganne pushed, she didn't push back—she retreated to her loom and donned a sour expression, refusing to speak for hours, sometimes days. Elowyn sensed that the balance of things had been altered, though she could not understand how, or why.

The day finally came when the order was complete, and their little cottage was on the verge of bursting. More anxious than ever, their mother went over the order item by item, inspecting each garment down to the last stitch to make sure that everything had been done precisely as requested. When she was satisfied that they could produce no better, she sent a message by courier to the castle, asking the lady's preferred day and method of delivery. She was fully expecting to have to hire out a cart and oxen and ferry the order herself. To everyone's surprise, the very next morning there came a loud, demanding rap on the door. Morganne opened it to find a man in an impressive, brightly colored uniform standing on the front step. Behind him was a large, elaborately decorated horse-drawn cart that displayed the crest of the Sovereign's House. But between him and the cart, mounted on a beautiful brown mare, was an even more impressive, richly dressed woman. She surveyed the surrounding area, the cottage, and Morganne, all in one careless, sweeping glance.

"Oh, how perfectly primitive! Isn't it charming?" She laughed in a way that indicated she thought herself to be rather clever, and everyone else would be well advised to think the same. Morganne nervously began to tuck back loose strands of hair, and brush the soot off her clothes. By contrast, their mother rose from her loom and stepped out to greet the woman without the slightest hesitation or appearance of self-consciousness.

Elowyn looked on in silence with great curiosity. This was by far the most exotic and imposing looking person she had ever encountered. Dark lines were boldly drawn along the bottom rims of her eyes, slanting upward to give them a cat-like shape. Her lips were unnaturally red, and her skin the color of milk. There were thin gold bracelets around her wrists that clanged together musically whenever she moved, and draped around her neck and head were brightly beaded strands of braided gold. Her blue-black hair flowed free instead of being covered or contained in netting. Only the young and the unseemly ever wore their hair loose in public. Yet none would dare to think of this Lady as unseemly. If anyone in Tyroc could claim to have noble blood, surely she could. Her posture was perfect, and her eyes commanded everything she saw as though it naturally belonged to her. Her clothes were of the same caliber as those of the completed order. The garment peeking out from beneath her summer cloak was of a thin, wispy material Elowyn had never seen before. She was sure that whatever it was, it had been bought at a very high price.

Elowyn found it hard to turn away—she felt as though she could stare at the Lady forever. She looked wild, but fascinatingly beautiful, like an untamed horse that no one could break. It was obvious she was not from Tyroc, or any other nearby town or village.

"We are in receipt of your courier's message, and have come to collect the garments commissioned," the uniformed man said in a dry, uninterested voice. "Payment will be made when all have been inspected and properly fitted to the Lady Isana. You will return with us now to the castle."

Their mother nodded graciously, but watched with a keen eye as the servant loaded everything into the cart, and Morganne frantically gathered together all of the supplies they would need. Elowyn was told to keep the house and care for Adelin while they were gone, but the Lady protested.

"No, no, that will not do at all. The whole family must come, or I shall be extremely displeased."

Their mother seemed perplexed for a moment, but she quickly recovered herself and said, "As you wish, my lady."

Elowyn's heart pulsed with anxiety as she covered the hearth fire and barred all the shutters. She grabbed Adelin's hand, her knees quivering as she walked slowly toward the cart. This was completely unexpected, and none of them were quite sure what to make of it. She and Adelin were lifted into the back of the cart, while Morganne and her mother were helped onto the narrow bench seat in front. The Lady Isana remained on her mare, riding beside them.

Elowyn could not imagine why she and Adelin were required to go along. She felt her tongue and throat going dry, all their moisture seemingly diverted to the palms of her hands. Every turn of the cart's wheels brought her closer to the evil looming within the Sovereign's castle walls. Neither her mother nor Morganne knew, and there was no way for her to warn them. All sorts of wild ideas were streaming through her mind to explain this unusual breech of the norm. What if Braeden, through some manner of sorcery, had discovered her relationship with Einar? What if the whole purpose of this venture was to capture her? Once they passed through the gates of the castle, they would be entirely at Braeden's mercy. If they simply disappeared, no one would ever know what became of them. Elowyn tried to calm herself, realizing how ridiculous those thoughts truly were. Even if Braeden knew of her existence, which was unlikely at best, what sort of threat was she, a mere child? Elowyn gazed at the lady intently, searching for any sign of malice or deception, and found neither.

Elowyn had ridden in carts before—mostly badly built carts lined with soggy straw that smelled like manure. This experience was nothing like that. This cart was clean, and freshly painted, and ran as smoothly as the road would allow. Entering Tyroc in such a fashion was wondrous, and she might have enjoyed it were she not so petrified of reaching their final destination. They received no suspicious looks from the guards as they passed through the city gates and rode along the narrow cobbled streets, shadowed by the massive city walls and towers that fortified them. There was none of the usual jostling or having to push through crowds of people. The crowds parted voluntarily to let them pass, many staring up with awe at the splendor of the cart, and the glorious beauty of the Lady Isana herself, who seemed thrilled to be attracting so much attention. She straightened her back more than Elowyn thought possible, and caused her mare to prance alongside the cart. The tilt of her head was regal as her glance took ownership of everything in sight.

Elowyn had never seen Tyroc from quite this vantage point before—she was getting a rare opportunity to see her home city with new eyes. Tyroc was alive with sounds, and colors, and especially smells, pleasant and unpleasant all mixed in together. To someone like this lady, who had unimaginable wealth and power, Tyroc must be a city full of delights. Anything in the world that was worth having could be found in Tyroc...for a price, of course. The city was a very different place for the poor and the working class, who labored their lives away in order to survive day by day.

Above them rose modest homes and workshops, their facades ornamented with moldings and painted with bright reds, blues and greens. They passed shops selling boots, pottery, purses, knives, tin pots and pans, pilgrim's trinkets and other wares. The signboards hanging out over the streets called out to passers-by in a language that anyone could understand. The road soon spilled them out onto the familiar central square, where merchants traded year round from makeshift stalls, the backs of their wagons, or the bags of their packhorses.

To the right, the Temple rose above the square. The sunlight peeking through the clouds glanced off its ceremonial pools and fountains, casting dancing reflections onto the warm sandstone walls and spires. There was a beauty about the place that Elowyn had not recognized for a long time. The Temple had become for her a common object in the midst of a dreary city that, on the whole, she utterly detested. Elowyn remembered that on the other side of those thick sandstone walls, beyond the public Temple, the abbey, and the honeycomb of private chambers no one was allowed to see, extensive grounds sprawled all the way to the outer city wall. There were carefully tended gardens where the monks grew their food and herbs, as well as tranquility gardens kept for their beauty and used for silent meditation. At the center of it all was a large hedge maze, the heart of which was a library filled with the Temple's most coveted Tomes of Knowledge. To find the library, one must solve the maze. Gareth had always told her that there was just as much spiritual wisdom to be found in the confusion of the maze as there was in the library itself, and so he was never disappointed when he got lost.

Elowyn had often watched the monks praying in the protective shade of gnarled, ancient trees when she was supposed to have been copying her letters. She could not help but look back on those peaceful times with longing. Those she had met at the Temple had always been kind to her, and they'd had such a warm, lovely golden glow all about them. She had felt close to Aviad when she was there. Had all of those kind people left with Gareth? Had Braeden covered the beautiful glow with darkness? Was Einar right to be bitter? She thought perhaps so about the Temple itself, but not about Aviad. Surely even Braeden could not produce a darkness so strong and deep as to envelop Aviad. Her knowledge of spiritual things was perhaps simple and childlike, but she knew in the core of her being that Aviad did not change, at least not in that way. In a world that was constantly shifting, blending, growing and decaying, that was the one truth that remained aloft, untouched.

The Temple was behind her now, as the cart swung to the left and bumped across the square. Radiating out from the square were numerous roads, some wide enough for several carts to pass, others so narrow that two people could barely squeeze past each other. The main thoroughfares were typically cobbled, like the square, but not all were. Many roads were still little more than beaten dirt paths, which at the moment were mucky pools of mud because of all the wet weather. Each road led to a different quarter of the city—the sooty blacksmiths quarter, the stench-filled tanners and butchers quarters, the bakers, the chandlers, the tinkers, the leatherworkers, and of course the clothiers, among others.

The road the lady chose was one that Elowyn had rarely been on. It housed many inns, taverns, breweries, and shops selling travel gear. These streets were bursting with visitors from the farthest reaches of the world, who had come to purchase from the great variety of goods available in Tyroc. The green southern fields and towns ferried their harvests up the coast to be sold in Tyroc's many food markets. The far northern mountains sent iron, copper, tin, silver and other materials to be beaten into submission in Tyroc's forges by its smiths. From the northwest came fine, heavy luxurious wools and flax, and from across the sea came more exotic wares, such as spices, gems, gold and silk. The world converged at Tyroc's ports not only at faire time, but year-round.

As the cart continued to move away from the center of Tyroc, the crowds thinned. Buildings began to stand separate from one another with green spaces in between. The road sloped to higher ground overlooking the river, where there were grand homes with spacious, well-tended grounds and gardens. Tyroc's hustle and bustle gradually diminished to nothing but a distant murmur, its strong odors washed away by a fresh breeze driving inland from the coast. From there Elowyn could see the ocean, shimmering on the horizon, stretching on seemingly without end. Elowyn had not realized that any part of the city held such simple splendor. But nearly as soon as they entered this quarter, they passed beyond it, coming to a bridge that spanned the river close to where it entered Tyroc from the Northeast. This part of the river was still pristine, untouched by the soils of the city. Not very far downstream, Elowyn could see the grain mill at work, people gathering water for their shops or houses, and ships ferrying merchandise.

They passed through the northern gate, which only served to remind her of her time with Einar, and of the danger she would soon be facing. The road continued to rise slowly, but relentlessly upward, first over open pasture land, then into the cool shadow of a forested mountain. That is to say, Elowyn thought of it as a mountain, because she had never seen a real one. With all of Tyroc being relatively flat and level with the sea, the hill on which Tyroc's castle had been built seemed immense to her. The road twisted upward and inward along the face of the hill in a zigzag pattern. With each hairpin curve, they rose higher. There was always a sheer wall of rock and tree on one side of her, and a steep drop on the other. The city below seemed distant and dreamlike.

As they rounded a final curve, the road broadened and they passed through a stone gateway flanked by massive towers. Beyond the gate, the road continued along a rough open field and then across a wooden bridge that spanned a deep ditch filled with rainwater and refuse. On the other side of the ditch began the outer defensive walls of the castle, which seemed to stretch up to the very clouds. Elowyn could not help but feel that they were being closely watched through the narrow slits carved into the walls. The towers and inner buildings rose even higher, dwarfing the trees that edged the hilltop. The sight was both majestic and oppressive at the same time.

Between the outer and inner defensive walls was a flat grassy area where sheep and other animals grazed, and where people and their livestock were gathered during times of war. Long, spiraling staircases rose from the ground to the tops of the walls. Elowyn couldn't help but wonder if it was from the top of one of these staircases that Avery had plummeted.

Shuddering, Elowyn realized more than ever that they were trapped, held captive at this lady's mercy until she saw fit to release them. She wished she could see Morganne's face, or even her mother's, in the hope of finding some comfort in their expressions. Elowyn swallowed hard when they finally passed beyond the outer and inner defensive walls, and through the main gate. She thought her heart would stop when the portcullis shut behind them with such a definitive clang, the sound continued to echo for several moments. She found herself in a poorly lit entryway that smelled strongly of damp stone. The gatekeepers kept a keen eye on them from open archways above, while the lady instantly began giving orders to servants waiting in the shadows.

"Have all of these garments delivered to my chambers immediately. Take the youngest child to the nursery, and show the remainder of my guests to the bath. Send handmaidens to see to their physical needs and comforts. Be sure that they are cared for as any personal friend of the Sovereign would have been, or I shall make my extreme displeasure known."

With that the lady swept past them, flinging open a single wooden door on the left, and disappearing down a rough stone corridor illuminated solely by torch light. Two servants stepped forward and indicated that they were to be followed. The entryway echoed again, this time with the sound of heavy chains being drawn, and loud groans and creaks as the two massive wooden doors before them were slowly drawn open. Such splendor as Elowyn could never have imagined awaited her. Thick woven rugs with bright, intricate patterns hung from the walls, as did banners displaying the family crest of the Sovereign. Overhead, arched and polished wooden beams supported great silver chandeliers holding a hundred or more candles each. The corridor represented such a small part of the castle's full glory, yet it was impressive enough to Elowyn who knew it could have easily held their little thatched roofed cottage many times over. She stood gaping in the doorway, unaware that everyone was waiting for her. Even once she realized it, her feet felt like stone, her knees like water. The servants stood without expression while Morgan glared fiercely in Elowyn's direction. She gave a pleading look to Morganne, who after a moment of contemplation seemed to understand. She grasped Elowyn by the hand, pulling her along beside her.

They were led through a series of rooms and corridors, each more impressive than the last, until they were finally brought into what the lady must have been referring to as the bath. The room was many times the size of their cottage, with a brightly colored tile floor, and a great hearth built into the outer wall. A huge fire roared and crackled, giving off incredible amounts of warmth. Before the hearth there was a thick fur rug, and three round wooden tubs, each separated by curtains for privacy. A group of young girls, not much beyond Elowyn's age, approached them. One of them scooped up Adelin and carried her off, presumably to the nursery. The others directed Elowyn, Morganne, and their mother to the three tubs.

Before she quite knew what was happening, Elowyn found that she had been discreetly stripped of all her clothing, and was being gently lowered into one of the baths. It was filled with hot, steaming water and had a soft cloth folded in the bottom for her to comfortably rest on. One of the girls scrubbed her hair clean, while the other washed the rest of her. Such treatment made Elowyn anxious at first. Everything was happening faster than she could anticipate, and was beyond her control. But the warmth of the water quickly soothed her. Her muscles began to relax as the weight lifted from her limbs, and her mind drifted off to more pleasant thoughts. So far, they were not being treated as prisoners.

When Elowyn had been thoroughly scrubbed and rinsed, the young girls helped her out of the tub, wrapping her tightly in a soft blanket, and guiding her over to the rug by the fire. Then she was rubbed all over with perfumed oil, and once her hair was dry, it was combed and braided with ribbons. Finally, she was taken into an adjoining room where she was dressed in the finest clothes she had ever hoped to wear—a soft linen undergarment trimmed with ribbons, and a beautiful green overdress, its edges and sleeves trimmed with embroidered flowers. She was amazed to see her reflection in a large mirror resting against the wall. She had caught wavy, distorted glimpses of herself in pools of water before, but she had never seen an actual mirror. Elowyn was stunned speechless by her appearance. She found it hard to believe that she was looking at herself, and yet she was. When she moved, the other Elowyn matched her movements with perfection.

Elowyn was then escorted through several more rooms into what appeared to be a waiting area. Morganne and her mother were already there, seated by a fire. Their hair and new clothes were equally stunning. Morganne wore a long blue gown that trailed on the floor behind her, with a bodice and sleeves that laced up with ribbons. Elowyn could not help but notice how well the color suited her. She was absolutely beautiful, with her hair shimmering in the firelight, and her complexion still rosy from the heat of the bath. Their mother had been dressed in a red gown trimmed with beads and needlework. It had long fluted sleeves and a beaded head covering that matched. Unlike Elowyn and Morganne, who felt very out of place in their new garments, their mother seemed to wear hers comfortably, as though she were quite accustomed to such luxury. Elowyn felt her mother to be even more imposing than usual dressed in red.

The Lady Isana soon appeared, inviting them into another adjoining room, which must have been her antechamber. There all the dresses Morganne had made were laid out for the lady to examine. Several attendants stood nearby, waiting graciously for her commands. Elowyn wondered about these young girls in the service of the castle. While it must be comforting to have all of one's needs attended to, and to live in such grandeur rather than in the squalor of a peasant cottage, it must also be a form of imprisonment. She could not imagine what it must be like, following a lord or lady around like a silent ghost, always ready to comply solemnly with whatever they wished.

"Begin with that one," the lady pointed to one of the silk gowns.

Thus began many tedious hours for Elowyn as the lady was undressed by her attendants, and re-dressed into the new garments to be properly fitted. As she stood, minor adjustments were made to each one by a flushed-faced Morganne. If the brunt of the pressure had been on their mother before, it was now squarely upon Morganne, whose needle must now work with speed and complete accuracy under the attentive eye of the lady. If she pleased the lady, they would be paid and sent on their way. If she did not...the thought of being turned out disgraced and empty-handed was unthinkable.

The whole time she was being fitted, the lady prattled and gossiped about anything that came to mind. Much of it was meaningless to Elowyn, as the lady kept referring to people and events that Elowyn knew nothing about...wealthy members of the court and their wives, her thoughts on what they wore to last week's feast, and what outlandish things she said just to watch their prim little mouths gape in disapproval. Then she did finally say something worth paying attention to.

"Is it not the biggest jest ever? All those insatiably wealthy Tyrocian families that have outdone themselves for years to get into the Sovereign's good graces, hoping that their daughters might be chosen to bear his descendants. Yet here am I, daughter of a far off land most of them have never heard of, nor will ever see. Indeed most of them would detest our ways as barbaric," she smirked dryly. "If only they truly knew how much I have already conformed to their way of life, including wearing these tight, burdensome garments. It is I who will sweep the throne out from under them by marrying the only son of the Sovereign who will ever father heirs. If that was not reason enough for them to resent me, I know that they also find me a contemptible heathen, entirely too wild and impulsive, and free with my opinions." She grinned merrily, "So let them hate me! Let them whisper behind my back. I will have the last satisfaction when they must come to me with their false smiles to attain the favor of the next Sovereign." The lady looked directly at Elowyn, who was at that moment in her line of vision, and winked. "In the meantime, why shouldn't I have the fun of fulfilling all of their expectations, and more? It might just make this new life interesting enough to be bearable."

Elowyn could feel her eyes widening to the point where she thought they must burst out of her head. She had a thousand questions she desperately wanted answers to, but she remembered her place enough to know she dare not ask even one of them.

Their mother lowered her eyes to the floor, fully aware that she had just been given private information not yet known to the general populace, and said, "My lady, we congratulate you on the good fortune of your upcoming marriage, which shall also be the good fortune of all Tyroc." She then spoke in a much lower voice, closer to the lady's ear. "What you say gives me great hope for the future. For though we are of a different class and upbringing, and without meaning any disrespect to my lady's status as my better in every respect, I understand your position all too well. My own eccentricities would not be so well tolerated were it not for my exceptional weaving skill, and the famous needle of my eldest daughter. I might very well be a penniless outcast among my peers, many of whom have traditionally fashioned all of the royal family's garments, and therefore boast far greater prestige. Your request for such humble services as I may offer is a great privilege and an honor that I shall not forget." With that she made a low bow before the lady, but not before she had given a sharp glance to her daughters indicating she expected them to follow her example.

The lady looked upon their mother with a mixture of surprise and amusement. She then did something none of them could have anticipated. She took hold of their mother's chin and lifted it so that she could stare directly into her eyes. Elowyn let out a little gasp of fear—she could not help it. Was the lady offended by what their mother had said? Would they be cast out, or imprisoned, or worse? That breathless moment seemed to go on forever, as she wondered what such strange behavior meant. If anyone else had touched Morgan in such a way, she would have instantly responded with violence. But what could she do? Even she was at the mercy of the Lady Isana.

"You do not speak nor act in the manner of a commonplace weaver, and I can tell by your eyes that you are not one of them." For the first time their mother looked truly uncomfortable. She initially seemed startled, then pained, before she quickly veiled her expression and carefully protested.

"My good lady, you have seen my home, and everything I have in this world. I have nothing more than a humble cottage and my work to show for my life's toil. But it should not surprise you my lady, that in my line of business, it pays to learn the ways and manners of my betters."

The lady let go of her face, giving her a skeptical glance, but choosing not to push the issue further. "You speak truly when you say there are many weavers and seamstresses in Tyroc of greater prestige. But my most trusted servant, whom I sent ahead to settle my affairs, found none of greater skill, and I settle for nothing less than perfection. The prestige of others is meaningless to me, unless I can use it in some way to further my own. You will do well to remember that.

"Now then," her tone changed. "I am weary of this and it is nearly time for the evening meal. We must all refresh ourselves before going to the Great Hall." As if her desires had been anticipated, three servant women suddenly appeared at the door.

"If it please you my lady, we have come to show your guests to their chambers." One of the servant women hung back in the shadow of the corridor, her head lowered.

The lady's sharp eye did not fail to notice her. She pointed accusingly in the servant's direction and called out sharply, "How is it that *you* have been sent to serve me? I thought that you had been relegated to scrubbing pots in the kitchens?"

"With all respect my lady, the kitchens would not have me," she choked on her words, obviously trying to hold back a gush of tears. "I am here by the Lord Braeden's will, and the son of my Lord Sovereign did say that I must obey Lord Braeden's every word as law if I wish to live."

The lady's expression was as cross as her tone, "Very well then. I shall take this matter up with him. In the meantime, you will tend to the young girl. Perhaps by the grace of youthful ignorance she will be able to suffer your presence. But if I hear that you have not treated her well, I will see to it that you spend the rest of your miserable days mucking out the privy pits."

"Yes, my lady. My only desire is to please you, and your guests."

Elowyn followed the servant down a maze of corridors until she was brought to the chambers that had been prepared for her. The servant, still teary eyed, drew a basin of water for her to wash up in, brought her some fresh clothes, then stood waiting to help her dress.

This sort of attention was embarrassing to Elowyn, who knew that the servant, however much she was despised by the lady, was probably still of higher birth than she was. Elowyn felt terrible for this poor woman, but she did not know what to say that would be of any comfort.

"You do not need to dress me…I would never say anything, you know."

The woman looked about nervously as though she felt she was being watched. "I must do my lady's bidding, or her wrath will surely fall upon me." Then she whispered so softly that Elowyn could barely hear her, "I trust your word, for you have the look of kindness about you. But these walls have eyes, and I am closely watched. I beg that you allow me to serve you."

Elowyn complied and allowed the servant woman to help her change, but she could not hold back her curiosity. "Why are you watched? Why is the lady so angry with you?"

The woman's features were overtaken with sorrow, and it took her so long to speak that Elowyn thought she was not going to answer. Finally she whispered again, very low under her breath, "My husband was beheaded as a traitor."

Elowyn's eyes got very wide, and before she remembered herself she had called out "Elias!"

The woman looked about for a moment in a wild panic and whispered fiercely, "These walls have also ears. If you mean to destroy me, you would be kinder to run me through where I stand."

"I am so sorry," Elowyn whispered, "I truly am. I was only surprised. I knew him...or rather, I knew one who knew him. A man called Einar was...my friend."

The woman searched Elowyn's face carefully for a moment, then said "We must speak, but not here. I will find a way. Until then, you should say not my husband's name, nor Einar's, to anyone. If the Lord Braeden ever found out, you and your kin would not leave this place alive."

Until that point, Elowyn's initial fears had been soothed away by the bath, and the fresh clothes, and even the lady's self-involved, but harmless prattling. Now she felt again with full intensity the gravity of their situation. She knew too much, certainly far more than anyone in the castle would suspect a fatherless weaver's daughter to know. The servant woman was right. If Braeden realized what he had so close to his grasp, he would never let them go. From some far off corridor a deep bell began to ring.

"Come, now," the woman's voice rose to its normal pitch. "It is time for me to take you to the Great Hall for the evening meal." In a much lower voice, she whispered, "Just keep your tongue quiet, mind your manners at the table, and don't let *him* sense your fear, whatever you do. Your best chance of saving your life is to simply go unnoticed."

Chapter 9
The Traitor's Wife

The Great Hall was not at all what Elowyn had expected. It was lit up with oil lamps, torches, candles, and an enormous blazing hearth set back in the wall near the high table. Many trestle tables had been laid out with cloths, knives, trenchers, chalices and finger bowls, and the room bustled with a good many people Elowyn did not know. By their clothes she presumed they were a mix of nobles, council members, and perhaps even high-level servants. The ruling family and Braeden were of course present, already seated and waiting for the first course to be presented. Elowyn recognized each of them from the day Elias was executed. Much to her horror, the lady proceeded to march her, Morganne and their mother right up to the high table, ordering the servants to make places for them.

Braeden looked up at the Lady Isana with a wry smile, and said in a tone of mock surprise, "These are most unusual guests you have brought, my dear. Are you certain they would not be more comfortable sitting at the table of honor already prepared for them?"

The Lady Isana flared back at him with heated tones, "Does having to sit with my guests displease you, my lord? Would you be more comfortable if they were seated in the kitchen with the servants? Shall I sit there as well? Or perhaps we should all take our meals with the traitor's wife you sent to my chambers earlier today, expressly against my wishes. Please tell me, Lord Braeden, if this is the kind of ill service and disrespect that I can look forward to my family and future guests receiving? Or does the treatment of guests depend solely on your *personal* evaluation of their worth?"

Allison D. Reid

Braeden did not look the least bit ruffled by her stinging accusations, and it seemed to Elowyn that he was even secretly amused by her outburst.

"A misunderstanding, my lady, to be sure. I did hear that you were quite unhappy, and I assure you that no offense was intended to you, or to your…guests. But this is a matter best resolved in private, do you not agree?"

The lady glared at him, but remained silent. She had apparently made her point and did not wish to press the issue further. Elowyn thought to herself that she would certainly be more comfortable sitting among the servants, and from the look on Morganne's face, Elowyn suspected that she must feel the same.

The lady turned to them with forced pleasantries and said there was no reason to be distressed by the Lord Braeden's poor manners—perhaps he had lived too long among sour, solitary scholars to have learned true hospitality. And Braeden shot back pointedly that if Tyrocian hospitality was not up to her standards, she was by no means obligated to fulfill her betrothal vows, and that he was certain her father would be pleased to have her back in his household once again. For a moment the lady looked quite alarmed, but she quickly brushed the comment off with a nervous laugh, remarking that he should leave humor to the jester and stick to his scholarly pursuits.

Braeden did once address their mother and Morganne directly, much to Elowyn's discomfort, but it was only to say that he heard the Lady Isana was pleased by their work on her new wardrobe, and that there might be more orders in the future. Braeden could not help but use the compliment to throw one more barb in Lady Isana's direction, saying how fortunate it was that their work had pleased her since she was obviously a difficult woman to satisfy. In this way the two of them insulted each other all through dinner while Darik looked on with disinterested silence, blankly tracing the rim of his chalice with his finger. The more the two bantered, and the more incensed the lady became, the greater Braeden's private amusement seemed to be. Elowyn remembered what
158

Einar had said about Braeden gradually, subtly shaping Darik into the kind of person he could manipulate to his will. She suddenly wondered if Braeden was doing the same thing to the Lady Isana. She would, after all, soon be Darik's wife, and the mother of Tyroc's heirs.

Elowyn tried very hard to avoid looking directly at Braeden. The darkened eyes, the pale, sallow, strange fitting skin, the crooked nose and twisted smile…everything about him repulsed her. Enduring his presence was like reliving a nightmare that even the strength of the midday sun could not chase away. With every bite Elowyn took, she was trying to choke down with it the terror rising steadily to the top of her throat. She remembered all too clearly the black aura that had enveloped Braeden at Elias' execution, even if she had been the only one to notice it. In but one fleeting moment, the directness of his gaze had seemed to penetrate all her defenses and left her feeling violated. If he'd had this effect on her from afar, how much more would he affect her now that he was just across the table? What would Braeden find should his probing eyes look directly into hers, and more importantly, what would he take? Would the darkness he exuded surround her too? She shuddered as she imagined it eating away, not at her flesh, but at the very essence of her being, until she was nothing more than an empty vessel, waiting to be filled by whatever horrors he saw fit to destroy her with.

Perhaps that was what had become of Darik, staring down at the food on his trencher as if he didn't really see it, the line of his jaw hardened and tense, his expression cold and empty. Though the Lady Isana seemed to want him as her future husband, Elowyn felt sorry for her. She could not imagine that life with such a man would ever be happy. Elowyn shifted her gaze to Avery. Now that she knew his woeful tale, her heart broke for him. She studied his face as he sat quietly by his brother's side. Avery was empty too, but in an innocent way. Though he of everyone at the table had the most to be bitter about, there was no trace of ill feeling about him. In a way, he was like an infant, or like the animals—aware of each moment as he lived it, without the ability to dwell on the past, or plan for the future, or engage in any kind of serious thought. He did little more than exist. Perhaps that was the key to getting through the meal. To turn off her thoughts and simply live in the moment as though there was no past, and no future, and nothing to be afraid of.

Elowyn focused instead on the glorious meal placed before her—mixed greens, meats, broths and gravies, bread with generous amounts of butter and honey, meat pies, fruit with cream, tortes, and wine that was not so inferior or watered down as what she sometimes got at home. Even when she was full, she wanted to keep right on eating, as she could not foresee having such a meal set before her again. When she could truly eat no more she sat back and took comfort in staring at the hearth fire and letting all of the conversation around her swirl into an indistinguishable hum.

By the time the remains on the table were all cleared away, and they were finally dismissed for the night, Elowyn was feeling rather sick. Her body was not accustomed to so much rich food. She said as much to Elias' wife on the way back to her chambers.

"I have just the remedy for that, don't you worry." She returned in a short while with a warm drink that smelled of mint leaves and said, "When you've finished that, the best thing for you would be a brisk walk in the gardens." Elowyn brightened at the suggestion and smiled gratefully.

It turned out to be a beautiful night for a walk. The moon shone so brightly, everything was clothed in its brilliance. Wisps of moonlit clouds drifted slowly across the night sky while the stars danced merrily overhead. The stepping stone path that wound its way through the castle gardens was cradled in an amazing abundance and variety of flourishing plants, trees and flowers. Many of them were new to Elowyn, as she knew far more about wild plants and herbs than cultivated pleasure gardens. She wished she could see the full array of breathtaking color in the light of the sun. But what really stood out to Elowyn were the smells, so many she could hardly distinguish them all from each other: floral perfumes, fruity aromas, and rich earthy musks, all mixed in with the tang of sea air wafting in from the coast. The world was still and pure, and its perfection cleared her mind as the fresh air being drawn into her body flushed out all the sick, heavy feeling she was there to purge herself of.

They soon came to a large open space circled by small flowering trees. In the center was a little carved bench and a looking pond that reflected the moon and stars on its surface. Elias' wife bade her to sit while she stood at a close distance, as she would normally do, waiting for direction. If anyone was watching them from the castle windows or the outer walls, they would not notice anything unusual.

"Are you feeling better, child?"

Elowyn nodded, "Thank you."

"Now, then, we may talk for a bit if we are careful. We are not truly safe, even here, but it is the best we can do without drawing attention." Her face softened and grew sad. "What has happened to them? To Einar, and the others? Since my husband's death there has been no one to bring us news, and there are many families here waiting, and hoping, and desperate to know if their loved ones are or dead or alive, or if they have any chance of seeing them again."

Elowyn answered truthfully, "I can only tell you that they were alive not so long ago, and that they have gone away to other places. They stayed in the wood and fought as long as they could, but then the Hounds came...they had no way to fight the Hounds." Elowyn stopped, wondering how much she should tell. She did not want to put Einar and the Circle in any further danger.

"They wanted to return...they tried their best," Elowyn shook her head sadly, not knowing what to say. Elias' wife nodded tearfully in understanding.

"They caught the man who betrayed your husband," Elowyn ventured cautiously.

The servant's interest perked up. "Who was it, and what became of him?"

"He was called Mavek. They voted to execute him. Einar did it himself with his bow...I was there, watching." Elowyn shuddered as the memory came back to her in full.

There was a long silence before the servant finally spoke again. "I know this may be too much to ask, and if it is, I understand. There is a courier in Tyroc that Elias knew well, and trusted completely. If I gave you a packet of letters, would you see that he gets it?"

"Yes," Elowyn nodded. "I will try to find him for you." She hesitated anxiously for a moment, and then asked in what was barely a whisper, "Is Braeden really the one who calls the Hounds? Are they coming to him with the storms?"

Elias' wife gaped at Elowyn with a mix of shock and fear, but would not answer.

"Please, I must know. Elias knew, didn't he? That was what he wrote to Einar just before he was captured. The dying monk they found gave the same warning." She lowered her voice even further. "What *is* Braeden?"

Whether it was coincidence or something more Elowyn would never know, but at that moment the wind changed direction and increased in strength. It came not from the coast, as it should have, but from the direction of the castle. The air was warm, heavy, moist, and smelled of rain. A soft, deep rumble of thunder vibrated throughout the garden. The moon and the stars, one by one, began to disappear under heavy cloud cover.

"Speak not of such things again, child," she whispered fiercely. "You know not what you say, or what danger you put yourself in by saying it. Do you not even now realize that such knowledge is what destroyed my husband's life, and mine? We must go back—at once!"

Elowyn found herself being hurried along the path back toward the castle at a rapid pace. They had barely gotten through the door when the skies began to pour. There was no longer any question in Elowyn's mind as to the truthfulness of Einar's tale. What to do with that knowledge was a different matter.

Watching the storm from within the castle was nothing like weathering it out from home would have been. During such storms, their little cottage shook with every gust of wind, and shuddered with each peal of thunder. On more than one occasion it had been flooded with water. But secure within the massive castle walls, Elowyn would not have even known there was a storm were it not for the strange whistling sounds the drafts made, the gentle pelting on her windows, and occasional flashes of light.

Even so, Elowyn barely slept that night. For one thing, she was not used to sleeping indoors alone, and on a soft bed rather than a floor mat. For another, she kept staring at the crack under her door, waiting for the guard to come for her. She half expected to be cast into the castle prisons under cover of night, never to be seen again. Even when she did manage to sleep, Braeden was always there, lurking in her dreams, shadowing her every move and thought. He desperately wanted something from her. Oh, he already knew about her connection with Einar, the quest he had embarked on, and the scattering of the Circle. All of that was of little consequence to him—it amused him, in fact. There was something more. Something that had gone awry, which was eating at him, infuriating him. What that something was, or why he thought she knew anything about it, she could not fathom.

Elowyn awoke in the early gray of morning feeling exhausted and confused. Had she only been dreaming? The heavy, haunting vision of Braeden's probing questions had seemed so real, staying with her more like a memory than a dream. It did not have the vague, disjointed, nonsensical quality that dreams so often do in the light of wakefulness.

Elias' wife did not come to her chamber that morning. Another servant, a prim-looking older lady with pursed lips, had been sent instead. She silently filled up the washing basin with hot water and began to bathe and dress Elowyn as though she had done it so many times she gave it no more thought than breathing. Elowyn instinctively knew that there would be no good protesting or trying to dress herself. This servant knew her duty and was determined to perform it.

"Where is the lady who cared for me yesterday?" Elowyn asked.

Without missing a step, the woman answered dryly, "It is not for me to question where my lord sends his servants. Where I am summoned

I go, where I am told to stay, I stay, and when no direction is given, I stand in silence waiting to learn my lord's will."

"Might I be able to visit the gardens today?" Elowyn asked, barely daring to hope. That hope was quickly dashed.

"The Lady Isana has requested your presence for the remainder of her fittings."

Elowyn breathed a heavy sigh of dread as she was escorted through the corridors, back to the lady's chambers where Morganne was already fast at work with thread and needle.

"That wretched storm kept me up half the night. Such tiresome weather you have here in Tyroc," the lady was saying as Elowyn was brought into the room. "How do you bear it?"

"It has been an unusual season, my lady," Morganne answered her softly as she worked. "Though sudden storms do come in off the sea now and again, our weather is normally quite pleasant during the summer months."

"Where I come from, the weather is always hot, no matter what the season. The rains are warm enough to bathe in. The plants grow huge and lush, in brilliant colors, and the seas stretch out clear, and blue, and calm, so far as your eyes can see." The lady's voice lost its commanding edge and became wistful. "I already miss the sight of the moon rising over the waters. I miss the openness of everything. Here, your buildings are all closed in, with small windows and stale, smoky air. Your clothes are heavy and restrictive, no doubt to keep out the cold. Even in summer you require a hearth fire to warm your halls and your baths. You have no hot springs, or steam caves in which to clear the mind and restore health to the body. I look out to your gardens and woodlands—to me they are dull, colorless. I don't know that I shall ever grow accustomed to this life. Had there been a family of suitable lineage and wealth for me to marry into, I should have stayed in the islands for the rest of my days."

Elowyn sat entranced, trying to envision the world the lady had described. She could not imagine a land so beautiful that it made Tyroc's gardens and woodlands look dull and colorless by comparison. She wondered what hot springs and steam caves were like, though she was not sure that she would appreciate the intense heat as the lady seemed to. Elowyn thought it was really too bad that she would never get to see such a wondrous place in her lifetime.

"Your people's ways are just as strange to me as your landscape," the lady continued. "So much lies hidden, so much that is spoken is false. A smile does not always mean benevolence. Polite words are spoken to the face, while insults are murmured behind the back. I do not understand that way. To speak directly, honestly, even when the words are unpleasant, is to show respect." She shook her head, laughing briefly with amusement. "But your people do make good sport, even if they are badly mannered. They are easily scandalized, aren't they? It takes so little to have their eyes bulging and their tongues wagging gossip to each other behind closed doors. Though they complain bitterly, I know they enjoy it. How dreary their lives must have been before my arrival!

"You would not believe the looks and the questioning I got when I gave orders to have you all brought here and treated as guests in the manner *I* saw fit. Who you were, or for what purpose I desired your presence close by should not have mattered. My word should have been enough. As the time of the wedding draws near, I shall have friends and family visiting me from my own homeland. The treatment of all guests, and their servants, is taken very seriously by my people. Deliberate breeches in our laws of hospitality have been enough to provoke wars between families that drenched our soil with blood for more than a hundred years. By bringing you here, I wanted to see in what manner I could expect that my future guests would be treated. No doubt they will be far more difficult to accommodate, and my demands shall also be far greater. This test should have been easily passed. I see now that much must change before I dare to invite my family to Tyroc. I would not wittingly allow them to be so dishonored."

The lady was finally interrupted by the arrival of a late breakfast, which she had ordered to be brought to her chambers as a way to avoid wasting time in the Great Hall. Her test concluded, and her new wardrobe nearing completion, she was eager to finish the fitting sessions all together. The novelty of their presence in the castle was no doubt wearing off, and the lady was ready to make a stir elsewhere. Elowyn was just as eager for these sessions to be over. The castle, great and beautiful as it was, felt no better than a tomb to her so long as Braeden's shadow hung over her soul. She was anxious to return home to her garden, to try to get back to the life she had before she knew about Einar and the Hounds, before the lady's order put such a strain on their household, and before the storms began. It was a deluded hope, but one that she clung to nonetheless.

It was late afternoon when the last hem had been set in place, the last knot tied off, and Morganne, with a satisfied smile, was finished with her work. The lady unlocked a metal chest in the corner of the room and brought out a cloth bag filled with money. Handing it to their mother, she said, "My servant chose well. The quality of your weave is unequaled. Consider this the fulfillment of our contract. You have been paid according to the terms of the agreement."

She then lifted another, smaller bag out of the chest and handed it to the astonished Morganne. "My people are both wealthy and generous. Much is demanded of a good servant, but she is also well rewarded when her work is done. You have a greater gift than I have ever seen in one so young. Your manner, your speed, and your skill have all pleased me greatly. Though I detest these clothes for what they are, they could not have been more beautifully made."

The lady then called to her attendant. "Bring the young child out of the nursery and have a cart readied to ferry my guests home." They were escorted to their rooms one last time, where they were changed back into their old clothes, now washed and pressed. Their time at Tyroc castle was over. An immense flood of relief swept over Elowyn as they passed back through the stone archway and began their journey down the twisting road that had brought them there. She could not believe that they had escaped unharmed, though she regretted that she had not been able to see Elias' wife one last time. No doubt the lady had spoken to Braeden in private and demanded her removal.

They were all in high spirits as they wound their way back through the streets of Tyroc, where afternoon activities were giving way to evening revelries. The taverns were filling with travelers and locals alike, with heavy mugs of ale being passed all around. Hearth fires were stoked, meals prepared, and sweet aromas wafted through the streets from shutters still open to the early evening air. One by one, the comforting glow of candles and oil lamps began to light up homes, and strains of music lilted on the fresh breeze coming in from the sea. Elowyn saw people greeting each other with friendly smiles, heard joyous laughter echoing down alley ways, and coins being charitably dropped into beggars' tins. She thought to herself that perhaps Tyroc was not so terrible as she had once believed. Having gotten away from Braeden's oppressive presence, the hazards of the city seemed much less threatening. The Lady Isana did not understand their ways, but this was the only life Elowyn had known—the only life she thought she would ever know. She had great hope that somehow Aviad would keep the darkness at bay, that what goodness existed in her time would prevail over the encroaching evil.

They were delivered to the doorstep of their cottage, which was just as they had left it. The driver lingered outside, bidding Morganne and her mother to make sure all was in order and that they had no further need of his services. As they went inside, he turned to Elowyn and silently slipped a sealed packet into her hand with a man's name written on the outside. He stared at her intently until she nodded in understanding. She had almost forgotten about the request Elias' wife had made of her in the garden the previous night. The driver must have also been a friend of Elias. Once her mother had declared everything was in order, the driver began his journey back to the castle.

Their hearth fire had completely gone out so that Elowyn had to start it with sparks and tinder. She did not mind this task, and she was better at it than most due to her frequent excursions into the wood. They had nothing except for coarse bread, dried fish and onions for their evening meal, but they all ate with good humor, knowing that the coming days would bring more promising fortune.

Chapter 10
Escape from Tyroc

The next morning was a glorious one. The sun shone brightly in a crystal blue and rose sky, and the air was warmer than it had been for weeks. Elowyn couldn't wait to spend the day working in her garden. The aroma of damp earth was as intoxicating to her as wine might be to another. Their mother woke earlier than usual, and in a fair mood. Elowyn actually thought she heard her mother humming to herself as she dressed to leave for Tyroc. She no doubt wanted to settle her debts and perhaps purchase a few items that she had long set her eyes on, before putting the rest of her earnings away for safekeeping. Morganne began her morning by cleaning up the cottage and starting a fresh kettle of pottage over the hearth fire.

Once their mother left, Morganne abruptly stopped her routine. She slowly, deliberately, took a satchel out of a storage chest and laid it out on the table, staring at it with a determined expression. She began to stuff it with what Elowyn instantly recognized as provisions for a journey. Simple, durable foods, tinder, candles, a blanket, sturdy clothes, Gareth's book…and of course, the bag of money the lady had given her.

Elowyn looked at Morganne, who stared back at her, silent and unwavering. Without words they understood each other perfectly.

"I want you to come with me," Morganne said. "I fear for the future you would have here, alone with her. But whether you come or not, Adelin and I must go. Here I will be no better than a slave for the rest of my days, and you know that our mother has no love for Adelin. This small bag of money may be the only chance I ever get. If I don't take it… oh, you have no idea how long I have hoped for this, dreamed of it…"

Elowyn saw tears forming in her sister's eyes, not of sorrow, but of joy, and the unspeakable elation of an impossible vision becoming blessed reality.

"Where would you take us?" Elowyn asked, knowing already that whatever Morganne's chosen destination, it was her fate to follow.

"We cannot go south. Those cities have too many connections with Tyroc, especially in the cloth and garment trade. We would be found out within a week. To the east there is naught but wasteland between here and the coast, and to the west we would have to walk much too far before finding a suitable place to settle down. I would eventually like to go there, to find out what became of Gareth. But we have neither the means nor provisions to get there just yet. We will have to go north. Along the way there are villages where we could stay and restock our supplies, though we will have to be careful with our money. There is a mining town on the northern sea called Minhaven, where I have heard that they are in need of a seamstress. It will be a new life, a hard life. . .but it will belong to us, and not to our mother."

"What of the Hounds?" Elowyn asked nervously. In ordinary times this journey would be dangerous enough for three young girls. In their present time, it would be much more so. Elowyn understood the darkness lurking out there more intimately than Morganne realized. If Morganne had been older and wiser, she might have never found the courage to even dream of such an escape. But there are times when, for good or for bad, the impulsiveness of youth persuades us to take those first steps, which forever forge the irreversible paths of our lives. Perhaps too, it is innocence that allows the young to hear Aviad more clearly when he calls, and encourages their hearts to follow Him, even when they do not recognize His voice for what it is.

Morganne paused thoughtfully, as though she had not before considered the Hounds a hindrance to her plan. "You said that you knew of them already, before Gareth's letter."

Elowyn nodded.

"Elowyn," Morganne's tone was earnest. "You *must* tell me all that you know, for my sake, and Adelin's…and yours too, if you decide to come with us."

Elowyn knew that it was now finally the time to explain everything that had happened. She started at the beginning, reliving the day she found the coin, the helm, and the bow and arrows. She even told her about the vision of the slain man (something she hadn't even told Einar), and how that vision had driven her to return to the stream. Only instead of casting away the coin as she had planned, she was attacked by a Hound and rescued by Einar. She recounted her conversation with Einar in the shelter below ground, her journey to the shrine, what she found there, and even the contents of her dreams. She though it especially important that what Aviad told her through her dream was also written to them in Gareth's letter. She told Morganne about following Einar to his camp, and Mavek's execution. She also explained everything Einar had said to her later about his growing up, the two brothers, the fate of the Circle, Braeden's dark influence, the probable murder of the Sovereign, and the true identity of the man Braeden had executed. Elowyn told Morganne every last detail, right down to the previous day, when the driver had silently thrust the packet of letters in her hand, which so many hoped would find their way into the hands of loved ones. When she had finally finished her tale, Morganne could only stare at her little sister in awed silence for a good long while.

"All this time…all that happened," she finally spoke, "and you never told me any of it, not even when we were right there in the castle. And to think, we sat at the same table with Braeden and Darik…and still you said nothing." Elowyn watched Morganne's expression as she slowly pieced everything together, realizing the danger they might have faced had Elowyn not kept her silence.

Elowyn shrugged apologetically—she thought for certain that Morganne would be angry, or hurt, or even disappointed that Elowyn had not taken her into her confidence sooner. At the very least she expected a scolding for all the times when she could have gotten herself

Allison D. Reid

killed, or worse. But the Morganne standing in front of her was also changed, no longer bound by the cares of a weaver's daughter. She had resolved herself to be finished with this life and with their mother. That decision had already freed her, though she had yet to take that first step beyond the threshold of the cottage.

"I shall have to remember not to underestimate you." She smiled admiringly at Elowyn, and from that point on their relationship changed, at least from Elowyn's point of view. For the first time she felt that Morganne needed her, and that she had been accepted as she was.

"From what you have told me, the Hounds seem to travel only at night, and they are gathering around the west of Tyroc, in the direction of the castle. I've heard no tale from the traveling merchants about the Hounds plaguing other cities, at least not yet. People come and go between Tyroc and other cities every day without incident. So long as we get well away before nightfall, we should be able to avoid them all together, should we not?"

"I cannot promise safety," Elowyn answered truthfully. "They move where they will, and devour who they will, whether anyone knows the tale or not. Surely no tales of Nevon or the traveling monks will ever be told among Tyroc's shopkeepers. But you are right—when I last saw Einar, he did say that they had moved west of here, heading in the direction of the Circle's old camp and the castle. I can only hope they have not returned. Do we risk the roads, or the wilderness?"

Morganne smiled with relief. "So, you are coming then."

Elowyn nodded. What choice had she? To remain alone with their mother? She, who was unwanted? How would she explain her sisters' disappearance? No doubt to remain would mean a miserable, lonely, pain-filled existence, with no hope for the future. She despised Tyroc, and it equally despised her. Einar and Gareth were gone, the Hounds haunted the forests, and evil reigned in the Sovereign's castle. She had no reason to stay.

"I've looked at a number of maps, and over the years have heard many of the merchants speaking at length of their travels," Morganne

172

continued. "To take the north road, we would have to pass through all of Tyroc, the North Gate, and the main crossroads beyond it that branches out to all the western villages. You might get by if you were alone, but too many people along the way could recognize me and tell mother which way we went. Besides, taking the road would considerably lengthen our trip. We would have to loop all the way back to the east, in the very direction we came from, before the road veers to the north again. But if we go directly north from here, through the wilds, we will meet the road eventually, and we will be far beyond the crossroads. From there, we can decide if we want to continue through the wilds or follow the road."

Elowyn felt a strong sense of urgency to get moving—if they were going to go through with this plan, every moment lost was a precious one. Not only did they need to get well beyond Tyroc's woodlands by nightfall, there was no way of knowing when their mother might return.

"We need to hurry," she told Morganne. "Adelin will slow us. Leave the clothes, and leave the book. But bring your heavy rain cloak, your sewing needle and thread, water skins, dry tinder, a blanket, a few candles and some rope. Eat your fill and pack enough food to last a couple of days. I'll go see what can be harvested from the garden."

Without waiting for Morganne to speak, Elowyn ran outside. As she looked over the garden she had faithfully tended for as long as she could remember, her eyes filled with tears. She felt as though she were about to betray her dearest friends to a slow, withering death. Her mother would certainly never care for them. She took anything that was ripe enough, or grown enough to be of use. She tied the herbs carefully in bundles with twine, and strung them together so they could be hung from their belts or satchels to dry.

The last thing Elowyn did was go to the place where her treasures were hidden. Among the objects she had so carefully saved, the only one of real meaning to her in that moment was the pair of old trousers she thought to be her father's. Gingerly she picked them up and brought them back with her into the cottage, where she found that Morganne had finished packing their satchels and was making a make-shift cloth carrier to tie around her waist and back, so that she could more easily bear Adelin's weight. It was finally time to leave.

Elowyn hung her pouch on her left side, and her dagger on her right, now that she had no need to hide it. With her satchel slung across her back, she stepped out the cottage door for what would be the last time. Elowyn could not help but look back thoughtfully at the life she was leaving behind so unexpectedly, and wonder what kind of future lay ahead. Morganne did not look back once, not even a glance. She walked boldly to the edge of the forest and waited patiently for Elowyn to catch up and take the lead. Elowyn was apprehensive, knowing that Morganne was depending on her to guide them safely through the wilds, and hoping that Morganne's faith in her was not misplaced. Elowyn knew this region of Tyroc's woodlands rather well, but she knew nothing of the lands and dangers that waited beyond, nor did she have the skills necessary to protect herself or her sisters.

The start of their journey was difficult for Elowyn. She was trying to sort through the jumble of memories and emotions flooding through her mind, while at the same time watching out for any sign of danger. Elowyn knew every tree, every stone, and every hill of the path they were on. So many lovely memories they held, of peaceful, innocent times—times that would never come again. Elowyn was noticeably uncomfortable allowing Morganne and Adelin to share in that path and add to those memories. For so long she had separated her wilderness life and her home life. To have them converge in such a way felt strange to her. Of course there were fearful memories too—feelings of dread that resurfaced as Elowyn remembered the weight of the Hound pressing upon her back, and the stench of its breath. She saw no trace of their recent presence, but knowing the Hounds had once been there was bothersome enough.

Morganne, on the other hand, was positively glowing with joy. She sung softly to herself as she walked, in spite of the obvious physical burden she was trying to overcome. Between Adelin's weight, her satchel (which carried Gareth's book, despite Elowyn's advice), and having spent far too many months sitting with her needle, she was constantly struggling to catch her breath and keep up with Elowyn.

In time they reached the place where Elowyn's part in this tale had begun...and Nevon's had violently ended. She could not help but cross the stream and pause at the stone his comrades had placed in his honor.

"Rest here for a bit," she told Morganne, who was grateful to set down her load and allow Adelin to run about and splash in the shallow water for a short while. Elowyn took the coin out of her pouch and fingered it thoughtfully.

"Is this the place?" Morganne asked gently.

Elowyn nodded. She knew this would be her last chance to rid herself of the coin that had brought her so much trouble. There had been a time when she couldn't wait to cast it back into the stream. Yet now she found it didn't seem right anymore. So few would remember what had happened to Nevon, to the monks, to Einar and the Circle. So few knew the truth about Elias. Perhaps the coin had belonged to Nevon, perhaps not, as Einar thought. But in her mind, they were all one. Every time she looked at the coin, every time she felt its cool smooth surface between her fingertips, she would remember, and hope that someday Elias' final words would come true, that through his death, Braeden and all of his wicked plots would be exposed. Elowyn placed the coin back into her pouch and pulled the drawstring tight. She plucked a yellow wildflower growing nearby and placed it reverently on the stone. It was her way of saying good-bye to this man she had never met, whose life had so profoundly changed hers.

"We must keep moving on," she said, quietly picking up her satchel and crossing the stream once more. They were soon in territory wholly unfamiliar to Elowyn. She had never been so far from the cottage. Signs of other travelers were quickly disappearing, while signs of wildlife, particularly large wildlife, were increasing. Fruit bearing and edible plants had not been entirely picked clean either, and when she spotted anything that might be of use, she took it. This gave Morganne brief moments of respite as well, which Elowyn could see she was beginning to need more often as the day wore on.

Adelin, too, was getting restless and tired of being carried. She struggled against Morganne, whimpering to be put down. Morganne tried for small bouts to let her walk before she got frustrated with her slow, aimless, stumbling pace and scooped her up again. Whenever she cried, Elowyn became greatly agitated. As if Morganne's untrained foot-falls weren't noisy enough, how could she be expected to listen for danger amidst that clamor? Surely every predator in the forest had been made aware of their presence.

By late afternoon, Elowyn could see that Morganne was already nearing the end of her strength. Her face was hot and flushed, her breathing labored and her steps heavy. She tripped a number of times on her skirts and on tree roots, nearly falling and dropping Adelin. Elowyn was tiring as well, unaccustomed to carrying so much with her. Even so, she knew she still had the strength to last until nightfall if necessary. She took Morganne's satchel from her in an attempt to lighten her load and allow her to last longer, but the bulk of her endurance had been already been spent. Elowyn was now only waiting out Morganne's resolve. She knew that Morganne would not ask to stop until she felt that she was utterly defeated.

When the afternoon sun began to weaken and make its evening descent, Morganne dropped down onto a fallen tree and gasped, "I cannot go on much further. Are we away enough?"

Elowyn nodded. Their pace had been fairly steady and she had yet to see any sign of Hounds. She had no idea how much further the road might be. This was as suitable a place as any to camp for the night. Elowyn left Morganne to rest while she surveyed the area and collected firewood. As far as she could see there was nothing remarkable to note. They were in gently rolling, untouched forestland, with the stream flowing close by to the east. Elowyn had decided that loosely following its course would give them a reliable guide, and a ready source of fresh water.

Elowyn built a fire, which was a warm and soothing companion that they could huddle close against in the coolness of the evening.

"We can never go back, you know," Morganne stated the fact as though she had just now fully understood what that meant.

"I know," Elowyn nodded.

"No doubt by now mother has realized we are gone. I'll bet she is furious." Morganne laughed nervously, looking about the wood as darkness crept slowly upon them. Elowyn was certain that Morganne had never spent the night out in the open, as she herself had done countless times. She wondered if Morganne was having second thoughts about their escape.

"We cannot go back," Elowyn stated emphatically. Nothing would compel Elowyn to return to Tyroc. For her, the only choice was to see this through to the end, whatever end that might be. Certainly one dark night in a so-far-benevolent wilderness was not going to send her running back to the enemy.

Morganne agreed with a silent nod. "There is no forgiveness in her soul. She would destroy us. If not all at once, she would do it one day at a time, until we became as bitter and tormented as she. I do not want to suffer that end. If this journey is folly, and its fruit is my death, at least I will die knowing my life was lost to hope and not despair. I cannot help but believe that we are meant for something, Elowyn, something greater than we know. Perhaps greater than we will ever know."

Morganne held a sleepy Adelin close in her arms and focused her eyes on the dancing flames of light before her. Elowyn smiled to herself, knowing full well what kind of comfort Morganne sought there.

"We should sleep now," Elowyn reminded her. Without thinking, she climbed up into the tree beside her and made herself comfortable on an outstretched limb.

"What are you doing?" Morganne asked in a confused tone.

"Going to sleep."

"In the tree?"

"Yes."

"But won't you fall out?"

"No. This is how I always sleep. You and Adelin can share my blanket. I will not need it."

She pulled her cloak tightly around her and closed her eyes, leaving a bewildered Morganne blinking in the firelight. This was the Elowyn that Morganne had always wondered about, but could never quite grasp—the Elowyn who disappeared for days at a time, with no cares, and no explanations. The mystery of her sister's other life was slowly being revealed to Morganne in a way that never would have happened had they lived out their lives in Tyroc.

The night passed without incident. Elowyn roused Morganne from sleep as soon as the first dim gray of morning gave them enough light to walk by. Morganne found that she was stiff, sore, and cold. She welcomed the warmth movement brought to her limbs. The day progressed as uneventfully as the night had, and they alternated steady walks with short rests. When Morganne needed longer rests, Elowyn replenished their water supply at the stream and scavenged the surrounding area for anything that might be useful. In that way they were able to stretch their meager food supplies with edible plants, wild onions, roots, and fruit. More than once Elowyn wished that they had a pot for cooking in.

By nightfall they had still not found the road, so they made camp a little closer to the stream than they had the night before. Elowyn listened contentedly as it gurgled to her a sweet, watery lullaby. The sky was bright and clear and the stars winked at her through the gently swaying branches overhead. She knew that the nights were worrisome for Morganne, who pressed as close to their small fire as she dared and shifted positions restlessly under her blanket. But to Elowyn this was almost like old times. To her the night sky was full of joy and mystery and it served once again as a reminder of Aviad's watchful, loving presence. Her lungs welcomed the cool dampness of the air. Her eyes delighted in tracing the subtle beams of moonlight that filtered down through gaps in the forest canopy above them. It was almost easy to forget the dangers they were running from, as well as those that most certainly lay ahead. But making herself anxious over such troubled thoughts served no good purpose. She slept well, with a peaceful heart and mind, full of growing dreams about what wonderful things might await them in Minhaven.

Chapter II
Respite Along the East Road

The dawn came late, and Elowyn woke to the sound of rain dripping on the leaves above her. It was a harmless, steady, late-summer rain, and not one of Braeden's conjured storms. Morganne and Adelin were still asleep under a wet bundle of blankets, curled up next to the muddy heap of cold ash that had once been their fire. Elowyn woke her and they donned their rain cloaks before starting out once again. Elowyn supposed that the weather could not have been expected to hold out all the way to Minhaven, though she wished they could have made it to the road before it changed. The girls plodded onward, heads down against the rain for what seemed like an endless age. Their shoes were drenched and caked in mud. The bottoms of their dresses were soaking up water and mud too, slowing them down and adding to their discomfort.

Elowyn wanted to move faster and more discreetly, but could not with Morganne and Adelin following behind. Her impatience was increasing and she wondered how much farther the road might be. Though she realized they were nowhere near Minhaven, and the condition of the road was likely to be even worse than the path they were on, it was a milestone she was anxious to reach. Deep down, she felt these woods were still too closely tied with Tyroc, their mother, and their old life. Every part of her being was ready to break free. For her, the road was the symbolic point where she could finally purge Tyroc, and the shadow of Braeden, from her soul.

The girls stumbled upon the road quite unexpectedly—a narrow, muddy scar along the forest floor, stretching from west to east. Though it was just barely wide enough for two small carts to pass each other, and was full of ruts and great pools of muddy water, the sight of it was a great relief. For Elowyn, who was trusting in Morganne's direction, this was finally some confirmation of what she had described. No doubt reaching the road boosted Morganne's confidence as well, for her step increased with renewed energy.

"I know I said that I wanted to avoid roads, but let's continue on this one for a while. Tyroc and the main crossroads are well to the west of here, and if what I have heard is right, we should soon come to a trading post. There we may be able to spend a night indoors, purchase some supplies and gather information. I must admit, I know very little about what lies beyond that point, either by road or wilderness. Maybe you will find a courier to take those letters you're carrying. We should rid ourselves of them as soon as possible, rather than taking them all the way to Minhaven. I am wary of having them traced back to us."

Elowyn was content with this plan, and so they trudged onward. It was much easier to keep a steady pace without having to scramble over fallen trees and skirt thick tangles of brush. Only twice did they share the way with others. Once with two men on horseback who paid them no heed, and once with a horse-drawn cart. Both parties were headed west. As they passed, Morganne kept her head down so that her hood covered her face. She saw no reason to take chances. Their anticipation grew as they walked. Morganne wondered what merchants there might be at the trading post, and hoped that she would be able to purchase a sturdy pair of boots. Elowyn had hopes of trading some of the rarer herbs she had collected along the way for others that might be more practical.

When the girls finally did arrive at the trading post, they nearly missed it. The only visible indication that they were in the right place was the mud splattered sign hanging outside the front door. Accustomed to the varied and brightly painted shops in Tyroc, they were shocked to discover that the trading post was nothing more than a large, dilapidated shack. Stunned by this blow to their expectations, the girls cautiously opened the door and peered inside, half expecting this to be a mistake. Though it hadn't been a bright day, their eyes still needed a few moments to adjust to the dark interior. The windows were sealed shut, covered with oiled parchment that had been stained black with smoke from the hearth.

Only a few quiet patrons lingered among the many tables and benches crowded into the main room. Not one of them bothered to glance in the direction of the doorway as the girls entered. To their left, a long counter ran the length of the wall. Behind the counter, from floor to ceiling, were stacked ale and wine kegs, shelves with crudely made drinking vessels, large storage jars, bags of grain, and other assorted items. A woman was standing behind the counter, wiping dry a newly washed ale mug.

"Ay! Whot's this?" She said in a surprised tone, "I never seen the like walk through my door. Yer must be lost then?" The woman, who they now took to be the matron of the establishment, put down the mug and came out from behind the counter. She was a slow moving, heavy-set woman with large, blunt features and a booming voice. Her thick accent was completely unfamiliar. Her limp brown hair was carelessly held back by a frayed wimple that had probably once been white. Despite her sluggish air, her eyes, and her tongue, were sharp enough. There was no doubt that she kept close watch over everything that went on. Morganne spoke up, though her voice sounded dry.

"No, we are not lost...at least, I do not think we are. Is this the trading post we have heard lies along this road?"

"Ay, and you'll not find another for many a day's walk, whot ever way yer fare." Her voice swelled with pride, her statement challenging anyone in earshot to prove her wrong. She looked the three girls over with careful scrutiny. "Yer be city folk from Tyroc—no denying it now," she shook her finger at them as though she expected them to protest. "Yer all carry the same look. I could spot one of yer of a bow shot. Tell me straight now. What be two young peeps and a babe doin' out on the road alone? I'm no nursemaid, and I won't take no trouble for yer."

Morganne's tone stiffened. "Meaning no disrespect, we would prefer to keep our business to ourselves. We have no intention of causing trouble. We seek only to purchase a meal, some travel supplies, and possibly lodging for the night if your establishment offers it."

The matron laughed coarsely, saying "Oh I can see that *yer* won't be no trouble. As if I couldnae drag the three of yer out with one hand!

It's the trouble that may come after looking for yer that I wonder about. What are yer runnin' from, ay?" Morganne gave Elowyn a look of alarm, but remained silent.

"Ay, I thought as much. Well, if yer won't tell me yer business, I've got no room available, see? If yer do tell me, and I like yer story, I just might."

"Their business is with me, Griselda," a deep voice resonated from the other side of the room. The voice belonged to a large man with thick auburn hair that fell across his forehead. Elowyn thought that he had a strong, but kindly face. He wore a dark red tunic, leather leggings, and a heavy belt with a sheathed sword hanging from it. He rose imposingly from his place by the hearth where he had been seated with an older woman. Her long braided hair had once been the same color as his, but was now streaked with silver.

"Is it now?" The matron gave him a skeptical look, "And whot might that be then?"

"Come now, Griselda," he chided, "You know that I never divulge that sort of information. Makes for bad business. Since when is my word, or that of any of my kin, not enough?" His tone indicated that she dare not go so far as to suggest it wasn't.

"Very well then," the matron grudgingly gave in, "Yer can have a room—on the good word of Tervaise."

"Wonderful," the man said light-heartedly. "Now, if you will be so kind, I would like to have cheese and wine brought to my table—nothing too strong, if you please, and fresh milk for the little one if you have it. There's a good woman. You will join us, won't you?" Tervaise looked at Morganne. It was an invitation she was glad to accept.

"Don't think too badly of Griselda," he said softly and winked as they walked away. "It is only wise to watch one's back when you're running a place like this in the wilderness. She does, however, lack courtesy and discretion, and for that I fault her."

Tervaise's companion rolled her eyes and grumbled at his remark. "Sour old crone, is what she is. She'd do well to get out of this place every so often. I wouldn't have even stopped here had not that flighty, peas-for-brains mare of mine startled and thrown me," she winced and shifted painfully in her seat. "I'm getting too old for falls like that." Turning to Morganne, the woman said, "My name is Reyda, by the by, and you've already met my son. You'll forgive me if I don't stand up."

"Of course," Morganne said softly, "I hope you aren't badly hurt."

"Nay, just a bit shaken and bruised. I'll rest tonight and we'll be on our way again in the morning. You three would be well advised to be on your way by then as well." Reyda gave them a stern, motherly look. "This is no place for children. Griselda won't be the only one who takes an interest in you and wonders why you're out here alone. The roads are plagued by murderers, thieves, and worse. There are wild beasts about, too, that stray out of the Shadow Wood looking for easy prey. We are headed toward Tyroc. If you are going our way, you would be safer to journey with us."

"We are not going that way," Morganne said regretfully, "though I thank you for your offer...and for your assistance a few moments ago. But why did you help us? We are but strangers to you."

"It would be a sad world if men came only to the aid of their friends and family," Tervaise replied. "It is both my pleasure, and the solemn oath I swore before the Kinship, that I would offer help to any innocent in need. You three seemed to fit that description well enough. I would not have slept soundly this night, or any other for the rest of my days, had I stood silent while children were being cast out to fend for themselves."

"We are in your debt. We do not have much with us as you can see, but we do have some means, and some modest skills between us. If there is anything you need, only ask. Perhaps my lady, we could ease the pains from your fall with herbal poultices, or perhaps you have clothes that need mending? There must be some way we can repay you."

"You offer is touching, my dear, it truly is. But we have all that we need in this world, and more," Reyda replied. "And my pains will go away well enough on their own. I only need a bit of rest."

"We desire nothing in return," Tervaise said, waving his hand dismissively. "My only request, and it is one that I ask you to take seriously, is that once Griselda has prepared your room, you remain in it until your departure. We will make sure that you are fed when the evening meal is served. Can you promise me that?"

Morganne nodded disappointedly, "Yes, but we were hoping that we could get some information, perhaps trade for some goods, and find a courier to take a parcel for us. That is mainly why we stopped here. Not that we aren't grateful to have shelter for the night, but my sister is very wood-wise, and we have already spent several nights out in the open. If there is nothing to be gained by staying, we would be better off to continue on our way. We have a long journey ahead of us yet."

"What is it you are seeking?" Tervaise inquired. "I am a merchant by trade, and well-traveled."

"I am in need of better footwear, for one," Morganne said, revealing the battered, mud-stained slippers on her feet. While they had been perfectly adequate to wear about the cottage, or to take quick walks into Tyroc, they were now coming apart upon hard use. "We could also use a warmer blanket for the little one, food, herbs, and whatever else my sister says we need. She would know better than I."

"A small hatchet," Elowyn said timidly. It was the first time she had spoken since they sat down. She was somewhat awed by Tervaise and Reyda, and was quite used to being ignored by adults in general. Morganne, on the other hand, had spoken with such people quite often in the shops of Tyroc. Elowyn was more than content to allow Morganne to speak for them both.

"I am afraid that I cannot help with the footwear, but the other items I may be able to procure before you set out. By nightfall, this place will be full of travelers who are more than happy to trade goods for food and ale. Leave that to me. As for the information, what sort do you require?"

"Information about what lies east and north of here."

"I see," Tervaise said thoughtfully. It was clear to Elowyn that he was trying to piece together their story without asking them anything too obvious. They needed supplies, and direction, to be sure, but it was difficult to ask for such without revealing both their weaknesses and their destination. She got the sense that Morganne trusted these strangers, and hoped that she would not say too much. Even if their intent was pure, a slip of the tongue to the wrong person in Tyroc could very well get back to their mother.

"I can tell you this much...that if you continue on this road eastward, you will pass through a small village and several hamlets before you get to Port's Keep, where many docked ships are being loaded with goods from the northern regions on their way toward Tyroc and the south. From Port's Keep the road turns due north, stretching all the way to the mountains and the cold northern seas. It passes through any number of towns and villages, some memorable, some not."

"And what is between here and the northern mountains if you do not take the road?" Elowyn asked, unable to let the opportunity slip away. Again, Tervaise gave them a somewhat puzzled, searching look.

"I don't know much of that first-hand, as I most often travel by road. But from what I have heard, there are mainly woodlands, meadows and farmlands. Farther north are the great pine forests and seven lakes that stretch across the foothills of the mountains. To get to the northernmost cities, one must take the road. I have been told there are several passes over the mountains, but few have ever gotten through them alive. They are quite treacherous."

"Thank you," Morganne said. "You have been most helpful."

"Now last of all, you said that you were in need of a courier?"

"Yes, to send something to Tyroc."

"Since that is our present destination, I could take whatever it is that you wish to be delivered."

"No," Elowyn shook her head fiercely, "you mustn't. It would be too..." she was about to say "dangerous," but stopped herself. A courier who regularly went to Tyroc would possibly already know the man the packet was addressed to. The delivery would be made quietly, with any instructions she gave kept in strict confidence. She could imagine Tervaise, on the other hand, waving the packet about, asking questions, possibly answering questions about who had given him the packet in the first place. And if someone loyal to Braeden or Darik ever discovered what the packet contained, countless lives would be endangered in addition to those of Tervaise and Reyda. Aside from all that, Elowyn had no assurance that this man wouldn't open the packet out of curiosity, perhaps read its contents. If he had pledged his loyalty to the Sovereign, he might think they were part of some treasonous plot, aligned with the renegades. He might even turn them in, not realizing his loyalty to the royal family was misplaced under the current leadership. She was reminded of how precious few knew the truth. No, he could not be asked to take the letters.

"It would be too much to ask," Morganne tried to finish Elowyn's statement. "You have helped us enough already."

"Nonsense!" Tervaise protested, now convinced that he had at last stumbled upon something interesting.

"We cannot tell you where to find the person we are seeking. We know only that he is a courier himself."

"Even better—I have used Tyroc's couriers often to send messages regarding my business ventures. I'm sure I would have no trouble finding the courier you seek."

Elowyn saw Morganne's resolve begin to waver. She knew that Morganne was eager to distance herself from anything that might be traced back to them, and this packet was particularly dangerous to hold onto. Morganne's purpose was mainly to escape, but Elowyn knew that she must not ignore the pleas of the dead, the imprisoned and the outcast. It was rare that she spoke out so forcibly against Morganne's wishes, and so Morganne was too startled to protest when Elowyn stated in a firm tone, "No, I will not give my package up to anyone but a courier." Her voice quivered with emotion. "I was given this task with great trust. I will not bring more suffering upon those who trusted in me."

Morganne glanced apologetically at Tervaise and Reyda. "Your offer is appreciated, but it seems that we must find a true courier."

"Very well," Tervaise said graciously. "There are many couriers in Port's Keep that make the journey to Tyroc on a regular schedule. However, be warned that as you travel farther north, the price for such services rises considerably." Looking up over Morganne's shoulder, he suddenly lightened his tone and expression, saying, "Ah, Griselda has returned. Is their room now prepared? It is getting on toward evening and it is about time they were tucked away for the night."

"Ay, on that we're of the same mind. Come, then." The girls followed Griselda to a very small, dark room at the back of the building. It contained nothing more than an open hearth and a single bed that sagged pitifully in the middle. The room was not very clean either. The floor had not been swept, the walls were dingy, and the ceiling was black with soot. While Morganne was just happy to be indoors, Elowyn would have preferred a nice tree branch with a thick canopy of leaves overhead to keep her dry. She loved to fall asleep to the gentle tapping sound of the rain falling through the forest.

Elowyn began a fire in the hearth while Morganne put Adelin, who was now full of warm milk and very tired, to bed for the night.

"Perhaps we should have told them more," Morganne mused quietly. "They seemed so kind, and willing to help…"

Elowyn shook her head in protest. "They cannot repeat what they do not know."

There seemed not much more to be said, and so they sat in silence before the fire, absorbed in their own thoughts, waiting for the meal they had been promised. As daylight faded, they could hear the trading post come to life through the thin walls that separated them from the rest of the building. There were raised voices, some in boisterous laughter, some in angry shouts, and some in pure drunken revelry. They could hear the scrape of benches being moved across the floor, the pounding of heavy booted feet, drinking cups being thrown, songs being sung, and tales being told.

Elowyn understood why Tervaise and Reyda had asked them to remain in their rooms. The same sort of rough behavior was common enough in Tyroc's taverns, but the Sovereign's guards were also close by and able to handle anyone that got too far out of hand. Out here, there was no law save what you could enforce with your own strength, or the strength of any nearby stranger willing to stick his neck out in your defense. In the midst of all the clamor, what actually got their attention the most were the delicious smells of food wafting under their door. It had been days since a warm meal had filled their bellies. After a long time, they finally heard a firm rap on the door. Tervaise and Reyda had returned bearing trays loaded with all sorts of foods.

"Some of this you must eat now, but that which will keep you should place in your travel sacks for tomorrow, and the day after," Reyda advised. The tray of food set down before them would have been a king's feast compared even to the best meal they would have gotten at home. There were two very large bowls of pottage in addition to a hefty leg of meat, some bread, cheese, onions, various fruits and greens, and salt meat. After three days in the open, with all the uncertainty, fears, and the meager meals they'd faced, this bounty seemed like one sent by Aviad himself.

"Oh, thank you, thank you…" Morganne looked up at Reyda with tears threatening to spill past the rims of her eyes. She fumbled in her pouch, blinded by her tears, trying to pull out enough money to pay them. Tervaise wouldn't take it, and neither would Reyda. "You'd best keep that a little more tightly in your fist—you will need it."

"Oh, and I nearly forgot. Here are some of the other items you asked for," Tervaise said as he handed Morganne a rough wool blanket, then unfastened a small hatchet from his belt and handed it to Elowyn. "It isn't very well made, and the blade is quite dull, but it has some use left in it for simple tasks."

"Please, at least let me pay you for the hatchet," Morganne pleaded.

"No payment is necessary. It was given freely to me by one who had no more need of it."

190

"There now, it is time for us to leave so they may eat and rest before the sun rises," Reyda said to Tervaise. "My aching bones are ready to retire as well." To Morganne and Elowyn she said, "We've got the room next to this one, so if you need anything, we will be close at hand." Reyda and Tervaise then left, pulling the door firmly shut behind them.

Morganne and Elowyn ate as though it was their last meal, until their stomachs ached, and their eyes grew heavy. As Elowyn lay there full and content by the warmth of the fire, she realized that she could hear the hushed tones of Tervaise and Reyda through the thin inner wall. In spite of the sounds of the tavern breaking through, she managed to make out part of their conversation. Reyda spoke first.

"Now that we may have a small amount of privacy, do you think we are doing right by allowing those children to go forth alone? I worry that they plunge headlong into perils their innocence has not allowed them to fathom. I noticed that you declined to tell them that the hatchet given to you 'freely' was in truth spoils off a troll you met in battle and defeated not so very far from here."

"And I noticed also, dear mother, that you kept to yourself the fact that it was the very same troll which frightened your mare." There was silence for a few moments before Tervaise spoke again.

"I understand your concern, and I have mulled it over in my mind all through the evening, but I truly see no other choice. We have no claim to them, and I would not betray them blindly. I know not who or what they are fleeing, but their intent seems sincere and purposeful, even dire. They have obviously been schooled and mannered, and they speak with intelligence. This is clearly no rash whim they follow. Whatever circumstance has brought them here, I assure you that they will not be swayed by any amount of prying or advice from two strangers. We can only help them as much as they will allow. We must honor their desire for discretion. Indeed, the fact that they guard themselves so fiercely gives me hope."

"I know you speak the truth, but this whole business leaves a sick feeling in my stomach. I will wonder for the rest of my days what became of them."

"As will I, mother. If I knew where they were going, I could direct them to others who would help them. The innkeeper at Greywalle owes me more gold than he can ever repay. Surely he would house and feed them on my word. I know a number of merchants who would be more than happy to ferry them from town to town in the backs of their carts along with their goods. At least they wouldn't have to go by foot, and they would have trustworthy companionship. Certainly our kin would take them in and do anything for them. Alas, if they flee in secret, their destination is the one piece of information they will guard most fiercely, and understandably so. I think we have done just about all that we can for them. And now Mother, you must forget your troubles for the night and rest your injuries. You won't admit it, but these trips are becoming too much for you."

"Rubbish! One nasty fall slows me down, and you're ready to start digging my grave."

Tervaise chuckled fondly. "I've got my shovel in hand, but it's not for your grave. When this trip is over, I have a surprise for you involving a bit of land I recently acquired. I wager that once the builders are finished, you'll no longer want to go on these long and dreary excursions with me."

"Oh, Tervaise! Is it the plot we were looking at? The one overlooking the sea?"

"The very one..."

From that point on, Elowyn could no longer make out the conversation. A fight broke out in the trading post, and all she could hear were drunken shouts, the clang of metal, and the crash of furniture being overturned. By the time the fight was over, there was nothing more to be heard from the other room.

Chapter 12
Emergence at Deep Lake

Morning came all too soon, and the girls still hadn't discussed which route to take. They had a quiet, sleepy breakfast and packed the remaining food in their bags.

"Which way?" Elowyn finally asked, hoping Morganne had already decided.

"Do you think you could get us there through the wood?" Morganne asked.

"I don't know. I would feel better about trying if I had been that way before." Elowyn was more anxious about choosing that route since she had heard the word "troll" surface in Tervaise and Reyda's conversation. She had heard tales of such creatures, but had never encountered any in Tyroc's tame outskirts. Alone, she might be able to sense and evade a troll, or blend in and hide from it. Morganne and Adelin were not equipped to do this. She could only hope that if they met a troll on the road, other travelers might offer some protection. Of course, after listening to the commotion from the previous night, she wondered if men were not equally dangerous. Still, a decision needed to be made, and Elowyn was more and more inclined to take the road, or at least stick close to it.

"You will need boots before long," Elowyn pointed out. "And a map would be helpful."

"I suppose we had best follow the road at least until we get to the next village."

When the girls emerged from their room, they found Tervaise and Reyda waiting to see them off.

"Griselda has been paid in full for your room, and don't let her tell you otherwise. I have one last thing to give you which may be of use." Tervaise handed them a piece of parchment with two wax seals pressed onto it. "One is my personal seal, which many merchants along this and the northern road will recognize from my business dealings with them. The other is the seal of the Kinship, which is also known and well-regarded by many. Perhaps if you say that you were sent by me, and that you are friends of the Kinship, you will be able to get some assistance along your way."

"You have both been so kind to us, and have asked for nothing in return," Morganne said gratefully. "Someday I hope to find a way to repay you for your generosity."

"The best way to do that, my dear," Reyda stated, "is to do the same for others when you are able." She kissed each of them on the cheek and held them together in a long, motherly embrace. "Be well, and stay safe..."

"Come, Mother," Tervaise said, gently pulling her away. "We must all be going—we want to get as far as we can before nightfall. Farewell!"

Tervaise and Reyda mounted their horses, and they reluctantly parted ways with the girls. The heavy rain of the previous day had been replaced by a fine, cold, prickly one that stung their faces. For the girls, it meant a day's march in soaked, muddy shoes and skirts, with heads bent low, and cloaks shimmering with tiny beads of rain. They spoke little. Even Adelin was quiet and still in Morganne's arms, peeking out from under her protective wrappings. It was a day that would have been happily spent indoors by a warm hearth fire. They encountered nothing remarkable that day. All Elowyn remembered seeing afterward were endless stretches of muddy road, marred by prints from horse's shoes and men's boots, wagon wheel ruts, stones, fallen twigs, puddles reflecting the grey sky overhead, and running rivulets of water. Other travelers who passed them seemed just as anxious as they were to move along and get out of the wet. When by early evening they had seen no sign of a town nearby, Elowyn found a sheltered place for them to camp away from the road.

By morning, the even blanket of gray that had covered the whole expanse of the sky had broken up into alternating patches of blue, and large scrubby clouds that looked like they had been drawn with charcoal. The sun was a comforting sight that lifted their spirits considerably as they trudged along the mucky road. As the day wore on, the girls began to see smaller foot-worn paths veering off from the main road every so often, and traffic on the road increased. Late in the afternoon, the girls reached a place where the wilderness on their right side suddenly gave way to open sky and a huge lake. Much to their relief, they could see a town resting on the far side of the shoreline. The road curved along the water's edge, bringing them to the town's gates just before dusk.

The town was primitive looking, surrounded by a wooden wall made of young felled trees that had been stripped of their branches and lashed together. The top end of each tree had been shaved down to form a sharp spike. A pair of scruffy guards with studded leather armor and long handled spears were the only watchmen looking down at them from the top of the wall as they approached. Certainly whatever town this was, it bore little resemblance to Tyroc. A large wooden door swung open for them as one of the guards called out with the same strange accent as Griselda's.

"Ay, yer peeps must be favored o' Aviad. Another few bits and yer would've been shut out for the night. We've had trouble o' late with trolls."

As the gate closed firmly behind them and they looked around, the girls could see that the place was really little more than a fort. The lake formed the western and southern borders, and the rest was encased by the same wooden walls that made up the gate. There was only one main road, made of packed earth. It stretched in a straight line from the gate to the boat docks on the lake. Branching out from the main road were smaller beaten footpaths that connected it to the larger buildings, and to shops and homes. Most homes had small signboards hanging from their doors with painted symbols to show what services the resident who lived there could offer. There did not seem to be an inn, or even a tavern. Morganne stopped in the street and looked around with a somewhat bewildered expression, unsure of where to go for the night.

Nearby there was a small home with a shoemaker's sign. An elderly man with fluffy white hair and knobby fingers was sweeping dirt off of his doorstep.

"Good sir," Morganne called out to him as they approached, "Do you know where we might find lodging for the night?"

The man surveyed them with squinting eyes, watery with age.

"Ay. There's a squatter's camp o'er by the docks if yer only want a fire an' a bit o' dry ground. Or if yer have the means, yer can go to any home that has a lamp lit outside the door. That's a sign that they'll board strangers for a price. But if the lamp is blown out, tha' is no more room."

"Thank you. Tomorrow we shall return to see what services you may be able to provide. I am in need of sturdy footwear before we continue on our way." Morganne extended her foot, revealing a slipper that had been reduced to rags and secured around her feet with twine. Elowyn noticed patches of dried blood through the caked on mud, where her feet had been worn raw or torn by twigs and stones on the road. She had apparently been enduring the pain all along without complaint.

"Oh, may the Ancients have mercy!" He exclaimed excitedly, "Whot have yer don' to 'em then?" They weren't sure if he was bemoaning the state of Morganne's shoes or her feet, but they suspected it was the shoes.

"Com' in, Com' in, I can't send yer away in that state. Whot would people say? If yer don't mind sleepin' on the floor in my shop, I'll take yer for the night an' get to work."

And so he took them in, giving them a place on a plush bear rug in front of the hearth, and a bowl of leek and fish soup from his pottage kettle. Morganne commissioned an order of new leather boots for herself, shoes for Adelin to keep her feet warm and dry, and repairs on Elowyn's boots which were starting to show wear. They haggled a price that included the additional cost of their board, and allowed Morganne to work off a portion of their bill by mending the man's clothes. That settled, the old shoemaker went eagerly to work. At his direction, Elowyn warmed up some water, gently bathed Morganne's damaged feet, and soaked them in a mineral bath. The shoemaker had quite adamantly proclaimed that it would not do to have those feet "muckin' up" his new boots. When he grew weary, he retired to his room, leaving the girls to pass a restful night in front of the fire, warm and secure with full stomachs.

When morning came, the shoemaker went back to work on Morganne's boots, and Morganne got out her needle. Not wanting to spend her day trapped indoors, Elowyn decided to take a look around outside. The sky was a promising blue, and the fresh breeze lifting off the lake was calling her to the water's edge. Approaching the docks, she noticed a crowd was starting to gather. A man wearing a rough hooded monk's robe was standing atop a wooden crate and calling out to anyone in earshot. There seemed to be a good mix of townsfolk and travelers from what the shoemaker had referred to as the squatter's camp.

"Too long have we, the children of Aviad, slept, allowing His fertile fields to lie fallow when we should have been planting and preparing for harvest. Too long have we shut out His calls, and ignored His warnings that there is danger lurking nearby, preparing to devour us where we lay. Have none seen the signs of change upon the horizon? Do you not wonder why there is a sudden resurgence of trolls bearing down upon you? For many hundreds of years, their emergence from the Shadow Wood was a rarity, a curiosity even. There was no need to shut your gates by night and double your watch. I know too, that you have heard the strange howlings and bayings emerging from that accursed wilderness that few dare to enter. I tell you, I know what beast makes those sounds, and it is a beast that has not been seen in these lands for more than an age, not since the Rift was sealed and the dreaded Alazoth, Lord of Destruction, was trapped inside.

"We must awaken, and remember our history, our heritage. We must rekindle our faith in the Ancients—true faith that goes beyond simply uttering hollow words. We must go back to the old ways when all lived and died for Aviad's glory, when our lives were spent fighting against evil instead of killing each other over petty squabbles. I tell you truly, it is time to rise together against the greatest darkness our generation has ever seen, or may ever see again. It is bearing down upon us even as we stand here. Alazoth has been released from the Rift; he has returned and desires nothing less than to claim our very souls for his own!"

Some people in the crowd threw rotten food at the man and jeered insults at him. "Go peddle your nonsense elsewhere, holy man. We've no use for it here."

Others argued that if this were true, the Temple in Tyroc would have surely told them, or taken action on their behalf.

"Cling not to the Temple, for the Temple cannot save us," the monk protested. "The men there may be learned, and they may perform sacred rituals, and speak with eloquence, and scribe our texts, but they cannot change what is in our hearts. There is no ritual they can perform over us that will cause us to live pure and faithful lives. Look to the Temple for spiritual guidance on worldly matters. But search your souls, and look to none other than the Ancients themselves for your salvation."

A rough looking man dressed in armor pushed his way up through the crowd. He spat at the monk, kicked the crate out from under his feet and smashed it to bits with his hatchet. "Tha's the end of it then. We already got 'nough trouble with the trolls without this sort 'o thing. Everyone clear out, before I summon the rest of the watch to deal with yer."

The crowd quickly cleared away, but Elowyn stayed until the guard left and she helped the monk to his feet. "I believe you," she said softly. "I have seen them."

The monk turned his hazel eyes upon her with surprise. "What have you seen, child?"

"The Hounds. They are on the move, southwest of here, closing in around Tyroc. I was nearly devoured by one."

He gave her a dumbfounded look before gathering his composure. "I'm sorry, I have been on the road for many months—you are the first true believer I have met. And one so young...it comes as quite a shock, that does." He stared at her in disbelief for a few moments, before a great smile broke out across his face, and he exclaimed, "Well, what is wrong with me then! Blessed be to Aviad!" He clasped her hand in his and shook it vigorously. "My name is Brenate."

"I'm Elowyn," she said, smiling. "But don't tell anyone else what I've said, or my sister will be angry with me."

"Not to worry," the Monk winked at her. "With the luck I've had so far, I doubt that any would believe me even if I did tell. It would seem that truth is poorly received, while fantasy is sought after. Though perhaps if the Hounds have been seen in Tyroc, my message will carry greater weight there."

Elowyn shook her head with alarm. "I'm afraid it will be even worse for you in Tyroc. Those from the Temple who would have believed you were cast out and are on their way to another place, I know not where. You must not trust the Temple, or the Sovereign's house with your message. You would put yourself in great danger."

The monk's smile dissolved into a very serious expression. "How is it that you, a mere child, know about such things?"

"Please do not ask that of me," Elowyn said with pain in her voice. "The tale is too long, and it is one that I must keep to myself for now. Just trust that I know. It is by no accident that the Hounds are gathering at Tyroc."

"I see," the monk said, visibly perplexed. "I will go with caution, but go I must. Three others from my Order are to meet me there. I am told they came this way a while ago, and went on toward Tyroc through the Shadow Wood rather than by the road. They were looking for something of great importance."

Elowyn asked wide-eyed, "Are you one of the Guardians of the Ancients?"

"Aye," the Monk said with surprise. "How did you know?"

Elowyn shook her head sadly. "You will not find your brethren in Tyroc."

Without speaking directly of Einar or their flight from home, Elowyn told Brenate about the dying monk found by Einar, and of the others who had fallen and were buried. He bowed his head in silence, uttering prayers under his breath for the sake of his fallen brothers.

Allison D. Reid

With tears in his eyes, he finally asked, "What, then, became of the relic they carried?"

"I don't know," Elowyn answered truthfully. "The man who had agreed to deliver it to your people was killed by the Hounds as he tried to leave Tyroc. There are others, friends of his, who are trying to find it and finish his quest. But I do not know what has become of them either. I am sorry that I cannot tell you more." Her regret was genuine. No doubt Morganne would have chastised her for being so free with Brenate, but this was an unexpected opportunity for her to set at least one thing right in the midst of a long series of terrible wrongs. She felt that she needed desperately to take it, for her own sake as well as that of Brenate, Einar, Nevon, and all the others.

"Grieve not. You have told me more than I dared to expect, and for that I thank you. No doubt Aviad himself placed you in my path to guide my way. It would be folly to continue on toward Tyroc now. I must instead return home and share this news with my brethren. This may change everything for us."

Then the monk did something quite unexpected. He laid his hand on the top of her head and spoke a blessing over her. He finished by saying, "Believe and remember. The journey begins."

Elowyn gasped and drew back from him.

"What is it, child?" he asked in a bewildered tone.

"You must tell me what those words mean."

"They are nothing to fear," Brenate said, confused by her reaction. "The phrase is a shortened version of an old saying among Aviad's followers, going back to the days of the Prophets. Now it is used mainly among the monastic community as a blessing, and as a reminder of the oaths we swore when we left our old lives behind to follow whatever path the Ancients laid out for us. The full verse says, 'Believe in the Ancients, the givers of everlasting life, for they are our constant guides. Remember those who came before us in righteousness, forging the path to truth with their blood and their wisdom. The journey begins when in faithful humility, our feet meet that path, walking it to its end as our will becomes

200

one with the divine.' The verse has many different levels of meaning for those who care to study it in depth..."

"You don't understand." Elowyn's skin was tingling, and her heart was pounding hard. Dared she tell the monk? Would he think her mad? Yet if anyone could answer this riddle, it was he, a faithful follower of Aviad.

Cautiously she told him of her nights at Aviad's shrine, of her dream, and of hearing those words again from Gareth after he had been expelled from the Temple a short time later.

Brenate's expression grew serious. "And you had never heard the phrase before? Are you certain?" Elowyn nodded.

"Such a dream is rare, and a special revelation not to be taken lightly—I would even dare to call it a vision rather than a dream. Aviad must have a part for you in all of this. But I cannot tell you what that part is. No doubt it will be revealed to you in time, at His leisure."

Elowyn could not hide her feelings of disappointment, or her anxiety over this unknown responsibility that Aviad had placed upon her.

"Worry not, child," Brenate said with the most jovial tone he could muster. "Aviad always takes care of his own. When He calls you, He does so with good purpose, and He will remain with you to whatever end. Now, I must get on my way. My road is long, and I would like to get well away from here before the sun sets. The wilds here are not safe at night—too close to the Shadow Wood and the many evils that lurk within it. When you do continue on your way, I would advise you to get up with the dawn and travel quickly, without respite, for as long as you can."

"Can you tell me what lies east and north of here?"

"Along the road, there is little else between here and Port's Keep, which is about four days' journey by foot. You will need to be well supplied and prepared to make camp amongst the trees."

After the monk left, Elowyn sat for a while on the docks, looking out over the water. The lake was very different from the churning ocean she knew so well. It was a frigid, black mirror, with a tiny island at the center that looked as though it were full of tangled trees and brambles.

Deep and still, the only thing that broke the lake's perfection were occasional breaths of wind that threw tiny ripples across its surface. This was not a place that invited bathing. Anything at all could be lurking below the surface, unseen through the murky waters. Gazing uneasily across the lake and into the Shadow Wood, she was glad there was some sort of barrier between them, even though this body of water seemed much more a part of its treacherous tangles of vine and tree than it did the civilized world. She wondered at those who had been brazen enough to build a settlement along its border and remain there.

All her life Elowyn had lived on the edge of the Shadow Wood, in awe-filled respect of its perils, hearing tale after tale of untold terror. No longer content to remain within their own territory, those terrors were now emerging. Tyroc was perhaps large and powerful enough to stand its ground, but this ramshackle fort was certainly not. She felt that the sooner they were on the move again, and away from this place, the better.

When she grew tired of the docks, Elowyn explored what little there was to see of the village. It was a disorganized jumble of poorly constructed homes and shops, all clustered between the road and the lake's edge. There were no mapmakers that she could find. Before heading back to the shoemaker's shop, she traded some of her herbs for a small tin cooking pot and some cured meat. She spent the rest of the afternoon looking after Adelin and preparing the evening meal while the old man finished their order, and Morganne took care of his mending. In the end both were well pleased with each other's work, and it seemed as though their dealings in that town were at an end. By the time the sun had darkened, and the meal was finished, their satchels had been packed and set by the door. The girls were prepared to leave at first light, when the town's gates were opened and they were free to continue on their way. But as Elowyn thought later, however much she longed to break free, the Shadow Wood was not yet ready to release her from its long, fast grip.

Elowyn was wakened in the night by a hard and frantic pounding at the shoemaker's door. She could hear commands being shouted, along with yells, and screams, and the frightened cries of very small children.

She cautiously unlatched the door, unable to push back the memory of the apparition that had once made itself known to her in the same way. The man standing in the doorway was no apparition. He was one of the watchmen, and the tone of his voice left no room for questioning.

"Awake yer household and get to the docks. The gate's about to breech! Don' stand there starin.' Fly, *now!*"

In a panic, Elowyn woke Morganne and the shoemaker, telling them what the guard had said. The old man began cursing, but moved faster than Elowyn thought he would be capable of at his age. Morganne grabbed Adelin while Elowyn snatched their packs and flew out the door. There were dozens of men surrounding the gate, trying to brace it with wooden beams. A large crash echoed down the street as something heavy rammed into it from the other side. It shuddered and groaned as a dying beast about to breathe its last.

"Away from the gate!" someone called out. "It won't stand another blow. Into position and weapons ready!" He had barely finished speaking when the next blow came. A wooden ram came crashing through, and the gate was breeched. The rest of the wall began to give way as well, and through the opening Elowyn got her first sight of a troll. Towering above everything, the troll was massive and hideously ugly, with a grey, sickly complexion. It had huge yellow teeth and merciless eyes. The first one through the breech called out triumphantly in a guttural tone that froze Elowyn's blood. It snatched up one of the watchmen with its huge hands. As Elowyn looked on in sickening horror, it ripped him in two with its teeth and devoured him—armor, bones and all. It turned its head, grinning at the rest of the men who were scattering at its feet. Blood still dripped from the corners of its mouth

Elowyn's knees suddenly unlocked themselves, and she ran with all that was in her. Morganne, Adelin, and the shoemaker were close behind. Elowyn realized that she had never truly known what fear was until that very moment in her life. It was a moment that forever changed her. As she reached the docks, she saw that those not able to fight the trolls were being loaded onto boats. They were broad boats with flat bottoms that

Allison D. Reid

would not have stood up long to the ocean's pounding waves, but which were perfect for the still, currentless waters of Deep Lake. Once packed onto the boats, the people were rowed well away from shore and in the direction of the tiny island she had seen during the day.

With wide silent eyes, Morganne squeezed Adelin tightly in her arms until Adelin squirmed uncomfortably in protest. In the bright moonlight, Elowyn could see that Morganne was trembling as she stared across the water toward the town. Flames began to leap up, exactly from where could not be told, but from that point the fire spread rapidly. The settlement at Deep Lake was burning. The shoemaker began to curse again under his breath, this time more out of grief and fear than out of annoyance at having been disturbed from sleep.

"A troll breeched the gate once before, but he was felled before he could get very far. I fear this time all's lost. I hope the watch 'ave the sense to get away, and don' stand there like fools even after everyone else is safe on the water. I've never seen so many trolls come together like tha'..."

"What will we do now? How long can we stay out here?" Elowyn asked.

"We have 'nough emergency stores on tha' little island to keep the entire town's number for a fortnight. Tha's long 'nough for help to come, anyway. But the trolls cannot swim, nor can they abide daylight. We need only wait for dawn an' then see what is left. Not much, I'll wager, from the look of it."

Everyone on the boat huddled together through the dead of night. No one spoke. One could only hear the soft whimpering of children pressed securely against their mothers, and the gentle sobs of those who feared for the safety of the watch, which had defended them and guided them to safety. Elowyn slipped in and out of wakefulness. Each time she awoke it took her a few moments to remember where she was, and to realize that this was real, and not just a passing nightmare. When the blessed dawn finally broke across the sky, they cautiously rowed back to shore to face whatever awaited them.

204

Much of the town was devastated, either smashed to bits or burned to the ground. Precious few buildings were left standing. Nearly all the watch had gotten onto boats themselves once the rest of the townsfolk had been set safely adrift, but a few lay dead near the gate where the heaviest part of the battle had taken place. They were bitterly mourned by their families, and hailed as great heroes by all. No doubt tales of their sacrifice would be told for generations in that place. Lying next to them were the remains of two trolls that had also been brought down. Upon that sight many proud cheers and calls rose from the bedraggled crowd. A few even dared to kick the carcasses, or hurl stones and insults at them.

The shoemaker's home was only partially destroyed. The roof had been smashed in, and the walls that had made up his personal chambers had collapsed. The workshop was still mostly intact—somehow it had escaped the fire. Once the general damage was surveyed, there was no question that most of the town's population would need to be relocated, at least for the time being. The town was defenseless against further onslaught, and with so many of the buildings gone or damaged beyond repair, there was inadequate shelter, food, or supplies to sustain them all. Several carts and horses were brought to the center of town, and the very young, the very old, and the infirm were loaded into them. The rest would have to walk alongside them for however many days it would take to reach Port's Keep. The old shoemaker refused to go, saying that he still had something left to salvage, and he was too old to begin anew elsewhere. He would rather risk perishing at the hand of a troll than risk finding himself a beggar and die just the same. And so they parted ways. But Morganne and Elowyn held onto the hope that the old man rebuilt his workshop, and that his remaining days were long and peaceful, and free of trolls.

The caravan was slow and cumbersome, and strangely silent. The only voices to be heard were those of the younger children playing together in the carts. There was no singing, or storytelling, or idle conversation to pass the time as one might expect on a journey of that sort. All wore a haggard look—eyes red-rimmed, and expressions numb. Elowyn

thought these people looked very much like animals stunned by a predator's venom, stumbling about in shock and confusion, slowly and unwittingly marching on towards their inevitable demise. Elowyn realized that
she probably wore the same expression, exhausted from lack of sleep, and
unable to forget the image of the troll and the watchman being eaten
alive. That moment in time kept replaying itself over and over in her
mind, until the images became so surreal and strange that she wondered
if they had really happened at all. She could almost convince herself that
it had been a nightmare, except there she still was, marching along with
a group of complete strangers, on a road she had never traversed before.
If it was only a nightmare, she was still in it, praying desperately to be
wakened.

When after a long day of walking the group finally camped for the
night, Elowyn lit her own fire a short distance away. She was weary of the
crowd and of feeling the weighty burden of everyone's sorrows crushing
down upon her soul. But she found that Morganne's company was equally mournful. The fire had been fed and stoked many times before she
would say anything at all, and even then she spoke with a broken voice.

"I never knew such things existed before today. Even had I known. . .
I don't think that I would have really understood without seeing. And as
horrific as the trolls were, from what Gareth told us, the Hounds are
far, far worse. I know in my mind that his word is true, but I fear that
without seeing, I do not truly understand their danger either, and that
frightens me even more than what I have just witnessed."

Morganne grew quiet again for a few moments, and then with great
brokenness said, "I am sorry. I should never have brought us. Nothing
our mother could do would ever come close to the terror I saw unleashed
by a single troll, let alone a Hound. It was wrong of me to think that
I could make this journey, that you and Adelin were safer away from
Tyroc. What I do not understand is why you came. You have seen a
Hound—you were nearly slain by one. You knew the danger in a way
that I could not, and yet you came."

Elowyn gathered her thoughts carefully for a few moments, answering truthfully, "Tyroc was not so safe as you imagined it to be. Our cottage was no stronghold, and our mother no sure protector from danger. It is around Tyroc that the Hounds gather their strength. When they have overrun the woodlands, and Braeden has darkened the skies, who there would be strong enough to protect us?"

Morganne mused on this response for a long while before she finally let go some of her anguish and said in a very different tone, "Gareth once told me a story about a bird that was captured and put in a cage. From his perch he could see through an open window and into the glorious free world beyond. The bird caught glimpses of blue sky for soaring, and inviting leafy green branches for resting, and he could hear the happy sounds of other birds singing songs to each other all day long. More than anything, he desired to be free of the cage so that he could join those birds on the other side of the open window. Yet every day the cage remained locked.

"One day the cage door was left open, and the bird realized this was his chance to escape. But as he prepared to fly away, he saw that the cat was watching the open cage too, crouched and ready to pounce. I asked Gareth what happened after that, and he said that he couldn't tell me—it was up to me to finish the story. I remember protesting greatly at the time. It was unfair, I thought, to be told a story that seemingly had no end. He explained that the point was not the story itself. How each listener finished the tale was supposed to give him a glimpse into his own spiritual state.

"He told me that the cage symbolizes our own fears and limitations, the cottage the world around us, and the cat the dangers within that world, which threaten both our physical and spiritual lives. The window is the gateway through which we leave this world to enter the next, and the world beyond the window symbolizes the perfected spirit and the realm of Aviad. Would the bird in my version of the story remain in her cage, safe and well fed, but a slave to her own fears and tormented by longing for the rest of her days? Or would she make an attempt at flight and risk the danger for the sake of something more, whatever the outcome? What would that outcome be? Would she be injured, or devoured, or would she fly free without hindrance?

"He told me the tale also reminds young members of his Order that true spiritual freedom involves courage, strength of character, and even sometimes sacrifice. That little story of Gareth's has always stayed with me, but until now, I do not think I took it seriously enough. Never have I felt more like that little bird in the cage. Only I took the plunge from the cage, and now I'm flying wildly about the room, nearly blind in my panic, with the cat close behind. Gareth said that I must finish the story. It sounds like such a simple thing, does it not? I feel instead as though the story is telling itself, and I have no control over how it will end."

Elowyn wanted to say something comforting, but was at a loss. She understood how Morganne felt. Despite their restless, anxious thoughts, and the discomfort of the hard earth they were camped upon, exhaustion eventually overcame them. They fell into a deep, dreamless sleep, knowing nothing until the early light of morning stirred the camp, and their caravan was on the move once more. In some ways this unexpected turn of events had been a great blessing. For one thing, Morganne had been relieved of the burden of carrying Adelin, who was enjoying some freedom of movement and the company of other children her age. For another, they felt more secure than they had before. They blended in nicely with this group of refugees, who were still in such a state of shock that they had no thought of asking any personal questions regarding who the girls were, and where they had come from. They also felt safer—perhaps not from trolls or Hounds, but certainly from the ordinary hazards of wild animals and robbers on the road. But the constant presence of the crowd, and the weight of their sorrows, pressed upon Elowyn's spirit until she could hardly bear it. She longed to be rid of the caravan and looked forward to the day when they would leave it behind.

Chapter 13

Living Fire

Evening was quickly descending upon the fifth day of the caravan's journey from Deep Lake. Elowyn began to wonder why they hadn't already stopped to make camp, when she saw an immense torch-lit stone wall and gate looming ahead in the blue twilight. They had finally reached Port's Keep.

A guard called down from high above, asking their business, and a voice from their group responded. "We've come from Deep Lake. Our settlement was attacked and nearly destroyed by trolls. We send you our women and children, our elderly and our infirm, to seek shelter in your fair city, and ask for the protection of your lord."

They were immediately ushered in through the main gate then guided to a large grassy area between the outer and inner wall. There they were told to make camp for the night while the lord of the city was notified of their situation, and until better accommodations could be made.

Morganne grabbed Adelin out of the cart and whispered fiercely in Elowyn's ear, "Keep going into the city—don't follow them." Elowyn gave her a confused look.

"These are not ordinary travelers simply passing through; they are seeking long-term refuge. No doubt a census will be taken for the lord to give an account of who is here. I don't want to have our names recorded, or have to answer questions about where we came from."

So they walked boldly up to the inner gate that led into the city. Two guards barred their way.

Morganne straightened herself and spoke firmly to the guard, looking, for a brief moment, very much like her mother. "We are not from the settlement. We have the means and would like to seek our own lodging in the city."

Allison D. Reid

"Looked like you came with them to me," the guard said brusquely.

"We had only stopped at Deep Lake to replenish our supplies and were caught up in their misfortune. We traveled with them for safety, but would have passed through your city either way. We do not intend to stay for long."

The guard replied in a patronizing manner, "Even so, you'll stay with them until daylight. The city streets are no place for young girls at night, and the lord's servants will take care of everything tomorrow." He looked away as though the matter was closed. The girls felt as if they had just been scolded and sent to bed without supper. But Morganne was not going to give up so easily, and she could sense that the crowd was listening to the exchange carefully.

"Meaning no disrespect, we are well aware of the hazards of the city. The hazards of the road have been far greater. We will risk a walk through your streets if we may find among them an inn where we can rest for the night."

The movement of the crowd had stopped and all eyes were on the guard, who looked as though he wasn't sure what to do. No doubt he was under orders to keep this displaced group from Deep Lake contained for the night, and yet he had not been told what to do in such a situation as this. If the group grew restless and frightened, he would be to blame. And if he let these girls go, and the rest of the group decided to follow, he would also be to blame.

Morganne saw the guard teetering on the edge of decision and decided to give him one last shove. "It was my understanding that Port's Keep was a city that welcomed travelers, and that its lord was under the Sovereign of Tyroc's authority. Are we to be treated as prisoners, or as guests and free citizens of the Sovereign?"

Every breath was stilled, waiting anxiously for the guard's answer.

"You are all guests, of course," the guard said gruffly as he stepped aside, visibly unnerved by the fact that his authority had been successfully challenged. "But I still advise those from Deep Lake to remain here for their own benefit. There are not enough inns to house all of you. I give

210

my word that those who stay will receive good help, and will be treated as any other citizen of Port's Keep…or of the Sovereign's realm for that matter," he said, giving Morganne a hard look. Morganne did not care. She was relieved to pass through the city gates and be on her way. A few other travelers who had also been caught up in the troll attack followed them. But most chose to set up camp in the green space between the city walls, grateful for the security they afforded. Morganne and Elowyn found a moderately priced inn where they were finally able to cast off their packs and sleep comfortably through the night.

By the light of morning the girls ventured out into the city of Port's Keep. As large as it was, the city could not compare with Tyroc in terms of size and wealth. The largest of its buildings were not nearly so grand, and there was no temple. Most buildings were small to modest shops and homes. The central square was little more than an open area of packed earth surrounded by a jumble of hastily constructed buildings, most of which had open stalls on the first floor with living quarters on the second. Rising above the entire city, set atop a cliff overlooking the sea, was a rough stone keep. It had one main rectangular tower, and smaller towers branching off of it that appeared to have been added on through the years. The keep looked very old—the archaic remnant of an age long passed. Elowyn sensed that its walls must echo with generations of voices, holding fast to the keep's darkest secrets. Elowyn could hardly take her eyes from it. She was wary of turning her back on the keep's imposing form as though it were an untamed and dangerous creature that could not be trusted. She was glad that she did not live in the shadow of its presence year upon year.

The innkeeper had told the girls that a courier could be found on the edge of the city near the coast, and that they would know the right place by the signboard hanging outside the door. As they walked briskly along the city streets, Elowyn breathed deeply, realizing suddenly how much she had missed the pungent, briny smell of the sea. Flocks of gulls called out to each other as they circled the blue expanse of sky overhead and lighted on everything like heaps of snow. The docks and the coastline were the most familiar sights they had seen on their journey thus far. Ships of all sizes were lined up, moving slowly in and out of the harbor. Groups of people were embarking, and disembarking, and cargo was being hoisted to and fro both in nets and by hand, or passed along from person to person over wooden ramps.

The mix of people was quite diverse. Poor sailors and deckhands rubbed shoulders with great lords and ladies, who had commissioned ships to carry them back and forth between exotic places and the mainland. There were merchants inspecting shipments, scholars seeking passage on cargo ships, artisans and farmers hauling their wares to be sent down the coast to Tyroc and other cities, and women and children lined up to greet those who were coming off the sea after working long, hard voyages. Morganne tried to avoid the crowds as much as possible, and kept looking down to hide her face. She had recognized a couple of the merchants, though she was sure they hadn't seen her. The girls were reminded though, that while they might be safe from trolls in Port's Keep, there were other dangers to be wary of. Morganne had worked closely with well-known cloth merchants and other wealthy customers of her mother's from all over the mainland, and it was quite possible any one of them might recognize her on sight.

At the entrance to a narrow alley, the girls finally happened upon a shabby little building with a courier's sign hanging above the door. When they walked in, they found the front room was empty except for a table against the far wall. Behind it sat a stocky, scruffy looking man with a curly beard that nearly covered his whole face. He was busy writing in a huge ledger that nearly covered the table.

"Yes?" the man asked, without looking up.

"We're looking for a courier," Morganne said.

"Aye. Destination?"

"Well, we're not quite sure..."

He raised an eyebrow, waiting for an explanation as he continued to write.

"We need to get a package to a specific courier. We know that he is often in Tyroc, but we're not sure where he is now. We were hoping that if this is delivered to the courier's office in Tyroc, they would know where to find him."

"Most of the couriers from Tyroc pass through here eventually, some more often than others. Whom do you seek?"

"One called Raife," Elowyn said, placing the packet of letters gingerly on the table.

As the man caught a glimpse of the packet and the wax seal that held it together, he finally looked up with a startled expression.

"Where did you get this?"

Morganne gave Elowyn a sideward glance, not wanting to say the wrong thing. This was Elowyn's quest to fulfill, not hers. Elowyn spoke softly, "It was given to me by a friend, who asked me to find the courier whose name is written on it."

The man called over his apprentice, who had appeared in the doorway of the adjoining room. "If Raife is still here, bid him come to me immediately. Then bar the back door and go home. You will no longer be needed this day."

The boy did as he was told, and a few moments later, a young man rushed in, still fastening on pieces of leather armor while he walked. In stark contrast to the man at the table, he was tall and slim, and well groomed with finely trimmed hair and beard. A satchel was slung over his shoulder, and a cloak was folded over one arm.

"You've got one more, have you? If it is along the western road, I've had to change my route based on the news we got this morning."

"You may be changing your entire route today," the man with the beard said in a carefully guarded tone.

Raife finally looked up, catching a glimpse of the package on the table. He stopped what he was doing and stood motionless for a moment, staring at it with disbelief. He first locked eyes with the man at the table, then swung around to face Morganne and Elowyn. He quickly surveyed them, and asked abruptly, "How did you come upon this package?"

"It was given to me," Elowyn answered. "I was asked to deliver it to you, and was told that once you opened it, you would know what to do."

"Who gave it to you?" Raife asked, his voice growing stern.

Elowyn was becoming more alarmed by the moment. This was not exactly the reception she had envisioned. She could sense the tension rising in the two men, and was not sure what to make of it. This man was supposed to be on the right side, a friend of Elias, and of the Circle. The presence of the man with the curly beard whose face she could not see only added to her apprehension. She wished that she could speak alone with Raife, as she was unsure of what she could safely say aloud.

"A friend and servant of the Sovereign," she said carefully, her throat going dry. "I was told to speak with you alone."

Raife nodded to the man with the curly beard, and they both took action so quickly that the girls hardly knew what was happening before it was done. The bearded man had circled around behind them, barring the door and fastening the shutters. Raife blocked the remaining doorway with his body and Elowyn could hear the unmistakable rasp of a weapon being drawn from its sheath. A long, polished dagger glinted in the dim lamp light. Elowyn suddenly remembered her own dagger, the one Einar had given her, and shakily withdrew it, holding it out before her. It was probably both the bravest, and most foolish thing she had ever done. She frantically tried to recall everything Einar had taught her, wishing that she had heeded his advice to continually practice, and knowing just the same that she had no chance of winning a fight against two fully grown men who knew their business. Elowyn's heart pounded so heavily that her ears rang. She felt a sickening mixture of fear, and of bewildered indignation. Had she been betrayed by the wife of Elias? Had she been Elias' wife at all? Was it all an elaborate trap, or was Raife not the friend Elias' wife had thought he was?

"Anything that is fit for my ears may be spoken in the presence of my friend. Play me not as a fool—I well know the emblem on that seal. We have no desire to harm you if you are innocents, and not willing tools and spies of our greatest enemy. Speak truth to us and you shall go free.

214

Speak falsely, and your journey ends here, at the points of our blades. Now, I shall ask one last time. Who gave you this package?"

Elowyn swallowed hard, knowing that whatever became of them as a result, there was nothing else she could answer but the truth. "The wife of one called Elias, who was killed as a traitor to Tyroc."

Raife relaxed his weapon slightly, but carefully continued his questioning. "How do you come to know her, and by what means did you acquire this package?"

"It is a long and strange tale that I fear you will not believe," Elowyn replied honestly.

"Strange or not, if it is the truth, I will know it. Tell me the short of it, and we shall see."

"I was a guest of the Lady Isana. My mother is a weaver and my sister a seamstress, both well-known in Tyroc. We were there only to fit the lady for clothing that her servants had commissioned. It was by chance that Elias' wife was the servant sent to look after me."

"Why would she give a stranger, a guest of her lady and mistress, a package with such instruction?"

"Because I was a friend of one who Elias had loved as a brother. I told her also what had become of her husband's betrayer. She believed in me, and trusted me with the package, knowing that I might be the only way for her to get it beyond the castle walls undetected."

"And who might that one be, that Elias loved as a brother?"

"Einar," the man with the curly beard answered for her with a gruff sigh. "I now know who you are. You are the girl who happened upon Nevon's remains, and the one whom Einar saved from the Hound, are you not?"

"Yes," Elowyn answered brightly. "How did you know?"

"I stood with him in exile, until we were forced to abandon our fight and go our separate ways. I did not care to continue Nevon's quest as Einar felt he must, and so I came here to begin a new life. I count myself fortunate that I did not leave behind a wife and children, or any other family. Just the same I have not forgotten the sting of treachery. Someday

I will find a way to repay my enemies tenfold. But how is it that you came to be here in Port's Keep, looking for Raife?" His question held a trace of remaining suspicion that needed to be satisfied.

"I can answer that," Morganne finally spoke. "It is my doing. When our order for the lady was completed, she was generous with me, and gave me a reward separate from the payment that she owed my mother. I saw it as my chance to escape Tyroc and our mother, who would have kept me as little better than a slave for the rest of my days, and at whose hand, my sisters and I have known nothing but violence. We too, are seeking a new life—we hope a better life. Our chance to flee undetected came swiftly, the very morning after we returned from the castle, and we did not have time to seek a courier in Tyroc. We have carried this packet with us all the while, hoping to find some way of faithfully delivering it without exposing the path of our flight to any who might come after us on our mother's behalf. Now that we have fulfilled our oath, and kept your secrets, we must trust your word that you will keep ours and not betray us. We wish only to continue on our way unhindered."

The two men put their weapons back in their sheaths, and Raife bowed graciously. "My apologies to you all. I assure you, it is not my custom to threaten young girls at knife point. But I had to know that you were friends, and not a clever ruse sent by Braeden. I helped Elias on many occasions, delivering messages, bringing him supplies, weapons, even gold, which he then took to the camp. It was a dangerous line we both walked. When he was caught and executed, I feared that my head would be the next one on the block. I still do not know for certain if Braeden has any evidence against me, but I will most likely spend the rest of my life looking over my shoulder, as will you I'm afraid. No matter how far you journey from Tyroc's borders, do not underestimate Braeden. There is no limit to his reach. He may just be the one who is fated to bring about the end of all things.

"From all I hear, he is still quietly seeking to destroy what is left of the Circle and its allies. He fears us because of what we know, and because we are prepared to resist him, and teach others to resist him, no matter what the cost. He is furious that we managed to elude his grasp at all—he had not figured that into his plan. But your story gives me hope that he does not yet know of your relationship with Einar, else he would have destroyed you when he had the chance. Even should all the rest of us perish silently in this struggle, someone will be left who knows our story."

Raife picked up the packet tenderly and ran his fingers along the seal. "Elias was a good man, and is sorely missed by those who knew him. Seeing his seal again brings back many memories—some that I cherish...and others I long to forget." He lingered in thought for a moment longer before he broke the seal. Inside the outer wrapping were bundles of individually addressed letters, and a note for Raife from Elias' wife that he did not read aloud, but which seemed to touch him deeply. He then said the last thing Elowyn expected.

"I cannot deliver these—I will not."

"But you must!" Elowyn replied. "I've brought them all this way. She trusted you—all those families are counting on you!"

"Aye. And that will be yet another burden I must carry upon my soul. Even so, it must be."

"But, why?"

"I doubt not your good intentions, nor those of Elias' wife. But I do not trust Braeden. I have no way of knowing if all these letters truly escaped his attention and that of his vast network of spies, or if he allowed them to be leaked out, hoping that each letter would find its way, leaving a path for him to follow.

"I have long suspected that I am watched, but that my life has been spared because Braeden still hopes I can be useful to him in some way. Surely he knows by now that I was helping Elias, and yet he has not come after me. Why, if not to use me to ferret out the rest? I will not do it."

Angry tears of frustration began to well in Elowyn's eyes. She knew by his face that there was nothing she could say that would change Raife's mind.

"Come, Elowyn," Morganne said firmly. "We have done what we've been asked. There is nothing more for us here."

They left the courier's office feeling discouraged, and Elowyn in particular felt outraged and betrayed. Even though part of her knew that Raife was in the right, another part of her felt that she had failed in the one important mission that had been entrusted to her. Her chance to bring some comfort to the outcast had been thwarted—and not by some evil force, but by the very person who was supposed to help her. Stewing in their thoughts as they walked, the girls nearly ran straight into a man who was hurrying in their direction along the crowded street. Morganne automatically glanced up at him and apologized, then abruptly looked down and brushed past him with her hood draped over her face. She grabbed Elowyn's arm so hard that it pinched, and dragged her along the street as fast as she could.

"We must leave this place, quickly," she hissed under her breath.

"Why?" Elowyn asked, trying to reclaim her arm from Morganne's tight grasp.

"I knew that man. He got a good look at my face, and I could tell that he was trying to place me. I want to be well away from here before he realizes who I am. If we are fortunate, he will remain uncertain. I don't want to give him the chance of a second look."

The girls hastily purchased some bread, dried fish and onions from vendors along the road toward the inn. They shoved everything into their packs, paid the innkeeper, and departed through the gate of Port's Keep without looking back. Elowyn felt apprehensive about leaving in such a rush, without asking any questions about what they might encounter on the road ahead, but nothing could be done about it.

For the first few days, the terrain was similar to what they had encountered on the road toward Port's Keep—the same thick woodlands stretching as far as one could see in any direction. The summer insects were outpouring the last of their energy into song, somehow aware that their days were ending. The lands resonated with their music, and with the calls of birds beginning their seasonal migrations. Every so often, groups of them could be seen gathering together in the sky, circling, landing and taking flight again. Elowyn felt the shift, too. It was in the air, in the sky, and in the movements of the animals. The nights began to get cooler, and the warmth of day shorter.

"We must press harder," Elowyn told Morganne apologetically.

Morganne gritted her teeth and nodded in understanding. The reprieve she had received when Adelin was being ferried in the cart was over. Elowyn could see that carrying Adelin for long hours was hard on Morganne. When they stopped at the end of the day, she fairly collapsed at their campsite. Elowyn often had to prod Morganne to eat before she fell asleep. At the least, in her utter exhaustion, the ground did not feel quite so hard as it otherwise might have. But when Elowyn woke her in the mornings, she was stiff, and sore, and had difficulty getting her limbs moving.

As the weather began to change, so did the landscape. The woodlands were gradually melting into gently sloping meadows, pasturelands and cultivated fields. They had better visibility, but lacked shelter and firewood. The days were sometimes long and hot with little shade to block the sun. At night, they huddled together under their cloaks and blankets to keep warm. There was nothing to break the force of the wind, or disburse the rain. Sometimes when they made camp they were able to find small bits of wood, and they cut and twisted the tall grasses into logs to add to their fire. But this sort of fire gave more smoke than flame and heat, and it did not last through the night. Much of the time it was simply not worth the effort.

There were no more large towns, only tiny farming hamlets that were nearly deserted during the day. Every able bodied person was working in the fields, bringing in the last of the harvest, winnowing, haying, and generally preparing for the impending winter months. Sometimes the girls were offered hospitality for the night in a home or barn, sometimes not. But they were always able to refresh their water from deep cool wells, and the farmers' wives gave them food for their packs, and warm goat's milk for Adelin. There were no taverns or shops. Morganne tried to pay for their food with money from her purse and got strange looks in return. What use was money in such a place? But where one might have food, another might have leather, or woodcraft, or some other useful thing. Everything worth having was bartered for. Days were governed by the trail of the sun across the sky, weeks by the weather, months by the seasons, seasons by the tasks of the field, and by the festivals of the Ancients.

Morganne and Elowyn had never before been so far removed from city life. The nights seemed brighter with nothing to hide the moon and the sky's full array of stars. But they were eerier somehow, at least for Elowyn, who was used to sleeping in the protective arms of the trees, and who was accustomed to the ways of the woodlands.

A good many nights after they had left Port's Keep, Elowyn had what she thought was the strangest dream. Her senses had perceived something that roused her from sleep. She looked about in the night-time stillness. The moon shone brightly above, washing the fields around them in its soft bluish light. A low fog was rising from the earth, swirling through the tall grasses, and over the hills, set aglow by the moon. Every detail seemed particularly crisp, and stunningly beautiful in a lonely sort of way, but nothing was out of place or disturbing. Just as she was about to close her eyes and go back to sleep, Elowyn saw what she could only describe as a hovering ball of white fire. It slowly circled their camp, then floated before her face, just within arm's reach. She stretched out a cautious hand to touch it, but it shifted its position evasively. As it moved, it seemed to speak to her in a musical voice that sounded like tinkling bells or chimes. She had never seen or heard anything like it before.

The ball of white fire flew about their camp several more times before diving into one of their bags. It disappeared inside it for a moment, passed through it and out the other side. It did the same to another bag. It moved its way along Morganne's cloak, looking for her pouch and passing through it before Elowyn had the chance to raise any alarm. Lastly, it hovered before Elowyn. It said something to her in its lovely musical language before flying at her own pouch. Elowyn gave an involuntary gasp as the creature flashed past her side. Her skin tingled at its touch, feeling much as a limb that has fallen to sleep, but no other bad thing befell her. It spoke one last time, disappearing among the tall grasses. She watched for a while to see if it might come back. When it did not, she allowed herself to fall asleep once more, certain that whatever the creature had wanted, it had not appeared to have any ill intent. When she awoke in the morning, she had nearly forgotten about her dream. It was far too strange and difficult to explain to Morganne, and so she said nothing.

The road began to bear eastward again, toward the coast. Trees once again littered the landscape. The soil became harder and stonier, strewn with large boulders, and the gentle slopes of hills transformed into rocky terraces. Elowyn thought no more about her dream, until one evening when they found themselves approaching a place in the road that wound its way in between two steep ledges. As they approached it, Elowyn's instincts were all on edge. She stopped suddenly in the middle of the road and stood motionless. Her eyes carefully took in their surroundings, her ears listening attentively to every sound. She breathed in deeply, smelling every scent that was carried on the wind.

"What is it?" Morganne asked.

"I don't know…something doesn't feel right."

The daylight was quickly waning, and Morganne was visibly exhausted, growing more impatient by the moment as Elowyn stood frozen in place.

"I don't want to go through there," Elowyn said, pointing to the path ahead, "but I can't tell you why."

"Well, we can't just remain here," Morganne said anxiously. "Would it be better to make camp and have it looming ahead of us in the dark? We cannot go back—the last homes we passed were two days ago."

"I know," Elowyn replied grimly, while she desperately searched for any way around the steep rock faces. She saw none. The only thing to do was move forward.

The passageway was just wide enough for a work cart to squeeze through, and no wider. Elowyn watched the ledges above for any sign of danger, but in the growing dusk there was little of anything to be seen. The moon hadn't yet risen, so they were feeling their way half blind, drawn toward the dim blue opening ahead where the rock fell away from the path.

As they passed through to the other side they saw three men crouched in the shadows of the trees. One was just starting a fire; the other two instantly stood and turned at the sound of the girls' approach.

"Greetings young travelers!" one of the men called out as he walked up to Morganne. He was rough looking, with an unshaven face and a ragged wool cloak that smelled like old ale. "Night's getting on, and the open road is no place for any man after dark. Make camp with us."

"No thank you," Elowyn said, pressing close to Morganne.

"Come now, we only want to protect you," the second man said in a wheedling voice. "Lots of wild beasts out there that will tear you to pieces before you even see them coming." He looked as rough as the first man did and smelled even worse. He grinned at them with a mouth full of blackened teeth, trying unsuccessfully to appear friendly and harmless.

"I'm sure we will be fine," Morganne said, trying to hurry past them.

The first man drew his sword and used it to bar her way. "You'll at least sit and have a meal with us before you go on."

Morganne and Elowyn looked at each other fearfully.

"I'm afraid that we must go on—we've no time for a meal," Morganne said as forcefully as she could.

The first man lowered his sword, but did not re-sheath it, saying, "Well then, if you cannot stay, we won't keep you. Just pay the toll and you're free to go on."

"What toll?" Morganne asked.

The second man laughed gruffly, "The toll for using this road, of course. You'll pay us...what should we charge them, hey?" he called out to his companions.

"Why don't you go easy on them," the man working on the fire shouted out. "Only charge them a thousand in gold."

The first man looked upon their stunned expressions and said, "What? You don't have a thousand gold?" He clicked his tongue and shook his head at them.

"Lucky for you I'm a generous man, and fond of children. We'll simply take whatever you have, and I'll forgive the difference," he said, finally exposed as the cold thief that he was. He pointed the end of his sword at them. "Drop everything where you stand. Money, food, packs, and all."

"And if we refuse?" Morganne prodded cautiously.

"Then I'll run you all through with my blade and take what I want just the same. It is, of course, your choice." The cruel edge to his voice left no doubt in their minds that he would make good this threat.

"Please, at least let us keep our water skins, and something to feed the baby with," Morganne pleaded. "That would be worth nothing to you." No doubt Morganne was fearful now as to how they would manage the rest of their journey with no food or money, even should these men let them live.

As Morganne tried to bargain with the men, Elowyn noticed something strange. There were white points of light moving through the trees all around them. As the lights came closer, and emerged from the wood, she recognized them for what they were—the balls of white fire she had seen in her dream, though now she realized it had not been a dream at all.

The white fire hovered between the children and the men. The first one exclaimed, "What's this, then? I've never seen the like." With the men distracted, Morganne grasped Elowyn's hand tightly and slowly began to back away, pulling them a good distance before the man noticed his victims were getting away.

"Where do you think you're going?" he scowled. "You'll pay for that." He lunged his sword toward them, but as he did so, a ball of fire intercepted the blow. Blinding white light traveled down the sword and into the man's arm. He screamed in pain as his body convulsed. He

dropped the sword, lying panting on the ground for a few moments trying to recover his strength. At last, he rose up once more, snarling in an
animal-like rage. Grasping his sword again, he flew at the light with full
fury. The white fire struck him again and again with its agonizing blows
until he lay motionless in the road, unable to rise, with saliva running
from the corners of his mouth. His two companions grabbed their own
swords and made a half-hearted attempt to come to his defense. After
feeling the first sting of the white fire themselves, and seeing what it had
done to their companion, they gave up and fled into the woods, leaving
all they had behind.

Morganne and Elowyn clung to each other, watching the lights ap-
prehensively. One of them approached Elowyn and spoke in the musical
voice she had remembered from their last encounter.

"I'm sorry," she spoke softly. "I don't understand...I'm trying..."
She shook her head apologetically.

The light moved ahead along the path, then stopped and spoke,
and moved ahead again.

"I think it wants us to follow," Elowyn said.

As soon as the girls moved forward, the remaining lights formed a
moving circle around them. They dared not try to push past the beings
to either go back or run ahead. The balls of fire pressed right up against
their backs, attempting to nudge them forward along the path. The only
thing to do was to go on, and hope that the intent of these strange creatures was more benevolent than that of the thieves. In spite of the darkness, and their obvious fatigue, the girls were only allowed occasional
short rests before they were prodded to continue walking.

Morganne was nearing the end of her strength. Numerous times
she stumbled on the path and whispered to Elowyn that she didn't think
she could go on any further. She was exceedingly pale and looked as
though she might fall over at any moment. Yet she managed to keep moving. Even Elowyn's practiced endurance was nearly spent. She wondered
where they were being led, and why they were not permitted to make
camp for the night. There were moments when she realized that she had

fallen asleep on her feet, and her legs were still moving only because she had commanded them to.

"Please," she begged. "We must rest. We have been walking all the day long. We cannot go on!" The beings of fire would let them rest for a short while, then gently nudge them forward once more.

The night seemed endless and unmerciful, and Elowyn felt sick with fatigue. In that moment, all past miseries were forgotten. She began to believe that nothing else ever had been, or would ever be, so terrible as this. The stars were no comfort. She could not focus on their glorious display. Her eyes were too blurred to focus, her head too heavy to lift up.

Eventually she did notice that the sky was a little lighter than it had been, and then lighter again, and then pinker, and brighter, until the horizon was splashed with full, vibrant color. Rays of warm sunshine peeked over the rim of the world and softly caressed her cold face and arms. She closed her tired eyes for just a moment, allowing her spirit to be refreshed by the cheery red color of the sun pressed against her eyelids. Surprisingly, even the sun could not quell the searing white of the fiery beings leading them onward. Suddenly they stopped. One of them approached Elowyn and spoke, though it must have known that she could not understand it. Then the lights vanished into the lingering shadows of the wood, leaving the girls alone on the path. Too tired to speak, Morganne's face lit up with hope and she pointed forward, past the trees and into the clearing beyond. Where the trees ended, the road sloped downward into an open valley. Across that valley, Elowyn saw the walls and gates of a city rising before them, and just beyond that, the vast blue expanse of the sea. Elowyn now understood that the lights, whatever matter of creatures they were, had brought them through the night and safely into the hands of the next city. With the last of their strength, the girls crossed the valley and passed through the gates. The large banner hanging from the walls beside the gate read Greywalle.

As they stumbled through the cobbled streets toward what was apparently the only inn, Elowyn was trying desperately to remember something important. She knew nothing about Greywalle except that the

Allison D. Reid

name had awakened something in her mind that she needed to focus on. However, focusing on anything in that moment was close to impossible. Every muscle in her body ached. Faces, buildings, signs...all blurred before her into a confusing swirl of color. Sounds seemed loud and disjointed, making her nauseous. For the first time Elowyn knew what it felt like to reach the point where she could truly be pushed no further. She marveled that Morganne was standing. She who was not accustomed to this kind of life, and who had borne the extra burden of carrying Adelin, had somehow matched her endurance, step for step.

It was with great relief and joy that they at last came to the doors of the inn and pushed their way inside. They were greeted by a short, round, red-faced man with a kindly look about him. "Looks as though we have some weary travelers, mother," he called out to a woman that was as round and ruddy as he. A young girl about Adelin's age was clinging shyly to her skirts.

"Weary is not the word, father. They look half dead on their feet. Come over here my dears. Sit down by the fire while we find you a room." The woman took Adelin gently out of Morganne's tight grasp, as Morganne nodded compliantly. But Morganne never made it over to the fire. Once she saw that Adelin was securely held by the innkeeper's wife, she collapsed onto the floor, and nothing they did could rouse her.

Chapter 14
The Inn at Greywalle

The innkeeper lifted Morganne in his arms, carried her to one of the rooms and carefully lowered her onto a freshly changed bed. While he ran to fetch the village healer, Elowyn removed Morganne's boots and the innkeeper's wife covered her with a warm blanket. The innkeeper soon returned with the healer, who also happened to be one of the local monks. After examining Morganne and hearing the tale of their night-long flight, he concluded that there was nothing seriously wrong with her. He left instructions to keep her in bed for at least three days, to feed her well when she woke, and to give her an herbal concoction to drink that he had made. The healer examined Elowyn as well. Food and rest were her prescription also, lest she succumb to the same collapse that Morganne had endured. He advised that the girls remain in Greywalle for a while, and then limit how many hours they spent on the road each day once they resumed their journey. His last request before he left was to be notified as soon as Morganne felt well enough to have visitors.

Thankfully, Elowyn had finally remembered what was so important about the name Greywalle. She had overheard Tervaise speak of the innkeeper as someone who owed him a great debt, and who would be happy to care for them on his word. She found the two seals Tervaise had given them in Morganne's bags and presented them to the innkeeper.

"Mother!" he called out excitedly. "These are friends of Tervaise and his kin."

His wife smiled genuinely. "Well, then, you are especially welcome. His friends are indeed ours. Do not fret for a thing! While you are here you will not be guests of the inn, but family."

Elowyn was given her own room, with her own soft bed filled with fresh straw and covered in clean linens. Adelin was well taken care of, and content to play with the little girl, who kept her amused and out of trouble.

Morganne did not awaken until the next morning, and only then was she finally able to sit up in bed, eat, and drink. Elowyn rubbed Morganne's bruised feet and swollen legs with a special herbal poultice she had concocted in the inn's kitchen, then wrapped them in cool damp rags. Elowyn was still sore and tired herself, but comfortable. She was faring the physical strain as well as she dared to hope.

"I suppose that I am not meant for this sort of journey," Morganne said in a frustrated tone. "My spirit tells me that I must go on, that something special is waiting for me in Minhaven. But my body is giving up on ever reaching that place."

"We will get there, if it is Aviad's will," Elowyn said thoughtfully. "Perhaps the innkeeper knows of someone who can ferry us by cart the rest of the way. I heard Tervaise say that he knew of merchants who would be willing, and he did give us his seal."

"I am glad that you remembered it. I had forgotten."

When Morganne was feeling well enough that she could rise out of bed to take meals with the innkeeper and his family, she sent word for the healer who had tended to her. He gave her one final examination and declared that she would recover fully in no time. He told her to begin taking regular walks about Greywalle for increasing lengths of time until she felt ready to continue on the road. Morganne thanked him profusely for attending to her and insisted that he take payment for his services.

"I will confess," he said sheepishly when everyone else but Elowyn had left the room, "there is another reason for my visit. I wanted to speak with you further about the beings of light that guided you here. I know of no other creature that appears as you describe except for what we call wisps. They are considered to be sacred by many who follow the old ways. Rarely are they seen in these times, and even then, only in the most remote wilds or in the ancient places of power. To have seen a wisp once in a lifetime is a wonder, and some say, a sign of Aviad's blessing. To have one speak to you is a dream. To have seen and heard more than one at a time is simply unheard of. To have actually been protected and guided by a whole host of them...the mere thought makes my knees quake! I know not whether I should fear you, or venerate you. Whether or not you believe in the teachings of the Prophets, my advice to you is that you seek out one of the shrines and give in prayer an offering of thanksgiving, for you have been profoundly blessed."

"If you could give us direction, we would be happy to leave an offering at whatever temple you have here," Morganne said.

"Temple? We have no temple here, child. I am speaking of the shrines of power, blessed by the Ancients and revered by the Prophets themselves in days of old.

"Do such places really still exist? I thought they had vanished along with the Prophets," Morganne said.

"Most of the shrines are now buried in the wilderness—they are difficult and dangerous to find without a knowledgeable guide. But there are the remains of one not very far to the north, in the village of Evensong. There was once nothing there but a monastery on the cliffs overlooking the sea, and the orchards tended by its monks. They built a shrine there dedicated to Immar, the Lord of Divine Love and Mercy. It was destroyed when the Prophets were scattered during the Great War. The monastery is still in ruins to this day, but eventually a town was built below it that took its name. All that remains of the original shrine is a fountain. The spring that fed it went dry with the destruction of the monastery, and many consider it to be a dead shrine that has lost favor with Aviad. Very few pay it the honor it is due, even among those who live under its shadow in present day Evensong. But there are those among my brethren who believe it is still a significant place of power by virtue of its history, and when we cannot make pilgrimage to the greater shrines, we journey to Evensong. I think it would be perfectly appropriate for you to take your offering there."

"Then that is where we shall go," Morganne said. "What sort of offering do we leave?"

"That I cannot tell you. You must ask in prayer at the shrine, and no doubt the answer will come. I will pray for your safe journey, though if the wisps watch over you, I am certain you are already blessed."

As directed, Morganne began a regimen of daily walks about the city, with Elowyn always at her side to watch over her. Greywalle was a small, but lovely town. The streets were cobbled, and most of the buildings were fashioned of a dark gray stone that seemed to be in plentiful supply in that region. The coastline and surrounding fields were littered with it. There was no harbor, only a few scattered docks used by small fishing vessels. The waters were apparently too treacherous for shipping, and so everything that came into Greywalle came by road through the main gate. Morganne had noticed that there was no tower, no castle, and no visible presence of guards standing watch along the wall. In her usual practical way, she asked the innkeeper by what means the city was guarded.

"We're not, exactly," he told her. "It's not like we're of any interest to the Sovereign, with no port, and no other source of wealth to catch his eye. You'll find that the order of things is somewhat different out here on the edge of the wilderness. We take care of ourselves, or we don't survive for very long. We were once at the mercy of marauding orders of knights who were either vying for territory of their own, or trying to take territory for their lords in exchange for other favors. But the Kinship put a stop to that, and we're under their protection now. It has been a long while since we had to defend our gates against our own countrymen. Against the terrors of the wilds, we have found our own swords to be sufficient."

As Elowyn gazed about Greywalle's charming central square, edged by small shops on three sides and a community herb garden on the fourth, she felt a sense of grateful wonder that this peaceful little village had so far escaped Braeden's destructive gaze. Though they had invoked the name of the Kinship in order to find the innkeeper's favor, Elowyn still wondered what the Kinship might be, and to what power it gave its loyalty. She had never heard its name before they had met Tervaise and Reyda at the trading post.

When she was able, Elowyn enjoyed sitting quietly in the herb gar-den. She breathed deeply of its earthy scents, wistfully missing her own garden back in Tyroc. Morganne, on the other hand, had found the local seamstress and was determined to make some heavier clothing to pro-tect them through the next stage of their journey. The locals had given fair warning that winter always came on fast and early, and as the girls progressed northward into the foothills of the mountains, the nights would grow bitter cold. The innkeeper thought that they should winter in Greywalle and promised them a room should they decide to stay.

Though Morganne prepared their winter clothing in earnest and spoke of leaving as soon as she felt well enough, Elowyn saw that her needle did not fly as swiftly as she knew it could. Morganne was fast making friends with the seamstress, who was predictably impressed by her skill and practically begged her to stay and work at the shop. Elowyn wondered at the back of her mind if Morganne was considering it, now that Greywalle was beginning to feel like home. The innkeeper and his wife, true to their word, treated the girls as their own family. They were gentle spirited, jovial, and hardworking people, though Morganne and Elowyn began to see that the inn was not very profitable, and the couple was wont to spend more on their guests than they got back in return. But the people of Greywalle liked it that way, and they were proud of the fact that they had an inn at all, so everyone in the village helped in whatever way they could to ensure that the inn remained, and that the innkeeper's family was cared for.

Since the innkeeper would not take their money, Morganne and Elowyn found other ways to help repay him. Morganne took care of all their mending and made the innkeeper's wife a new dress that so pleased her she nearly wept over it. Elowyn prepared their garden for the com-ing winter and helped make tallow candles. As much as she had dreaded helping with that chore back in Tyroc, she found that the innkeeper's wife made it bearable. She sang merrily and told stories to help the time pass.

The girls might have stayed happily at Greywalle for the rest of their days were it not for a strange and sudden visitor who appeared at the inn. He wore the crest of the Sovereign and the uniform of the castle guard. He had a rough, unshaven face, with a dark beard and thin, cruel lips. His presence alone sent a chill wind blowing through the usually cheery inn and sent guests scuttling off to their rooms in haste. The guard approached the innkeeper, and with a gravelly voice asked if any guests from Tyroc had recently stayed at the inn. He claimed that he was searching for a rebel sympathizer who was in possession of a valuable heirloom that had been smuggled out of the castle at Tyroc. He was charged with the task of finding the heirloom before it could be sold, and bringing the sympathizer to justice.

"Sympathizers come in many forms," the man growled. "Even women and children have been known to carry such items." He gave a long glance in the direction of Morganne, who was sitting by the fire with her sewing.

The man slowly walked over to her, the floorboards creaking under the weight of his steps. "You, there. Where are you from? What is your business here?" Morganne stared at him in fearful shock, unable to speak or move, her mind drawing a complete blank in her panic.

His face red with anger, the innkeeper called out to the stranger. "You'll leave my daughter be and direct your questions to me, if you please. I'll not have you frightening my family and my guests. We've not had any visitors from Tyroc in more months than I can remember."

The guard planted his leather-gloved hands on the counter and leaned across it, towering threateningly over the portly innkeeper and staring him in the face for what seemed like an eternity. But the innkeeper stood his ground and stared back at him with unwavering eyes until the stranger finally stepped back and went on his way.

With a quivering voice, Morganne thanked the innkeeper.

"You have become daughters to me, and I would not have fed you to that beast of a man wherever you may have come from. It is of no consequence to me."

"I can assure you that we do not have any heirloom of the Sovereign, nor are we criminals on the run. But we are from Tyroc and would rather not have to answer questions about where we came from or where we are going. I had begun to hope that we could make Greywalle our new home, but it seems we must continue on for your sake as much as ours."

Once Morganne had finished making their winter clothing, they packed their satchels, filled with generous amounts of food from the inn's kitchen. They departed Greywalle with tearful hugs and farewells from the friends they had made during their stay, setting out by foot once again on the road to Minhaven.

Chapter 15
The Offering

Once again the landscape began to change and the girls found that their pace was considerably slowed. The terrain was stonier and swelled in gentle rolls. All around them the trees were showering the woodlands in reds, golds, and oranges. The days were cool, and the nights frigid. Instead of sleeping in a tree as she normally would, Elowyn found herself huddling under blankets in front of the fire with Morganne and Adelin through the long nights. When they rose in the morning, their breath showed in the crisp air, a sure sign that the winter months were closing in quickly. Morganne worried that perhaps they had dallied too long at Greywalle, and said with some regret in her voice that they might have been better off wintering there after all.

Elowyn could tell that the region they now traversed was wilder than anything she had ever experienced in Tyroc's outskirts, and was becoming thicker, deeper, and wilder still as they pressed on. The trees were so old, and so tall, that they choked out most of thick underbrush, leaving a clear view across much of the forest floor. Elowyn could sense how alone they were out there on the road. It was a source of both worry and wonder to her. They had no weapons except for Einar's dagger, and nothing to guide them aside from her meager wood skills, which felt woefully inadequate in these foreign lands. And yet, the landscape was so pristine, so imposingly beautiful, it left her gaping in awed silence. The destructive hand of man's ingenuity had not yet found its way there to disrupt the glory of Aviad's creation. She could distinguish the work of His hands so clearly it frightened her. The trees, the earth, the sky, all seemed too perfect to be real, as though they had been painted by Aviad upon a shimmering curtain, hovering in the air just before her eyes. Elowyn felt that were she to reach out and draw the curtain aside, the barrier between earth and Aviad's realm would be torn away, and she would find herself whisked away to that other place, beyond the reach of any road made by man. Oh, how vast, and how good His power truly was, and how small and fragile was she by comparison. How could it be that He had bestowed His blessing upon her?

For many days, there was nothing but wilderness before them. There were no villages, no people, nor indeed any sign that people had ever been there, save the obvious presence of the road itself. It was many more days still before they reached Evensong. The village was little more than a loose group of stone buildings edged by cultivated fields, the ancient orchards of the old monastery, and the sea, which churned far below. The coastline was sheer cliff for as far as one could see, with the waves crashing against moss covered rocks rather than sand. They could see the ruins of the old monastery on a rise above the town. The crumbled remains of its once solid foundation stood watch like gravestones keeping vigil over the dead.

Evensong had a rugged, lonely sort of beauty about it that made Elowyn want to sit in silence among the ruins, close her eyes, and feel the sea wind against her skin. There was, of course, no inn. They were given the use of a one-room cottage nestled among the orchards. It had an open roof with a central hearth, and a bare earthen floor. At least it provided shelter from the elements, and there was an ample supply of firewood stacked outside which they were grateful for. The long-abandoned cottage had been kept in repair by an old farmer, who sometimes used it as a place to warm himself while he harvested apples in the fall.

Elowyn found that the people of Evensong were very different from those of Greywalle, or anyplace else she had been for that matter. They were a friendly, but silent and contemplative people. They wore the weathered looks of those who have learned to overcome hardship with nothing but their fortitude and their faith. Their hands were rough from hard work, their minds keen, their eyes proud. It was almost as though the old monastery looking down upon them still held its influence over the surrounding land.

After they had thoroughly rested, the girls decided that Morganne should find her way to the shrine alone to make her offering. She was the eldest, and better versed in the lessons of the Temple, so Elowyn kept Adelin and waited. Morganne returned several hours later, discouraged and frustrated.

"What happened?" Elowyn asked.

"I don't know..." Morganne replied in a confused tone. "Nothing, really. I sat by the shrine and prayed all of the prayers of thanks I could recall from Gareth's lessons, asked what sort of offering I should leave, and waited for the answer to come to me. No answer came. Perhaps I did something wrong...said the wrong prayers, or said them in the wrong way. I finally just left, not knowing what else to do. Perhaps you should go, and Aviad will speak to you. He has before...in the other ruins outside of Tyroc."

Elowyn gave Morganne a startled look. "That was only a dream."

"But perhaps it wasn't. It certainly doesn't seem like you had a dream of the ordinary kind. Please, at least try? I cannot go back up there, not just yet. I need to rest."

And so Elowyn went. She made her way through the orchards, along an old dirt path that wound its way up to the crest of the hill where the ruins spread out before her on a flat plateau. The sea winds grabbed at her clothes, and tossed her hair wildly about her face. She welcomed the taste of salt in the air, and the faint warmth of the autumn sun on her skin. The ruins were completely undisturbed and silent, save the sounds of the waves, and the birds calling out to each other.

It was not difficult to find the shrine, set apart from the ruins and overlooking the cliff edge. All that was left was a simple stone basin, held upwards in the arms of a variety of carved figures, both male and female. Rising above the figures was the larger figure of a man in flowing robes, tipping a chalice on its side. No doubt when the fountain worked, water poured from the chalice into the basin. Elowyn stared at it for a long while before she got the courage to approach it. Once again, she felt as though she had set foot in a place she was not worthy of entering. She stared up at the carved figure of the man with the chalice. She supposed he was Immar. Gareth had told Elowyn that Immar had been born of Aviad's grief over the evils of the world, embodying all of His perfect goodness, and remaining both distinct and one with Him. She never quite understood how the three Ancients could each be different and yet the same all at once. But she trusted Gareth and hoped that one day it would all become clear to her.

Elowyn tried to clear her mind and simply listen for Aviad's voice. She didn't know any of the prayers Morganne did, nor did she know what to say. A few clumsily spoken words of thanks uttered by a grubby child did not seem adequate. The longer she sat there, the more self-conscious she became, until she too, got up and fairly fled down the hillside. Over the next couple of days she and Morganne made further attempts to leave an offering at the shrine and returned disheartened. Morganne was taking their failure especially hard. She felt that they needed to follow the monk's instruction, but had not expected it would be so difficult. Elowyn pointed out that the monk had never told them how long it would take for them to make the offering. He only said they should offer whatever they were told to while in prayer at the shrine.

Help finally came in a most unexpected form. The old farmer who had let them use the cottage came by to visit one afternoon, bringing them more firewood and some fresh apples. He warned them that if they wanted to spend the winter in Evensong they would need to find someone in town who had enough food stored to take them in.

"This would be no safe place when winter comes," he said. "You would likely either freeze to death or starve. When the squalls come in, you would be cut off from the rest of the town by blinding snow. Once the snows start, no one goes up on the plateau again until spring, and for good reason. Best find whatever you are looking for up there quickly."

"What makes you think we are looking for something?" Morganne asked.

"I've seen you both trudging up the hill every day since you arrived here. Why so, if you are not seeking something there that has not yet been found?"

"We seek only answers, so that we may leave an offering to the shrine and be on our way. But this has proved more difficult than we expected." Morganne went on to explain what the monk in Greywalle had instructed them to do, and about their difficulty in getting an answer.

"Well," the old farmer said as he scratched his face thoughtfully, "I don't know about all the fancy prayers. Never had a need for those out in the orchards. But I do need company now and then. I'm not always a good listener, mind you, but I can't think of a time when I needed Aviad's company and He wasn't there to talk to. There's no use in trying to impress Him, you know. Just go up there and be. You'll find Him quick enough."

Elowyn found that she liked the old farmer very much. He was a simple yet contemplative man, who was quite happy spending his days with only Aviad for company. Through his eyes she saw Aviad in a new and profound way. As huge and powerful as she knew Aviad to be, she could also see Him walking along quietly through the orchards with this old farmer, the two of them as comfortable with each other as dear friends who had always been together. With all the time she had spent alone in the wilds, she could understand Aviad in this way, and hoped that He would walk along with her just the same.

The next morning, Morganne went alone to the ruins while Elowyn cared for Adelin and waited for her return. As the day went on, Elowyn became more anxious, pacing about the cottage, her thoughts consumed by her own imaginings about what might be happening at the shrine.

When Morganne did return, she had a peaceful glow about her, but remained silent. When Elowyn finally couldn't bear it any longer, she asked what had happened.

"I don't really know. I tried to do what the farmer had told me, and found that I couldn't. My thoughts would not stop long enough. The harder I tried to quiet them, the more frustrated I became, until…"

Allison D. Reid

"Until what?" Elowyn asked after a long silence.

"I'm ashamed to tell it, but I began to cry. Not gentle silent tears, either. From somewhere deep inside of me, all of my anger against mother, and the pain and fear we've endured on our journey, welled up and gushed forth. I cried much harder and longer than I had any right to, and if anyone had found me there in that state I would have been completely horrified. But eventually I reached a point where there were no more tears. I grew weary, and silent, and my eyes lost their focus. I sat with my knees held close against me, staring out into the empty sky beyond the cliff's edge. In that place, I found Him—or rather, He found me. He had been there all along, only I hadn't been listening. Even then, at first I did not recognize Him. A small thought simply came to my mind—a phrase that kept repeating. It was bothersome, like a biting insect that just kept coming back all the more persistently each time I tried to brush it away. Then I simply gave in to the thought and embraced it rather than trying to purge it. 'Drink from my cup, for it is filled with living water.'

"I had no idea what the phrase meant, or why it was so unrelenting. I seemed to recall hearing it before, though I couldn't remember from where. As I focused on it a little longer, I almost thought that I could see the phrase in writing, on a page that looked familiar. Perhaps a page from the book Gareth gave me, or one of the other books he loaned me to read. Once that thought entered my mind the phrase stopped repeating, and other thoughts began to flow. I cannot express them to you, because they were not in words and it would be too confusing. I only felt their message, like pictures inscribed on my heart. Oh, Elowyn, He was so real in that moment. I almost believed that I could reach out my hand and feel His physical presence seated beside me. You know what it feels like to come in out of the cold and wrap yourself in the warmth of a soft blanket that has been heated by fire? Or imagine drinking the purest, sweetest water you've ever tasted just at the moment when you are so parched you think that you must surely die of thirst. That is the best way I can describe the experience. Never have I felt such purity of joy, and peace, and wonder.

240

"I know now that we are on the right path. Whatever happens, this journey was meant for us to take. And I know, too, what we are supposed to leave behind as our offerings; the drinking cup from my belt, which I have already left at the shrine, and some meadowsweet, which we will have to find somewhere. I wanted to go into the village and purchase a new cup to leave, perhaps a silver chalice...something far more worthy to give as a sacrifice than my old worn out wooden cup. But it was the wooden one He wanted, I do not know why."

"I have some dried meadowsweet that I brought from my garden. It grew well this year with all the rain we had. Will that be good enough?" Elowyn asked.

Morganne considered it for a moment. "Dried will do nicely. But I think you should go tomorrow and place it on the shrine yourself."

Elowyn nodded in agreement. It was only right that she should go. After all, the wisps had come to her twice.

Morganne pulled Gareth's book from her bag and sat with it by the fire while Elowyn prepared a meager meal from what little food remained in their bags. They would need to supply themselves well before continuing on their way.

It was not long before Morganne exclaimed in an excited voice, "I found it! The phrase that came to me...it is from one of the tales of Varol."

"Who is Varol?" Elowyn asked.

Morganne shot her a scolding look. "Who is Varol? Did all of Gareth's lessons teach you no more than that? He is only the greatest of the old heroes—the only man to read the Tome of Truth, written by the very hand of Emeth, and remain unscathed."

Elowyn gave her a blank look and shrugged apologetically. She did remember some of the stories Gareth had read to them, but those days seemed so distant to her now, and there were, of course, many times when the sights and sounds of the gardens had captured her attention far more completely than the lessons had. Sometimes Gareth noticed and rapped his pen across her knuckles to get her attention. At other times, he and Morganne had shared such mutual interest and excitement that he failed to noticed Elowyn's wandering gaze.

"If you do not remember Varol, come sit beside me, and I shall read to you from Gareth's book. Knowing such stories is important, especially now."

Elowyn made a face. "I remember some of his readings. They were so difficult to understand."

"This one is not. It is a primer, written for young boys entering the Temple for the first time."

Elowyn settled in comfortably by the warmth of the fire as night descended up on them. The sea winds grew stronger, whistling through the cracks in the cottage and causing the flames of their candles to dance.

"Perhaps it would be best to start at the beginning. I've had little time to read since Gareth gave me the book, and I've only gotten through short bits of it here and there. I'm sure there are many tales I have forgotten or that I never knew."

Morganne opened to the first page and began to read. "The oldest of writings reveals the creation in this way. That before there were such things as earth, and moon, and sun, there was nothingness. Then the light of Aviad, the Creator, appeared, and within the light, the Realm of the Spirit was first formed, like a pale, shifting mist, stretching out its fingers into eternity. Beyond the edges of the light, a deep darkness grew, where all who despised the light fled from it and gathered in the shadows.

"At Aviad's word, the heavens were formed, swirling about Him in their hot, fiery dance. He gathered some of the stars together in his arms, and began to combine their masses. With His hands, He formed a single flaming ball, allowing it to grow large and hot before He separated it into three glowing spheres. The first sphere drew nearly all of the flame away from the others, but the second He cupped tightly in his hands, extinguishing all of its remaining heat until it was a lifeless sphere of ashen rock. The third sphere He cupped lightly, so that the surface was cooled, yet the flames still burned far beneath. He set the three together in the heavens, and so were formed the sun, the moon, and the earth. The earthen sphere was still nothing more than a barren landscape, but it was Aviad's own creation, and He loved it.

"He immediately set to work, giving the earth life, and health. At the sound of His laughter, the ground rumbled joyously and rushed to meet Him, thus forming all the mountain ranges. The soft whisper of His voice formed the waters that rose up from the deep valleys left behind by the ground's movement. His breath formed the winds and the clouds that still roam the skies. He reached one hand into the waters, and another onto the mountain peaks. From the points where He touched, all the green and growing things spread outward in lush abundance, until they covered the whole of the earth. In the oceans were formed all the life which breathe of water, and in the young forests formed all the life which breathe of air. His glorious creation, when all was done, was crowned with a single flower, growing on the highest mountaintop.

"Even with all the animals, and the new life that surrounded Him, there were still none like Aviad. So He created the first humans, blessing them with intelligence beyond that of animals, and the ability to love, and laugh, and form coherent speech. Together they kept good company, and Aviad was content. He loved his children and blessed them with his presence, yet they were soon lured and deceived by the darkness. For the first time evil's shadow passed over Aviad's perfect creation and corrupted it. Each living thing suddenly began to age, eventually returning into the earth from where it had come. Separated from Aviad, His human companions grew frail and perished, and Aviad was sorely grieved. He wept to himself atop the hill—the first tears He had ever cried.

"Much more than human tears, the droplets shed by Aviad further revealed His unique nature, for they were vibrant and living, at once part of Aviad's grand being, and yet distinct and individual. As the first tear fell into a world bathed in shadow, it reflected the brilliant glow of Aviad's perfect love. Momentarily, the tear hung in the sky, a new morning star illuminating all of creation, breaking evil's hold and heralding a new dawn. But mankind had been blind for so long, that few recognized the face of the Creator shining through that first tear, whose name has been revealed to us as Immar. As the tear fell, it was broken on jagged cliffs that marred the surface of the world like a scar. Blood ran down the cliffs from the place where the tear was broken, and the agonized cries of Aviad and Immar rang out in unison over the whole world. Through the breaking of the tear, Aviad felt the same pain His children endured at the hands of sickness and death. The thirsty soil tried to swallow Immar, but death was no match for Him. He sprang forth again, rejoining Aviad to sit at His side, and revealing Aviad's full power and majesty. Immar's blood had washed away all that separated humanity from its creator.

"A second tear fell behind the first, only this one was swept up in the wind before hitting the ground. All of Aviad's love for his creation, and the pain of its separation from Him, welled up in the tear. His passion was so intense that it ignited the tear, sending a bright flame across the sky. Many looked up and exalted in Aviad's glory, allowing the flame's brilliance to drive the Shadow from their hearts. Those who accepted the light, revealed to us as Emeth, found themselves bathed in its gentle warmth and were healed by it.

"But there were others who feared the flame. They fled as far as they could into the Shadow's waiting arms, denying that there could ever be hope in such searing brilliance, even trying to convince themselves that the light never existed. Those who thought they were seeking protection in the Shadow found instead that the farther they fled into its depths, the more they feared the light until they could hardly bear to even look upon it. In this way, they allowed the Shadow to falsely claim them for his own.

"The light of Aviad's flame could not be extinguished by the Shadow. It continued to penetrate the darkness, ever seeking the lost, reaching out to illuminate the homeward path. The heat of the flame and the wetness of Aviad's second tear together formed a fine mist that filled the air. Aviad's children breathed it in, as newborns taking in their first breath of life. The mist re-ignited in their hearts, burning together in unison with the Creator and bestowing upon each spiritual gifts. With them we are called to serve one another as we journey through the shadows and into Aviad's light. And so, in the form of Aviad's tears, Immar, the Lord of Divine Love, and Emeth, the Lord of Truth, were first revealed to us. Because they are of Aviad, and remain one with Aviad, they embody all of His perfect goodness. It is these that the Prophets call the Ancients.

"The Shadow's corruptive influence continued to spread so long as humanity allowed itself to be swayed by it, for even those who knew and loved the Ancients sometimes stumbled into the twilight or were lured into the darkness. The Shadow therefore continued to cause the creation to slowly age and die. Yet through Aviad's perfect love, Immar's life-giving sacrifice, and the Spirit of Emeth, humanity may be cleansed and made new, so that even in death Aviad's children can live on forever with Him in His realm, beyond the earth, and even the stars of the heavens.

"Under the Ancients' care, the human race grew and increased their number. They began to form small communities and learned to farm the land. They also built shrines to the Ancients out of worshipful devotion. In each shrine were housed Tomes of Wisdom, scribed in the hands of the Ancients themselves. Very few of mortal blood could read or wield these powerful Tomes without falling into madness, and so the first monastic orders were founded. The Prophets who formed them guarded the Tomes, and the few who could read them taught their wisdom to the rest of the order. This wisdom was scribed by human hand into those books we know of as the Tomes of the Prophets, which could be read by anyone with the desire for knowledge, and could be taught to the people. When those with adventurous hearts began to wander into the untamed wilds, establishing new homes and forming new cities, orders began to send their followers out into the world to teach, provide ritual services, and perform works of great charity.

"As the years passed, the Shadow and his forces of evil grew in strength. He raised up two shadow spirits to aid him and to serve as a twisted mockery of the Ancients. They were Destruction and Deceit, and he called them Alazoth and Tieced. Their impact resounded through the whole of the earth, forming a great rift through the peaceful surface, and into the hot flaming core. Up from those teeming depths rose billowing gasses, and raging storms that flooded the lands. The trees were ripped apart, the oceans swelled in anger, the earth trembled. Famine, and plagues, and all types of pestilence swept through the land. Dark, strange creatures, not of Aviad's making, began to spawn, ambushing travelers and assaulting villages. Aviad's glorious creation was plunged into utter chaos and despair, but He did not abandon it. He willed with Immar and Emeth, to ever fight against the Shadow's devastating presence. Many men rose to aid them in the fight. Most joined with willing hearts, and were blessed. However, there were some who could not resist the Shadow's wiles, and fell into darkness, choosing to become vile minions of evil whose offspring still roam to this day.

"Many great battles were waged, as generation upon generation of humanity's blood was spilled keeping back the Shadow. No matter how many warriors and prophets stood on the side of the Ancients, others were swayed to following the false promises of the Shadow, and thus no victory was truly decisive.

"It was during one such battle that the course of history was forever changed. Among the armies of the Ancients was a young boy with a great desire to serve Emeth, the Lord of Truth. He had been turned away from the abbey year upon year, because he was poor and of no great lineage. Only by his persistence was he eventually given a sword and a purpose; to fight the Shadow. The captain who sent him into battle had assumed that survival would be the greatest achievement this young man could hope for in such times.

"As many of the great abbeys and monasteries fell, vital relics and tomes were moved to areas of protection. So it happened that the Tome of Truth was set to be moved to a newly built shrine, dedicated to Emeth. The Tome was accompanied by high ranking officers, monks, and a large complement of fighting men. Before they had gotten very far, they were ambushed by Tieced's forces. The monks, the officers, and many of the men were systematically targeted and slaughtered. Those who remained were young, untrained fighters who had been pressed into service out of sheer need, and Tieced found it easy to confuse their minds. Without their battle-hardened leaders to guide them, they were quickly succumbing to the terrors the enemy was unleashing upon them, and they were ready to simply desert the Tome and flee.

"Varol alone was able to see through Tieced's deceptions. He knew that if he did not do something quickly, all was lost. Boy though he was, no one questioned him as he took command and pulled the men together. He rallied them, urging them onward, breaking the hold Tieced had on their minds. In the end, it was the enemy who abandoned the Tome and scattered into the hills.

"When the Tome was securely in Varol's hands, he looked upon it with amazement, knowing that he would never again hold such a treasure. Poor though he was, he had always aspired to serve the abbey, and had taught himself to read in the hopes that he might one day be accepted. Worried that the enemy might have somehow defiled the Tome, he dared to release the silver clasp, open the leather binding, and leaf through its pages. In reverent amazement, he could not help but read some of the words out loud to himself before he closed and clasped the book again, relieved that it had not apparently suffered any damage.

"When Varol's men reached the new shrine, the Tome was handed over to the monk who was to give the dedication. He had reportedly spent years in meditation and practice so that he could read but a few lines from it. When word reached the abbot that Varol had been able to read far more than that, Varol was summoned to his chambers. Fearing that he had done something wrong, Varol dropped to his knees before the abbot and began to apologize for his transgression, asking for leniency. But the abbot was a wise man with a faithful heart. He handed Varol the open Tome and asked him to read it. Varol did so flawlessly. The abbot explained that his reading of the Tome was not forbidden, merely unexpected, and he offered to make Varol a monk at the abbey if he so desired. Varol instead chose to remain as one of the monastic guard and often asked to be sent on missions to move other relics, tomes, and even Prophets who were being relocated for the sake of their safety.

"Over time, Varol grew to be a great warrior and scholar. He was a valiant man who never raised his sword out of anger, but only in service to the Ancients. Many a battle was won by his sword and his cunning. Among the Ancients, he was favored more than any other man before or since, and yet he remained humble, turning away countless worldly honors and special favors.

"There came a time when the world was in the greatest desperation it had yet faced. The Shadow had for the first time erected a shrine of its own, one from which darkness and chaos spewed forth, and where evil's slain minions could be resurrected. From this shrine, the Shadow filled the ranks of his armies so that no matter how many were killed in battle, they only returned the next day to resume their fight. To strengthen their position, each Order called for all of the Tomes of Wisdom to be brought to Aviad's shrine in the south. In that way their powers could be combined, and, it was hoped, that both the evil shrine and the dark forces bearing down upon them would be destroyed. The Shadow learned of this plot, and he ordered Alazoth to launch an attack on Aviad's Shrine, while Tieced launched an assault on the Shrine of Truth. He needed to force Emeth's Order to choose between taking the Tome to Aviad's Shrine, or standing to protect the Shrine of Truth and those loyal followers who were defending it with their lives.

"In the midst of the fray stood Varol, his golden hair flowing in the light of righteousness. Many of Tieced's minions fell to his blade that day. But as evening began to fall, it was evident that under such continued brutal assault, the Shrine of Truth would not stand for much longer. Tieced was a wily opponent and had the ability to cloud the minds of Emeth's warriors. Many of them fell not to the enemy's blades, but to those of their comrades. Since Varol was the only one who could read Emeth's Tome without coming to harm, and who could also protect it with his sword, it was his task to make the journey. Although Tieced was powerful, he knew better than to attack Varol directly while he held the Tome of Truth in his hand. He had not forgotten his previous encounters with Varol, nor had he forgotten that by its nature, the Tome possessed great power of its own. Tieced knew that should it so much as

248

touch him, he would be cast into oblivion. Instead he appeared in many forms before Varol, trying his utmost to trick the young warrior. But Varol's heart was pure, and Emeth protected him from Tieced's deceptions as he had so many times before. After many failed attempts, Tieced called upon his minions to prevent Varol from reaching Aviad's Shrine.

"Little did he know that Aviad's Order was already on the move. While they could not destroy the Shadow's shrine without the Tome of Truth, they had managed to do two very significant things. First, by the power of the Tomes of Aviad and Immar, and with much prayer and sacrifice, they were able to trap Alazoth within the confines of a magically sealed stone chest. Without Alazoth to lead them, his armies fell into disarray, and Aviad's forces were able to drive them all the way back to the rift in the earth from whence they had come. Though in the heat of battle the chest fell into the hands of Alazoth's followers, certain protections had been placed upon the chest to ensure that his followers could not release him. Only one of innocent blood, whose heart was willing, could open the chest and set Alazoth free again.

"Meanwhile, Varol became trapped between those retreating from the victory of Aviad's Order, and those who were pursuing him from the direction of the Shrine of Truth. Even as Alazoth's warriors were licking their wounds, Tieced's were telling the tale of the fall of Emeth's Shrine, and reveling over how many of His followers and Prophets they had slaughtered. Full of anguish, and having no way of escape, Varol charged upon the two armies, fully prepared to meet his death by taking out as many of his enemies as he could on the way. Seeing Varol with Emeth's Tome shining bright in his hands, they fled into the rift, with Varol at their heels. When the last of the beasts vanished into the Rift, Varol raised the Tome and called upon its power to seal it.

"As the Rift closed before his eyes, Varol stumbled for the first time in his life. He allowed himself to be consumed with pride, as though he had single-handedly driven evil from the world. He imagined the honor and status that he would now be blessed with among his people. And as these thoughts entered his heart, the Tome wrenched itself from his hands and was torn in two. Realizing what had happened, Varol kneeled before it and wept with shame and grief. He begged Emeth's forgiveness with a truly repentant heart, picked up the remains of the Tome, and returned home with a heavy heart.

"When Varol entered his home village and looked upon the carnage there, he knew how foolish his pride had been. Many had perished in the attempt to drive evil back, including most of the Monks who had cared for him as a brother, and who had taught him the ways of righteousness.

"Varol rebuilt the Shrine of Truth with his own hands, stone by stone, as an act of penance. As he was in the midst of setting the stones of the altar, a haggard looking man emerged and approached him from the wood. The man looked as though he had been walking for many days without rest or food.

"'Is there a well nearby?' the man asked. 'My water skin is empty and needs to be filled.'

"'There was once a well here, but the dark ones defiled it so that it is no longer fit for drinking,' Varol replied. 'There is no stream, and the village is yet half a day's walk.' Varol took the skin from his own belt and handed it to the stranger. 'Your need appears to be greater than mine. I will wait for the rains to quench my thirst, else I will return to the village if they do not come.'

"'Your compassion is great, and your sacrifice noble.' The man removed from his belt a beautifully carved wooden cup and set it on the ground. 'Please take this in payment. It is all I have to give. May you be blessed by more than rain water.'

"Varol reached down for another stone to continue with his building, telling the man as he did so to keep his cup, that payment was not necessary. But when he stood back up again, he saw that beside the cup the stranger had placed on the ground, a fresh new spring had erupted, with clear, cool water. The man took the cup, filled it from the spring, and handed it to Varol.

"'You must drink from my cup, for it is filled with living water. Once you drink it, you will never again thirst for any water but mine, which will sustain you, and nourish you for the rest of your days, and in the days of true life beyond that.'

"Varol then knew that he was in the presence of Immar, the Lord of Divine Love and Mercy, and kneeled before Him in prayer. He knew that he had indeed been blessed with more than rain water, and that his transgressions had been forgiven. When he finally looked up, he saw that Immar had vanished and he was once again alone. Varol tore down the half-built altar and instead erected a fountain with a basin to contain the water. He left the cup there on a little shelf he built into the fountain's wall, so that anyone who made pilgrimage to the shrine could drink from it. Though Varol kept the tale to himself, many who traveled to the shrine thereafter claimed that water taken from the cup healed wounds and cured sickness. But it was best known for clearing the mind and re-storing lost sight."

Morganne paused in her reading and stared with wide eyes into the flames of the hearth fire. "I think I understand now..." she said in a low voice. "At least some things, though much less than I ought. I never knew this part of the story. And yet there it was, before the eyes of my mind as I sat on the cliff top. How did it get there, if not by Aviad's desire that I act upon it?" Her voice was barely a whisper, and Elowyn realized that Morganne was speaking only to herself, as though Elowyn were not even in the room.

Though Morganne appeared to be somewhat shaken, Elowyn wanted her to read on further. She found comfort in this time they were sharing together. Certainly had they remained at home, their mother would not have allowed such a reading to take place, and Elowyn's inter-est in the old stories had been renewed by the events unfolding around her. They were no longer simply ancient tales, meant to be quietly kept in leather-bound volumes on dusty shelves. They were lessons in history that had begun to merge with the present in ways she could not have imagined in her days of sitting through lessons at the Temple.

"Is there more?" Elowyn asked timidly.

"Yes," Morganne replied with an expression of wonder on her face. "There is much more. We have barely begun this little book of Gareth's. I could study books and scrolls every day for the remainder of my life, and still there would be more. If a simple primer can make my heart quicken so, what other wonders must there be? If only I could go back, and read again the many books Gareth lent me through the years," she said with wistful regret. "I had no idea at the time what treasures he had placed in my hands. My mind embraced them, but my heart did not believe. Until today, my faith in the Ancients was as lifeless as the pages themselves, though I did not realize it. Today the words of this book have been written on my heart, where they shall live, and grow, and cause me to grow."

Elowyn could see that this was a moment of transformation for Morganne. She had recognized the look once before, when Morganne had defied their mother, taken a bad beating for it, and laughed with her last conscious breath. Only this transformation had not been borne of perseverance through cruelty, but of a love more pure than the human heart could ever grasp. Elowyn did not fully understand what was happening, and yet she knew that her life was also being touched. She liked this new feeling that made her skin tingle, her face glow with warmth, and her tired body feel weightless. She knew that she wanted more.

"Please go on with the book," Elowyn pleaded fervently. "I want to know what happened to Varol."

"Very well," Morganne said as she continued. "Varol also rebuilt the monastery, helping the remaining Prophets to enlist new followers until their home was once again full of life. His lesson well learned, the Prophets bestowed upon Varol a signet ring with a brilliant blue stone at the center. He was made the Lord High Protector of Truth, a title of honor that was to be passed down through his descendants for as long as his line lasted. In all matters of authority, Varol and his line were to stand as an equal to the Abbott. His honor, valor, honesty, and sense of justice were to balance the Abbott's compassion, humility, spiritual discipline, and sacrifice.

"Humanity's battle with the dark forces was not at an end, for evil had not been banished from the world, only temporarily diminished. The Shadow and Tieced still roamed freely, using the dark shrine to rebuild their armies. Many more battles were waged, but their effects were not nearly as devastating without Alazoth's destructive powers. Varol's forces were always victorious with the remnants of the Tome of Truth in his hand. However, his victories came at a price, for its lessons aged him before his years. When he died, the Prophets of Emeth's order did not know what to do with it. Since Varol had been the only one ever to read it without succumbing to madness, they feared it was not meant for any mortal but Varol. They agreed that it would be entombed with him. The only relic of it they kept was the silver clasp, which had been ripped off the book when it had been torn in two. It was ceremonially purified at the Shrine, then shaped into a talisman by a master metal smith. The talisman was then fitted onto a long staff, and this was carried into battle by Varol's descendants for hundreds of years. It served as a reminder of the days when the Ancients walked the earth, and a reminder of Varol, the great hero who sealed the rift to the underworld. The talisman remained an object of great power, though it did not by any means contain the full power of the Tome of Truth. The Prophetic Orders scribed in their histories that it leveled entire armies when wielded by one of Varol's line. Those creatures that had been given false life by the Shadow Shrine were extinguished by it forever, unable to be resurrected.

"In that way the Shadow's armies were gradually diminished, until the final war, the Great War, which came to be known as the final battle between humanity and the Shadow. The cost was high, for during this time the shrine of Aviad was utterly destroyed. The staff met its demise along with its bearer, and though the pieces were carefully brought home with the fallen warrior, the talisman mysteriously disappeared and was never seen again. This also marked the end of the Prophets, who were nearly hunted to extinction—but only nearly. They carefully took their Tomes of Wisdom and hid them in secret places throughout the world, where they would be kept safe from evil's hand.

"After that, history records that they simply vanished. But the year the Prophets left was the same year that a strange new creature was reported to have been seen. These creatures were like balls of white fire floating through the air, and they spoke in a strange, musical tongue that no one could decipher. Some thought they were the Prophets themselves, but no one knew for sure. They seemed to be most concentrated in the oldest places of power...the mountain where Aviad had with his hand begun life, the places where the original Shrines of the Ancients had been constructed, and the places where the Prophets had first formed their orders. It was rare to see one close to bustling cities or in dark, murky places of evil. It was said that to come across one and hear it speak was a sign of blessing or good fortune."

Morganne slowly closed the book, and she and Elowyn stared at one another in stunned silence.

"I think I have perhaps read enough for tonight," Morganne said, her voice quivering with emotion. Elowyn nodded in agreement, unable to speak. They both made pretense of going to bed, but neither could sleep very well. For much of the night, they stared at the fire, consumed by thought in quiet communion with Aviad.

Chapter 16
Endings and Beginnings

When the morning came, it felt different. Not because the event of the sun's rising was anything more or less than it had always been, but because something inside of them had changed. They dressed in the crisp autumn air with renewed purpose, and with a sense of closeness to Aviad they had not known before. They felt as if a tangible presence was enveloping them—embracing, shielding, guiding, listening, comforting, and gently correcting. Elowyn took the meadowsweet from her bag and went alone to the cliff top. Resting on the edge of the shrine's basin was Morganne's drinking cup. A strong surge of reverent awe welled up inside of Elowyn. This was not the shrine that Varol had built with his hands, but she could imagine that it was. She held the cup, and it did not feel like the commonplace, well-worn drinking vessel that it was. To Elowyn, it might as well have been placed there by Immar himself. She, too, heard the words from the previous night's tale in her mind. *You must drink from my cup, for it is filled with living water. Once you drink it, you will never again thirst for any water but mine. . .*

"If only this basin was filled with the living water you gave to Varol, I would gladly drink," Elowyn whispered. She ran her fingers along the bottom of the dry basin, trying to imagine that instead of hard granules of sand and dust, cool, clean water met her fingertips. She tried to see the entire cliff top as it had once been, full of life, with the prayers of the monks carrying softly on the sea winds. Though this place had not been entirely forgotten as had the shrine outside of Tyroc, it had still been abandoned to the abuse of nature. There was nothing she could do to restore it to its former glory, but she did at least gather up her skirts to wipe the dust from the basin. With her fingers, she tenderly cleaned the sand out of the dry opening from where water once freely flowed. After she had done this, she took the sprig of meadowsweet and placed it solemnly in the basin. There seemed nothing more to be done.

As she stared out to sea, Elowyn sensed again the seasonal cycle of the earth in motion, building up to the moment when the world would be cast over the edge into winter's grasp. A sudden sense of urgency pressed upon her to either prepare for the last stage of their journey, and move on quickly, or resolve to wait out the winter in the village. In her heart, she knew that Morganne would not want to wait, and so she returned with hastened steps to the cottage.

"I have left the meadowsweet. If we are going to press on, we must replenish our supplies and go. Winter will not wait for us."

Morganne agreed, and so they spent the rest of that day making preparations. Late in the afternoon the old farmer came to the cottage. "I don't suppose anyone could convince you to delay your departure until spring."

"How did you know we were leaving?" Morganne asked.

"I may be old dear one, but I'm not blind or daft. You've found whatever it is you sought in the ruins, and now you're preparing to continue on."

"Yes, I'm afraid it is true. We have very much appreciated your hospitality, but to stay longer would only make us a burden, and we must press onward before the weather turns."

The old man nodded, "I understand. The one who hears His instruction and dares to say 'no' is worse than a fool. If you're headed north, I may be able to help you along. I've a mind to take one last load of apples to Minhaven. I owe the tavern keeper several barrels yet, and I know what having apples through the winter means to the men. It's the only fresh fruit they'll see until summer. I wanted to go earlier, but my health wouldn't have it. If you don't mind sharing a cart with a load of barrels, I certainly wouldn't mind the company."

"That is a most welcome offer," Morganne said with a smile. "Please allow us to take care of your provisions for the journey as payment." When she saw that he was ready to protest, she continued, "We've

256

already stayed in your cottage, used your firewood, and benefited from your wisdom. Now you will spare us from having to walk the rest of our journey, and carrying the little one has been hard on me. It is the least we can do."

"Very well, then. Tomorrow a group of young men from the village are coming to load the barrels into my cart, as I am no longer strong enough to do it. We shall leave just before dawn the following day. That will ensure we need only spend one night on the road. The way the wind has turned, you had best buy some extra blankets."

The next day was an exciting one for Morganne and Elowyn. Their journey was finally coming to a close. In another three days' time they would be in Minhaven, beginning their new lives. They had managed to spend very little of their money along the way, and so they purchased extra blankets as the farmer had suggested, some nice looking cured meats from the butcher, cheese, a flask of wine to help keep them warm, and a new drinking cup for Morganne. They knew that they ought to spend their last day in Evensong resting, and yet they couldn't. They found themselves walking about, browsing the various shops, and the small but busy market in the center of the village. While doing this, they heard a great commotion taking place. A man in a monk's robe was calling out emphatically to anyone who would listen, "The shrine is alive! Glory be to Aviad, the shrine is alive!"

"What are you saying?" an old woman called out to him from one of the vendor stalls.

The monk tried very hard to calm himself, but his eyes shone with jubilant tears and his entire face beamed like the sun and could not be extinguished.

"I came to Evensong just yesterday, as a pilgrim to the shrine on the cliff top. I went there first for evening prayer, and it was dry and lifeless as it has been for hundreds of years. Except that I noticed someone had placed a cup there, and a sprig of meadowsweet, which I know to be the sacred herb of the Abbey that once stood beside it. I thought it curious, as I know the herb is not native to this region, but I left it untouched and went on my way. Today, when I returned, the dead spring had come to life. There was water flowing from the fountain, spilling into the basin, and even overflowing onto the ground. I took the cup and drank of the water. It was pure, and sweet. Surely this is a wondrous sign from the Ancients—a blessing, and an omen of good in uncertain times. The restoration of the shrine was foretold in prophecy, which is why my order has continued to honor it for so long. But never did I imagine that it would be fulfilled in my lifetime." Everyone in the market stopped what they were doing, glancing at each other with skeptical expressions.

"I see that you do not believe me," the monk said with exasperation. "Go look for yourselves, then—go, and you will see I am telling the truth. Rejoice, friends! Your shrine has been blessed by Aviad once again!"

The monk began to walk toward the road leading to the shrine with a curious group following him. Morganne and Elowyn turned to follow as well, but not before Morganne had whispered in Elowyn's ear, "No matter what, say nothing about what we did there yesterday."

When they got to the shrine, they found everything just as the monk had described it. The fountain was flowing with water, beautiful, clear and cold. Remembering the words she had said in prayer the previous day, Elowyn was the first to approach the basin, grasp the cup, and with trembling fingers, draw water. She stared at it for a brief moment, hardly daring to believe that what she saw was real. Could she and Morganne have done this? Such an event was perhaps something she could imagine reading about in Gareth's books. But she could not conceive of such a thing taking place in the present day. She put the cup to her lips and drank long, sweet draughts. In reverent silence, she then handed the cup to Morganne, who also gladly drank. Morganne handed the cup back to the monk and whispered a grateful "thank you." He gave her a perplexed look, but was too surrounded by people asking for the cup to question her.

Elowyn's face suddenly lit up with excitement. She reached down into her pouch, pulled out the coin, and showed it to Morganne. "I could not bring myself to leave it in the stream. Do you think perhaps I should leave it here? If this is Nevon's, and his spirit has not yet found rest, surely Aviad would bring him peace."

Morganne seemed as though she were about to say yes, but her look of affirmation rapidly dissolved into one of alarm.

"No, put it away, quickly," she said, pulling Elowyn well away from the other people there. "Did anyone see it?"

Elowyn was confused by Morganne's reaction, but did as she was told. "No, no one saw it."

"You must keep it a while longer. There will come a time when Aviad calls upon you to release it, but that time is not now."

"How do you know this?" Elowyn asked with great curiosity.

"Honestly, I don't know. . .I just have a strong feeling, the same way I did yesterday when I knew that I must leave my drinking cup behind. I followed that feeling, and today the dead shrine is alive. Dare I not follow it this time?"

Morganne grasped Elowyn's hand. "Come, it is time for us to leave this place." She led Elowyn back to the path, past the crowd of people, which was growing larger by the moment as word spread through the village. They both looked back only long enough to see the fountain full of shimmering water, surrounded by people whose faces were glowing with jubilation.

Elowyn asked quietly, "Why did you not want anyone to know that we left the cup and the meadowsweet? The people here will always wonder where they came from."

"Yes, I suppose they will," Morganne said, smiling. "And if we told them what we had done, some might think that we had brought the fountain to life ourselves, as though my old travel cup and your bit of dried plant from an ordinary cottage garden held some sort of magic in themselves. We did nothing to make the water flow again. We only brought the offerings Aviad told us to. It was He who made the water flow, and He is the only one whom they should praise and think of when they drink that water. I would not have anyone led away from the truth by our words or deeds."

Elowyn understood the wisdom behind Morganne's words and returned with her to the cottage in thoughtful silence. They dared not leave it again until in the chill air of early dawn the farmer arrived with his cart. Barely awake yet, they put out the remains of the fire, loaded their few belongings, and huddled together under the blankets in sleepy silence as the cart jerked forward. The last stage of their journey to Minhaven had begun.

The girls peered upward through the branches of the trees, watching the early morning sky gradually change from gray to pale blue. And then as though a fire had been lit beneath the horizon, the world was illuminated in vivid pinks, oranges and yellows. A warm red glow spread over the whole wood just before the golden sun emerged, so bright they could not look in its direction for more than a fleeting second. But as bright as the sun was, Elowyn noticed that it held no warmth. She watched the forceful breaths of the horses curling outward like smoke as they steadily bore their heavy load. There was no question now that winter was closing in upon the northern reaches of the world.

With cold, stiff fingers, Morganne served everyone fresh bread, spread with butter and a currant jam that she had purchased in Evensong as a special treat for them to share. She was the first to break the silence of the morning, by asking the old farmer the question that had been pressing on their hearts from the moment they stepped beyond the confines of their mother's cottage.

"What is Minhaven like? Is it anything like Evensong?"

"Bless me, no. Evensong is a quiet place, still living in the shadow of what it once was when the monastery was there. Even after all this time, I suppose it is impossible to purge what is mixed in with the blood. The people of Minhaven live under a shadow too, but it is that of the mountains. They may hold riches, to be sure, but the mountains show no mercy to man. The first people there were miners and metal smiths, drawn by the prospects of finding ore; iron, silver and gold. As more of them came, the town emerged out of necessity. I would feel more at ease had you stayed in Evensong until spring. As rough as our winters are, Minhaven's are far more perilous, especially for those not accustomed to them. Once the first heavy snows fall, you'll be cut off from the rest of the mainland except by boat over very treacherous waters."

"We will manage somehow," Morganne said brightly. While to some this news would have been disheartening, Morganne felt it was an added ray of hope. Should anyone attempt to trace their flight, at least they would remain securely cradled in Minhaven through the winter.

"You'll find the people of Minhaven are a suspicious lot, and superstitious too," the farmer went on. "I suppose that comes of having to stare the dangers of the mountains in the face day by day. No doubt they'll look upon you strangely at first, and they may even seem unfriendly. They're only hanging back to make sure you're not a bad luck charm," he said, chuckling softly. "If it happens that you turn out to be a good one, you'll make fast friends. But the best piece of advice I can offer you is do nothing to offend the Kinship. They make and enforce the law in Minhaven. Without the Kinship, Minhaven would be at the mercy of every marauding group looking to draw fast wealth from the points of their swords. Stay on their good side and you'll have all the help and protection you need."

"Doesn't the Sovereign defend these lands?" Morganne asked, suddenly remembering that Greywalle was also under the Kinship's protection.

"The Sovereign?" the farmer huffed. "He claims these lands well enough, and takes his share of taxes, but expending his resources to defend them is another matter. We've had to make our own protection out here. The Sovereign's interests lie elsewhere, but we each have something the other needs, and so there remains a stiff peace between us. If I were you, I wouldn't throw too much talk about the Sovereign about. It won't gain you anything, and might make you any number of enemies."

"Are the Kinship traitors against the Sovereign, then?"

"No, they're not traitors. In fact, some of them are lords under the Sovereign's house."

"What are they then? We've heard their name spoken a number of times, and have met two of their kin who showed us great kindness. But we don't really know anything about them."

"I can't say that I know so much myself—they don't show in Evensong all that often. From what I understand, the Kinship began in the early days of Minhaven, when great stores of fine ore, including gold, were being brought out of the mountains. The miners found themselves being robbed again and again by different groups who wanted the smelted ore to make weapons and armor for themselves. Calls upon the Sovereign for help brought little result. And so a local lord who had some means and fighting men of his own, a handful of local citizens, and the miners, all came together to form the Kinship as a means of protecting themselves. Over time they grew in size and power, and by now few are fool enough to openly stand against them. They are greatly loved and respected by the citizens of Minhaven, and feared by the wicked. If you've already befriended one of their kind, you're sure to befriend more."

As the day wore on, the landscape abruptly changed. Elowyn noticed that leafy trees, bearing the dusty brown and yellow leaves of late autumn, were being replaced by fine evergreens. The forest was deep, but sparse. There was so little undergrowth, she could see through the pines with unexpected clarity. Even the air seemed different. It was clearer, sharper—almost lighter in her chest as she breathed it in. The road grew rough. It curved and twisted along the edges of steep hillsides, lifting the cart higher at each bend. The old farmer grew quiet, intently focused on maneuvering the horses along the dangerously uneven road. The earth was no longer made up of soft, rich farming soil, but was hard and full of stones. Immense boulders towered above the forest floor all around them. This part of the world seemed completely untouched by time, as though nothing had changed since the very dawn of creation. Elowyn could envision Aviad setting each boulder in place with the loving hand of an artist laboring over a masterpiece.

By late afternoon the weather began to change as well. A soft grey blanket of clouds washed over them from the north and Elowyn could smell moisture on the wind that carried them. She thought for certain there would be rain before morning. As daylight faded, the farmer steered the horses into a small area off the road that was barely large enough for them and the cart.

"I always stop here," he said. "Further on, the road grows even more difficult, and there are no safe places to pull a heavy cart off to the side. We can light a fire and stretch our legs a bit, but we'll not sleep on the ground. The earth is hard, and your bones would chill. You'll see, the nights get bitter cold up here."

They enjoyed a roaring fire for a time, with satisfying food, and tales, and even a few songs in the old farmer's raspy voice. When it came time for sleep, they all bundled together in the back of the cart and drew their new blankets over them for warmth. The old farmer had not misled them as to how frigid the night air would be. When Elowyn woke in the night feeling that she was suffocating under her wrappings, she lifted her face to the fresh air and found that the sheer coldness of it made her lungs gasp and her heart quicken. She felt a soft tickle on her face—a dusting of snow, gently falling from a moonless sky. She ducked her head back within the warmer confines of her blankets and finished the night in a restless sleep.

The dawn was draped in heavy cloud, but the snow had stopped. Before Morganne and Elowyn were awake enough to be fully aware of where they were, they felt the cart moving once again beneath them. The old farmer had already hitched his horses and turned them onto the road. Elowyn was in no hurry to greet the cold when there was naught to do but stare out upon a vast wilderness that felt completely foreign to her. The closer they got to Minhaven, the more apprehensive Elowyn became about what awaited them there. It certainly didn't sound like any other place she had known. She could hear Morganne's muffled voice, asking the farmer if there was a monastery in Minhaven.

"There is no formal monastery," she could hear him reply. "But there is a small community of monks who provide charity and serve as healers for the sick and injured." Elowyn surmised from his response that there would be no temple in Minhaven either. She pulled the blankets tighter around her. As much as she had wanted to get away from Braeden's influences, she didn't much like the thought of having none of the benefits or protections that Tyroc had afforded. If nothing else, this journey had made her realize just how small her life had been thus far, and how big and different the world was from anything she had previously imagined.

Elowyn couldn't even take comfort in her surroundings. These woodlands seemed so harsh and unforgiving, with the tall, untouchable pines standing as rigid sentries along the edge of the road. They were thick, and very old, with high branches that blocked out the sun's light instead of tenderly filtering it down to the forest floor. Certainly these trees were not the right kind for tree sailing. Where was the jolly mother with her giggling saplings? Where were the gentle green woodlands, the soft rich soils, the lushness of leaves, the graceful swaying trees?

Eventually Elowyn became horribly hungry and knew that she would have to leave the protection of her wrappings. Reluctantly, she lifted the blanket and looked ahead. In that moment, she forgot all of her sorrows and simply stared, her mouth gaping, and her eyes wide with wonder. The clouds had thinned away toward the north. She saw, for the first time in her life, a line of snow covered mountains. The remaining cloud cover, hovering low to the earth, created the illusion that those massive peaks were floating on the air. To Elowyn, this was a miraculous sight. In silent awe she stared at the rugged peaks for the remainder of the day, learning their shapes and colors, watching how the clouds formed and dissolved around them, and how the light played upon them. It was amazing to her that they could look so close, and yet so distant, all at the same time.

The afternoon eventually waned into twilight. The last of the sun's rays lit up the mountains like a beacon, while the rest of the woodlands began to diminish into shadow. When even that light began to fade, and they were nearly plunged into total darkness, Elowyn began to see other lights. Warm, yellow, flickering human lights made by lanterns, torches, and the white hot fires of great forges. They had, at last, entered the streets of Minhaven.

Spread out before them was a small village that had sprung up like a mushroom in the midst of a vast, hard, mountain wilderness. There were no walls, not even the primitive kind that had surrounded the settlement at Deep Lake. There were no gates or watch towers. None of the streets were cobbled—they were little more than beaten footpaths connecting clusters of buildings together. So far as Elowyn could see, most of the structures were made of stone or roughly cut logs. A very few others were timber frame like those she was more accustomed to seeing in the south-ern regions. The only ones with open stalls were the blacksmith's work-shops, whose fires constantly churned forth heat and billowing smoke, staining all the buildings around with streaks of gray soot. Minhaven was not an unpleasant looking place, though it lacked the charm of Grey-walle and the austere beauty of Evensong. It had a comfortable quality about it, like a well-worn leather shoe that has already been broken in by the elements and conforms perfectly to your foot. Elowyn sensed that they would have little trouble blending in if the people were friendly.

At the farthest end of town, before this last northern foothold gave way to the wilderness once again, they came to a large stone structure that looked as though it had been expanded upon several times over. Morganne and Elowyn recognized by the sign post that it was the local tavern. The farmer brought the cart to a stop, eased his stiff legs over the side and secured the horses before helping the girls out.

"We've arrived," he said. "Is anyone expecting you here? Do you have a place to go for the night?"

Morganne shook her head regretfully.

"I thought as much," the farmer said. "Well, in we go."

He swung the heavy doors open onto a large room with a wide-planked wooden floor and a great stone hearth on the far wall. The warmth emanating from it was a welcome relief to Elowyn's cold face and fingers. There were many tables, all full of men merrily drinking from frothy mugs that were instantly raised to the old farmer in greeting. The tavern keeper came over to give him a hearty welcome.

"Hail, my old friend! I feared you would not make another trip this season."

The tavern keeper was a tall man with dark brown hair and a thick, wooly beard. His eyes had a youthful twinkle, but his face was heavily lined, as though he had been aged by tribulation rather than time.

"I nearly didn't," the old farmer responded. "My health has been poor of late, but I wouldn't have left you to fare the winter without one more load of apples," he said, smiling with satisfaction as though he had defeated a great foe. "These are the last of the season."

"I promise you'll be well paid for your trouble, but worry no more about your load this night. I'll see to it that the barrels are unloaded and your horses are stabled and fed. Come, warm yourself by the fire and have a drink with me. Tell me all the news from Evensong and the southern cities—we get precious little of it these days."

"Aye, that I will. But there is one other thing I must take care of first." The old farmer nudged Morganne, Elowyn and Adelin forward. "I brought some passengers with me on this trip. They are in need of hospitality for the night and may need a place to stay through the winter months. Have you any room?"

The tavern keeper looked upon the girls with kindness, but it was obvious that this request was worrisome to him. "I've the room, but I'm not sure that this is such a fine place for young girls. They might be better off staying with the monks, as I won't be able to keep a proper eye on them. I've barely even time to take regular meals."

Morganne responded in a firm voice, "We don't need to be looked after. We've journeyed alone a very long way, and we have the means to take care of ourselves."

The tavern keeper seemed both surprised and amused by Morganne's forthrightness. "Of that I've no doubt," he said with a smirk.

"Only the bold and the foolish would dare to journey here at the onset of winter with two young girls in tow. If you've made it this far unscathed, it is highly unlikely that you're a fool, else you're just a very lucky one."

"I suppose time will be my witness either way," Morganne replied.

"Aye, that it will," he nodded in agreement. "Do you intend to make Minhaven your home, or are you merely passing through?"

"I have heard that Minhaven is in need of a seamstress. If that is true, we mean to make this our home. Should you decide to let us stay here until spring, we will gladly pay you for our room and also help with the cooking and mending until we find a place of our own."

The tavern keeper shook his head with uncertainty. "Your offer is fair, but sometimes this place can get mighty rough on dark, cold days. There's nothing good for you here, just the smell of ale and pipe smoke, and coarse talk not fit for young ears."

"If that is so, then we shall find a more suitable place all the more quickly. But for now, we only need a warm place to sleep, and we have nowhere else to go." Morganne could see that he was not convinced, and so she pulled one last bit of hope from her bag. "Perhaps this will ease your mind. We met a friend on our journey, who said that his seal is well regarded in this region, and that it might aid us along our way." Morganne pulled out Tervaise's seal and showed it to the tavern keeper, remembering the effect it had once before upon the innkeeper at Greywalle and knowing how the Kinship was regarded in Minhaven.

The moment he saw the seal, the tavern keeper grinned and shrugged in a helpless fashion. "Well, you've won me over," he said loudly enough for everyone to hear. "If you're friends of the Kinship, you're most welcome to all that I have. No doubt you'll be watched after and under their protection."

His voice returned to normal as he said, "Come with me, and I'll show you where to sleep."

He led them down a short hallway, through the kitchen, and down another hallway where he had private living quarters. He opened the door onto a cozy room with a single bed, a chair and a bearskin rug on the floor.

"This was my brother's. Mine is the next door down if you ever need anything. Though it won't take long now for the whole town to know you're under the Kinship's protection, I will still sleep more soundly with you close by. They're not a bad lot, but they sometimes lose their wits in their ale, and I can't say as they are used to having young women about the tavern."

"Where is your brother now?" Elowyn asked timidly.

"He was a miner. The mountain buried him two winters ago, but I never had the heart to take his room. It is clean and mostly as he left it. You've had a long journey in the cold. Are you hungry? I must return to my work, but I could have some food brought to you from the kitchen."

"We still have food in our bags," Morganne said. "We will be fine until morning. Thank you for your hospitality, and thank the farmer for us as well. We didn't get the chance to say good bye, and he was so very kind to us."

"Aye, I will tell him."

"And please, if you would," Morganne continued, "also tell him that he should visit the shrine when he returns to Evensong. There is something there which will do him good."

The tavern keeper nodded in acknowledgment. "Until morning then," he said graciously and left.

And so it was that Elowyn, Morganne and Adelin made their escape from Tyroc and arrived safely in Minhaven. Elowyn brought the hearth to life while Morganne prepared the evening meal. To anyone looking on it would have seemed a meager fare, but Morganne and Elowyn relished it as a feast great enough to rival the one they had enjoyed at Tyroc Castle. Though Elowyn's heart was still uncertain about many things in this strange place that would be their new home, Morganne's face beamed with a glow that only Aviad could have lit, and the sureness of her faith comforted Elowyn. When they had filled their stomachs, and Adelin had been put to bed, Morganne took out Gareth's book. She sat with Elowyn by the fire and they read together, tales of the Ancients, of Varol, and of the Prophets, long into the night, until sleep finally claimed them.

I am quite certain that Morganne and Elowyn felt their hardships and adventures had come to a close—or so they revealed to me many years later upon honest reflection. Time would teach them differently, as we must all learn such lessons through the unfolding of our lives. But the wise farmer always knows when he should let his fields lie fallow. Beyond sight, the soil gathers its strength until it is time once more to endure the plow, and nourish the seeds that will sprout forth into a bountiful harvest. And so for a time, the Ancients granted Elowyn and Morganne respite from their journey. Weary and spent, they rested securely cradled in the cold mountain village of Minhaven.

As I glance out of my office window, I can see that the dawn long ago passed into day and is about to fall again into darkness. My eyes are blurred and my hand is pained from long hours of writing. I too, must allow my body and mind to rest. But soon I shall return to pick up my pen and resume my work, for there is far more to this tale than a single tome can hold.

No journey begun by Aviad's hand ever truly ends, and the path of Morganne and Elowyn's lives had only just begun.

Made in the USA
Charleston, SC
08 December 2011